Green Longmans

Lothair by the Right Honorable B. Disraeli

Green Longmans

Lothair by the Right Honorable B. Disraeli

ISBN/EAN: 9783742832214

Manufactured in Europe, USA, Canada, Australia, Japa

Cover: Foto ©Andreas Hilbeck / pixelio.de

Manufactured and distributed by brebook publishing software
(www.brebook.com)

Green Longmans

Lothair by the Right Honorable B. Disraeli

COLLECTED EDITION

OF THE

NOVELS AND TALES

BY

THE RIGHT HONORABLE

B. DISRAELI.

———

VOL. I.—LOTHAIR.

LONDON: PRINTED BY
SPOTTISWOODE AND CO., NEW-STREET SQUARE
AND PARLIAMENT STREET

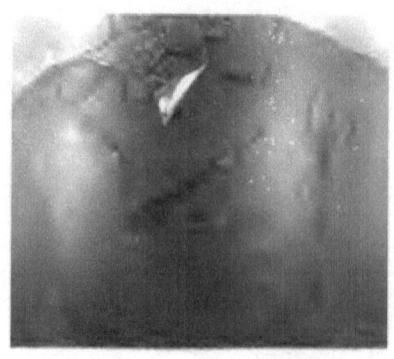

The Lighthouse: Lumads

LOTHAIR.

BY THE

RIGHT HONORABLE B. DISRAELI.

'Nisso omnia haeo simo cui adolescentiala.'

TERENTIUS.

NEW EDITION.

LONDON:

LONGMANS, GREEN, AND CO.

1870.

TO

HIS ROYAL HIGHNESS

THE DUKE OF AUMALE

WITH

RESPECT AND AFFECTION.

GENERAL PREFACE.

AN AMERICAN GENTLEMAN, with more than courtesy, has forwarded to me a vast number of notices of LOTHAIR which have appeared in the leading journals of his country. He tells me that, irrespective of literary 'organs,' there are in the Union five thousand newspapers, and it is not impossible that some notice of 'Lothair' might appear in each of these. However various may be the opinions of those which I thus possess, they appear to me generally to be sincere, and in point of literary ability; taste, style, and critical acumen; I think they need not fear competition with the similar productions of our own land.

My English publishers also have made a collection of the notices of this work in our own country, and though we have not yet five thousand newspapers, the aggregate of articles is in amount perhaps unprecedented. I have nothing to complain of in their remarks. One could hardly expect at home the judicial impartiality of a foreign land. Personal influences inevitably mingle in some degree with such productions. There are critics who, abstractedly, do not approve of successful books, particularly if they have failed in the same style; social acquaintances also of lettered taste,

and especially cotemporaries whose public life has not
exactly realised the vain dreams of their fussy existence, would seize the accustomed opportunity of
welcoming with affected discrimination about nothing,
and elaborate controversy about trifles, the production
of a friend; and there is always, both in politics and
literature, the race of the Dennises, the Oldmixons,
and Curls, who flatter themselves that by systematically
libelling some eminent personage of their times, they
have a chance of descending to posterity; but, so far as
I am concerned, they have always been disappointed.

A distinguished individual has suggested that, in a
preface to this edition of my collected works, I might
give my own views of the purport of 'Lothair.' It
strikes me, with all deference, that it would be not a
little presumptuous for an author thus to be the self-
critic of volumes which appeared only a few months ago.
Their purport to the writer seems clear enough, and
as they have been more extensively read both by the
people of the United Kingdom and the United States
than any work that has appeared for the last half century, I will even venture to assume that on this point
they are of the same opinion as myself.

But on some other works, the youngest of which
were written a quarter of a century ago, it would perhaps be in me not impertinent now to make a few
remarks. CONINGSBY, SYBIL, and TANCRED form a real
Trilogy; that is to say, they treat of the same subject,
and endeavour to complete that treatment. The
origin and character of our political parties, their
influence on the condition of the people of this country,
some picture of the moral and physical condition of

that people, and some intimation of the means by which it might be elevated and improved, were themes which had long engaged my meditation.

Born in a library, and trained from early childhood by learned men who did not share the passions and the prejudices of our political and social life, I had imbibed on some subjects conclusions different from those which generally prevail, and especially with reference to the history of our own country. How an oligarchy had been substituted for a kingdom, and a narrow-minded and bigoted fanaticism flourished in the name of religious liberty, were problems long to me insoluble, but which early interested me. But what most attracted my musing, even as a boy, were the elements of our political parties, and the strange mystification by which that which was national in its constitution had become odious, and that which was exclusive was presented as popular.

What has mainly led to this confusion of public thought and this uneasiness of society is our habitual carelessness in not distinguishing between the excellence of a principle and its injurious or obsolete application. The feudal system may have worn out, but its main principle, that the tenure of property should be the fulfilment of duty, is the essence of good government. The divine right of kings may have been a plea for feeble tyrants, but the divine right of government is the keystone of human progress, and without it governments sink into police, and a nation is degraded into a mob.

National institutions were the ramparts of the multitude against large estates exercising political power derived from a limited class. The Church was in theory, and once it had been in practice, the spiritual and intellectual trainer of the people. The privileges of the multitude and the prerogatives of the Sovereign had grown up together, and together they had waned. Under the plea of liberalism, all the institutions which were the bulwarks of the multitude had been sapped and weakened, and nothing had been substituted for them. The people were without education, and, relatively to the advance of science and the comfort of the superior classes, their condition had deteriorated, and their physical quality as a race was threatened. Those who in theory were the national party, and who sheltered themselves under the institutions of the country against the oligarchy, had, both by a misconception and a neglect of their duties, become, and justly become, odious; while the oligarchy, who had mainly founded themselves on the plunder of the popular estate, either in the shape of the possessions of the Church or the domains of the Crown, had by the patronage of certain general principles which they only meagerly applied, assumed, and to a certain degree acquired, the character of a popular party. But no party was national: one was exclusive and odious, and the other liberal and cosmopolitan.

The perverse deviation of political parties from their original significance may at first sight seem only subjects of historical curiosity, but they assume a different character when they practically result in the degradation of a people.

To change back the oligarchy into a generous aristocracy round a real throne; to infuse life and vigour

into the Church, as the trainer of the nation, by the
revival of Convocation, then dumb, on a wide basis,
and not, as has been since done, in the shape of a
priestly section; to establish a commercial code on
the principles successfully negotiated by Lord Boling-
broke at Utrecht, and which, though baffled at the
time by a Whig Parliament, were subsequently and
triumphantly vindicated by his political pupil and
heir, Mr. Pitt; to govern Ireland according to the
policy of Charles I. and not of Oliver Cromwell; to
emancipate the political constituency of 1832 from its
sectarian bondage and contracted sympathies; to elevate
the physical as well as the moral condition of the people,
by establishing that labour required regulation as much
as property; and all this rather by the use of ancient
forms and the restoration of the past than by political
revolutions founded on abstract ideas, appeared to be
the course which the circumstances of this country
required, and which, practically speaking, could only,
with all their faults and backslidings, be undertaken
and accomplished by a reconstructed Tory Party.

When I attempted to enter public life, I expressed
these views, long meditated, to my countrymen, but they
met with little encouragement. He who steps out of the
crowd is listened to with suspicion or with heedless-
ness: and forty years ago there prevailed a singular
ignorance of the political history of our country. I
had no connection either in the press or in public life.
I incurred the accustomed penalty of being looked on
as a visionary, and what I knew to be facts were treated
as paradoxes.

Ten years afterwards affairs had changed. I had

been some time in Parliament and had friends who
had entered public life with myself, and who listened
always with interest and sometimes with sympathy to
views which I had never ceased to enforce.   Living
much together, without combination we acted together.
Some of those who were then my companions have, like
myself, since taken some part in the conduct of public
affairs: two of them, and those who were not the least
interested in our speculations, have departed.   One
was GEORGE SMYTHE, afterwards seventh Lord Strang-
ford, a man of brilliant gifts; of dazzling wit, infinite
culture, and fascinating manners.   His influence over
youth was remarkable, and he could promulgate a new
faith with graceful enthusiasm.   HENRY HOPE, the
eldest son of the author of ' Anastasius,' was of a different nature, but he was learned and accomplished,
possessed a penetrating judgment and an inflexible
will.   Master of a vast fortune, his house naturally
became our frequent rendezvous; and it was at the
DEEPDENE, that he first urged the expediency of my
treating in a literary form those views and subjects
which were the matter of our frequent conversation.

This was the origin of CONINGSBY OR THE NEW
GENERATION, which I commenced under his roof, and
which I inscribed to his name.

The derivation and character of political parties; the
condition of the people which had been the consequence
of them; the duties of the Church as a main remedial
agency in our present state; were the three principal
topics which I intended to treat, but I found they were
too vast for the space I had allotted to myself.

These were all launched in ' Coningsby,' but the

origin and condition of political parties, the first portion of the theme, was the only one completely handled in that work.

Next year (1845), in SYBIL OR THE TWO NATIONS, I considered the condition of the people, and the whole work, generally speaking, was devoted to that portion of my scheme. At that time the Chartist agitation was still fresh in the public memory, and its repetition was far from improbable. I had mentioned to my friend, the late THOMAS DUNCOMBE, and who was my friend before I entered the House of Commons, something of what I was contemplating; and he offered and obtained for my perusal the whole of the correspondence of Feargus O'Connor when conductor of the 'Northern Star,' with the leaders and chief actors of the Chartist movement. I had visited and observed with care all the localities introduced; and as an accurate and never exaggerated picture of a remarkable period in our domestic history, and of a popular organisation which in its extent and completeness has perhaps never been equalled, the pages of SYBIL may, I venture to believe, be consulted with confidence.

In recognising the Church as a powerful agent in the previous development of England, and possibly the most efficient means of that renovation of the national spirit which was desired, it seemed to me that the time had arrived when it became my duty to ascend to the origin of that great ecclesiastical corporation, and consider the position of the descendants of that race who had been the founders of Christianity. Some of the great truths of ethnology were necessarily involved in such discussions. Familiar as we all are now with such

themes, the house of Israel being now freed from the
barbarism of mediæval misconception, and judged, like
all other races, by their contributions to the existing
sum of human welfare, and the general influence of
race on human action being universally recognised as
the key of history, the difficulty and hazard of touching for the first time on such topics cannot now be
easily appreciated. But public opinion recognised both
the truth and sincerity of these views, and, with its
sanction, in TANCRED OR THE NEW CRUSADE, the third
portion of the Trilogy, I completed their development.

It will be seen that the general spirit of these productions ran counter to the views which had been long
prevalent in England, and which may be popularly,
though not altogether accurately, described as utili-
tarian. They recognised imagination in the government
of nations as a quality not less important than reason.
They trusted much to a popular sentiment, which
rested on an heroic tradition and was sustained by the
high spirit of a free aristocracy. Their economic principles were not unsound, but they looked upon the
health and knowledge of the multitude as not the least
precious part of the wealth of nations. In asserting the
doctrine of race, they were entirely opposed to the
equality of man, and similar abstract dogmas, which
have destroyed ancient society without creating a satisfactory substitute. Resting on popular sympathies and
popular privileges, they held that no society could be
durable unless it was built upon the principles of loyalty
and religious reverence.

The writer and those who acted with him looked,
then, upon the Anglican Church as a main machinery by

which these results might be realised. There were
few great things left in England, and the Church was
one. Nor do I now doubt that if, a quarter of a century
ago, there had arisen a churchman equal to the occasion,
the position of ecclesiastical affairs in this country
would have been very different from that which they
now occupy. But these great matters fell into the
hands of monks and schoolmen; and little more than a
year after the publication of CONINGSBY, the secession
of DR. NEWMAN dealt a blow to the Church of England
under which it still reels. That extraordinary event
has been ' apologised ' for, but has never been explained.
It was a mistake and a misfortune. The tradition of
the Anglican Church was powerful. Resting on the
Church of Jerusalem, modified by the divine school of
Galilee, it would have found that rock of truth which
Providence, by the instrumentality of the Semitic race,
had promised to St. Peter. Instead of that, the
seceders sought refuge in mediæval superstitions, which
are generally only the embodiments of pagan ceremonies and creeds.

It cannot be denied that the aspect of the world and
this country, to those who have faith in the spiritual
nature of man, is at this time dark and distressful.
They listen to doubts, and even denials, of an active
Providence; what is styled Materialism is in the
ascendant. To those who believe that an atheistical
society, though it may be polished and amiable, involves the seeds of anarchy, the prospect is full of
gloom.

This disturbance in the mind of nations has been
occasioned by two causes: firstly, by the powerful assault

on the divinity of the Semitic literature by the Germans; and, secondly, by recent discoveries of science, which are hastily supposed to be inconsistent with our long-received convictions as to the relations between the Creator and the created.

One of the consequences of the Divine government of this world, which has ordained that the sacred purposes should be effected by the instrumentality of various human races, must be occasionally a jealous discontent with the revelation entrusted to a particular family. But there is no reason to believe that the Teutonic rebellion of this century against the Divine truths entrusted to the Semites will ultimately meet with more success than the Celtic insurrection of the preceding age. Both have been sustained by the highest intellectual gifts that human nature has ever displayed; but when the tumult subsides, the Divine truths are found to be not less prevalent than before, and simply because they are divine. Man brings to the study of the oracles more learning and more criticism than of yore: and it is well that it should be so. The documents will yet bear a greater amount both of erudition and examination than they have received; but the word of God is eternal, and will survive the spheres.

The sceptical effects of the discoveries of science, and the uneasy feeling that they cannot co-exist with our old religious convictions, have their origin in the circumstance, that the general body who have suddenly become conscious of these physical truths are not so well acquainted as is desirable with the past history of man. Astonished by their unprepared emergence from ignorance to a certain degree of information, their amazed intelligence takes refuge in the theory of what is conveniently called Progress, and every step in scientific discovery seems further to remove them from the path of primæval inspiration. But there is no fallacy so flagrant as to suppose that the modern ages have the peculiar privi lege of scientific discovery, or that they are distinguished as the epochs of the most illustrious inventions. On the contrary, scientific invention has always gone on simultaneously with the revelation of spiritual truths; and more, the greatest discoveries are not those of modern ages. No one for a moment can pretend that printing is so great a discovery as writing, or algebra as language. What are the most brilliant of our chymical discoveries compared with the invention of fire and the metals? It is a vulgar belief that our astronomical knowledge dates only from the recent century when it was rescued from the monks who imprisoned Galileo; but Hipparchus, who lived before our Divine Master, and who among other sublime achievements discovered the precession of the equinoxes, ranks with the Newtons and the Keplers; and Copernicus, the modern father of our celestial science, avows himself, in his famous work, as only the champion of Pythagoras, whose system he enforces and illustrates. Even the most modish schemes of the day on the origin of things, which captivate as much by their novelty as their truth, may find their precursors in ancient sages, and after a careful analysis of the blended elements of imagination and induction which characterise the new theories, they will be found mainly to rest on the atom of Epicurus and the monad of Thales. Scientific like spiritual truth has ever from the beginning been descending from

Heaven to man. He is a being who organically demands direct relations with his Creator, and he would not have been so organised if his requirements could not be satisfied. We may analyse the sun and penetrate the stars, but man is conscious that he is made in God's own image, and in his perplexity he will ever appeal to our Father which art in Heaven.

I had been in Parliament seven years when this Trilogy was published, and during that period I had not written anything; but in 1837, the year I entered the House of Commons, I had published two works, HENRIETTA TEMPLE and VENETIA. These are not political works, but they would commemorate feelings more enduring than public passions, and they were written with care, and some delight. They were inscribed to two friends, the best I ever had, and not the least gifted. One was the inimitable D'ORSAY, the most accomplished and the most engaging character that has figured in this century, who, with the form and universal genius of an Alcibiades, combined a brilliant wit and a heart of quick affection, and who, placed in a public position, would have displayed a courage, a judgment, and a commanding intelligence which would have ranked him with the leaders of mankind. The other was one who had enjoyed that public opportunity which had been denied to COMTE D'ORSAY. The world has recognised the political courage, the versatile ability, and the masculine eloquence of LORD LYNDHURST; but his intimates only were acquainted with the tenderness of his disposition, the sweetness of his temper, his ripe scholarship, and the playfulness of his bright and airy spirit.

And here I cannot refrain from mentioning that in

1837 I accompanied Lord Lyndhurst to Kensington
Palace, when, on the accession of the Queen, the peers
and privy councillors and chief personages of the
realm pledged their fealty to their new Sovereign.
He was greatly affected by the unusual scene: a
youthful maiden receiving the homage of her subjects,
most of them illustrious, in a palace in a garden,
and all with a sweet and natural dignity. He gave
me, as we drove home, an animated picture of what
had occurred in the Presence Chamber, marked by all
that penetrating observation, and happy terseness of
description, which distinguished him. Eight years
afterwards, with my memory still under the influence
of his effective narrative, I reproduced the scene in
SYBIL, and I feel sure it may be referred to for its
historical accuracy.

There was yet a barren interval of five years of my
life, so far as literature was concerned, between the
publication of 'Henrietta Temple,' and 'Venetia,' and
my earlier works. In 1832 I had published CONTARINI
FLEMING and ALROY. I had then returned from two
years of travel in the Mediterranean regions, and I
published 'Contarini Fleming' anonymously, and in
the midst of a revolution. It was almost stillborn,
and having written it with deep thought and feeling,
I was naturally discouraged from further effort. Yet
the youthful writer who may, like me, be inclined
to despair, may learn also from my example not to
be precipitate in his resolves. Gradually 'Contarini
Fleming' found sympathising readers; GOETHE and
BECKFORD were impelled to communicate their un-
solicited opinions of this work to its anonymous author,

and I have seen a criticism on it by HEINE, of which
any writer might be justly proud. Yet all this does
not prevent me from being conscious that it would
have been better if a subject so essentially psycho-
logical had been treated at a more mature period of
life.

I had commenced 'Alroy' the year after my first
publication, and had thrown the manuscript aside.
Being at Jerusalem in the year 1831, and visiting the
traditionary tombs of the kings, my thoughts recurred
to the marvellous career which had attracted my boyhood, and I shortly after finished a work which I began
the year after I wrote VIVIAN GREY.

What my opinion was of that my first work, written
in 1826, was shown by my publishing my second anonymously. Books written by boys, which pretend to give
a picture of manners and to deal in knowledge of human
nature, must be affected. They can be, at the best, but
the results of imagination acting on knowledge not acquired by experience. Of such circumstances exaggeration is a necessary consequence, and false taste accom-
panies exaggeration. Nor is it necessary to remark
that a total want of art must be observed in such
pages, for that is a failing incident to all first efforts.
'Vivian Grey' is essentially a puerile work, but it has
baffled even the efforts of its creator to suppress it. Its
fate has been strange; and not the least remarkable
thing is, that forty-four years after its first publication,
I must ask the indulgence of the reader for its continued and inevitable re-appearance.

D.

HUGHENDEN MANOR: October 1870.

LOTHAIR.

CHAPTER I.

'I REMEMBER HIM a little boy,' said the Duchess, 'a pretty
little boy, but very shy. His mother brought him to us
one day. She was a dear friend of mine; you know she
was one of my bridesmaids?'

'And you have never seen him since, mamma?' enquired a married daughter, who looked like the younger
sister of her mother.

'Never; he was an orphan shortly after: I have often
reproached myself, but it is so difficult to see boys. Then,
he never went to school, but was brought up in the High-
lands with a rather savage uncle; and if he and Bertram
had not become friends at Christchurch, I do not well see
how we ever could have known him.'

These remarks were made in the morning-room of
Brentham, where the mistress of the mansion sate surrounded by her daughters, all occupied with various works.
One knitted a purse, another adorned a slipper, a third
emblazoned a page. Beautiful forms in counsel leant over
frames glowing with embroidery, while two fair sisters
more remote occasionally burst into melody, as they tried
the passages of a new air, which had been communicated
to them in the manuscript of some devoted friend.

The Duchess, one of the greatest heiresses of Britain,

D

singularly beautiful and gifted with native grace, had married in her teens one of the wealthiest and most powerful of our nobles, and scarcely older than herself. Her husband was as distinguished for his appearance and his manners as his bride, and those who speculate on race were interested in watching the development of their progeny, who in form, and colour, and voice, and manner, and mind were a reproduction of their parents, who seemed only the elder brother and sister of a gifted circle. The daughters with one exception came first, and all met the same fate. After seventeen years of a delicious home they were presented, and immediately married; and all to personages of high consideration. After the first conquest, this fate seemed as regular as the order of nature. Then came a son, who was now at Christchurch, and then several others, some at school, and some scarcely out of the nursery. There was one daughter unmarried, and she was to be presented next season. Though the family likeness was still apparent in Lady Corisande, in general expression she differed from her sisters. They were all alike with their delicate aquiline noses, bright complexions, short upper lips, and eyes of sunny light. The beauty of Lady Corisande was even more distinguished and more regular, but whether it were the effect of her dark-brown hair or darker eyes, her countenance had not the lustre of the rest, and its expression was grave and perhaps pensive.

The Duke, though still young, and naturally of a gay and joyous temperament, had a high sense of duty, and strong domestic feelings. He was never wanting in his public place, and he was fond of his wife and his children; still more proud of them. Every day when he looked into the glass, and gave the last touch to his consummate toilette, he offered his grateful thanks to Providence that his family was not unworthy of him.

His Grace was accustomed to say that he had only one

misfortune, and it was a great one; he had no home. His
family had married so many heiresses, and he, conse-
quently, possessed so many halls and castles, at all of
which, periodically, he wished, from a right feeling, to
reside, that there was no sacred spot identified with his life
in which his heart, in the bustle and tumult of existence,
could take refuge. Brentham was the original seat of his
family, and he was even passionately fond of it; but it was
remarkable how very short a period of his yearly life was
passed under its stately roof. So it was his custom always
to repair to Brentham the moment the season was over, and
he would exact from his children, that, however short
might be the time, they would be his companions under
these circumstances. The daughters loved Brentham, and
they loved to please their father; but the sons-in-law,
though they were what is called devoted to their wives,
and, unusual as it may seem, scarcely less attached to their
legal parents, did not fall very easily into this arrangement.
The country in August without sport was unquestionably
to them a severe trial: nevertheless, they rarely omitted
making their appearance, and if they did occasionally
vanish, sometimes to Cowes, sometimes to Switzerland,
sometimes to Norway, they always wrote to their wives,
and always alluded to their immediate or approaching return; and their letters gracefully contributed to the fund
of domestic amusement.

And yet it would be difficult to find a fairer scene than
Brentham offered, especially in the lustrous effulgence of a
glorious English summer. It was an Italian palace of freestone; vast, ornate, and in scrupulous condition; its spacious
and graceful chambers filled with treasures of art, and
rising itself from statued and stately terraces. At their foot
spread a gardened domain of considerable extent, bright
with flowers, dim with coverts of rare shrubs, and musical
with fountains. Its limit reached a park, with timber such

as the midland counties only can produce. The fallow
deer trooped among its ferny solitudes and gigantic oaks;
but beyond the waters of the broad and winding lake the
scene became more savage, and the eye caught the dark
form of the red deer on some jutting mount, shrinking
with scorn from communion with his gentler brethren.

CHAPTER II.

LOTHAIR was the little boy whom the Duchess remembered.
He was a posthumous child, and soon lost a devoted mother.
His only relation was one of his two guardians, a Scotch
noble, a Presbyterian and a Whig. This uncle was a
widower with some children, but they were girls, and,
though Lothair was attached to them, too young to be his
companions. Their father was a keen, hard man, honourable and just, but with no softness of heart or manner.
He guarded with precise knowledge and with unceasing
vigilance Lothair's vast inheritance, which was in many
counties and in more than one kingdom; but he educated
him in a Highland home, and when he had reached boyhood thought fit to send him to the High School of Edinburgh. Lothair passed a monotonous if not a dull life;
but he found occasional solace in the scenes of a wild and
beautiful nature, and delight in all the sports of the field
and forest, in which he was early initiated and completely
indulged. Although an Englishman, he was fifteen before
he revisited his country, and then his glimpses of England
were brief, and to him scarcely satisfactory. He was
hurried sometimes to vast domains, which he heard were
his own; and sometimes whisked to the huge metropolis,
where he was shown St. Paul's and the British Museum.
These visits left a vague impression of bustle without

kindness, and exhaustion without excitement; and he was glad to get back to his glens, to the moor and the mountain-stream.

His father, in the selection of his guardians, had not contemplated this system of education. While he secured, by the appointment of his brother-in-law, the most competent and trustworthy steward of his son's fortune, he had depended on another for that influence which should mould the character, guide the opinions, and form the tastes of his child. The other guardian was a clergyman, his father's private tutor and heart-friend; scarcely his parent's senior, but exercising over him irresistible influence, for he was a man of shining talents and abounding knowledge, brilliant and profound. But unhappily, shortly after Lothair became an orphan, this distinguished man seceded from the Anglican communion, and entered the Church of Rome. From this moment there was war between the guardians. The uncle endeavoured to drive his colleague from the trust: in this he failed, for the priest would not renounce his office. The Scotch noble succeeded, however, in making it a fruitless one: he thwarted every suggestion that emanated from the obnoxious quarter; and indeed the secret reason of the almost constant residence of Lothair in Scotland, and of his harsh education, was the fear of his relative, that the moment he crossed the border he might, by some mysterious process, fall under the influence that his guardian so much dreaded and detested.

There was, however, a limit to these severe precautions even before Lothair should reach his majority. His father had expressed in his will that his son should be educated at the University of Oxford, and at the same college of which he had been a member. His uncle was of opinion he complied with the spirit of this instruction by sending Lothair to the University of Edinburgh, which would give the last tonic to his moral system; and then commenced a

celebrated chancery suit, instituted by the Roman Catholic
guardian, in order to enforce a literal compliance with the
educational condition of the will. The uncle looked upon
this movement as a Popish plot, and had recourse to every
available allegation and argument to baffle it, but ultimately in vain. With every precaution to secure his Protestant principles, and to guard against the influence, or
even personal interference, of his Roman Catholic guardian,
the Lord Chancellor decided that Lothair should be sent to
Christchurch.

Here Lothair, who had never been favoured with a companion of his own age and station, soon found a congenial
one in the heir of Brentham. Inseparable in pastime, not
dissociated even in study, sympathising companionship soon
ripened into fervent friendship. They lived so much together that the idea of separation became not only painful
but impossible; and, when vacation arrived, and Brentham
was to be visited by its future lord, what more natural than
that it should be arranged that Lothair should be a visitor
to his domain?

CHAPTER III.

ALTHOUGH Lothair was the possessor of as many palaces
and castles as the Duke himself, it is curious that his first
dinner at Brentham was almost his introduction into refined
society. He had been a guest at the occasional banquets
of his uncle, but these were festivals of the Picts and
Scots; rude plenty and coarse splendour, with noise instead
of conversation, and a tumult of obstructive dependants,
who impeded, by their want of skill, the very convenience
which they were purposed to facilitate. How different the
surrounding scene! A table covered with flowers, bright

with fanciful crystal, and porcelain that had belonged to sovereigns, who had given a name to its colour or its form. As for those present, all seemed grace and gentleness, from the radiant daughters of the house to the noiseless attendants that anticipated all his wants, and sometimes seemed to suggest his wishes.

Lothair sat between two of the married daughters. They addressed him with so much sympathy that he was quite enchanted. When they asked their pretty questions and made their sparkling remarks, roses seemed to drop from their lips, and sometimes diamonds. It was a rather large party, for the Brentham family were so numerous that they themselves made a festival. There were four married daughters, the Duke and two sons-in-law, a clergyman or two, and some ladies and gentlemen who were seldom absent from this circle, and who, by their useful talents and various accomplishments, alleviated the toil or cares of life from which even princes are not exempt.

When the ladies had retired to the Duchess's drawing-room, all the married daughters clustered round their mother.

'Do you know, mamma, we all think him very good-looking,' said the youngest married daughter, the wife of the listless and handsome St. Aldegonde.

'And not at all shy,' said Lady Montairy, 'though reserved.'

'I admire deep blue eyes with dark lashes,' said the Duchess.

Notwithstanding the decision of Lady Montairy, Lothair was scarcely free from embarrassment when he rejoined the ladies; and was so afraid of standing alone, or talking only to men, that he was almost on the point of finding refuge in his dinner companions, had not he instinctively felt that this would have been a social blunder. But the Duchess relieved him: her gracious glance caught his at

the right moment, and she rose and met him some way as
he advanced. The friends had arrived so late, that Lothair
had had only time to make a reverence of ceremony before
dinner.

'It is not our first meeting,' said her Grace; 'but that
you cannot remember.'

'Indeed I do,' said Lothair, 'and your Grace gave me a
golden heart.'

'How can you remember such things,' exclaimed the
Duchess, 'which I had myself forgotten!'

'I have rather a good memory,' replied Lothair; 'and it
is not wonderful that I should remember this, for it is the
only present that ever was made me.'

The evenings at Brentham were short, but they were
sweet. It was a musical family, without being fanatical
on the subject. There was always music, but it was not
permitted that the guests should be deprived of other
amusements. But music was the basis of the evening's
campaign. The Duke himself sometimes took a second;
the four married daughters warbled sweetly; but the great
performer was Lady Corisande. When her impassioned
tones sounded, there was a hushed silence in every chamber; otherwise, many things were said and done amid
accompanying melodies that animated without distracting
even a whistplayer. The Duke himself rather preferred a
game of piquet or écarté with Captain Mildmay, and sometimes retired with a troop to a distant but still visible
apartment, where they played with billiard balls games
which were not billiards.

The ladies had retired, the Duke had taken his glass of
seltzer water, and had disappeared. The gentlemen lingered
and looked at each other, as if they were an assembly of
poachers gathering for an expedition, and then Lord St.
Aldegonde, tall, fair, and languid, said to Lothair, 'Do you
smoke?'

'No!'

'I should have thought Bertram would have seduced you by this time. Then let us try. Montairy will give you one of his cigarettes, so mild that his wife never finds him out.'

CHAPTER IV.

THE breakfast-room at Brentham was very bright. It opened on a garden of its own, which, at this season, was so glowing, and cultured into patterns so fanciful and finished, that it had the resemblance of a vast mosaic. The walls of the chamber were covered with bright drawings and sketches of our modern masters, and frames of interesting miniatures, and the meal was served on half-a-dozen or more round tables, which vied with each other in grace and merriment; brilliant as a cluster of Greek or Italian republics, instead of a great metropolitan table, like a central government absorbing all the genius and resources of the society.

Every scene in this life at Brentham charmed Lothair, who, though not conscious of being of a particularly gloomy temper, often felt that he had, somehow or other, hitherto passed through life rarely with pleasure, and never with joy.

After breakfast the ladies retired to their morning-room, and the gentlemen strolled to the stables, Lord St. Aldegonde lighting a Manilla cheroot of enormous length. As Lothair was very fond of horses, this delighted him. The stables at Brentham were rather too far from the house, but they were magnificent, and the stud worthy of them. It was numerous and choice, and, above all, it was useful. It could supply a readier number of capital riding horses than any stable in England. Brentham was a great riding

family. In the summer season the Duke delighted to head
a numerous troop, penetrate far into the country, and
scamper home to a nine o'clock dinner. All the ladies of
the house were fond and fine horsewomen. The mount of
one of these riding parties was magical. The dames and
damsels vaulted on their barbs, and genets, and thorough-
bred hacks, with such airy majesty; they were absolutely
overwhelming with their bewildering habits and their bewitching hats.

Everything was so new in this life at Brentham to
Lothair, as well as so agreeable, that the first days passed
by no means rapidly; for, though it sounds strange, time
moves with equal slowness whether we experience many
impressions or none. In a new circle every character is
a study, and every incident an adventure; and the multi-
plicity of the images and emotions restrains the hours.
But after a few days, though Lothair was not less delighted, for he was more so, he was astonished at the
rapidity of time. The life was exactly the same, but
equally pleasant; the same charming companions, the same
refined festivity, the same fascinating amusements; but to
his dismay Lothair recollected that nearly a fortnight had
elapsed since his arrival. Lord St. Aldegonde also was
on the wing; he was obliged to go to Cowes to see a sick
friend, though he considerately left Bertha behind him.
The other son-in-law remained, for he could not tear himself
away from his wife. He was so distractedly fond of Lady
Montairy that he would only smoke cigarettes. Lothair
felt it was time to go, and he broke the circumstance to
his friend Bertram.

These two 'old fellows,' as they mutually described each
other, could not at all agree as to the course to be pursued.
Bertram looked upon Lothair's suggestion as an act of
desertion from himself. At their time of life, the claims of
friendship are paramount. And where could Lothair go

to? And what was there to do? Nowhere, and nothing. Whereas, if he would remain a little longer, as the Duke expected and also the Duchess, Bertram would go with him anywhere he liked, and do anything he chose. So Lothair remained.

In the evening, seated by Lady Montairy, Lothair observed on her sister's singing, and said, 'I never heard any of our great singers, but I cannot believe there is a finer voice in existence.'

'Corisande's is a fine voice,' said Lady Montairy, 'but I admire her expression more than her tone; for there are certainly many finer voices, and some day you will hear them.'

'But I prefer expression,' said Lothair very decidedly.

'Ah, yes! doubtless,' said Lady Montairy, who was working a purse, 'and that is what we all want, I believe; at least we married daughters, they say. My brother, Granville St. Aldegonde, says we are all too much alike, and that Bertha St. Aldegonde would be perfect if she had no sisters.'

'I do not at all agree with Lord St. Aldegonde,' said Lothair with energy. 'I do not think it is possible to have too many relatives like you and your sisters.'

Lady Montairy looked up with a smile, but she did not meet a smiling countenance. He seemed what is called an earnest young man, this friend of her brother Bertram.

At this moment the Duke sent swift messengers for all to come, even the Duchess, to partake in a new game just arrived from Russia, some miraculous combination of billiard-balls. Some rose directly, some lingering a moment arranging their work, but all were in motion. Corisande was at the piano, and disencumbering herself of some music. Lothair went up to her rather abruptly:

'Your singing,' he said, 'is the finest thing I ever heard.

I am so happy that I am not going to leave Brentham to-morrow. There is no place in the world that I think equal to Brentham.'

'And I love it too, and no other place,' she replied; 'and I should be quite happy if I never left it.'

CHAPTER V.

LORD MONTAIRY was passionately devoted to croquêt. He flattered himself that he was the most accomplished male performer existing. He would have thought absolutely the most accomplished, were it not for the unrivalled feats of Lady Montairy. She was the queen of croquêt. Her sisters also used the mallet with admirable skill, but not like Victoria. Lord Montairy always looked forward to his summer croquêt at Brentham. It was a great croquêt family, the Brentham family; even listless Lord St. Alde-gonde would sometimes play, with a cigar never out of his mouth. They did not object to his smoking in the air. On the contrary, 'they rather liked it.' Captain Mildmay, too, was a brilliant hand, and had written a treatise on croquêt, the best going.

There was a great croquêt party one morning at Brent-ham. Some neighbours had been invited who loved the sport. Mr. Blenkinsop, a grave young gentleman, whose countenance never relaxed while he played, and who was understood to give his mind entirely up to croquêt. He was the owner of the largest estate in the county, and it was thought would very willingly have allied himself with one of the young ladies of the House of Brentham; but these flowers were always plucked so quickly, that his relations with the distinguished circle never grew more intimate than croquêt. He drove over with some fine

horses and several cases and bags containing instruments
and weapons for the fray. His sister came with him, who
had forty thousand pounds, but, they said, in some mysterious manner dependent on his consent to her marriage;
and it was added that Mr. Blenkinsop would not allow his
sister to marry because he would miss her so much in his
favourite pastime. There were some other morning visitors,
and one or two young curates in cassocks.

It seemed to Lothair a game of great deliberation and of
more interest than gaiety, though sometimes a cordial
cheer, and sometimes a ringing laugh of amiable derision,
notified a signal triumph or a disastrous failure. But the
scene was brilliant: a marvellous lawn, the Duchess's
Turkish tent with its rich hangings, and the players themselves, the prettiest of all the spectacle, with their coquet-
tish hats, and their half-veiled and half-revealed under-
raiment, scarlet and silver, or blue and gold, made up a
sparkling and modish scene.

Lothair, who had left the players for awhile and was
regaining the lawn, met the Duchess.

'Your Grace is not going to leave us, I hope?' he said,
rather anxiously.

'For a moment. I have long promised to visit the new
dairy; and I think this a good opportunity.'

'Might I be your companion?' said Lothair.

They turned into a winding walk of thick and fragrant
shrubs, and, after a while, they approached a dell, surrounded with high trees that enveloped it with perpetual
shade; in the centre of the dell was apparently a Gothic
shrine, fair in design and finished in execution, and this
was the Duchess's new dairy. A pretty sight is a first-
rate dairy, with its flooring of fanciful tiles, and its cool
and shrouded chambers, its stained windows and its
marble slabs, and porcelain pans of cream, and plenteous
platters of fantastically formed butter.

'Mrs. Woods and her dairymaids look like a Dutch picture,' said the Duchess. 'Were you ever in Holland?'

'I have never been anywhere,' said Lothair.

'You should travel,' said the Duchess.

'I have no wish,' said Lothair.

'The Duke has given me some Corcean fowls,' said the Duchess to Mrs. Woods, when they had concluded their visit. 'Do you think you could take care of them for me?'

'Well, Grace, I am sure I will do my best; but then they are very troublesome, and I was not fortunate with my Cochin. I had rather they were sent to the aviary, Grace, if it were all the same.'

'I should like to see the aviary,' said Lothair.

'Well, we will go.'

And this rather extended their walk, and withdrew them more from the amusement of the day.

'I wish you would do me a great favour,' said Lothair, abruptly breaking a rather prolonged silence.

'And what is that?' said the Duchess.

'It is a very great favour,' repeated Lothair.

'If it be in my power to grant it, its magnitude would only be an additional recommendation.'

'Well,' said Lothair, blushing deeply, and speaking with much agitation, 'I would ask your Grace's permission to offer my hand to your daughter.'

The Duchess looked amazed. 'Corisande!' she exclaimed.

'Yes, to Lady Corisande.

'Corisande,' replied the Duchess, after a pause, 'has absolutely not yet entered the world. Corisande is a child; and you, you, my dear friend; I am sure you will pardon me if I say so, you are not very much older than Corisande,'

'I have no wish to enter the world,' said Lothair, with much decision.

'1 am not an enemy to youthful marriages,' said the Duchess. 'I married early myself, and my children married early; and I am very happy, and I hope they are; but some experience of society before we settle is most desirable, and is one of the conditions I cannot but believe of that felicity which we all seek.'

'I hate society,' said Lothair. 'I would never go out of my domestic circle if it were the circle I contemplate.'

'My dear young friend,' said the Duchess, 'you could hardly have seen enough of society to speak with so much decision.'

'I have seen quite enough of it,' said Lothair. 'I went to an evening party last season; I came up from Christchurch on purpose for it, and if ever they catch me at another, they shall inflict any penalty they please.'

'I fear it was a stupid party,' said the Duchess, smiling, and glad to turn, if possible, the conversation into a lighter vein.

'No, it was a very grand party, I believe, and not exactly stupid; it was not that; but I was disgusted with all I saw and all I heard. It seemed to me a mass of affectation, falsehood, and malice.'

'Oh! dear,' said the Duchess, 'how very dreadful! But I did not mean merely going to parties for society; I meant knowledge of the world, and that experience which enables us to form sound opinions on the affairs of life.'

'Oh! as for that,' said Lothair, 'my opinions are already formed on every subject; that is to say, every subject of importance; and, what is more, they will never change.'

'I could not say that of Corisande,' said the Duchess.

'I think we agree on all the great things,' said Lothair, musingly. 'Her Church views may be a little higher than mine, but I do not anticipate any permanent difficulty on that head. Although my uncle made me go to kirk, I always hated it, and always considered myself a churchman. Then, as to churches themselves, she is in favour of building churches, and so am I; and schools, there is no number of schools I would not establish. My opinion is, you cannot have too much education, provided it be founded on a religious basis. I would sooner renounce the whole of my inheritance than consent to secular education.'

'I should be sorry to see any education but a religious education,' remarked the Duchess.

'Well, then,' said Lothair, 'that is our life, or a great part of it. To complete it, there is that to which I really wish to devote my existence, and in which I instinctively feel Lady Corisande would sympathise with me, the extinction of pauperism.'

'That is a vast subject,' said the Duchess.

'It is the terror of Europe, and the disgrace of Britain,' said Lothair; 'and I am resolved to grapple with it. It seems to me that pauperism is not an affair so much of wages as of dwellings. If the working classes were properly lodged, at their present rate of wages, they would be richer. They would be healthier and happier at the same cost. I am so convinced of this, that the moment I am master I shall build 2,000 cottages on my estates. I have the designs all ready.'

'I am much in favour of improved dwellings for the poor,' said the Duchess; 'but then you must take care that your dwellings are cottages, and not villas like my cousin's, the Duke of Luton.'

'I do not think I shall make that mistake,' replied Lothair. 'It constantly engages my thought. I am wearied of hearing of my wealth, and I am conscious it has never brought me any happiness. I have lived a great deal alone, dearest Duchess, and thought much of these things, but I feel now I should be hardly equal to the effort, unless I had a happy home to fall back upon.'

'And you will have a happy home in due time,' said the

Duchess; 'and with such good and great thoughts you deserve one. But take the advice of one who loved your mother, and who would extend to you the same affection as to her own children: before you take a step which cannot be recalled, see a little more of the world.'

Lothair shook his head. 'No,' he said, after a pause. 'My idea of perfect society is being married as I propose, and paying visits to Brentham; and when the visits to Brentham ceased, then I should like you and the Duke to pay visits to us.'

'But that would be a fairy tale,' said the Duchess.

So they walked on in silence.

Suddenly and abruptly Lothair turned to the Duchess and said, 'Does your Grace see any objection to my speaking to your daughter?'

'Dear friend, indeed yes. What you would say would only agitate and disturb Corisande. Her character is not yet formed, and its future is perplexing, at least to me,' murmured the mother. 'She has not the simple nature of her sisters. It is a deeper and more complicated mind, and I watch its development with fond but anxious interest.' Then in a lighter tone she added, 'You do not know very much of us. Try to know more. Everybody under this roof views you with regard, and you are the brother friend of our eldest son. Wherever we are, you will always find a home; but do not touch again upon this subject, at least at present, for it distresses me.' And then she took his arm and pressed it, and by this time they had gained the croquet ground.

CHAPTER VI.

ONE of the least known squares in London is Hexham Square, though it is one of the oldest. Not that it is very remote from the throng of existence, but it is isolated in a dingy district of silent and decaying streets. Once it was a favoured residence of opulence and power, and its architecture still indicates its former and prouder destiny. But its noble mansions are now divided and broken up into separate dwellings, or have been converted into chambers and offices. Lawyers, and architects, and agents dwell in apartments where the richly-sculptured chimneypieces, the carved and gilded pediments over the doors, and sometimes even the painted ceilings, tell a tale of vanished stateliness and splendour.

A considerable portion of the north side of the square is occupied by one house standing in a courtyard, with iron gates to the thoroughfare. This is Hexham House, and where Lord Hexham lived in the days of the first Georges. It is reduced in size since his time, two considerable wings having been pulled down about sixty years ago, and their materials employed in building some residences of less pretension. But the body of the dwelling-house remains, and the courtyard, though reduced in size, has been retained.

Hexham House has an old oak entrance hall panelled with delicacy, and which has escaped the rifling arts of speculators in furniture; and out of it rises a staircase of the same material, of a noble character, adorned occasionally with figures; armorial animals holding shields, and sometimes a grotesque form rising from fruits and flowers, all doubtless the work of some famous carver. The staircase leads to a corridor, on which several doors open, and through one of these, at the moment of our history, a man,

dressed in a dark cassock and holding a card in his hand,
was entering a spacious chamber, meagerly, but not shab-
bily, furnished. There was a rich cabinet and a fine picture.
In the next room, not less spacious, but which had a more
inhabited look, a cheerful fire, tables covered with books
and papers, and two individuals busily at work with their
pens, he gave the card to a gentleman who wore also the
cassock, and who stood before the fire with a book in his
hand, and apparently dictating to one of the writers.

'Impossible!' said the gentleman, shaking his head;
'I could not even go in, as Monsignore Berwick is with his
Eminence.'

'But what shall I do?' said the attendant; 'his
Eminence said that when Mr. Giles called he never was to
be denied.'

'The Monsignore has been here a long time; you must
beg Mr. Giles to wait. Make him comfortable; give him
a newspaper; not the "Tablet," the "Times;" men like
Mr. Giles love reading the advertisements. Or stop, give
him this, his Eminence's lecture on geology; it will show
him the Church has no fear of science. Ah! there's my
bell, Mr. Giles will not have to wait long.' So saying, the
gentleman put down his volume and disappeared through
an antechamber into a further apartment.

It was a library, of moderate dimensions, and yet its
well-filled shelves contained all the weapons of learning
and controversy which the deepest and the most active of
ecclesiastical champions could require. It was unlike
modern libraries, for it was one in which folios greatly
predominated; and they stood in solemn and sometimes
magnificent array, for they bore, many of them, on their
ancient though costly bindings the proofs that they had
belonged to many a prince and even sovereign of the Church.
Over the mantelpiece hung a portrait of his Holiness

c 2

Pius IX., and on the table, in the midst of many papers,
was an ivory crucifix.

The master of the library had risen from his seat when
the chief secretary entered, and was receiving an obeisance.
Above the middle height, his stature seemed magnified by
the attenuation of his form. It seemed that the soul never
had so frail and fragile a tenement. He was dressed in a
dark cassock with a red border, and wore scarlet stockings;
and over his cassock a purple tippet, and on his breast a
small golden cross. His countenance was naturally of an
extreme pallor, though at this moment slightly flushed
with the animation of a deeply interesting conference. His
cheeks were hollow, and his grey eyes seemed sunk into
his clear and noble brow, but they flashed with irresistible
penetration. Such was Cardinal Grandison.

'All that I can do is,' said his Eminence, when his visitor
was ushered out, and slightly shrugging his shoulders, ' is
to get it postponed until I go to Rome, and even then I
must not delay my visit. This crossing the Alps in winter
is a trial ; but we must never repine, and there is nothing
which we must not encounter to prevent incalculable mischief. The publication of the Scotch hierarchy at this
moment will destroy the labours of years. And yet they
will not see it ! I cannot conceive who is urging them,
for I am sure they must have some authority from home.
You have something for me, Chidiock,' he added, enquiringly, for his keen eye caught the card.

'I regret to trouble your Eminence when you need
repose, but the bearer of this card seems to have been
importunate and to have appealed to your name and personal orders;' and he gave the Cardinal the card.

'Yes,' said the Cardinal looking at the card with much
interest; ' this is a person I must always see.'

And so in due course they ushered into the library a
gentleman with a crimson and well-stuffed bag, of a com-

posed yet cheerful aspect, who addressed the Cardinal with respect but without embarrassment, saying, 'I am ashamed to trouble your Eminence with only matters of form, absolutely mere matters of form; but I obey, sir, your own instructions.'

'It is not for me to depreciate form,' replied the Cardinal; 'and in business there are no mere matters of form.'

'Merely the wood accounts,' continued the visitor; 'they must be approved by both the guardians, or the money cannot be received by the bankers. Your Eminence, you see, has sanctioned the felling, and authorized the sales, and these are the final accounts, which must be signed before we pay in.'

'Give them to me,' said the Cardinal, stretching out both his hands as he received a mass of paper folios. His Eminence resumed his chair, and hastily examined the sheets. 'Ah!' he said, 'no ordinary felling; it reaches over seven counties. By the bye, Bracewood Forest; what about the enclosure? I have heard no more of it.' Then, murmuring to himself, 'Grentham Wood; how well I remember Grentham Wood, with his dear father!'

'If we could sign to-day,' said the visitor in a tone of professional cajolery: 'time is important.'

'And it shall not be wasted,' replied the Cardinal. 'But I must look over the accounts. I doubt not all is quite regular, but I wish to make myself a little familiar with the scene of action; perhaps to recall the past,' he added. 'You shall have them to-morrow, Mr. Giles.'

'Your Eminence will have very different accounts to settle in a short time,' said Mr. Giles, smiling. 'We are hard at work; it takes three of our clerks constantly occupied.'

'But you have yet got time.'

'I don't know that,' said Mr. Giles. 'The affairs are very large. And the mines, they give us the greatest

trouble. Our Mr. James Roundell was two months in
Wales last year about them. It took up the whole of his
vacation. And your Eminence must remember that time
flies. In less than eight months he will be of age.'

'Very true,' said the Cardinal ; 'time indeed flies, and
so much to be done ! By the bye, Mr. Giles, have you by
any chance heard anything lately of my child ?'

'I have heard of him a good deal of late, for a client of
ours, Lord Montairy, met him at Brentham this summer,
and was a long time there with him. After that, I hear,
he went deer-stalking with some of his young friends ; but
he is not very fond of Scotland ; had rather too much of it,
I suspect ; but the truth is, sir, I saw him this very day.'

'Indeed !'

'Some affairs have brought him up to town, and I
rather doubt whether he will return to Oxford ; at least,
so he talks.'

'Ah ! I have never seen him since he was an infant, I
might say,' said the Cardinal. 'I suppose I shall see him
again, if only when I resign my trust ; but I know not.
And yet few things would be more interesting to me than
to meet him !'

Mr. Giles seemed moved, for him almost a little embarrassed ; he seemed to blush, and then he cleared his throat.
'It would be too great a liberty,' said Mr. Giles, 'I feel
that very much ; and yet, if your Eminence would con-
descend, though I hardly suppose it possible, his Lordship
is really going to do us the honour of dining with us to-
day ; only a few friends, and if your Eminence could make
the sacrifice, and it were not an act of too great presumption to ask your Eminence to join our party.'

'I never eat and I never drink,' said the Cardinal. 'I
am sorry to say I cannot. I like dinner society very much.
You see the world, and you hear things which you do not
hear otherwise. For a time I presumed to accept invita-

tions, though I sat with an empty plate; but though the
world was indulgent to me, I felt that my habits were an
embarrassment to the happier feasters: it was not fair, and
so I gave it up. But I tell you what, Mr. Giles: I shall be
in your quarter this evening; perhaps you would permit
me to drop in and pay my respects to Mrs. Giles: I have
wished to do so before.'

CHAPTER VII.

MR. GILES was a leading partner in the firm of Roundells,
Giles, and Roundell, among the most eminent solicitors of
Lincoln's Inn. He, in these days of prolonged maturity,
might be described as still a young man. He had inherited from his father a large share in a first-rate business,
and no inconsiderable fortune; and he had a wife, celebrated in her circle, but no children. He was opulent and
prosperous, with no cares and anxieties of his own, and
loved his profession, for which he was peculiarly qualified,
being a man of uncommon sagacity, very difficult to deceive,
and yet one who sympathised with his clients, who were
all personally attached to him, and many of whom were
among the distinguished personages of the realm.

During an important professional visit to Ireland, Mr.
Giles had made the acquaintance of Miss Apollonia
Smylie, the niece of an Irish peer; and though the lady
was much admired and courted, had succeeded, after a
time, in inducing her to become the partner of his life.

Mrs. Giles, or as she described herself Mrs. Putney Giles,
taking advantage of a second and territorial Christian
name of her husband, was a showy woman; decidedly
handsome, unquestionably accomplished, and gifted with
energy and enthusiasm which far exceeded even her

physical advantages. Her principal mission was to destroy the Papacy and to secure Italian unity. Her lesser impulses were to become acquainted with the aristocracy, and to be herself surrounded by celebrities. Having a fine house in Tyburnia, almost as showy as herself, and a husband who was never so happy as when gratifying her wishes, she did not find it difficult in a considerable degree to pursue and even accomplish her objects. The Putney Giles gave a great many dinners, and Mrs. Putney received her world frequently, if not periodically. As they entertained with profusion, her well-lighted saloons were considerably attended. These assemblies were never dull; the materials not being ordinary, often startling, sometimes even brilliant, occasionally rather heterogeneous. For though being a violent Protestant and of extreme conservative opinions, her antipapal antipathies and her Italian predilections frequently involved her with acquaintances not so distinguished as she deemed herself for devotion to the cause of order and orthodoxy. It was rumoured that the brooding brow of Mazzini had been observed in her rooms, and there was no sort of question that she had thrown herself in ecstatic idolatry at the feet of the hero of Caprera.

On the morning of the day on which he intended to visit Cardinal Grandison, Mr. Giles, in his chambers at Lincoln's Inn, was suddenly apprised by a clerk, that an interview with him was sought by a client no less distinguished than Lothair.

Although Mr. Giles sat opposite two rows of tin boxes, each of which was numbered, and duly inscribed with the name of Lothair and that of the particular estate to which it referred, Mr. Giles, though he had had occasional communications with his client, was personally unacquainted with him. He viewed therefore with no ordinary curiosity the young man who was ushered into his room; a shapely youth above the middle height, of simple but distinguished mien, with a countenance naturally pale, though

somewhat bronzed by a life of air and exercise, and a profusion of dark auburn hair.

And for what could Lothair be calling on Mr. Giles ?

It seems that one of Lothair's intimate companions had
got into a scrape, and under these circumstances had what
is styled ' made a friend ' of Lothair; that is to say, con-
fided to him his trouble, and asked his advice, with a view,
when given, of its being followed by an offer of assistance.

Lothair, though inexperienced and very ingenuous, was
not devoid of a certain instinctive perception of men and
things, which rendered it difficult for him to be an easy
prey. His natural disposition, and his comparatively solitary education, had made him a keen observer, and he was
one who meditated over his observations. But he was
naturally generous and sensible of kindness; and this was
a favourite companion, next to Bertram his most intimate.

Lothair was quite happy in the opportunity of soothing
a perturbed spirit whose society had been to him a source
of so much gratification.

It was not until Lothair had promised to extricate his
friend from his overwhelming difficulties, that, upon reflection and examination, he found the act on his part was not
so simple and so easy as he had assumed it to be. His
guardians had apportioned to him an allowance in every
sense adequate to his position; and there was no doubt,
had he wished to exceed it for any legitimate purpose, not
the slightest difficulty on their part would have been
experienced.

Such a conjuncture had never occurred. Lothair was
profuse, but he was not prodigal. He gratified all his
fancies, but they were not ignoble ones; and he was not
only sentimentally, but systematically, charitable. He had
a great number of fine horses, and he had just paid for an
expensive yacht. In a word, he spent a great deal of
money, and until he called at his bankers to learn what

sums were at his disposition he was not aware that he had
overdrawn his account.

This was rather awkward. Lothair wanted a considerable sum, and he wanted it at once. Irrespective of the
consequent delay, he shrunk from any communication with
his guardians. From his uncle he had become, almost insensibly, estranged, and with his other guardian he had
never had the slightest communication. Under these circumstances he recalled the name of the solicitor of the
trustees, between whom and himself there had been occasional correspondence; and being of a somewhat impetuous
disposition, he rode off at once from his hotel to Lincoln's
Inn.

Mr. Giles listened to the narrative with unbroken interest and unswerving patience, with his eyes fixed on his
client, and occasionally giving a sympathetic nod.

'And so,' concluded Lothair, 'I thought I would come
to you.'

'We are honoured,' said Mr. Giles. 'And certainly it
is quite absurd that your Lordship should want money, and
for a worthy purpose, and not be able to command it.
Why! the balance in the name of the trustees never was so
great as at this moment; and this very day, or to-morrow
at farthest, I shall pay no less than eight-and-thirty
thousand pounds timber money to the account.'

'Well, I don't want a fifth of that,' said Lothair.

'Your Lordship has an objection to apply to the
trustees?' enquired Mr. Giles.

'That is the point of the whole of my statement,' said
Lothair, somewhat impatiently.

'And yet it is the right and regular thing,' said Mr.
Giles.

'It may be right and it may be regular, but it is out of
the question.'

'Then we will say no more about it. What I want to

prevent,' said Mr. Giles, musingly, 'is anything absurd happening. There is no doubt if your Lordship went into the street and said you wanted ten thousand pounds, or a hundred thousand, fifty people would supply you immediately; but you would have to pay for it. Some enormous usury! That would be bad; but the absurdity of the thing would be greater than the mischief. Roundells, Giles, and Roundell could not help you in that manner. That is not our business. We are glad to find money for our clients at a legal rate of interest, and the most moderate rate feasible. But then there must be security, and the best security. But here we must not conceal it from ourselves, my Lord, we have no security whatever. At this moment your Lordship has no property. An insurance office might do it with a policy. They might consider that they had a moral security; but still it would be absurd. There is something absurd in your Lordship having to raise money. Don't you think I could see these people,' said Mr. Giles, 'and talk to them, and gain a little time. We only want a little time.'

'No,' said Lothair, in a peremptory tone. 'I said I would do it, and it must be done, and at once. Sooner than there should be delay, I would rather go into the street, as you suggest, and ask the first man I met to lend me the money. My word has been given, and I do not care what I pay to fulfil my word.'

'We must not think of such things,' said Mr. Giles, shaking his head. 'All I want your Lordship to understand is the exact position. In this case we have no security. Roundells, Giles, and Roundell cannot move without security. It would be against our articles of partnership. But Mr. Giles, as a private individual, may do what he likes. I will let your Lordship have the money, and I will take no security whatever, not even a note of hand. All that I will ask for is that your Lordship should write me a

letter, saying you have urgent need for a sum of money
(mentioning amount) for an honourable purpose, in which
your feelings are deeply interested; and that will do. If
anything happens to your Lordship before this time next
year, why, I think the trustees could hardly refuse repay-
ing the money; and if they did, why then,' added Mr.
Giles, 'I suppose it will be all the same a hundred years
hence.'

'You have conferred on me the greatest obligation,' said
Lothair, with much earnestness. 'Language cannot express what I feel. I am not too much used to kindness,
and I only hope that I may live to show my sense of yours.'

'It is really no great affair, my Lord,' said Mr. Giles. 'I
did not wish to make difficulties, but it was my duty to put
the matter clearly before you. What I propose to do is
really nothing. I could do no less; I should have felt
quite absurd if your Lordship had gone into the money
market.'

'I only hope,' repeated Lothair, rising and offering Mr.
Giles his hand, 'that life may give me some occasion to
prove my gratitude.'

'Well, my Lord,' replied Mr. Giles, 'if your Lordship
wish to repay me for any little interest I have shown in
your affairs, you can do that, over and over again, and at
once.'

'How so?'

'By a very great favour, by which Mrs. Giles and
myself would be deeply gratified. We have a few friends
who honour us by dining with us to-day in Hyde Park
Gardens. If your Lordship would add the great distinction of your presence ——'

'I should only be too much honoured,' exclaimed
Lothair; 'I suppose about eight;' and he left the room;
and Mr. Giles telegraphed instantly the impending event
to Apollonia.

CHAPTER VIII.

It was a great day for Apollonia; not only to have Lothair on her right hand at dinner, but the prospect of receiving a Cardinal in the evening. But she was equal to it; though so engrossed, indeed, in the immediate gratification of her hopes and wishes, that she could scarcely dwell sufficiently on the coming scene of triumph and social excitement.

The repast was sumptuous; Lothair thought the dinner would never end, there were so many dishes, and apparently all of the highest pretension. But if his simple tastes had permitted him to take an interest in these details, which they did not, he would have been assisted by a splendid menu of gold and white typography, that was by the side of each guest. The table seemed literally to groan under vases and gigantic flagons, and, in its midst, rose a mountain of silver, on which apparently all the cardinal virtues, several of the pagan deities, and Britannia herself, illustrated with many lights a glowing inscription which described the fervent feelings of a grateful client.

There were many guests: the Dowager of Farringford, a lady of quality, Apollonia's great lady, who exercised under this roof much social tyranny; in short, was rather fine; but who, on this occasion, was somewhat cowed by the undreamt-of presence of Lothair. She had not yet met him, and probably never would have met him, had she not had the good fortune of dining at his lawyer's. However, Lady Farringford was placed a long way from Lothair, having been taken down to dinner by Mr. Giles, and so, by the end of the first course, Lady Farringford had nearly resumed her customary despotic vein, and was beginning

to indulge in several kind observations, championing her
host and hostess and indirectly exalting herself; upon
which Mr. Giles took an early easy opportunity of ap-
prising Lady Farringford that she had nearly met Cardinal
Grandison at dinner, and that his Eminence would certainly pay his respects to Mrs. Putney Giles in the evening.
As Lady Farringford was at present a high ritualist,
and had even been talked of as 'going to Rome,' this intelligence was stunning, and it was observed that her
Ladyship was unusually subdued during the whole of the
second course.

On the right of Lothair sate the wife of a Vice-Chancellor, a quiet and pleasing lady, to whom Lothair, with
natural good breeding, paid snatches of happy attention,
when he could for a moment with propriety withdraw himself from the blaze of Apollonia's coruscating conversation.
Then there was a rather fierce-looking Red Ribbon, medal-
led as well as be-starred, and the Red Ribbon's wife, with
a blushing daughter, in spite of her parentage not yet
accustomed to stand fire. A partner and his unusually
numerous family had the pleasure also of seeing Lothair
for the first time, and there were no less than four M.P.'s,
one of whom was even in office.

Apollonia was stating to Lothair, with brilliant perspi-
cuity, the reasons which quite induced her to believe that
the Gulf Stream had changed its course, and the political
and social consequences that might accrue.

'The religious sentiment of the Southern races must be
wonderfully affected by a more rigorous climate,' said
Apollonia. 'I cannot doubt,' she continued, 'that a series
of severe winters at Rome might put an end to Romanism.'

'But is there any fear that a reciprocal influence might
be exercised on the Northern nations?' enquired Lothair.
'Would there be any apprehension of our Protestantism
becoming proportionately relaxed?'

'Of course not,' said Apollonia. 'Truth cannot be affected by climate. Truth is truth alike in Palestine and Scandinavia.'

'I wonder what the Cardinal would think of this,' said Lothair, 'who, you tell me, is coming to you this evening.'

'Yes, I am most interested to see him, though he is the most puissant of our foes. Of course he would take refuge in sophistry; and science, you know, they deny.'

'Cardinal Grandison is giving some lectures on science,' said the Vice-Chancellor's lady, quietly.

'It is remorse,' said Apollonia. 'Their clever men can never forget that unfortunate affair of Galileo, and think they can divert the indignation of the nineteenth century by mock zeal about red sandstone or the origin of species.'

'And are you afraid of the Gulf Stream?' enquired Lothair of his calmer neighbour.

'I think we want more evidence of a change. The Vice-Chancellor and I went down to a place we have near town on Saturday, where there is a very nice piece of water; indeed, some people call it a lake; it was quite frozen, and my boys wanted to skate, but that I would not permit.'

'You believe in the Gulf Stream to that extent,' said Lothair; 'no skating.'

The Cardinal came early; the ladies had not long left the dining-room. They were agitated when his name was announced; even Apollonia's heart beat; but then that might be accounted for by the inopportune recollection of an occasional correspondence with Caprera.

Nothing could exceed the simple suavity with which the Cardinal appeared, approached, and greeted them. He thanked Apollonia for her permission to pay his respects to her, which he had long wished to do; and then they were all presented, and he said exactly the right thing to every-one. He must have heard of them all before, or read their characters in their countenances. In a few minutes they were all listening to his Eminence with enchanted ease, as, sitting on the sofa by his hostess, he described to them the ambassadors who had just arrived from Japan, and with whom he had relations of interesting affairs. The Japanese Government had exhibited enlightened kindness to some of his poor people who had barely escaped martyrdom. Much might be expected from the Mikado, evidently a man of singular penetration and elevated views; and his Eminence looked as if the mission to Yokohama would speedily end in an episcopal see; but he knew where he was, and studiously avoided all controversial matter.

After all, the Mikado himself was not more remarkable than this Prince of the Church in a Tyburnian drawing-room, habited in his pink cassock and cape, and waving, as he spoke, with careless grace his pink barrette.

The ladies thought the gentlemen rejoined them too soon; but Mr. Giles, when he was apprised of the arrival of the Cardinal, thought it right to precipitate the symposium. With great tact, when the Cardinal rose to greet him, Mr. Giles withdrew his Eminence from those surrounding, and, after a brief interchange of whispered words, quitted him, and then brought forward and presented Lothair to the Cardinal, and left them.

'This is not the first time that we should have met,' said the Cardinal; 'but my happiness is so great at this moment that, though I deplore, I will not dwell on, the past.'

'I am, nevertheless, grateful to you, sir, for many services, and have more than once contemplated taking the liberty of personally assuring your Eminence of my gratitude.'

'I think we might sit down,' said the Cardinal, looking around; and then he led Lothair into an open but interior saloon, where none were yet present, and where they seated

themselves on a sofa, and were soon engaged in apparently
interesting converse.

In the meantime the world gradually filled the principal
saloon of Apollonia, and when it approached overflowing,
occasionally some persons passed the line, and entered the
room in which the Cardinal and his ward were seated, and
then, as if conscious of violating some sacred place, drew
back. Others, on the contrary, with coarser curiosity, were
induced to invade the chamber from the mere fact that the
Cardinal was to be seen there.

'My geographical instinct,' said the Cardinal to Lothair,
'assures me that I can regain the staircase through these
rooms, without rejoining the busy world; so I shall bid you
good night, and even presume to give you my blessing;'
and his Eminence glided away.

When Lothair returned to the saloon it was so crowded
that he was not observed; exactly what he liked; and he
stood against the wall watching all that passed, not without amusement. A lively, social parasite, who had dined
there, and had thanked his stars at dinner that fortune had
decreed he should meet Lothair, had been cruising for his
prize all the time that Lothair had been conversing with the
Cardinal, and was soon at his side.

'A strange scene this!' said the parasite.

'Is it unusual?' enquired Lothair.

'Such a medley! How they can be got together, I
marvel: priests and philosophers, legitimists and car-
bonari! Wonderful woman, Mrs. Putney Giles!'

'She is very entertaining,' said Lothair, 'and seems to
me clever.'

'Remarkably so,' said the parasite, who had been on the
point of satirising his hostess, but, observing the quarter of
the wind, with rapidity went in for praise. 'An extraordinary woman. Your Lordship had a long talk with the
Cardinal.'

D

'I had the honour of some conversation with Cardinal Grandison,' said Lothair, drawing up.

'I wonder what the Cardinal would have said if he had met Mazzini here?'

'Mazzini! Is he here?'

'Not now; but I have seen him here,' said the parasite, 'and our host such a Tory! That makes the thing so amusing;' and then the parasite went on making small personal observations on the surrounding scene, and every now and then telling little tales of great people with whom, it appeared, he was intimate: all concocted fire to gain the very great social fortress he was now besieging. The parasite was so full of himself, and so anxious to display himself to advantage, that with all his practice it was some time before he perceived he did not make all the way he could wish with Lothair, who was courteous, but somewhat monosyllabic and absent.

'Your Lordship is struck by that face?' said the parasite.

Was Lothair struck by that face? And what was it?

He had exchanged glances with that face during the last ten minutes, and the mutual expression was not one of sympathy, but curiosity, blended, on the part of the face, with an expression, if not of disdain, of extreme reserve.

It was the face of a matron, apparently of not many summers, for her shapely figure was still slender, though her mien was stately. But it was the countenance that had commanded the attention of Lothair: pale, but perfectly Attic in outline, with the short upper lip and the round chin, and a profusion of dark chesnut hair bound by a Grecian fillet, and on her brow a star.

'Yes, I am struck by that face. Who is it?'

'If your Lordship could only get a five-francpiece of the last French Republic, 1850, you would know. I dare say the moneychangers could get you one. All the artists of

Paris, painters, and sculptors, and medallists, were competing to produce a face worthy of representing "La République française;" nobody was satisfied, when Ondine caught a girl of not seventeen, and, with a literal reproduction of nature, gained the prize with unanimity.'

'Ah!'

'And though years have passed, the countenance has not changed; perhaps improved.'

'It is a countenance that will bear, perhaps even would require, maturity,' said Lothair; 'but she is no longer "La République française;" what is she now?'

'She is called Theodora, though married, I believe, to an Englishman, a friend of Garibaldi. Her birth unknown; some say an Italian, some a Pole; all sorts of stories. But she speaks every language, is ultracosmopolitan, and has invented a new religion.'

'A new religion!'

'Would your Lordship care to be introduced to her? I know her enough for that. Shall we go up to her?'

'I have made so many new acquaintances to-day,' said Lothair, as it were starting from a reverie, 'and indeed heard so many new things, that I think I had better say good night;' and he graciously retired.

CHAPTER IX.

ABOUT the same time that Lothair had repaired to the residence of Mr. Giles, Monsignore Berwick, whose audience of the Cardinal in the morning had preceded that of the legal adviser of the trustees, made his way towards one of the noblest mansions in St. James's Square, where resided Lord St. Jerome.

It was a mild winter evening; a little fog still hanging

about, but vanquished by the cheerful lamps, and the voice
of the muffin bell was just heard at intervals; a genial
sound that calls up visions of trim and happy hearths. If
we could only so contrive our lives as to go into the
country for the first note of the nightingale, and return to
town for the first note of the muffin bell, existence, it is
humbly presumed, might be more enjoyable.

Monsignore Berwick was a young man, but looking
younger from a countenance almost of childhood; fair, with
light blue eyes, and flaxen hair and delicate features. He
was the last person you would have fixed upon as a born
Roman; but nature, in one of the freaks of race, had
resolved that his old Scottish blood should be re-asserted,
though his ancestors had sedulously blended it, for many
generations, with that of the princely houses of the eternal
city. The Monsignore was the greatest statesman of
Rome, formed and favoured by Antonelli, and probably his
successor.

The mansion of Lord St. Jerome was a real family
mansion, built by his ancestors a century and a half ago,
when they believed that from its central position, its happy
contiguity to the Court, the senate, and the seats of
Government, they at last in St. James's Square had discovered a site which could defy the vicissitudes of fashion,
and not share the fate of their river palaces, which they
had been obliged in turn to relinquish. And in a considerable degree they were right in their anticipation,
for although they have somewhat unwisely permitted the
Clubs to invade too successfully their territory, St. James's
Square may be looked upon as our Faubourg St. Germain,
and a great patrician residing there dwells in the heart of
that free and noble life of which he ought to be a part.

A marble hall and a marble staircase, lofty chambers
with silk or tapestried hangings, gilded cornices, and
painted ceilings, gave a glimpse of almost Venetian splen-

door, rare in our metropolitan houses of this age; but the first dwellers in St. James's Square had tender and inspiring recollections of the Adrian bride, had frolicked in St. Mark's, and glided in adventurous gondolas. The Monsignore was ushered into a chamber bright with lights and a blazing fire, and welcomed with extreme cordiality by his hostess, who was then alone. Lady St. Jerome was still the young wife of a nobleman not old. She was the daughter of a Protestant house, but, during a residence at Rome after her marriage, she had reverted to the ancient faith, which she professed with the enthusiastic convictions of a convert. Her whole life was dedicated to the triumph of the Catholic cause; and being a woman of considerable intelligence and of an ardent mind, she had become a recognised power in the great confederacy which has so much influenced the human race, and which has yet to play perhaps a mighty part in the fortunes of the world.

'I was in great hopes that the Cardinal would have met you at dinner,' said Lady St. Jerome, 'but he wrote only this afternoon to say unexpected business would prevent him, but he would be here in the evening, though late.'

'It must be something sudden, for I was with his Eminence this morning, and he then contemplated our meeting here.'

'Nothing from abroad?'

'I should think not, or it would be known to me. There is nothing new from abroad this afternoon: my time has been spent in writing, not receiving, despatches.'

'And all well, I hope?'

'This Scotch business plagues us. So far as Scotland is concerned it is quite ripe; but the Cardinal counsels delay on account of this country, and he has such a consummate knowledge of England, that ——'

At this moment Lord St. Jerome entered the room: a grave but gracious personage, polished but looking silent, though he immediately turned the conversation to the weather. The Monsignore began denouncing English fogs; but Lord St. Jerome maintained that, on the whole, there were not more fogs in England than in any other country; 'and as for the French,' he added, 'I like their audacity, for when they revolutionised the calendar, they called one of their months Brumaire.'

Then came in one of his Lordship's chaplains, who saluted the Monsignore with reverence, and immediately afterwards a beautiful young lady, his niece, Clare Arundel.

The family were living in a convenient suite of small rooms on the ground-floor, called the winter rooms, so dinner was announced by the doors of an adjoining chamber being thrown open, and there they saw, in the midst of a chamber hung with green silk and adorned with some fine cabinet-pictures, a small round table bright and glowing.

It was a lively dinner. Lord St. Jerome loved conversation, though he never conversed. 'There must be an audience,' he would say, 'and I am the audience.' The partner of his life, whom he never ceased admiring, had originally fascinated him by her conversational talents; and even if nature had not impelled her, Lady St. Jerome was too wise a woman to relinquish the spell. The Monsignore could always, when necessary, sparkle with anecdote or blaze with repartee; and all the chaplains, who abounded in this house, were men of bright abilities, not merely men of reading but of the world, learned in the world's ways, and trained to govern mankind by the versatility of their sympathies. It was a dinner where there could not be two conversations going on, and where even the silent take their share in the talk by their sympathy.

And among the silent, as silent even as Lord St. Jerome, was Miss Arundel; and yet her large violet eyes, darker even than her dark brown hair, and gleaming with intelligence, and her rich face mantling with emotion, proved she was not insensible to the witty passages and the bright and interesting narratives that were sparkling and flowing about her.

The gentlemen left the dining-room with the ladies in the continental manner. Lady St. Jerome, who was leaning on the arm of the Monsignore, guided him into a saloon farther than the one they had re-entered, and then seating herself said, ' You were telling me about Scotland, that you yourself thought it ripe.'

'Unquestionably. The original plan was to have established our hierarchy when the Kirk split up; but that would have been a mistake; it was not then ripe. There would have been a fanatical reaction. There is always a tendency that way in Scotland : as it is, at this moment, the Establishment and the Free Kirk are mutually sighing for some compromise which may bring them together again ; and if the proprietors would give up their petty patronage, some flatter themselves it might be arranged. But we are thoroughly well-informed, and have provided for all this. We sent two of our best men into Scotland some time ago, and they have invented a new Church, called the United Presbyterians. John Knox himself was never more violent, or more mischievous. The United Presbyterians will do the business : they will render Scotland simply impossible to live in ; and then, when the crisis arrives, the distracted and despairing millions will find refuge in the bosom of their only mother. That is why, at home, we wanted no delay in the publication of the bull and the establishment of the hierarchy.'

' But the Cardinal says no ?'

' And must be followed. For these islands he has no equal. He wishes great reserve at present. Affairs here are progressing, gradually but surely. But it is Ireland where matters are critical, or will be soon.'

'Ireland! I thought there was a sort of understanding there, at least for the present.'

The Monsignore shook his head, 'What do you think of an American invasion of Ireland?'

'An American invasion!'

'Even so; nothing more probable, and nothing more to be deprecated by us. Now that the civil war in America is over, the Irish soldiery are resolved to employ their experience and their weapons in their own land; but they have no thought for the interest of the Holy See, or the welfare of our Holy religion. Their secret organisation is tampering with the people and tampering with the priests. The difficulty of Ireland is that the priests and the people will consider everything in a purely Irish point of view. To gain some local object, they will encourage the principles of the most lawless liberalism, which naturally land them in Fenianism and Atheism. And the danger is not foreseen, because the Irish political object of the moment is alone looked to.'

'But surely they can be guided?'

'We want a statesman in Ireland. We have never been able to find one; we want a man like the Cardinal. But the Irish will have a native for their chief. We caught Churchill young, and educated him in the Propaganda; but he has disappointed us. At first all seemed well; he was reserved and austere; and we heard with satisfaction that he was unpopular. But now that critical times are arriving, his peasant blood cannot resist the contagion. He proclaims the absolute equality of all religions, and of the power of the state to confiscate ecclesiastical property, and alienate it for ever. For the chance of subverting the Anglican Establishment, he is favouring a policy which will subvert religion itself. In his eagerness he cannot see that the Anglicans have only a lease of our property, a lease which is rapidly expiring.'

'This is sad.'

'It is perilous, and difficult to deal with. But it must be dealt with. The problem is to suppress Fenianism, and not to strengthen the Protestant confederacy.'

'And you left Rome for this? We understood you were coming for something else,' said Lady St. Jerome in a significant tone.

'Yes, yes, I have been there, and I have seen him.'

'And have you succeeded?'

'No; and no one will; at least at present.'

'Is all lost then? Is the Malta scheme again on the carpet?'

'Our Holy Church is built upon a rock,' said the Monsignore, 'but not upon the rock of Malta. Nothing is lost; Antonelli is calm and sanguine, though, rest assured, there is no doubt about what I tell you. France has washed her hands of us.'

'Where then are we to look for aid,' exclaimed Lady St. Jerome, 'against the assassins and atheists? Austria, the alternative ally, is no longer near you; and if she were (that I should ever live to say it), even Austria is our foe.'

'Poor Austria!' said the Monsignore with an unctuous sneer. 'Two things made her a nation; she was German and she was Catholic, and now she is neither.'

'But you alarm me, my dear Lord, with your terrible news. We once thought that Spain would be our protector, but we hear bad news from Spain.'

'Yes,' said the Monsignore, 'I think it highly probable that, before a few years have elapsed, every government in Europe will be atheistical except France. Vanity will always keep France the eldest son of the Church, even if she wear a bonnet rouge. But if the Holy Father keep Rome, these strange changes will only make the occupier of the chair of St. Peter more powerful. His subjects will

be in every clime and every country, and then they will be
only his subjects. We shall get rid of the difficulty of the
divided allegiance, Lady St. Jerome, which plagued our
poor forefathers so much.'

'If we keep Rome,' said Lady St. Jerome.

'And we shall. Let Christendom give us her prayers
for the next few years, and Pio Nono will become the most
powerful monarch in Europe, and perhaps the only one.'

'I hear a sound,' exclaimed Lady St. Jerome. 'Yes!
the Cardinal has come. Let us greet him.'

But as they were approaching the saloon the Cardinal
met them, and waved them back. 'We will return,' he
said, ' to our friends immediately, but I want to say one
word to you both.'

He made them sit down. 'I am a little restless,' he
said, and stood before the fire. 'Something interesting
has happened; nothing to do with public affairs (do not
pitch your expectations too high), but still of importance,
and certainly of great interest, at least to me. I have
seen my child, my ward.'

'Indeed an event!' said Lady St. Jerome, evidently
much interested.

'And what is he like?' enquired the Monsignore.

'All that one could wish. Extremely good-looking,
highly bred, and most ingenuous; a considerable intelligence and not untrained; but the most absolutely unaffected person I ever encountered.'   *

'Ah! if he had been trained by your Eminence,' sighed
Lady St. Jerome. 'Is it too late?'

''Tis an immense position,' murmured Berwick.

'What good might he not do?' said Lady St. Jerome ;
'and if he be so ingenuous, it seems impossible that he can
resist the truth.'

'Your Ladyship is a sort of cousin of his,' said the Cardinal musingly.

'Yes; but very remote. I dare say he would not acknowledge the tie. But we are kin; we have the same blood in our veins.'

'You should make his acquaintance,' said the Cardinal.

'I more than desire it. I hear he has been terribly neglected, brought up among the most dreadful people, entirely infidels and fanatics.'

'He has been nearly two years at Oxford,' said the Cardinal. 'That may have mitigated the evil.'

'Ah! but you, my Lord Cardinal, you must interfere. Now that you at last know him, you must undertake the great task; you must save him.'

'We must all pray, as I pray every morn and every night,' said the Cardinal, 'for the conversion of England.'

'Or the conquest,' murmured Berwick.

CHAPTER X.

As the Cardinal was regaining his carriage on leaving Mrs. Giles' party, there was, about the entrance of the house, the usual gathering under such circumstances; some zealous linkboys marvellously familiar with London life, and some midnight loungers, who thus take their humble share of the social excitement, and their happy chance of becoming acquainted with some of the notables of the wondrous world of which they form the base. This little gathering, ranged at the instant into stricter order by the police to facilitate the passage of his Eminence, prevented the progress of a passenger, who exclaimed in an audible, but not noisy, voice, as if he were ejaculating to himself, 'À bas les prêtres!'

This exclamation, unintelligible to the populace, was noticed only by the only person who understood it. The

Cardinal, astonished at the unusual sound (for, hitherto, he had always found the outer world of London civil, or at least indifferent), threw his penetrating glance at the passenger, and caught clearly the visage on which the lamp-light fully shone. It was a square, sinewy face, closely shaven, with the exception of a small but thick moustache, brown as the well-cropped hair, and blending with the hazel eye; a calm, but determined countenance; clearly not that of an Englishman, for he wore ear-rings.

The carriage drove off, and the passenger, somewhat forcing his way through the clustering group, continued his course until he reached the cab-stand near the Marble Arch, when he engaged a vehicle and ordered to be driven to Leicester Square. That quarter of the town exhibits an animated scene towards the witching hour; many lights and much population, illuminated coffee-houses, the stir of a large theatre, bands of music in the open air, and other sounds, most of them gay, and some festive. The stranger, whose compact figure was shrouded by a long fur cape, had not the appearance of being influenced by the temptation of amusement. As he stopped in the square and looked around him, the expression of his countenance was moody, perhaps even anxious. He seemed to be making observations on the locality, and, after a few minutes, crossed the open space and turned up into a small street which opened into the square. In this street was a coffee-house of some pretension, connected indeed with an hotel, which had been formed out of two houses, and therefore possessed no inconsiderable accommodation.

The coffee-room was capacious, and adorned in a manner which intimated it was not kept by an Englishman, or much used by Englishmen. The walls were painted in frescoed arabesques. There were many guests, principally seated at small tables of marble, and on benches and chairs covered with a coarse crimson velvet. Some were sipping coffee, some were drinking wine, others were smoking or playing dominoes, or doing both; while many were engaged in reading the foreign journals, which abounded.

An ever-vigilant waiter was at the side of the stranger the instant he entered, and wished to know his pleasure. The stranger was examining with his keen eye every individual in the room, while this question was asked and repeated.

'What would I wish?' said the stranger, having concluded his inspection, and as it were summoning back his recollection. 'I would wish to see, and at once, one Mr. Perroni, who, I believe, lives here.'

'Why, 'tis the master!' exclaimed the waiter.

'Well, then, go and tell the master that I want him.'

'But the master is much engaged,' said the waiter; 'particularly.'

'I dare say; but you will go and tell him that I particularly want to see him.'

The waiter, though prepared to be impertinent to any one else, felt that one was speaking to him who must be obeyed, and with a subdued but hesitating manner said, 'There is a meeting to-night upstairs, where the master is secretary, and it is difficult to see him; but if I could see him, what name am I to give?'

'You will go to him instantly,' said the stranger, 'and you will tell him that he is wanted by Captain Bruges.'

The waiter was not long absent, and returning with an obsequious bow, he invited the stranger to follow him to a private room, where he was alone only for a few seconds, for the door opened and he was joined by Perroni.

'Ah! my General,' exclaimed the master of the coffee-house, and he kissed the stranger's hand. 'You received my telegram?'

'I am here. Now what is your business?'

'There is business, and great business; if you will do it, business for you.'

'Well, I am a soldier, and soldiering is my trade, and I do not much care what I do in that way, provided it is not against the good cause. But I must tell you at once, friend Perroni, I am not a man who will take a leap in the dark. I must form my own staff, and I must have my commissariat secure.'

'My General, you will be master of your own terms. The standing committee of the Holy Alliance of Peoples are sitting upstairs at this moment. They were unanimous in sending for you. See them; judge for yourself; and, rest assured, you will be satisfied.'

'I do not much like having to do with committees,' said the General. 'However, let it be as you like: I will see them.'

'I had better just announce your arrival,' said Perroni. 'And will you not take something, my General, after your travel? You must be wearied.'

'A glass of sugar and water. You know I am not easily tired. And, I agree with you, it is better to come to business at once: so prepare them.'

CHAPTER XI.

THE Standing Committee of the Holy Alliance of Peoples all rose, although they were extreme Republicans, when the General entered. Such is the magical influence of a man of action over men of the pen and the tongue. Had it been, instead of a successful military leader, an orator that had inspired Europe, or a journalist who had established the rights of the human race, the Standing Committee would have only seen one of their own kidney, who, having been

favoured with happier opportunities than themselves, had
reaped a harvest which, equally favoured, they might have
garnered.

'General,' said Felix Drolin, the president, who was
looked upon by the brotherhood as a statesman, for he had
been, in his time, a member of a Provisional Government,
'this seat is for you;' and he pointed to one on his right
hand. 'You are ever welcome; and I hope you bring
good tidings, and good fortune.'

'I am glad to be among my friends, and I may say,'
looking around, 'my comrades. I hope I may bring you
better fortune than my tidings.'

'But now they have left Rome,' said the President,
'every day we expect good news.'

'Ay, ay! he has left Rome, but he has not left Rome
with the door open. I hope it is not on such gossip you
have sent for me. You have something on hand. What
is it?'

'You shall hear it from the fountain-head,' said the
President, 'fresh from New York;' and he pointed to an
individual seated in the centre of the table.

'Ah! Colonel Finucane,' said the General, 'I have not
forgotten James River. You did that well. What is the
trick now?'

Whereupon a tall, lean man, with a decided brogue, but
speaking through his nose, rose from his seat and informed
the General that the Irish people were organised and ready
to rise; that they had sent their deputies to New York;
all they wanted were arms and officers; that the American
brethren had agreed to supply them with both, and amply;
and that considerable subscriptions were raising for
other purposes. What they now required was a com-
mander-in-chief equal to the occasion, and in whom all
would have confidence; and therefore they had telegraphed
for the General.

'I doubt not our friends over the water would send us plenty of rifles,' said the General, 'if we could only manage to land them; and I think I know men now in the States from whom I could form a good staff; but how about the people of Ireland? What evidence have we that they will rise, if we land?'

'The best,' said the President. 'We have a Head-Centre here, Citizen Desmond, who will give you the most recent and the most authentic intelligence on that head.'

'The whole country is organised,' said the Head-Centre; 'we could put 300,000 men in the field at any time in a fortnight. The movement is not sectarian; it pervades all classes and all creeds. All that we want are officers and arms.'

'Hem!' said the General. 'And as to your other supplies? Any scheme of commissariat?'

'There will be no lack of means,' replied the Head-Centre. 'There is no country where so much money is hoarded as in Ireland. But, depend upon it, so far as the commissariat is concerned, the movement will be self-supporting.'

'Well, we shall see,' said the General; 'I am sorry it is an Irish affair, though, to be sure, what else could it be? I am not fond of Irish affairs: whatever may be said, and however plausible things may look, in an Irish business there is always a priest at the bottom of it. I hate priests. By the bye, I was stopped on my way here by a Cardinal getting into his carriage. I thought I had burnt all those vehicles when I was at Rome with Garibaldi in '48. A Cardinal in his carriage! I had no idea you permitted that sort of cattle in London.'

'London is a roost for every bird,' said Felix Drolin.

'Very few of the priests favour this movement,' said Desmond.

'Then you have a great power against you,' said the General, 'in addition to England.'

'They are not exactly against; the bulk of them are too national for that; but Rome does not sanction : you understand?'

'I understand enough,' said the General, 'to see that we must not act with precipitation. An Irish business is a thing to be turned over several times.'

'But yet,' said a Pole, 'what hope for humanity except from the rising of an oppressed nationality. We have offered ourselves on the altar, and in vain ! Greece is too small, and Roumania, though both of them are ready to do anything; but they would be the mere tools of Russia. Ireland alone remains, and she is at our feet.'

'The peoples will never succeed till they have a fleet,' said a German. 'Then you could land as many rifles as you like, or anything else. To have a fleet we rose against Denmark in my country, but we have been betrayed. Nevertheless, Germany will yet be united, and she can only be united as a Republic. Then she will be the mistress of the seas.'

'That is the mission of Italy,' said Perroni. 'Italy, with the traditions of Genoa, Venice, Pisa ; Italy is plainly indicated as the future mistress of the seas.'

'I beg your pardon,' said the German ; 'the future mistress of the seas is the land of the Viking. It is the forests of the Baltic that will build the fleet of the future. You have no timber in Italy.'

'Timber is no longer wanted,' said Perroni. 'Nor do I know of what will be formed the fleets of the future. But the sovereignty of the seas depends upon seamen, and the nautical genius of the Italians——'

'Comrades,' said the General, 'we have discussed tonight a great subject. For my part I have travelled rather briskly as you wished it. I should like to sleep on this affair.'

''Tis most reasonable,' said the President. 'Our re

freshment at council is very spare,' he continued, and he
pointed to a vase of water and some glasses ranged round
it in the middle of the table; 'but we always drink one
toast, General, before we separate. It is to one whom you
love, and whom you have served well. Fill glasses, brethren, and now "To Mary-Anne."'

If they had been inspired by the grape nothing could be
more animated and oven excited than all their countenances
suddenly became. The cheer might have been heard in
the coffee-room, as they expressed, in the phrases of many
languages, the never-failing and never-flagging enthusiasm
invoked by the toast of their mistress.

CHAPTER XII

'Did you read that paragraph, mamma?' enquired Lady
Corisande of the Duchess, in a tone of some seriousness.

'I did.'

'And what did you think of it?'

'It filled me with so much amazement that I have hardly
begun to think.'

'And Bertram never gave a hint of such things!'

'Let us believe they are quite untrue.'

'I hope Bertram is in no danger,' said his sister.

'Heaven forbid!' exclaimed the mother, with unaffected
alarm.

'I know not how it is,' said Lady Corisande, 'but I
frequently feel that some great woe is hanging over our
country.'

'You must dismiss such thoughts, my child; they are
fanciful.'

'But it will come, and when least expected; frequently
in church, but also in the sunshine; and when I am riding

too, when once everything seemed gay. But now I often think of strife, and struggle, and war; civil war: the stir of our cavalcade seems like the tramp of cavalry.'

'You indulge your imagination too much, dear Corisande. When you return to London, and enter the world, these anxious thoughts will fly.'

'Is it imagination? I should rather have doubted my being of an imaginative nature. It seems to me that I am rather literal. But I cannot help hearing things, and reading things, and observing things, and they fill me with disquietude. All seems doubt and change, when it would appear that we require both faith and firmness.'

'The Duke is not alarmed about affairs,' said his wife.

'And if all did their duty like papa, there might be less, or no cause,' said Corisande, 'to be alarmed. But when I hear of young nobles, the natural leaders of the land, going over to the Roman Catholic Church, I confess I lose heart and patience. It seems so unpatriotic, so effeminate.'

'It may not be true,' said the Duchess.

'It may not be true of him, but it is true of others,' said Lady Corisande. 'And why should he escape? He is very young, rather friendless, and surrounded by wily persons. I am disappointed about Bertram too. He ought to have prevented this, if it be true. Bertram seemed to me to have such excellent principles, and so completely to feel that he was born to maintain the great country which his ancestors had created, that I indulged in dreams. I suppose you are right, mamma; I suppose I am imaginative without knowing it; but I have always thought and hoped, that when the troubles came the country might, perhaps, rally round Bertram.'

'I wish to see Bertram in Parliament,' said the Duchess. 'That will be the best thing for him. The Duke has some plans.'

This conversation had been occasioned by a paragraph in

E 2

the 'Morning Post,' circulating a rumour that a young
noble, obviously Lothair, on the impending completion of
his minority, was about to enter the Roman Church. The
Duchess and her daughter were sitting in a chamber of
their northern castle, and speculating on their return to
London, which was to take place after the Easter which
had just arrived. It was an important social season for
Corisande, for she was to be formally introduced into the
great world, and to be presented at Court.

In the meanwhile, was there any truth in the report
about Lothair?

After their meeting at their lawyer's, a certain intimacy
had occurred between the Cardinal and his ward. They
met again immediately and frequently, and their mutual
feelings were cordial. The manners of his Eminence were
refined and affectionate; his conversational powers were
distinguished; there was not a subject on which his mind
did not teem with interesting suggestions; his easy knowledge seemed always ready and always full; and whether it
were art, or letters, or manners, or even political affairs,
Lothair seemed to listen to one of the wisest, most enlightened, and most agreeable of men. There was only one
subject on which his Eminence seemed scrupulous never to
touch, and that was religion; or so indirectly, that it was
only when alone that Lothair frequently found himself
musing over the happy influence on the arts, and morals,
and happiness of mankind, of the Church.

In due time, not too soon, but when he was attuned to
the initiation, the Cardinal presented Lothair to Lady St.
Jerome. The impassioned eloquence of that lady germinated
the seed which the Cardinal had seemed so carelessly to
scatter. She was a woman to inspire crusaders. Not that
she ever condescended to vindicate her own particular
faith, or spoke as if she were conscious that Lothair did not
possess it. Assuming that religion was true, for otherwise

man would be in a more degraded position than the beasts
of the field, which are not aware of their own wretched-
ness, then religion should be the principal occupation of
man, to which all other pursuits should be subservient.
The doom of eternity, and the fortunes of life, cannot be
placed in competition. Our days should be pure, and holy,
and heroic, full of noble thoughts and solemn sacrifice.
Providence, in its wisdom, had decreed that the world
should be divided between the faithful and atheists; the
latter even seemed to predominate. There was no doubt
that, if they prevailed, all that elevated man would become
extinct. It was a great trial; but happy was the man who
was privileged even to endure the awful test. It might
develope the highest qualities and the most sublime conduct. If he were equal to the occasion, and could control
and even subdue these sons of Corah, he would rank with
Michael the Archangel.

This was the text on which frequent discourses were delivered to Lothair, and to which he listened at first with
eager, and soon with enraptured attention. The priestess
was worthy of the shrine. Few persons were ever gifted
with more natural eloquence; a command of language,
choice without being pedantic; beautiful hands that fluttered with irresistible grace; flashing eyes and a voice of
melody.

Lothair began to examine himself, and to ascertain
whether he possessed the necessary qualities, and was
capable of sublime conduct. His natural modesty and his
strong religious feeling struggled together. He feared he
was not an archangel, and yet he longed to struggle with
the powers of darkness.

One day he ventured to express to Miss Arundel a
somewhat hopeful view of the future, but Miss Arundel
shook her head.

'I do not agree with my aunt, at least as regards this

country,' said Miss Arundel; 'I think our sins are too great. We left His Church, and God is now leaving us.'

Lothair looked grave, but was silent.

Weeks had passed since his introduction to the family of Lord St. Jerome, and it was remarkable how large a portion of his subsequent time had passed under that roof. At first there were few persons in town, and really of these Lothair knew none; and then the house in St. James's Square was not only an interesting, but it was an agreeable house. All Lady St. Jerome's family connections were persons of much fashion, so there was more variety and entertainment than sometimes are to be found under a Roman Catholic roof. Lady St. Jerome was at home every evening before Easter. Few dames can venture successfully on so decided a step; but her saloons were always attended, and by 'nice people.' Occasionally the Cardinal stepped in, and, to a certain degree, the saloon was the rendezvous of the Catholic party; but it was also generally social and distinguished. Many bright dames and damsels, and many influential men, were there, who little deemed that deep and daring thoughts were there masked by many a gracious countenance. The social atmosphere infinitely pleased Lothair. The mixture of solemn duty and graceful diversion, high purposes and charming manners, seemed to realise some youthful dreams of elegant existence. All too was enhanced by the historic character of the roof and by the recollection that their common ancestors, as Clare Arundel more than once intimated to him, had created England. Having had so many pleasant dinners in St. James's Square, and spent there so many evening hours, it was not wonderful that Lothair had accepted an invitation from Lord St. Jerome to pass Easter at his country seat.

CHAPTER XIII.

VAUXE, the seat of the St. Jeromes, was the finest specimen of the old English residence extant. It was the perfection of the style, which had gradually arisen after the wars of the Roses had alike destroyed all the castles and the purpose of those stern erections. People said Vauxe looked like a college: the truth is, colleges looked like Vauxe, for when those fair and civil buildings rose, the wise and liberal spirits who endowed them, intended that they should resemble as much as possible the residence of a great noble.

There were two quadrangles at Vauxe of grey stone; the outer one of larger dimensions and much covered with ivy; the inner one not so extensive but more ornate, with a lofty tower, a hall, and a chapel. The house was full of galleries, and they were full of portraits. Indeed there was scarcely a chamber in this vast edifice of which the walls were not breathing with English history in this interesting form. Sometimes more ideal art asserted a triumphant claim: transcendental Holy Families, seraphic saints, and gorgeous scenes by Tintoret and Paul of Verona.

The furniture of the house seemed never to have been changed. It was very old, somewhat scanty, but very rich: tapestry and velvet hangings, marvellous cabinets, and crystal girandoles. Here and there a group of ancient plate; ewers and flagons and tall saltcellars a foot high and richly chiselled; sometimes a state bed shadowed with a huge pomp of stiff brocade and borne by silver poles.

Vauxe stood in a large park studded with stately trees; here and there an avenue of Spanish chesnuts or a grove of oaks; sometimes a gorsy dell and sometimes a great spread of antlered fern, taller than the tallest man.

It was only twenty miles from town, and Lord St.
Jerome drove Lothair down; the last ten miles through a
pretty land, which, at the right season, would have been
bright with orchards, oak woods, and hop gardens. Lord
St. Jerome loved horses and was an eminent whip. He
had driven four-in-hand when a boy, and he went on driving four-in-hand; not because it was the fashion, but because he loved it. Towards the close of Lent, Lady St.
Jerome and Clare Arundel had been at a convent in retreat, but they always passed Holy Week at home, and
they were to welcome Lord St. Jerome again at Vauxe.

The day was bright, the mode of movement exhilarating,
all the anticipated incidents delightful, and Lothair felt the
happiness of health and youth.

'There is Vauxe,' said Lord St. Jerome, in a tone of
proud humility, as a turn in the road first displayed the
stately pile.

'How beautiful!' said Lothair; 'ah! our ancestors
understood the country.'

'I used to think when I was a boy,' said Lord St.
Jerome, 'that I lived in the prettiest village in the world,
but these railroads have so changed everything, that Vauxe
seems to me now only a second town house.'

The ladies were in a garden, where they were consulting
with the gardener and Father Coleman about the shape of
some new beds, for the critical hour of filling them was
approaching. The gardener, like all head-gardeners, was
opiniated. Living always at Vauxe, he had come to believe that the gardens belonged to him, and that the family
were only occasional visitors; and he treated them accordingly. The lively and impetuous Lady St. Jerome had a
thousand bright fancies, but her morose attendant rarely
indulged them. She used to deplore his tyranny with
piteous playfulness. 'I suppose,' she would say, 'it is
useless to resist, for I observe 'tis the same everywhere.

Lady Roehampton says she never has her way with her gardens. It is no use speaking to Lord St. Jerome, for though he is afraid of nothing else, I am sure he is afraid of Hawkins.'

The only way that Lady St. Jerome could manage Hawkins was through Father Coleman. Father Coleman, who knew everything, knew a great deal about gardens; from the days of Le Notre to those of the fine gentlemen who now travel about, and when disengaged deign to give us advice.

Father Coleman had only just entered middle-age, was imperturbable and mild in his manner. He passed his life very much at Vauxe, and imparted a great deal of knowledge to Mr. Hawkins, without apparently being conscious of so doing. At the bottom of his mind, Mr. Hawkins felt assured that he had gained several distinguished prizes, mainly through the hints and guidance of Father Coleman; and thus, though on the surface a little surly, he was ruled by Father Coleman, under the combined influence of self-interest and superior knowledge.

'You find us in a garden without flowers,' said Lady St. Jerome; 'but the sun, I think, alway loves these golden yews.'

'These are for you, dear uncle,' said Clare Arundel, as she gave him a rich cluster of violets. 'Just now the woods are more fragrant than the gardens, and these are the produce of our morning walk. I could have brought you some primroses, but I do not like to mix violets with anything.'

'They say primroses make a capital salad,' said Lord St. Jerome.

'Barbarian!' exclaimed Lady St. Jerome. 'I see you want luncheon; it must be ready;' and she took Lothair's arm. 'I will show you a portrait of one of your ancestors,' she said; 'he married an Arundel.'

CHAPTER XIV.

'Now, you know,' said Lady St. Jerome to Lothair in a
hushed voice, as they sate together in the evening, 'you
are to be quite free here; to do exactly what you like, and
we shall follow our ways. If you like to have a clergyman
of your own Church visit you while you are with us, pray
say so without the slightest scruple. We have an excellent
gentleman in this parish; he often dines here; and I am
sure he would be most happy to attend you. I know that
Holy Week is not wholly disregarded by some of the
Anglicans.'

'It is the anniversary of the greatest event of time,'
said Lothair; 'and I should be sorry if any of my Church
did not entirely regard it, though they may show that
regard in a way different from your own.'

'Yes, yes,' murmured Lady St. Jerome; 'there should
be no difference between our Churches, if things were only
properly understood. I would accept all who really bow
to the name of Christ; they will come to the Church at
last; they must. It is the Atheists alone, I fear, who are
now carrying everything before them, and against whom
there is no rampart, except the rock of St. Peter.'

Miss Arundel crossed the room, whispered something to
her aunt, and touched her forehead with her lips, and then
left the apartment.

'We must soon separate, I fear,' said Lady St. Jerome;
'we have an office to-night of great moment; the Tenebræ
commence to-night. You have, I think, nothing like it;
but you have services throughout this week.'

'I am sorry to say I have not attended them,' said
Lothair. 'I did at Oxford; but I don't know how it is,
but in London there seems no religion. And yet, as you

sometimes say, religion is the great business of life; I
sometimes begin to think the only business.'

'Yes, yes,' said Lady St. Jerome, with much interest, 'if
you believe that you are safe. I wish you had a clergyman
near you while you are here. See Mr. Claughton if you
like; I would; and if you do not, there is Father Coleman.
I cannot convey to you how satisfactory conversation is
with him on religious matters. He is the holiest of men,
and yet he is a man of the world: he will not invite you
into any controversies. He will speak with you only on
points on which we agree. You know there are many
points on which we agree?'

'Happily,' said Lothair. 'And now about the office to-
night: tell me about these Tenebræ. Is there anything
in the Tenebræ that should prevent my being present?'

'No reason whatever; not a dogma which you do not
believe; not a ceremony of which you cannot approve.
There are psalms, at the end of each of which a light on
the altar is extinguished. There is the Song of Moses, the
Canticle of Zachary, the Miserere, which is the 51st
Psalm you read and chant regularly in your church, the
Lord's Prayer in silence; and then all is darkness and
distress: what the Church was when our Lord suffered,
what the whole world is now except His Church.'

'If you will permit me,' said Lothair, 'I will accompany
you to the Tenebræ.'

Although the chapel at Vauxe was, of course, a private
chapel, it was open to the surrounding public, who eagerly
availed themselves of a permission alike politic and gracious.

Nor was that remarkable. Manifold art had combined
to create this exquisite temple, and to guide all its ministrations. But to-night it was not the radiant altar and the
splendour of stately priests, the processions and the
incense, the divine choir and the celestial harmonies re-
sounding and lingering in arched roofs, that attracted

many a neighbour. The altar was desolate, the choir was dumb; and while the services proceeded in hushed tones of subdued sorrow, and sometimes even of suppressed anguish, gradually, with each psalm and canticle, a light of the altar was extinguished, till at length the Miserere was muttered, and all became darkness. A sound as of a distant and rising wind was heard, and a crash, as it were the fall of trees in a storm. The earth is covered with darkness, and the vail of the temple is rent. But just at this moment of extreme woe, when all human voices are silent, and when it is forbidden even to breathe 'Amen;' when everything is symbolical of the confusion and despair of the Church at the loss of her expiring Lord, a priest brings forth a concealed light of silvery flame from a corner of the altar. This is the light of the world, and announces the resurrection, and then all rise up and depart in silence.

As Lothair rose, Miss Arundel passed him with streaming eyes.

'There is nothing in this holy office,' said Father Coleman to Lothair, 'to which every real Christian might not give his assent.'

'Nothing,' said Lothair, with great decision.

CHAPTER XV.

THERE were Tenebræ on the following days, Maundy Thursday and Good Friday; and Lothair was present on both occasions.

'There is also a grant office on Friday,' said Father Coleman to Lothair, 'which perhaps you would not like to attend, the mass of the Pre-sanctified. We bring back the Blessed Sacrament to the desolate altar, and unveil the

Cross. It is one of our highest ceremonies, the adoration of the Cross, which the Protestants persist in calling idolatry, though I presume they will give us leave to know the meaning of our own words and actions, and hope they will believe us when we tell them that our genuflexions and kissing of the Cross are no more than exterior expressions of that love which we bear in our hearts to Jesus crucified; and that the words adoration and adore, as applied to the Cross, only signify that respect and veneration due to things immediately relating to God and His service.'

'I see no idolatry in it,' said Lothair, musingly.

'No impartial person could,' rejoined Father Coleman; 'but unfortunately all these prejudices were imbibed when the world was not so well-informed as at present. A good deal of mischief has been done, too, by the Protestant versions of the Holy Scriptures; made in a hurry, and by men imperfectly acquainted with the Eastern tongues, and quite ignorant of Eastern manners. All the accumulated research and investigation of modern times have only illustrated and justified the offices of the Church.'

'That is very interesting,' said Lothair.

'Now, this question of idolatry,' said Father Coleman, 'that is a fertile subject of misconception. The house of Israel was raised up to destroy idolatry, because idolatry then meant dark images of Moloch opening their arms by machinery, and flinging the beauteous firstborn of the land into their huge forms, which were furnaces of fire; or Ashtaroth, throned in moonlit groves, and surrounded by orgies of ineffable demoralisation. It required the declared will of God to redeem man from such fatal iniquity, which would have sapped the human race. But to confound such deeds with the commemoration of God's saints, who are only pictured because their lives are perpetual incentives to purity and holiness, and to declare that the Queen

of Heaven and the Mother of God should be to human
feeling only as a sister of charity or a gleaner in the fields,
is to abuse reason and to outrage the heart.'

'We live in dark times,' said Lothair, with an air of
distress.

'Not darker than before the deluge,' exclaimed Father
Coleman; 'not darker than before the Nativity; not
darker even than when the saints became martyrs. There
is a Pharos in the world, and its light will never be extinguished, however black the clouds and wild the waves.
Man is on his trial now, not the Church; but in the service
of the Church his highest energies may be developed, and
his noblest qualities proved.'

Lothair seemed plunged in thought, and Father Coleman
glided away as Lady St. Jerome entered the gallery,
shawled and bonneted, accompanied by another priest,
Monsignore Catesby.

Catesby was a youthful member of an ancient English
house, which for many generations had without a murmur,
rather in a spirit of triumph, made every worldly sacrifice
for the Church and Court of Rome. For that cause they
had forfeited their lives, broad estates, and all the honours
of a lofty station in their own land. Reginald Catesby
with considerable abilities, trained with consummate skill,
inherited their determined will, and the traditionary beauty
of their form and countenance. His manners were winning, and he was as well informed in the ways of the world
as he was in the works of the great casuists.

'My Lord has ordered the char-a-banc, and is going to
drive us all to Chart, where we will lunch,' said Lady St.
Jerome; ''tis a curious place, and was planted only seventy
years ago by my Lord's grandfather, entirely with spruce
firs, but with so much care and skill, giving each plant and
tree ample distance, that they have risen to the noblest
proportions, with all their green branches far-spreading on
the ground like huge fans.'

It was only a drive of three or four miles entirely in the park. This was a district that had been added to the ancient enclosure; a striking scene. It was a forest of firs, but quite unlike such as might be met with in the north of Europe or of America. Every tree was perfect, huge and complete, and full of massy grace. Nothing else was permitted to grow there except juniper, of which there were abounding and wondrous groups, green and spiral; the whole contrasting with the tall brown fern of which there were quantities about cut for the deer.

The turf was dry and mossy, and the air pleasant. It was a balmy day. They sate down by the great trees, the servants opened the luncheon baskets, which were a present from Balmoral. Lady St. Jerome was seldom seen to greater advantage than distributing her viands under such circumstances. Never was such gay and graceful hospitality. Lothair was quite fascinated as she playfully thrust a paper of lobster-sandwiches into his hand, and enjoined Monsignore Catesby to fill his tumbler with Chablis.

'I wish Father Coleman were here,' said Lothair to Miss Arundel.

'Why?' said Miss Arundel.

'Because we were in the midst of a very interesting conversation on idolatry and on worship in groves, when Lady St. Jerome summoned us to our drive. This seems a grove where one might worship.'

'Father Coleman ought to be at Rome,' said Miss Arundel. 'He was to have passed Holy Week there. I know not why he changed his plans.'

'Are you angry with him for it?'

'No, not angry, but surprised; surprised that anyone might be at Rome, and yet be absent from it.'

'You like Rome?'

'I have never been there. It is the wish of my life.'

'May I say to you what you said to me just now: why?'

'Naturally, because I would wish to witness the ceremonies of the Church in their most perfect form.'

'But they are fulfilled in this country, I have heard, with much splendour and precision.'

Miss Arundel shook her head.

'Oh! no,' she said; 'in this country we are only just emerging from the catacombs. If the ceremonies of the Church were adequately fulfilled in England, we should hear very little of English infidelity.'

'That is saying a great deal,' observed Lothair, enquiringly.

'Had I that command of wealth of which we hear so much in the present day, and with which the possessors seem to know so little what to do, I would purchase some of those squalid streets in Westminster, which are the shame of the metropolis, and clear a great space and build a real cathedral, where the worship of heaven should be perpetually conducted in the full spirit of the ordinances of the Church. I believe, were this done, even this country might be saved.'

CHAPTER XVI.

LOTHAIR began to meditate on two great ideas: the reconciliation of Christendom and the influence of architecture on religion. If the differences between the Roman and Anglican Churches, and between the Papacy and Protestantism, generally arose, as Father Coleman assured him, and seemed to prove, in mere misconception, reconciliation, though difficult, did not seem impossible, and appeared to be one of the most efficient modes of defeating the Atheists. It was a result which of course mainly depended on the authority of Reason; but the power of the imagination might also be enlisted in the good cause through the influence of the fine arts, of which the great mission is to excite, and at the same time elevate, the feelings of the human family. Lothair found himself frequently in a reverie over Miss Arundel's ideal fane; and feeling that he had the power of buying up a district in forlorn Westminster, and raising there a temple to the living God, which might influence the future welfare of millions, and even effect the salvation of his country, he began to ask himself, whether he could incur the responsibility of shrinking from the fulfilment of this great duty.

Lothair could not have a better adviser on the subject of the influence of architecture on religion than Monsignore Catesby. Monsignore Catesby had been a pupil of Pugin; his knowledge of ecclesiastical architecture was only equalled by his exquisite taste. To hear him expound the mysteries of symbolical art, and expatiate on the hidden revelations of its beauteous forms, reached even to ecstasy. Lothair hung upon his accents like a neophyte. Conferences with Father Coleman on those points of faith on which they did not differ, followed up by desultory remarks on those points of faith on which they ought not to differ; critical discussions with Monsignore Catesby on cathedrals, their forms, their purposes, and the instances in several countries in which those forms were most perfect and those purposes best secured, occupied a good deal of time; and yet these engaging pursuits were secondary in real emotion to his frequent conversations with Miss Arundel, in whose society every day he took a strange and deeper interest.

She did not extend to him that ready sympathy which was supplied by the two priests. On the contrary, when he was apt to indulge in those speculations which they always encouraged, and rewarded by adroit applause, she was often silent, throwing on him only the scrutiny of

F

those violet eyes, whose glance was rather fascinating than apt to captivate. And yet he was irresistibly drawn to her, and once recalling the portrait in the gallery, he ventured to murmur that they were kinsfolk.

'Oh! I have no kin, no country,' said Miss Arundel. 'These are not times for kin and country. I have given up all these things for my Master!'

'But are our times so trying as that?' enquired Lothair.

'They are times for new crusades,' said Miss Arundel, with energy, 'though it may be of a different character from the old. If I were a man I would draw my sword for Christ. There are as great deeds to be done as the siege of Ascalon, or even as the freeing of the Holy Sepulchre.'

In the midst of a profound discussion with Father Coleman on Mariolatry, Lothair, wrapt in reverie, suddenly introduced the subject of Miss Arundel. 'I wonder what will be her lot,' he exclaimed.

'It seems to me to be settled,' said Father Coleman. 'She will be the bride of the Church.'

'Indeed!' and he started, and even changed colour.

'She deems it her vocation,' said Father Coleman.

'And yet, with such gifts, to be immured in a convent,' said Lothair.

'That would not necessarily follow,' replied Father Coleman. 'Miss Arundel may occupy a position in which she may exercise much influence for the great cause which absorbs her being.'

'There is a divine energy about her,' said Lothair, almost speaking to himself. 'It could not have been given for little ends.'

'If Miss Arundel could meet with a spirit as exalted and as energetic as her own,' said Father Coleman, 'her fate might be different. She has no thoughts which are not great, and no purposes which are not sublime. But for the companion of her life she would require no less than a Godfrey de Bouillon.'

Lothair began to find the time pass very rapidly at Vauxe. Easter week had nearly vanished; Vauxe had been gay during the last few days. Every day some visitors came down from London; sometimes they returned in the evening; sometimes they passed the night at Vauxe and returned to town in the morning with large bouquets. Lothair felt it was time for him to depart, and he broke his intention to Lady St. Jerome; but Lady St. Jerome would not hear of it. So he muttered something about business.

'Exactly,' she said; 'everybody has business, and I dare say you have a great deal. But Vauxe is precisely the place for persons who have business. You go up to town by an early train, and then you return in time for dinner, and bring us all the news from the Clubs.'

Lothair was beginning to say something, but Lady St. Jerome, who, when necessary, had the rare art of not listening without offending the speaker, told him that they did not intend themselves to return to town for a week or so, and that she knew Lord St. Jerome would be greatly annoyed if Lothair did not remain.

Lothair remained; and he went up to town one or two mornings to transact business; that is to say, to see a celebrated architect, and to order plans for a cathedral, in which all the purposes of those sublime and exquisite structures were to be realised. The drawings would take a considerable time to prepare, and these must be deeply considered. So Lothair became quite domiciliated at Vauxe: he went up to town in the morning and returned, as it were, to his home; everybody delighted to welcome him, and yet he seemed not expected. His rooms were called after his name; and the household treated him as one of the family.

F 2

CHAPTER XVII.

A few days before Lothair's visit was to terminate, the Cardinal and Monsignore Berwick arrived at Vauxe. His Eminence was received with much ceremony; the marshalled household, ranged in lines, fell on their knees at his approach, and Lady St. Jerome, Miss Arundel, and some other ladies scarcely less choice and fair, with the lowest obeisance, touched with their honoured lips his princely hand.

The Monsignore had made another visit to Paris on his intended return to Rome, but in consequence of some secret intelligence which he had acquired in the French capital, had thought fit to return to England to consult with the Cardinal. There seemed to be no doubt that the Revolutionary party in Italy, assured by the withdrawal of the French troops from Rome, were again stirring. There seemed also little doubt that London was the centre of preparation, though the project and the projectors were involved in much mystery. 'They want money,' said the Monsignore; 'that we know, and that is now our best chance. The Aspromonte expedition drained their private resources; and as for further aid, that is out of the question; the galantuomo is bankrupt. But the Atheists are desperate, and we must prepare for events.'

On the morning after their arrival, the Cardinal invited Lothair to a stroll in the park. 'There is the feeling of spring this morning,' said his Eminence, 'though scarcely yet its vision.' It was truly a day of balm, and sweetness, and quickening life; a delicate mist hung about the huge trees and the masses of more distant woods, and seemed to clothe them with that fulness of foliage which was not yet theirs. The Cardinal discoursed much on forest trees, and

happily. He recommended Lothair to read Evelyn's
'Sylva.' Mr. Evelyn had a most accomplished mind;
indeed, a character in every respect that approached perfection. He was also a most religious man.

'I wonder,' said Lothair, 'how any man who is religious
can think of anything but religion.'

'True,' said the Cardinal, and looking at him earnestly,
'most true. But all things that are good and beautiful
make us more religious. They tend to the development of
the religious principle in us, which is our divine nature.
And, my dear young friend,' and here his Eminence put
his arm easily and affectionately into that of Lothair's, 'it
is a most happy thing for you that you live so much with
a really religious family. It is a great boon for a young
man, and a rare one.'

'I feel it so,' said Lothair, his face kindling.

'Ah!' said the Cardinal, 'when we remember that this
country once consisted only of such families!' And then,
with a sigh, and as if speaking to himself, 'and they made
it so great and so beautiful!'

'It is still great and beautiful,' said Lothair, but rather
in a tone of enquiry than decision.

'But the cause of its greatness and its beauty no longer
exists. It became great and beautiful because it believed
in God.'

'But faith is not extinct?' said Lothair.

'It exists in the Church,' replied the Cardinal with
decision. 'All without that pale is practical atheism.'

'It seems to me that a sense of duty is natural to man,'
said Lothair, 'and that there can be no satisfaction in life
without attempting to fulfil it.'

'Noble words, my dear young friend; noble and true.
And the highest duty of man, especially in this age, is to
vindicate the principles of religion, without which the
world must soon become a scene of universal desolation.'

'I wonder if England will ever again be a religious country,' said Lothair musingly.

'I pray for that daily,' said the Cardinal; and he invited his companion to seat himself on the trunk of an oak that had been lying there since the autumn fall. A slight hectic flame played over the pale and attenuated countenance of the Cardinal; he seemed for a moment in deep thought; and then in a voice distinct yet somewhat hushed, and at first rather faltering, he said, 'I know not a grandeur or a nobler career for a young man of talents and position in this age, than to be the champion and asserter of Divine truth. It is not probable that there could be another conqueror in our time. The world is wearied of statesmen, whom democracy has degraded into politicians, and of orators who have become what they call debaters. I do not believe there could be another Dante, even another Milton. The world is devoted to physical science, because it believes these discoveries will increase its capacity of luxury and self-indulgence. But the pursuit of science leads only to the insoluble. When we arrive at that barren term, the Divine voice summons man, as it summoned Samuel; all the poetry and passion and sentiment of human nature are taking refuge in religion; and he whose deeds and words most nobly represent Divine thoughts, will be the man of this century.'

'But who could be equal to such a task,' murmured Lothair.

'Yourself,' exclaimed the Cardinal, and he threw his glittering eye upon his companion. 'Anyone with the necessary gifts, who had implicit faith in the Divine purpose.'

'But the Church is perplexed; it is ambiguous, contradictory.'

'No, no,' said the Cardinal; 'not the Church of Christ; it is never perplexed, never ambiguous, never contradictory. Why should it be? How could it be? The Divine persons are ever with it, strengthening and guiding it with perpetual miracles. Perplexed churches are churches made by Act of Parliament, not by God.'

Lothair seemed to start, and looked at his guardian with a scrutinising glance. And then he said, but not without hesitation, 'I experience at times great despondency.'

'Naturally,' replied the Cardinal. 'Every man must be despondent who is not a Christian.'

'But I am a Christian,' said Lothair.

'A Christian estranged,' said the Cardinal; 'a Christian without the consolations of Christianity.'

'There is something in that,' said Lothair. 'I require the consolations of Christianity, and yet I feel I have them not. Why is this?'

'Because what you call your religion is a thing apart from your life, and it ought to be your life. Religion should be the rule of life, not a casual incident of it. There is not a duty of existence, not a joy or sorrow which the services of the Church do not assert, or with which they do not sympathise. Tell me, now; you have, I was glad to hear, attended the services of the Church of late, since you have been under this admirable roof. Have you not then found some consolation?'

'Yes; without doubt I have been often solaced.' And Lothair sighed.

'What the soul is to man, the Church is to the world,' said the Cardinal. 'It is the link between us and the Divine nature. It came from heaven complete; it has never changed, and it can never alter. Its ceremonies are types of celestial truths; its services are suited to all the moods of man; they strengthen him in his wisdom and his purity, and control and save him in the hour of passion and temptation. Taken as a whole, with all its ministrations, its orders, its offices, and the divine splendour of its ritual, it secures us on earth some adumbration of that ineffable glory which awaits the faithful in heaven, where the blessed Mother of God and ten thousand saints perpetually guard us with Divine intercession.'

'I was not taught these things in my boyhood,' said Lothair.

'And you might reproach me and reasonably, as your guardian, for my neglect,' said the Cardinal. 'But my power was very limited, and when my duties commenced, you must remember that I was myself estranged from the Church, I was myself a Parliamentary Christian, till despondency and study and ceaseless thought and prayer, and the Divine will, brought me to light and rest. But I at least saved you from a Presbyterian University; I at least secured Oxford for you; and I can assure you of my many struggles that was not the least.'

'It gave the turn to my mind,' said Lothair, 'and I am grateful to you for it. What it will all end in, God only knows.'

'It will end in His glory and in yours,' said the Cardinal. 'I have spoken perhaps too much and too freely, but you greatly interest me, not merely because you are my charge and the son of my beloved friend, but because I perceive in you great qualities; qualities so great,' continued the Cardinal with earnestness, 'that, properly guided, they may considerably affect the history of this country, and perhaps even have a wider range.'

Lothair shook his head.

'Well, well,' continued the Cardinal in a lighter tone, 'we will pursue our ramble. At any rate, I am not wrong in this, that you have no objection to join in my daily prayer for the conversion of this kingdom to —— religious truth,' his Eminence added after a pause.

'Yes; religious truth,' said Lothair, 'we must all pray for that.'

CHAPTER XVIII.

LOTHAIR returned to town excited and agitated. He felt that he was on the eve of some great event in his existence, but its precise character was not defined. One conclusion, however, was indubitable: life must be religion. When we consider what is at stake, and that our eternal welfare depends on our due preparation for the future, it was folly to spare a single hour from the consideration of the best means to secure our readiness. Such a subject does not admit of half measures or of halting opinions. It seemed to Lothair that nothing could interest him in life that was not symbolical of Divine truths and an adumbration of the celestial hereafter.

Could truth have descended from heaven ever to be distorted, to be corrupted, misapprehended, misunderstood? Impossible! Such a belief would confound and contradict all the attributes of the All-wise and the All-mighty. There must be truth on earth now as fresh and complete as it was at Bethlehem. And how could it be preserved but by the influence of the Paraclete acting on an ordained class? On this head his tutor at Oxford had fortified him; by a conviction of the Apostolical succession of the English bishops, which no Act of Parliament could alter or affect. But Lothair was haunted by a feeling that the relations of his Communion with the Blessed Virgin were not satisfactory. They could not content either his heart or his intellect. Was it becoming that a Christian should live as regards the hallowed Mother of his God in a condition of harsh estrangement? What mediatorial influence more awfully appropriate than the consecrated agent of the mighty mystery? Nor could he, even in his early days, accept without a scruple the frigid system that would class

the holy actors in the divine drama of the Redemption
as mere units in the categories of vanished generations.
Human beings who had been in personal relation with the
Godhead must be different from other human beings. There
must be some transcendent quality in their lives and careers,
in their very organisation, which marks them out from all
secular heroes. What was Alexander the Great, or even
Caius Julius, compared with that apostle whom Jesus
loved?

Restless and disquieted, Lothair paced the long and lofty
rooms which had been secured for him in a London hotel
which rivalled the colossal convenience of Paris and the
American cities. Their tawdry ornaments and their terrible
new furniture would not do after the galleries and portraits
of Vauxe. Lothair sighed.

Why did that visit over end? Why did the world con-
sist of anything else but Tudor palaces in ferny parks, or
time be other than a perpetual Holy Week? He never
sighed at Vauxe. Why? He supposed it was because
there religion was his life, and here: and he looked around
him with a shudder. The Cardinal was right: it was a
most happy thing for him to be living so much with so
truly a religious family.

The door opened, and servants came in bearing a large
and magnificent portfolio. It was of morocco and of pre-
latial purple with broad bands of gold and alternate ornaments of a cross and a coronet. A servant handed to
Lothair a letter, which enclosed the key that opened its
lock. The portfolio contained the plans and drawings of
the cathedral.

Lothair was lost in admiration of those designs and their
execution. But after the first fever of investigation was
over, he required sympathy and also information. In a
truly religious family there would always be a Father Coleman or a Monsignore Catesby to guide and to instruct.

But a Protestant, if he wants aid or advice on any matter, can only go to his solicitor. But as he proceeded in his researches, he sensibly felt that the business was one above even an Oratorian or a Monsignore. It required a finer and a more intimate sympathy; a taste at the same time more inspired and more inspiring; some one who blended with divine convictions the graceful energy of human feeling, and who would not only animate him to effort but fascinate him to its fulfilment. The counsellor he required was Miss Arundel.

Lothair had quitted Vauxe one week, and it seemed to him a year. During the first four-and-twenty hours he felt like a child who had returned to school, and the day after like a man on a desert island. Various other forms of misery and misfortune were suggested by his succeeding experience. Town brought no distractions to him; he knew very few people, and these he had not yet encountered; he had once ventured to White's, but found only a group of grey-headed men, who evidently did not know him, and who seemed to scan him with cynical nonchalance. These were not the golden youth who he had been assured by Bertram would greet him: so, after reading a newspaper for a moment upside downwards, he got away. But he had no harbour of refuge, and was obliged to ride down to Richmond and dine alone and meditate on symbols and celestial adumbrations. Every day he felt how inferior was this existence to that of a life in a truly religious family.

But of all the members of the family to which his memory recurred with such unflagging interest none more frequently engaged his thoughts than Miss Arundel. Her conversation, which stimulated his intelligence while it rather piqued his self-love, exercised a great influence over him, and he had omitted no opportunity of enjoying her society. That society and its animating power he sadly

missed; and now that he had before him the very drawings
about which they had frequently talked, and she was not
by his side to suggest and sympathise and criticise and
praise, he felt unusually depressed.

Lothair corresponded with Lady St. Jerome, and was
aware of her intended movements. But the return of the
family to London had been somewhat delayed. When this
disappointment was first made known to him his impulse
was to ride down to Vauxe; but the tact in which he was
not deficient assured him that he ought not to reappear on
a stage where he had already figured for perhaps too considerable a time; and so another week had to be passed,
softened, however, by visits from the Father of the Oratory and the Chamberlain of his Holiness, who came to
look after Lothair with much friendliness, and with
whom it was consolatory and even delightful for him to
converse on sacred art, still holier things, and also Miss
Arundel.

At length, though it seemed impossible, this second week
elapsed, and to-morrow Lothair was to lunch with Lady
St. Jerome in St. James's Square, and to meet all his friends.
He thought of it all day, and he passed a restless night.
He took an early canter to rally his energies, and his fancy
was active in the splendour of the spring. The chesnuts
were in silver bloom, and the pink May had flushed the
thorns, and banks of sloping turf were radiant with plots
of gorgeous flowers. The waters glittered in the sun, and
the air was fragrant with that spell which only can be
found in metropolitan mignionette. It was the hour and
the season when heroic youth comes to great decisions,
achieves exploits, or perpetrates scrapes.

Nothing could be more cordial, nothing more winning,
than the reception of Lothair by Lady St. Jerome. She
did not conceal her joy at their being again together.
Even Miss Arundel, though still calm, even a little demure,

seemed glad to see him : her eyes looked kind and pleased, and she gave him her hand with graceful heartiness. It was the sacred hour of two when Lothair arrived, and they were summoned to luncheon almost immediately. Then they were not alone ; Lord St. Jerome was not there, but the priests were present and some others. Lothair, however, sate next to Miss Arundel.

'I have been thinking of you very often since I left Vauxe,' said Lothair to his neighbour.

'Charitably, I am sure.'

'I have been thinking of you every day,' he continued, 'for I wanted your advice.'

'Ah! but that is not a popular thing to give.'

'But it is precious : at least, yours is to me, and I want it now very much.'

'Father Coleman told me you had got the plans for the cathedral,' said Miss Arundel.

'And I want to show them to you.'

'I fear I am only a critic,' said Miss Arundel, 'and I do not admire mere critics. I was very free in my comments to you on several subjects at Vauxe ; and I must now say I thought you bore it very kindly.'

'I was enchanted,' said Lothair, 'and desire nothing but to be ever subject to such remarks. But this affair of the cathedral, it is your own thought; I would fain hope your own wish, for unless it were your own wish I do not think I ever should be able to accomplish it.'

'And when the cathedral is built,' said Miss Arundel, 'what then ? '

'Do you not remember telling me at Vauxe that all sacred buildings should be respected, for that in the long run they generally fell to the professors of the true faith ? '

'But when they built St. Peter's, they dedicated it to a saint in heaven,' said Miss Arundel. 'To whom is yours to be inscribed ? '

'To a saint in heaven and on earth,' said Lothair, blushing; 'to St. Clare.'

But Lady St. Jerome and her guests rose at this moment, and it is impossible to say with precision whether this last remark of Lothair absolutely reached the ear of Miss Arundel. She looked as if it had not. The priests and the other guests dispersed. Lothair accompanied the ladies to the drawing-room: he lingered, and he was meditating if the occasion served to say more.

Lady St. Jerome was writing a note, Miss Arundel was arranging some work, Lothair was affecting an interest in her employment in order that he might be seated by her and ask her questions, when the groom of the chambers entered and enquired whether her Ladyship was at home, and being answered in the affirmative retired, and announced and ushered in the Duchess and Lady Corisande.

CHAPTER XIX.

IT seemed that the Duchess and Lady St. Jerome were intimate, for they called each other by their Christian names, and kissed each other. The young ladies also were cordial. Her Grace greeted Lothair with heartiness; Lady Corisande with some reserve. Lothair thought she looked very radiant and very proud.

It was some time since they had all met, not since the end of the last season, so there was a great deal to talk about. There had been deaths and births and marriages, which required a flying comment; all important events: deaths which solved many difficulties, heirs to estates which were not expected, and weddings which surprised everybody.

'And have you seen Selina?' enquired Lady St. Jerome.

'Not yet; except mamma, this is our first visit,' replied the Duchess.

'Ah! that is real friendship! She came down to Vauxe the other day, but I did not think she was looking well. She frets herself too much about her boys; she does not know what to do with them. They will not go into the Church, and they have no fortune for the Guards.'

'I understood that Lord Plantagenet was to be a civil engineer,' said Lady Corisande.

'And Lord Albert Victor to have a sheep-walk in Australia,' continued Lady St. Jerome.

'They say that a lord must not go to the bar,' said Miss Arundel. 'It seems to me very unjust.'

'Alfred Beaufort went the circuit,' said Lady Corisande, 'but I believe they drove him into Parliament.'

'You will miss your friend Bertram at Oxford,' said the Duchess, addressing Lothair.

'Indeed,' said Lothair, rather confused, for he was himself a defaulter in collegiate attendance. 'I was just going to write to him to see whether one could not keep half a term.'

'Oh! nothing will prevent his taking his degree,' said the Duchess, 'but I fear there must be some delay. There is a vacancy for our county: Mr. Sandstone is dead, and they insist upon returning Bertram. I hope he will be of age before the nomination. The Duke is much opposed to it; he wishes him to wait; but in these days it is not so easy for young men to get into Parliament. It is not as it used to be; we cannot choose.'

'This is an important event,' said Lothair to Lady Corisande.

'I think it is; nor do I believe Bertram is too young for public life. These are not times to be laggard.'

'There is no doubt they are very serious times,' said Lothair.

'I have every confidence in Bertram, in his ability and his principles.'

The ladies began to talk about the approaching Drawing-room and Lady Corisande's presentation, and Lothair thought it right to make his obeisance and withdraw. He met in the hall Father Coleman, who was in fact looking after him, and would have induced him to repair to the Father's room and hold some interesting conversation, but Lothair was not so congenial as usual. He was even abrupt, and the Father, who never pressed anything, assuming that Lothair had some engagement, relinquished with a serene brow, but not without chagrin, what he had deemed might have proved a golden opportunity.

And yet Lothair had no engagement, and did not know where to go or what to do with himself. But he wanted to be alone, and of all persons in the world at that moment, he had a sort of instinct that the one he wished least to converse with was Father Coleman.

'She has every confidence in his principles,' said Lothair to himself as he mounted his horse, 'and his principles were mine six months ago, when I was at Brentham. Delicious Brentham! It seems like a dream; but everything seems like a dream: I hardly know whether life is agony or bliss.'

CHAPTER XX.

THE Duke was one of the few gentlemen in London who lived in a palace. One of the half dozen of those stately structures that our capital boasts had fallen to his lot.

An heir apparent to the throne, in the earlier days of the present dynasty, had resolved to be lodged as became a prince, and had raised, amid gardens which he had diverted from one of the royal parks, an edifice not unworthy of Vicenza in its best days, though on a far more extensive scale than any pile that favoured city boasts. Before the palace was finished the prince died, and irretrievably in debt. His executors were glad to sell to the trustees of the ancestors of the chief of the house of Brentham the incomplete palace, which ought never to have been commenced. The ancestor of the Duke was by no means so strong a man as the Duke himself, and prudent people rather murmured at the exploit. But it was what is called a lucky family; that is to say, a family with a charm that always attracted and absorbed heiresses; and perhaps the splendour of CRECY HOUSE, for it always retained its original title, might have in some degree contributed to fascinate the taste or imagination of the beautiful women who, generation after generation, brought their bright castles and their broad manors to swell the state and rent-rolls of the family who were so kind to Lothair.

The centre of Crecy House consisted of a hall of vast proportion, and reaching to the roof. Its walls commemorated, in paintings by the most celebrated artists of the age, the exploits of the Black Prince; and its coved ceiling, in panels resplendent with Venetian gold, was bright with the forms and portraits of English heroes. A corridor round this hall contained the most celebrated private collection of pictures in England, and opened into a series of sumptuous saloons.

It was a rather early hour when Lothair, the morning after his meeting the Duchess at Lady St. Jerome's, called at Crecy House; but it was only to leave his card. He would not delay for a moment paying his respects there, and yet he shrank from thrusting himself immediately into the circle. The Duke's brougham was in the courtyard. Lothair was holding his groom's horse, who had

G

dismounted, when the hall-door opened and his Grace and Bertram came forth.

'Halloa, old fellow!' exclaimed Bertram, 'only think of your being here. It seems an age since we met. The Duchess was telling us about you at breakfast.'

'Go in and see them,' said the Duke, 'there is a large party at luncheon; Victoria Montairy is there. Bertram and I are obliged to go to Lincoln's Inn, something about his election.'

But Lothair murmured thanks and declined.

'What are you going to do with yourself to-day?' said the Duke. And Lothair hesitating, his Grace continued: 'Well then, come and dine with us.'

'Of course you will come, old fellow. I have not seen you since you left Oxford at the beginning of the year. And then we can settle about your term.' And Lothair consenting, they drove away.

It was nine o'clock before they dined. The days were getting very long, and soft, and sweet; the riding parties lingered amid the pink May and the tender twilight breeze. The Montairys dined that day at Crecy House, and a charming married daughter without her husband, and Lord and Lady Clanmorne, who were near kin to the Duchess, and themselves so good-looking and agreeable that they were as good at a dinner-party as a couple of first-rate entrées. There was also Lord Carisbrooke, a young man of distinguished air and appearance; his own master, with a large estate, and three years or so older than Lothair.

They dined in the Chinese saloon, which was of moderate dimensions, but bright with fantastic forms and colours, brilliantly lit up. It was the privilege of Lothair to hand the Duchess to her seat. He observed that Lord Carisbrooke was placed next to Lady Corisande, though he had not taken her out.

'This dinner reminds me of my visit to Brentham,' said Lothair.

'Almost the same party,' said the Duchess.

'The visit to Brentham was the happiest time of my life,' said Lothair moodily.

'But you have seen a great deal since,' said the Duchess.

'I am not so sure it is of any use seeing things,' said Lothair.

When the ladies retired, there was some talk about horses. Lord Carisbrooke was breeding; Lothair thought it was a duty to breed, but not to go on the turf. Lord Carisbrooke thought there could be no good breeding without racing; Lothair was of opinion that races might be confined to one's own parks, with no legs admitted, and immense prizes, which must cause emulation. Then they joined the ladies, and then, in a short time, there was music. Lothair hovered about Lady Corisande, and at last seized a happy opportunity of addressing her.

'I shall never forget your singing at Brentham,' he said; 'at first I thought it might be as Lady Montairy said, because I was not used to fine singing; but I heard the Venusina the other day, and I prefer your voice and style.'

'Have you heard the Venusina?' said Lady Corisande with animation; 'I know nothing that I look forward to with more interest. But I was told she was not to open her mouth until she appeared at the Opera. Where did you hear her?'

'Oh, I heard her,' said Lothair, 'at the Roman Catholic Cathedral.'

'I am sure I shall never hear her there,' said Lady Corisande, looking very grave.

'Do not you think music a powerful accessory to religion?' said Lothair, but a little embarrassed.

'Within certain limits,' said Lady Corisande, 'the limits

G 2

I am used to; but I should prefer to hear Opera singers at the Opera.'

'Ah! if all amateurs could sing like you,' said Lothair, 'that would be unnecessary. But a fine Mass by Mozart requires great skill as well as power to render it. I admire no one so much as Mozart, and especially his Masses. I have been hearing a great many of them lately.'

'So we understood,' said Lady Corisande rather dryly, and looking about her as if she were not much interested, or at any rate not much gratified, by the conversation.

Lothair felt he was not getting on, and he wished to get on; but he was socially inexperienced, and his resources not much in hand. There was a pause; it seemed to him an awkward pause; and then Lady Corisande walked away and addressed Lady Clanmorne.

Some very fine singing began at this moment; the room was hushed, no one moved, and Lothair, undisturbed, had the opportunity of watching his late companion. There was something in Lady Corisande that to him was irresistibly captivating; and as he was always thinking and analysing, he employed himself in discovering the cause. 'She is not particularly gracious,' he said to himself, 'at least not to me; she is beautiful, but so are others; and others, like her, are clever, perhaps more clever. But there is something in her brow, her glance, her carriage, which indicates what they call character, and interests me. Six months ago I was in love with her, because I thought she was like her sisters. I love her sisters, but she is not the least like them.'

The music ceased; Lothair moved away, and he approached the Duke.

'I have a favour to ask your Grace,' he said. 'I have made up my mind that I shall not go back to Oxford this term; would you do me the great favour of presenting me at the next Levée?'

CHAPTER XXI.

ONE's life changes in a moment. Half a month ago, Lothair, without an acquaintance, was meditating his return to Oxford. Now he seemed to know everybody who was anybody. His table was overflowing with invitations to all the fine houses in town. First came the routs and the balls; then, when he had been presented to the husbands, came the dinners. His kind friends the Duchess and Lady St. Jerome were the fairies who had worked this sudden scene of enchantment. A single word from them, and London was at Lothair's feet.

He liked it amazingly. He quite forgot the conclusion at which he had arrived respecting society a year ago, drawn from his vast experience of the single party which he had then attended. Feelings are different when you know a great many persons, and every person is trying to please you; above all, when there are individuals whom you want to meet, and whom, if you do not meet, you become restless.

Town was beginning to blaze. Broughams whirled and bright barouches glanced, troops of social cavalry cantered and caracolled in morning rides, and the bells of prancing ponies, lashed by delicate hands, gingled in the laughing air. There were stoppages in Bond Street, which seems to cap the climax of civilisation, after crowded clubs and swarming parks.

But the great event of the season was the presentation of Lady Corisande. Truly our bright maiden of Brentham woke and found herself famous. There are families whom everybody praises, and families who are treated in a different way. Either will do; all the sons and daughters of the first succeed, all the sons and daughters of the

last are encouraged in perverseness by the prophetic
determination of society. Half a dozen married sisters,
who were the delight and ornament of their circles, in
the case of Lady Corisande were good precursors of popularity; but the world would not be content with that: they
credited her with all their charms and winning qualities,
but also with something grander and beyond comparison;
and from the moment her fair cheek was sealed by the
gracious approbation of Majesty, all the critics of the Court
at once recognised her as the cynosure of the Empyrean.

Monsignore Catesby, who looked after Lothair, and was
always breakfasting with him without the necessity of an
invitation (a fascinating man, and who talked upon all subjects except High Mass), knew everything that took place
at Court without being present there himself. He led the
conversation to the majestic theme, and while he seemed to
be busied in breaking an egg with delicate precision, and
hardly listening to the frank expression of opinions which
he carelessly encouraged, obtained a not insufficient share
of Lothair's views and impressions of human beings and
affairs in general during the last few days, which had witnessed a Levée and a Drawing-room.

'Ah! then you were so fortunate as to know the beauty
before her début,' said the Monsignore.

'Intimately; her brother is my friend. I was at Brentham last summer. Delicious place! and the most agreeable
visit I ever made in my life, at least, one of the most agreeable.'

'Ah! ah!' said the Monsignore. 'Let me ring for some
toast.'

On the night of the Drawing-room, a great ball was given
at Crecy House to celebrate the entrance of Corisande into
the world. It was a sumptuous festival. The palace, resonant with fantastic music, blazed amid illumined gardens
rich with summer warmth.

A prince of the blood was dancing with Lady Corisande. Lothair was there, vis-à-vis with Miss Arundel.

'I delight in this hall,' she said to Lothair; 'but how superior the pictured scene to the reality!'

'What! would you like, then, to be in a battle?'

'I should like to be with heroes, wherever they might be. What a fine character was the Black Prince! And they call those days the days of superstition!'

The silver horns sounded a brave flourish. Lothair had to advance and meet Lady Corisande. Her approaching mien was full of grace and majesty, but Lothair thought there was a kind expression in her glance, which seemed to remember Brentham, and that he was her brother's friend.

A little later in the evening he was her partner. He could not refrain from congratulating her on the beauty and the success of the festival.

'I am glad you are pleased, and I am glad you think it successful; but, you know, I am no judge, for this is my first ball!'

'Ah! to be sure; and yet it seems impossible,' he continued, in a tone of murmuring admiration.

'Oh! I have been at little dances at my sisters;' half behind the door,' she added, with a slight smile. 'But to-night I am present at a scene of which I have only read.'

'And how do you like balls?' said Lothair.

'I think I shall like them very much,' said Lady Corisande; 'but to-night, I will confess, I am a little nervous.'

'You do not look so.'

'I am glad of that.'

'Why?'

'Is it not a sign of weakness?'

'Can feeling be weakness?'

'Feeling without sufficient cause is, I should think.' And then, and in a tone of some archness, she said, 'And how do you like balls?'

'Well, I like them amazingly,' said Lothair. 'They seem to me to have every quality which can render an entertainment agreeable: music, light, flowers, beautiful faces, graceful forms, and occasionally charming conversation.'

'Yes; and that never lingers,' said Lady Corisande, 'for see, I am wanted.'

When they were again undisturbed, Lothair regretted the absence of Bertram, who was kept at the House.

'It is a great disappointment,' said Lady Corisande; 'but he will yet arrive, though late. I should be most unhappy though, if he were absent from his post on such an occasion. I am sure if he were here I could not dance.'

'You are a most ardent politician,' said Lothair.

'Oh! I do not care in the least about common politics, parties and office and all that; I neither regard nor understand them,' replied Lady Corisande. 'But when wicked men try to destroy the country, then I like my family to be in the front.'

As the destruction of the country meditated this night by wicked men was some change in the status of the Church of England, which Monsignore Catesby in the morning had suggested to Lothair as both just and expedient and highly conciliatory, Lothair did not pursue the theme, for he had a greater degree of tact than usually falls to the lot of the ingenuous.

The bright moments flew on. Suddenly there was a mysterious silence in the hall, followed by a kind of suppressed stir. Everyone seemed to be speaking with bated breath, or, if moving, walking on tiptoe. It was the supper hour:

Soft hour which wakes the wish and melts the heart.

Royalty, followed by the imperial presence of ambassadors, and escorted by a group of dazzling duchesses and paladins of high degree, was ushered with courteous pomp by the host and hostess into a choice saloon, hung with rose-coloured tapestry and illumined by chandeliers of crystal, where they were served from gold plate. But the thousand less favoured were not badly off, when they found themselves in the more capacious chambers, into which they rushed with an eagerness hardly in keeping with the splendid nonchalance of the preceding hours.

'What a perfect family,' exclaimed Hugo Bohun, as he extracted a couple of fat little birds from their bed of aspic jelly; 'everything they do in such perfect taste. How safe you were here to have ortolans for supper!'

All the little round tables, though their number was infinite, were full. Male groups hung about; some in attendance on fair dames, some foraging for themselves, some thoughtful and more patient and awaiting a satisfactory future. Never was such an elegant clatter.

'I wonder where Carisbrooke is,' said Hugo Bohun. 'They say he is wonderfully taken with the beauteous daughter of the house.'

'I will back the Duke of Brecon against him,' said one of his companions. 'He raved about her at White's yesterday.'

'Hem!'

'The end is not so near as all that,' said a third wassailer.

'I do not know that,' said Hugo Bohun. 'It is a family that marries off quickly. If a fellow is obliged to marry, he always likes to marry one of them.'

'What of this new star?' said his friend, and he mentioned Lothair.

'Oh! he is too young; not launched. Besides he is going to turn Catholic, and I doubt whether that would do in that quarter.'

'But he has a greater fortune than any of them.'

'Immense! A man I know, who knows another man——' and then he began a long statistical story about Lothair's resources.

'Have you got any room here, Hugo?' drawled out Lord St. Aldegonde.

'Plenty, and here is my chair.'

'On no account; half of it and some soup will satisfy me.'

'I should have thought you would have been with the swells,' said Hugo Bohun.

'That does not exactly suit me,' said St. Aldegonde. 'I was ticketed to the Duchess of Salop, but I got a first-rate substitute with the charm of novelty for her Grace, and sent her in with Lothair.'

St. Aldegonde was the heir apparent of the wealthiest, if not the most ancient, dukedom in the United Kingdom. He was spoiled, but he knew it. Had he been an ordinary being, he would have merely subsided into selfishness and caprice, but having good abilities and a good disposition, he was eccentric, adventurous, and sentimental. Notwithstanding the apathy which had been engendered by premature experience, St. Aldegonde held extreme opinions, especially on political affairs, being a republican of the reddest dye. He was opposed to all privilege, and indeed to all orders of men, except dukes, who were a necessity. He was also strongly in favour of the equal division of all property, except land. Liberty depended on land, and the greater the landowners, the greater the liberty of a country. He would hold forth on this topic even with energy, amazed at anyone differing from him; 'as if a fellow could have too much land,' he would urge with a voice and glance which defied contradiction. St. Aldegonde had married for love, and he loved his wife, but he was strongly in favour of woman's rights and their extremest consequences. It was thought that he had originally adopted these latter views

with the amiable intention of piquing Lady St. Aldegonde;
but if so, he had not succeeded. Beaming with brightness,
with the voice and airiness of a bird, and a cloudless
temper, Albertha St. Aldegonde had, from the first hour of
her marriage, concentrated her intelligence, which was not
mean, on one object; and that was never to cross her
husband on any conceivable topic. They had been married
several years, and she treated him as a darling spoiled
child. When he cried for the moon, it was promised him
immediately; however irrational his proposition, she always
assented to it, though generally by tact and vigilance she
guided him in the right direction. Nevertheless, St. Aldegonde was sometimes in scrapes; but then he always went
and told his best friend, whose greatest delight was to
extricate him from his perplexities and embarrassments.

CHAPTER XXII.

ALTHOUGH Lothair was not in the slightest degree shaken
in his conviction that life should be entirely religious, he
was perplexed by the inevitable obstacles which seemed
perpetually to oppose themselves to the practice of his
opinions. It was not merely pleasure in its multiform ap-
pearances that he had to contend against, but business
began imperiously to solicit his attention. Every month
brought him nearer to his majority, and the frequent letters
from Mr. Putney Giles now began to assume the pressing
shape of solicitations for personal interviews. He had
a long conversation one morning with Father Coleman on
this subject, who greatly relieved him by the assurance
that a perfectly religious life was one of which the sovereign purpose was to uphold the interests of the Church;
of Christ, the Father added after a momentary pause.

Business, and even amusement, were not only compatible with such a purpose, but might even be conducive to its fulfilment.

Mr. Putney Giles reminded Lothair that the attainment of his majority must be celebrated, and in a becoming manner. Preparation, and even considerable preparation, was necessary. There were several scenes of action; some very distant. It was not too early to contemplate arrangements. Lothair really must confer with his guardians. They were both now in town, the Scotch uncle having come up to attend Parliament. Could they be brought together? Was it indeed impossible? If so, who was to give the necessary instructions?

It was much more than a year since Lothair had met his uncle, and he did not anticipate much satisfaction from the renewal of their intimacy; but every feeling of propriety demanded that it should be recognised, and to a certain degree revived. Lord Culloden was a black Scotchman, tall and lean, with good features, a hard red face and iron grey hair. He was a man who shrank from scenes, and he greeted Lothair as if they had only parted yesterday. Looking at him with his keen, unsentimental, but not unkind eye, he said, 'Well, sir, I thought you would have been at Oxford.'

'Yes, my dear uncle; but circumstances —— '

'Well, well, I don't want to hear the cause. I am very glad you are not there; I believe you might as well be at Rome.'

And then in due course, and after some talk of the past and old times, Lothair referred to the suggestions of Mr. Giles, and hinted at a meeting of his guardians to confer and advise together.

'No, no,' said the Scotch peer, shaking his head; 'I will have nothing to do with the Scarlet Lady. Mr. Giles is an able and worthy man; he may well be trusted to draw up a programme for our consideration, and indeed it is an affair in which yourself should be most consulted. Let all be done liberally, for you have a great inheritance, and I would be no curmudgeon in these matters.'

'Well, my dear uncle, whatever is arranged, I hope you and my cousins will honour and gratify me with your presence throughout the proceedings.'

'Well, well, it is not much in my way. You will be having balls and fine ladies. There is no fool like an old fool, they say; but I think, from what I hear, the young fools will beat us in the present day. Only think of young persons going over to the Church of Rome. Why, they are just naturals!'

The organising genius of Mr. Putney Giles had rarely encountered a more fitting theme than the celebration of the impending majority. There was place for all his energy and talent and resources: a great central inauguration; sympathetical festivals and gatherings in half a dozen other counties; the troth, as it were, of a sister kingdom to be pledged; a vista of balls and banquets, and illuminations and addresses, of ceaseless sports and speeches, and processions alike endless.

'What I wish to effect,' said Mr. Giles, as he was giving his multifarious orders, 'is to produce among all classes an impression adequate to the occasion. I wish the lord and the tenantry alike to feel they have a duty to perform.'

In the meantime, Monsignore Catesby was pressing Lothair to become one of the patrons of a Roman Catholic Bazaar, where Lady St. Jerome and Miss Arundel were to preside over a stall. It was of importance to show that charity was not the privilege of any particular creed.

Between his lawyers, and his monsignores, and his architects, Lothair began to get a little harassed. He was disturbed in his own mind, too, on greater matters, and seemed to feel every day that it was more necessary to take a decided step, and more impossible to decide upon what it should be. He frequently saw the Cardinal, who was very kind to him, but who had become more reserved on religious subjects. He had dined more than once with his Eminence, and had met some distinguished prelates and some of his fellow nobles who had been weaned from the errors of their cradle. The Cardinal perhaps thought that the presence of these eminent converts would facilitate the progress, perhaps the decision, of his ward; but something seemed always to happen to divert Lothair in his course. It might be sometimes apparently a very slight cause, but yet for the time sufficient; a phrase of Lady Corisande for example, who, though she never directly addressed him on the subject, was nevertheless deeply interested in his spiritual condition.

'You ought to speak to him, Bertram,' she said one day to her brother very indignantly, as she read a fresh paragraph alluding to an impending conversion. 'You are his friend. What is the use of friendship, if not in such a crisis as this?'

'I see no use in speaking to a man about love or religion,' said Bertram; 'they are both stronger than friendship. If there be any foundation for the paragraph, my interference would be of no avail; if there be none, I should only make myself ridiculous.'

Nevertheless, Bertram looked a little more after his friend, and disturbing the Monsignore, who was at breakfast with Lothair one morning, Bertram obstinately outstayed the priest, and then said: 'I tell you what, old fellow, you are rather hippish; I wish you were in the House of Commons.'

'So do I,' said Lothair, with a sigh; 'but I have come into everything ready-made. I begin to think it very unfortunate.'

'What are you going to do with yourself to-day? If you

be disengaged, I vote we dine together at White's, and then
we will go down to the House. I will take you to the
smoking-room and introduce you to Bright, and we will
trot him out on primogeniture.'

At this moment the servant brought Lothair two letters;
one was an epistle from Father Coleman, meeting Lothair's
objections to becoming a patron of the Roman Catholic
Bazaar in a very unctuous and exhaustive manner; and
the other from his stud-groom at Oxford, detailing some of
those disagreeable things which will happen with absent
masters who will not answer letters. Lothair loved his
stable, and felt particularly anxious to avoid the threatened
visit of Father Coleman on the morrow. His decision was
rapid. 'I must go down this afternoon to Oxford, my dear
fellow. My stable is in confusion. I shall positively
return to-morrow, and I will dine with you at White's, and
we will go to the House of Commons together or go to
the play.'

CHAPTER XXIII.

LOTHAIR's stables were about three miles from Oxford.
They were a rather considerable establishment, in which he
had taken much interest, and having always intended to
return to Oxford in the early part of the year, although he
had occasionally sent for a hack or two to London, his stud
had been generally maintained.

The morning after his arrival, he rode over to the
stables, where he had ordered his drag to be ready. About
a quarter of a mile before he reached his place of destination he observed at some little distance a crowd in the road,
and, hastening on, perceived as he drew nearer a number
of men clustered round a dismantled vehicle, and vainly

endeavouring to extricate and raise a fallen horse; its companion, panting and foaming, with broken harness but apparently uninjured, standing aside and held by a boy. Somewhat apart stood a lady alone. Lothair immediately dismounted and approached her, saying, 'I fear you are in trouble, madam. Perhaps I may be of service?'

The lady was rather tall and of a singularly distinguished presence. Her air and her costume alike intimated high breeding and fashion. She seemed quite serene amid the tumult and confusion, and apparently the recent danger. As Lothair spoke, she turned her head to him, which had been at first a little averted, and he beheld a striking countenance, but one which he instantly felt he did not see for the first time.

She bowed with dignity to Lothair, and said in a low but distinct voice, 'You are most courteous, sir. We have had a sad accident, but a great escape. Our horses ran away with us, and had it not been for that heap of stones I do not see how we could have been saved.'

'Fortunately my stables are at hand,' said Lothair, 'and I have a carriage waiting for me at this moment, not a quarter of a mile away. It is at your service, and I will send for it,' and his groom, to whom he gave directions, galloped off.

There was a shout as the fallen horse was on his legs again, much cut, and the carriage shattered and useless. A gentleman came from the crowd and approached the lady. He was tall and fair and not ill-favoured, with fine dark eyes and high cheek bones, and still young, though an enormous beard at the first glance gave him an impression of years the burthen of which he really did not bear. His dress, though not vulgar, was richer and more showy than is usual in this country, and altogether there was something in his manner which, though calm and full of self-respect, was different from the conventional refinement of

England. Yet he was apparently an Englishman, as he said to the lady, 'It is a bad business, but we must be thankful it is no worse. What troubles me is how you are to get back. It will be a terrible walk over these stony roads, and I can hear of no conveyance.'

'My husband,' said the lady, as with dignity she presented the person to Lothair. 'This gentleman,' she continued, 'has most kindly offered us the use of his carriage, which is almost at hand.'

'Sir, you are a friend,' said the gentleman. 'I thought there were no horses that I could not master, but it seems I am mistaken. I bought these only yesterday; took a fancy to them as we were driving about, and bought them of a dealer in the road.'

'That seems a clever animal,' said Lothair, pointing to the one uninjured.

'Ah! you like horses?' said the gentleman.

'Well, I have some taste that way.'

'We are visitors to Oxford,' said the lady. 'Colonel Campian, like all Americans, is very interested in the ancient parts of England.'

'To-day we were going to Blenheim,' said the Colonel; 'but I thought I would try these new tits a bit on a by-road first.'

'All's well that ends well,' said Lothair; 'and there is no reason why you should not fulfil your intention of going to Blenheim, for here is my carriage, and it is entirely at your service for the whole day, and, indeed, as long as you stay at Oxford.'

'Sir, there requires no coronet on your carriage to tell me you are a nobleman,' said the Colonel. 'I like frank manners, and I like your team. I know few things that would please me more than to try them.'

They were four roans, highly bred, with black manes

H

and tails. They had the Arab eye, with arched necks, and seemed proud of themselves and their master.

'I do not see why we should not go to Blenheim,' said the Colonel.

'Well, not to-day,' said the lady, 'I think. We have had an escape, but one feels these things a little more afterwards than at the time. I would rather go back to Oxford and be quiet; and there is more than one college which you have not yet seen.'

'My team is entirely at your service wherever you go,' said Lothair; 'but I cannot venture to drive you to Oxford, for I am there in statu pupillari, and a proctor might arrest us all. But perhaps,' and he approached the lady, 'you will permit me to call on you to-morrow, when I hope I may find you have not suffered by this misadventure.'

'We have got a professor dining with us to-day at seven o'clock,' said the Colonel, 'at our hotel; and if you are disengaged and would join the party, you would add to the favours which you know so well how to confer.'

Lothair handed the lady into the carriage, the Colonel mounted the box and took the ribbons like a master, and the four roans trotted away with their precious charge and their two grooms behind with folded arms and imperturbable countenances.

Lothair watched the equipage until it vanished in the distance.

'It is impossible to forget that countenance,' he said; 'and I fancy I did hear at the time that she had married an American. Well, I shall meet her at dinner, that is something.' And he sprang into his saddle.

CHAPTER XXIV.

The Oxford Professor, who was the guest of the American Colonel, was quite a young man, of advanced opinions on all subjects, religious, social, and political. He was clever, extremely well-informed, so far as books can make a man knowing, but unable to profit even by that limited experience of life from a restless vanity and overflowing conceit, which prevented him from ever observing or thinking of anything but himself. He was gifted with a great command of words, which took the form of endless exposition, varied by sarcasm and passages of ornate jargon. He was the last person one would have expected to recognise in an Oxford professor; but we live in times of transition.

A Parisian man of science, who had passed his life in alternately fighting at barricades and discovering planets, had given Colonel Campian, who had lived much in the French capital, a letter of introduction to the Professor, whose invectives against the principles of English society were hailed by foreigners as representative of the sentiments of venerable Oxford. The Professor, who was not satisfied with his home career, and, like many men of his order of mind, had dreams of wild vanity which the New World, they think, can alone realise, was very glad to make the Colonel's acquaintance, which might facilitate his future movements. So he had lionised the distinguished visitors during the last few days over the University, and had availed himself of plenteous opportunities for exhibiting to them his celebrated powers of exposition, his talent for sarcasm, which he deemed peerless, and several highly finished picturesque passages, which were introduced with extemporary art.

H 2

The Professor was much surprised when he saw Lothair enter the saloon at the hotel. He was the last person in Oxford whom he expected to encounter. Like sedentary men of extreme opinions, he was a social parasite, and instead of indulging in his usual invectives against peers and princes, finding himself unexpectedly about to dine with one of that class, he was content only to dazzle and amuse him.

Mrs. Campian only entered the room when dinner was announced. She greeted Lothair with calmness but amenity, and took his offered arm.

'You have not suffered, I hope?' said Lothair.

'Very little, and through your kindness.'

It was a peculiar voice, low and musical, too subdued to call thrilling, but a penetrating voice, so that however ordinary the observation it attracted and impressed attention. But it was in harmony with all her appearance and manner. Lothair thought he had never seen anyone or anything so serene; the serenity, however, not of humbleness, nor of merely conscious innocence; it was not devoid of a degree of majesty; what one pictures of Olympian repose. And the countenance was Olympian: a Phidian face, with large grey eyes and dark lashes; wonderful hair, abounding without art, and gathered together by Grecian fillets.

The talk was of Oxford, and was at first chiefly maintained by the Colonel and the Professor.

'And do you share Colonel Campian's feeling about Old England?' enquired Lothair of his hostess.

'The present interests me more than the past,' said the lady, 'and the future more than the present.'

'The present seems to me as unintelligible as the future,' said Lothair.

'I think it is intelligible,' said the lady, with a faint smile. 'It has many faults, but not, I think, the want of clearness.'

'I am not a destructive,' said the Professor, addressing the Colonel but speaking loudly; 'I would maintain Oxford under any circumstances with the necessary changes.'

'And what are those, might I ask?' enquired Lothair.

'In reality not much. I would get rid of the religion.'

'Get rid of the religion!' said Lothair.

'You have got rid of it once,' said the Professor.

'You have altered, you have what people call reformed it,' said Lothair, 'but you have not abolished or banished it from the University.'

'The shock would not be greater, nor so great, as the change from the Papal to the Reformed Faith. Besides, Universities have nothing to do with religion.'

'I thought Universities were universal,' said Lothair, 'and had something to do with everything.'

'I cannot conceive any society of any kind without religion,' said the lady.

Lothair glanced at her beautiful brow with devotion as she uttered these words.

Colonel Campian began to talk about horses. After that the Professor proved to him that he was related to Edmund Campian the Jesuit; and then he got to the Gunpowder Plot, which he was not sure, if successful, might not have beneficially influenced the course of our history. Probably the Irish difficulty would not then have existed.

'I dislike plots,' said the lady; 'they always fail.'

'And whatever their object, are they not essentially immoral?' said Lothair.

'I have more faith in ideas than in persons,' said the lady. 'When a truth is uttered, it will sooner or later be recognised. It is only an affair of time. It is better that it should mature and naturally germinate than be forced.'

'You would reduce us to lotus-eaters,' exclaimed the Professor. 'Action is natural to man. And what, after all, are conspiracies and revolutions but great principles in violent action?'

'I think you must be an admirer of repose,' said Lothair to the lady, in a low voice.

'Because I have seen something of action in my life,' said the lady, 'and it is an experience of wasted energies and baffled thoughts.'

When they returned to the saloon, the Colonel and the Professor became interested in the constitution and discipline of the American Universities. Lothair hung about the lady, who was examining some views of Oxford, and who was ascertaining what she had seen and what she had omitted to visit. They were thinking of returning home on the morrow.

'Without seeing Blenheim?' said Lothair.

'Without seeing Blenheim,' said the lady; 'I confess to a pang; but I shall always associate with that name your great kindness to us.'

'But cannot we for once enter into a conspiracy together,' said Lothair, 'and join in a happy plot and contrive to go? Besides I could take you to the private gardens, for the Duke has given me a perpetual order, and they are really exquisite.'

The lady seemed to smile.

'Theodora,' said the Colonel, speaking from the end of the room, 'what have you settled about your train to-morrow?'

'We want to stay another day here,' said Theodora, 'and go to Blenheim.'

CHAPTER XXV.

THEY were in the private gardens at Blenheim. The sun was brilliant over the ornate and yet picturesque scene.

'Beautiful, is it not?' exclaimed Lothair.

'Yes, certainly beautiful,' said Theodora. 'But, do you know, I do not feel altogether content in these fine gardens. The principle of exclusion on which they are all founded is to me depressing. I require in all things sympathy. You would not agree with me in this. The manners of your country are founded on exclusion.'

'But surely there are times and places when one would like to be alone?'

'Without doubt,' said the lady, 'only I do not like artificial loneliness. Even your parks, which all the world praises, do not quite satisfy me. I prefer a forest where all may go, even the wild beasts.'

'But forests are not at command,' said Lothair.

'So you make a solitude and call it peace,' said the lady, with a slight smile. 'For my part, my perfect life would be a large and beautiful village. I admire nature, but I require the presence of humanity. Life in great cities is too exhausting; but in my village there should be air, streams, and beautiful trees, a picturesque scene, but enough of my fellow-creatures to ensure constant duty.'

'But the fulfilment of duty and society founded on what you call the principle of exclusion, are not incompatible,' said Lothair.

'No, but difficult. What should be natural becomes an art; and in every art it is only the few who can be first-rate.'

'I have an ambition to be a first-rate artist in that respect,' said Lothair thoughtfully.

'That does you much honour,' she replied, 'for you necessarily embark in a most painful enterprise. The toiling multitude have their sorrows which, I believe, will some day be softened, and obstacles hard to overcome ; but I have always thought that the feeling of satiety, almost inseparable from large possessions, is a surer cause of misery than ungratified desires.'

'It seems to me that there is a great deal to do,' said Lothair.

'I think so,' said the lady.

'Theodora,' said the Colonel, who was a little in advance with the Professor, and turning round his head, 'this reminds me of Mirabel,' and he pointed to the undulating banks covered with rare shrubs and touching the waters of the lake.

'And where is Mirabel ?' said Lothair.

'It was a green island in the Adriatic,' said the lady, 'which belonged to Colonel Campian; we lost it in the troubles. Colonel Campian was very fond of it. I try to persuade him that our home was of volcanic origin, and has only vanished and subsided into its native bed.'

'And were not you fond of it ?'

'I never think of the past,' said the lady.

'Oxford is not the first place where I had the pleasure of meeting you,' Lothair ventured at length to observe.

'Yes, we have met before, in Hyde Park Gardens. Our hostess is a clever woman, and has been very kind to some friends of mine.'

'And have you seen her lately ?'

'She comes to see us sometimes. We do not live in London, but in the vicinity. We only go to London for the Opera, of which we are devotees. We do not at all enter general society ; Colonel Campian only likes people who interest or amuse him, and he is fortunate in having rather a numerous acquaintance of that kind.'

'Rare fortune!' said Lothair.

'Colonel Campian lived a great deal at Paris before we married,' said the lady, 'and in a circle of considerable culture and excitement. He is social, but not conventional.'

'And you, are you conventional?'

'Well, I live only for climate and the affections,' said the lady. 'I am fond of society that pleases me, that is accomplished and natural and ingenious; otherwise I prefer being alone. As for atmosphere, as I look upon it as the main source of felicity, you may be surprised that I should reside in your country. I should myself like to go to America, but that would not suit Colonel Campian; and if we are to live in Europe we must live in England. It is not pleasant to reside in a country where, if you happen to shelter or succour a friend, you may be subject to a domiciliary visit.'

The Professor stopped to deliver a lecture or address on the villa of Hadrian. Nothing could be more minute or picturesque than his description of that celebrated pleasaunce. It was varied by portraits of the Emperor and some of his companions, and, after a rapid glance at the fortunes of the imperial patriciate, wound up with some conclusions favourable to communism. It was really very clever, and would have made the fortune of a literary society.

'I wonder if they had gravel walks in the villa of Hadrian,' said the Colonel. 'What I admire most in your country, my Lord, are your gravel walks, though that lady would not agree with me in that matter.'

'You are against gravel walks,' said Lothair.

'Well, I cannot bring myself to believe that they had gravel walks in the garden of Eden,' said the lady.

They had a repast at Woodstock, too late for luncheon, too early for dinner, but which it was agreed should serve as the latter meal.

'That suits me exactly,' said the lady; 'I am a great
foe to dinners, and indeed to all meals. I think when the
good time comes we shall give up eating in public, except
perhaps fruit on a green bank with music.'

It was a rich twilight as they drove home, the lady
leaning back in the carriage silent. Lothair sat opposite
to her, and gazed upon a countenance on which the moon
began to glisten, and which seemed unconscious of all
human observation.

He had read of such countenances in Grecian dreams:
in Corinthian temples, in fanes of Ephesus, in the radiant
shadow of divine groves.

CHAPTER XXVI.

WHEN they had arrived at the hotel, Colonel Campian proposed that they should come in and have some coffee, but
Theodora did not enforce this suggestion, and Lothair
feeling that she might be wearied gracefully, though un-
willingly, waved the proposal. Remembering that on the
noon of the morrow they were to depart, with a happy
inspiration, as he said farewell, he asked permission to accompany them to the station.

Lothair walked away with the Professor, who seemed in
a conservative vein, and graciously disposed to make several concessions to the customs of an ancient country.
Though opposed to the land laws, he would operate
gradually, and gave Lothair more than one receipt how
to save the aristocracy. Lothair would have preferred
talking about the lady they had just quitted, but as he
soon found the Professor could really give him no information about her he let the subject drop.

But not out of his own mind. He was glad to be alone and brood over the last two days. They were among the most interesting of his life. He had encountered a character different from any he had yet met, had listened to new views, and his intelligence had been stimulated by remarks made casually in easy conversation, and yet to him pregnant with novel and sometimes serious meaning. The voice, too, lingered in his ear, so hushed and deep and yet so clear and sweet. He leant over his mantelpiece in teeming reverie.

'And she is profoundly religious,' he said to himself; 'she can conceive no kind of society without religion. She has arrived at the same conclusion as myself. What a privilege it would be to speak to her on such subjects!'

'After a restless night the morrow came. About eleven o'clock Lothair ventured to call on his new friends. The lady was alone; she was standing by the window reading an Italian newspaper, which she folded up and placed aside when Lothair was announced.

'We propose to walk to the station,' said Theodora; 'the servants have gone on. Colonel Campian has a particular aversion to moving with any luggage. He restricts me to this,' she said, pointing to her satchel, in which she had placed the foreign newspaper, 'and for that he will not be responsible.'

'It was most kind of you to permit me to accompany you this morning,' said Lothair; 'I should have been grieved to have parted abruptly last night.'

'I could not refuse such a request,' said the lady; 'but do you know I never like to say farewell, even for four-and-twenty hours. One should vanish like a spirit.'

'Then I have erred,' said Lothair, 'against your rules and principles.'

'Say my fancies,' said the lady, 'my humours, my whims. Besides this is not a farewell. You will come and see

us. Colonel Campian tells me you have promised to give
us that pleasure.'

'It will be the greatest pleasure to me,' said Lothair; 'I
can conceive nothing greater.' And then hesitating a little,
and a little blushing, he added, 'When do you think I
might come?'

'Whenever you like,' said the lady, 'you will always find
me at home. My life is this: I ride every day very early,
and far into the country, so I return tamed some two or
three hours after noon, and devote myself to my friends.
We are at home every evening, except opera nights, and
let me tell you, because it is not the custom generally among
your compatriots, we are always at home on Sundays.'

Colonel Campian entered the room; the moment of departure was at hand. Lothair felt the consolation of being
their companion to the station. He had once hoped it
might be possible to be their companion in the train; but
he was not encouraged.

'Railways have elevated and softened the lot of man,'
said Theodora, 'and Colonel Campian views them with
almost a religious sentiment. But I cannot read in a railroad, and the human voice is distressing to me amid the
whirl and the whistling, and the wild panting of the
loosened megatheria who drag us. And then those terrible
grottoes; it is quite a descent of Proserpine; so I have no
resource but my own thoughts.'

'And surely that is sufficient,' murmured Lothair.

'Not when the past is expelled,' said the lady.

'But the future?' said Lothair.

'Yes, that is ever interesting, but so vague that it sometimes induces slumber.'

The bell sounded, Lothair handed the lady to her com-
partment.

'Our Oxford visit,' she said, 'has been a great success
and mainly through you.'

The Colonel was profuse in his cordial farewells, and it seemed they would never have ended had not the train moved.

Lothair remained upon the platform until it was out of sight, and then exclaimed, 'Is it a dream, or shall I ever see her again?'

CHAPTER XXVII.

LOTHAIR reached London late in the afternoon. Among the notes and cards and letters on his table was a long and pressing despatch from Mr. Putney Giles awaiting his judgment and decision on many points.

'The central inauguration, if I may use the term,' said Mr. Putney Giles, 'is comparatively easy. It is an affair of expense and of labour, great labour; I may say unremitting labour. But your Lordship will observe the other points are not mere points of expense and labour. We have to consult the feelings of several counties where your Lordship cannot be present, at least certainly not on this occasion, and yet where an adequate recognition of those sentiments which ought to exist between the proprietor and all classes connected with him ought to be secured. Then Scotland: Scotland is a very difficult business to manage. It is astonishing how the sentiment lingers in that country connected with its old independence. I really am quite surprised at it. One of your Lordship's most important tenants wrote to me only a few days back, that great dissatisfaction would prevail among your Lordship's friends and tenantry in Scotland, if that country on this occasion were placed on the same level as a mere English county. It must be recognised as a kingdom. I almost think it would be better if we could persuade Lord Culloden

not to attend the English inauguration, but remain in the
kingdom of Scotland, and take the chair and the lead
throughout the festal ceremonies.   A peer of the realm,
and your Lordship's guardian, would impart something of
a national character to the proceedings, and this, with a
judicious emblazoning on some of the banners of the royal
arms of Scotland, might have a conciliatory effect.   One
should always conciliate.   But your Lordship on all these
points, and especially with reference to Lord Culloden, must
be a much better judge than I am.'

Lothair nearly gave a groan. ' I almost wish,' he thought,
' my minority would never end.   I am quite satisfied with
things as they are.   What is the kingdom of Scotland to
me, and all these counties?   I almost begin to feel that
satiety which she said was inseparable from vast possessions.'

A letter from Bertram reminding him that he had not
dined at White's as he had promised, and suggesting some
new arrangement, and another from Monsignore Catesby
earnestly urging him to attend a most peculiar and solemn
function of the Church next Sunday evening, where the
Cardinal would officiate and preach, and in which Lady
St. Jerome and Miss Arundel were particularly interested,
did not restore his equanimity.

A dinner at White's!   He did not think he could stand
a dinner at White's.   Indeed he was not sure that he could
stand any dinner anywhere, especially in this hot weather.
There was a good deal in what she said : ' One ought to
eat alone.'

The ecclesiastical function was a graver matter.   It had
been long contemplated, often talked about, and on occasions looked forward to by him even with a certain degree
of eagerness.   He wished he had had an opportunity of
speaking with her on these matters.   She was eminently
religious ; that she had voluntarily avowed.   And he felt

persuaded that no light or thoughtless remark could fall from those lips. He wondered to what Church she belonged? Protestant or Papal? Her husband, being an American, was probably a Protestant, but he was a gentleman of the South and with nothing puritanical about him. She was a European, and probably of a Latin race. In all likelihood she was a Roman Catholic.

It was Wednesday evening, and his valet reminded him that he was engaged to dine with Lord and Lady Montairy.

Lothair sighed. He was so absorbed by his new feelings, that he shrunk from society with a certain degree of aversion. He felt it quite out of his power to fulfil his engagement. He sent an excuse. It was Lothair's first excuse. In short, he 'threw over' the Montairys, to whom he was so much attached, whom he so much admired, and whose society he had hitherto so highly prized.

To 'throw over' a host is the most heinous of social crimes. It ought never to be pardoned. It disjoints a party, often defeats the combinations which might affect the results of a season, and generally renders the society incoherent and unsatisfactory. If the outrage could ever be condoned it might be in the instance of a young man very inexperienced, the victim of some unexpected condition of nervous feelings over which the defaulter has really no control.

It was evening, and the restless Lothair walked forth without a purpose, and in a direction which he rarely visited. 'It is a wonderful place,' said he, 'this London; a nation, not a city; with a population greater than some kingdoms, and districts as different as if they were under different governments and spoke different languages. And what do I know of it? I have been living here six months, and my life has been passed in a park, two or three squares, and half a dozen streets!'

So he walked on and soon crossed Oxford Street, like the Rhine a natural boundary, and then got into Portland Place, and then found himself in the New Road, and then he hailed a cruising Hansom, which he had previously observed was well-horsed.

''Tis the gondola of London,' said Lothair as he sprang in.

'Drive on till I tell you to stop.'

And the Hansom drove on, through endless boulevards, some bustling, some dingy, some tawdry and flaring, some melancholy and mean; rows of garden gods, planted on the walls of yards full of roses and divinities of concrete, huge railway halls, monster hotels, dissenting chapels in the form of Gothic churches, quaint ancient almshouses that were once built in the fields, and tea-gardens and stingo houses and knackers' yards. They were in a district far beyond the experience of Lothair, which indeed had been exhausted when he had passed Euston, and from that he had been long separated. The way was broad but ill-lit, with houses of irregular size but generally of low elevation, and sometimes detached in smoked-dried gardens. The road was becoming a bridge which crossed a canal, with barges and wharves and timber yards, when their progress was arrested by a crowd. It seemed a sort of procession; there was a banner, and the lamp-light fell upon a religious emblem. Lothair was interested, and desired the driver not to endeavour to advance. The procession was crossing the road and entering a building.

'It's a Roman Catholic chapel,' said a bystander in answer to Lothair. 'I believe it is a meeting about one of their schools. They always have banners.'

'I think I will get out,' said Lothair to his driver. 'This I suppose will pay your fare.'

The man stared with delight at the sovereign in his astonished palm, and in gratitude suggested that he should remain and wait for the gentleman, but the restless Lothair declined the proposal.

'Sir, sir,' said the man, leaning down his head as low as possible from his elevated seat, and speaking in a hushed voice, 'you are a real gentleman. Do you know what all this is?'

'Yes, yes; some meeting about a Roman Catholic school.'

The man shook his head. 'You are a real gentleman, and I will tell you the truth. They meet about the schools of the order of St. Joseph, over the left. It is a Fenian meeting.'

'A Fenian meeting!'

'Ay, ay, and you cannot enter that place without a ticket. Just you try! However, if a gentleman like you wants to go, you shall have my ticket,' said the cabdriver; 'and here it is. And may I drive to-morrow as true a gentleman as I have driven to-day.'

So saying he took a packet from his breast pocket, and opening it offered to Lothair a green slip of paper which was willingly accepted. 'I should like above all things to go,' he said, and he blended with the rear of those who were entering the building. The collector of the tickets stared at Lothair and scrutinised his pass, but all was in order, and Lothair was admitted.

He passed through a house and a yard, at the bottom of which was a rather spacious building. When he entered it, he saw in an instant it was not a chapel. It was what is called a temperance hall, a room to be hired for public assemblies, with a raised platform at the end, on which were half a dozen men. The hall was tolerably full, and Lothair came in among the last. There were some children sitting on a form placed against the wall of the room, each with a bun which kept them quiet; the banner belonged to this school, and was the banner of St. Joseph.

A man dressed like a priest, and known as Father

I

O'Molloy, came forward. He was received with signs of much sympathy, succeeded by complete silence. He addressed them in a popular and animated style on the advantages of education. They knew what that was, and then they cheered. Education taught them to know their rights. But what was the use of knowing their rights unless they enforced them? That was not to be done by prayer books but by something else, and something else wanted a subscription.

This was the object of the meeting and the burthen of all the speeches which followed, and which were progressively more outspoken than the adroit introductory discourse. The Saxon was denounced, sometimes with coarseness, but sometimes in terms of picturesque passion; the vast and extending organisation of the brotherhood was enlarged on, the great results at hand intimated; the necessity of immediate exertion on the part of every individual pressed with emphasis. All these views and remarks received from the audience an encouraging response; and when Lothair observed men going round with boxes, and heard the clink of coin, he felt very embarrassed as to what he should do when asked to contribute to a fund raised to stimulate and support rebellion against his Sovereign. He regretted the rash restlessness which had involved him in such a position.

The collectors approached Lothair, who was standing at the end of the room opposite to the platform, where the space was not crowded.

'I should like to speak to Father O'Molloy,' said Lothair; 'he is a priest and will understand my views.'

'He is a priest here,' said one of the collectors with a sardonic laugh, 'but I am glad to say you will not find his name in the directory. Father O'Molloy is on the platform and engaged.'

'If you want to speak to the Father, speak from where

you are,' said the other collector. 'Here, silence! a gentleman wants to address the meeting.'

And there was silence, and Lothair felt extremely embarrassed, but he was not wanting, though it was the first time in his life that he had addressed a public meeting.

'Gentlemen,' said Lothair, 'I really had no wish to intrude upon you; all I desired was to speak to Father O'Molloy. I wished to tell him that it would have given me pleasure to subscribe to these schools. I am not a Roman Catholic, but I respect the Roman Catholic religion. But I can do nothing that will imply the slightest sanction of the opinions I have heard expressed this evening. For your own sakes——' but here a yell arose which for ever drowned his voice.

'A spy, a spy!' was the general exclamation. 'We are betrayed! Seize him! Knock him over!' and the whole meeting seemed to have turned their backs on the platform and to be advancing on the unfortunate Lothair. Two of the leaders on the platform at the same time leapt down from it, to direct as it were the enraged populace.

But at this moment a man who had been in the lower part of the hall, in the vicinity of Lothair and standing alone, pushed forward, and by his gestures and general mien arrested somewhat the crowd, so that the two leaders who leapt from the platform and bustled through the crowd came in contact with him.

The stranger was evidently not of the class or country of the rest assembled. He had a military appearance, and spoke with a foreign accent when he said, 'This is no spy. Keep your people off.'

'And who are you?' enquired the leader thus addressed.

'One accustomed to be obeyed,' said the stranger.

'You may be a spy yourself,' said the leader.

'I will not undertake to say that there are no spies in this room,' said the stranger, 'but this person is not one, and

I 2

anybody who touches this person will touch this person at his peril. Stand off, men!' And they stood off. The wave retreated backward, leaving the two leaders in front. A couple of hundred men, a moment before apparently full of furious passion and ready to take refuge in the violence of fear, were cowed by a single human being.

'Why, you are not afraid of one man?' said the leaders, ashamed of their following. 'Whatever betides, no one unknown shall leave this room, or it will be Bow Street to-morrow morning.'

'Nevertheless,' said the stranger, 'two unknown men will leave this room, and with general assent. If anyone touches this person or myself I will shoot him dead,' and he drew out his revolver; 'and as for the rest, look at that,' he added, giving a paper to the leader of the Fenian Lodge, 'and then give it me back again.'

The leader of the Fenian Lodge glanced at the paper; he grew pale, then scarlet, folded the paper with great care and returned it reverentially to the stranger, then looking round to the assembly and waving his hand he said, 'All right, the gentlemen are to go.'

'Well, you have got out of a scrape, young sir,' said the stranger to Lothair when they had escaped from the hall.

'And how can I express my gratitude to you?' Lothair replied.

'Poh!' said the stranger, 'a mere affair of common duty. But what surprises me is how you got your pass ticket.'

Lothair told him all.

'They manage their affairs in general wonderfully close,' said the stranger, 'but I have no opinion of them. I have just returned from Ireland, where I thought I would go and see what they really are after. No real business in them. Their treason is a fairy tale, and their sedition a child talking in its sleep.'

They walked together about half a mile, and then the stranger said, 'At the end of this we shall get into the City Road, and the land again of omnibus and public conveyances, and I shall wish you good night.'

'But it is distressing to me to part thus,' said Lothair. 'Pray let me call and pay my respects to my benefactor.'

'No claim to any such title,' said the stranger; 'I am always glad to be of use. I will not trouble you to call on me, for, frankly, I have no wish to increase the circle of my acquaintance. So, good night; and as you seem to be fond of a little life, take my advice and never go about unarmed.'

CHAPTER XXVIII.

THE Fenian adventure furnished the distraction which Lothair required. It broke that absorbing spell of sentiment which is the delicious but enervating privilege of the youthful heart: yet when Lothair woke in the morning from his well-earned slumbers, the charm returned, and he fell at once into a reverie of Belmont, and a speculation when he might really pay his first visit there. Not to-day, that was clearly out of the question. They had separated only yesterday, and yet it seemed an age, and the adventure of another world. There are moods of feeling which defy alike time and space.

But on the morrow, Friday, he might venture to go. But then would to-morrow ever come? It seemed impossible. How were the intervening hours to pass? The world, however, was not so void of resources as himself, and had already appropriated his whole day. And, first, Monsignore Catesby came to breakfast with him, talking of everything that was agreeable or interesting, but in reality bent on securing his presence at the impending ecclesiastical

ceremony of high import, where his guardian was to
officiate, and where the foundation was to be laid of the
reconciliation of all Churches in the bosom of the true one.
Then in the afternoon Lothair had been long engaged to a
match of pigeon-shooting, in which pastime Bertram ex-
celled. It seemed there was to be a most exciting sweep-
stakes to-day, in which the flower of England were to
compete; Lothair among-them, and for the first time.

This great exploit of arms was to be accomplished at the
Castle in the Air, a fantastic villa near the banks of the
Thames, belonging to the Duke of Brecon. His Grace had
been offended by the conduct or the comments of the outer
world, which in his pastime had thwarted or displeased him
in the free life of Battersea. The Duke of Brecon was a
gentleman easily offended, but not one of those who ever
confined their sense of injury to mere words. He prided
himself on 'putting down' any individual or body of men
who chose to come into collision with him. And so in the
present instance he formed a club of pigeon-shooters, and
lent them his villa for their rendezvous and enjoyment.
The society was exquisite, exclusive, and greatly sought
after. And the fine ladies, tempted of course by the beauty
of the scene, honoured and inspired the competing con-
federates by their presence.

The Castle in the Air was a colossal thatched cottage,
built by a favourite of King George the Fourth. It was
full of mandarins and pagodas and green dragons, and
papered with birds of many colours and with vast tails.
The gardens were pretty, and the grounds park-like, with
some noble cedars and some huge walnut trees.

The Duke of Brecon was rather below the middle size,
but he had a singularly athletic frame not devoid of symmetry. His head was well placed on his broad shoulders,
and his mien was commanding. He was narrow-minded
and prejudiced, but acute, and endowed with an unbending

will. He was an eminent sportsman, and brave even to
brutality. His boast was that he had succeeded in everything he had attempted, and he would not admit the
possibility of future failure. Though still a very young
man he had won the Derby, training his own horse; and
he successfully managed a fine stud in defiance of the ring,
whom it was one of the secret objects of his life to extirpate.
Though his manner to men was peremptory, cold, and
hard, he might be described as popular, for there existed a
superstitious belief in his judgment, and it was known that
in some instances when he had been consulted he had
given more than advice. It could not be said that he was
beloved, but he was feared and highly considered. Para-
sites were necessary to him, though he despised them.

The Duke of Brecon was an avowed admirer of Lady
Corisande, and was intimate with her family. The Duchess
liked him much, and was often seen at ball or assembly on
his arm. He had such excellent principles, she said; was
so straightforward, so true and firm. It was whispered
that even Lady Corisande had remarked that the Duke of
Brecon was the only young man of the time who had
'character.' The truth is the Duke, though absolute and
hard to men, could be soft and deferential to women, and
such an exception to a general disposition has a charm.
It was said also that he had, when requisite, a bewitching
smile.

If there were any thing or any person in the world that
St. Aldegonde hated more than another it was the Duke of
Brecon. Why St. Aldegonde hated him was not very
clear, for they had never crossed each other, nor were the
reasons for his detestation, which he occasionally gave,
entirely satisfactory: sometimes it was because the Duke
drove piebalds; sometimes because he had a large sum in
the Funds, which St. Aldegonde thought disgraceful for a
Duke; sometimes because he wore a particular hat, though,

with respect to this last allegation, it does not follow that St. Aldegonde was justified in his criticism, for in such matters St. Aldegonde was himself very deficient, and had once strolled up St. James's Street with his dishevelled locks crowned with a wide-awake. Whatever might be the cause, St. Aldegonde generally wound up, ' I tell you what, Bertha, if Corisande marries that fellow I have made up my mind to go to the Indian Ocean. It is a country I never have seen, and Pinto tells me you cannot do it well under five years.'

' I hope you will take me, Granville, with you,' said Lady St. Aldegonde, ' because it is highly probable Corisande will marry the Duke; mamma, you know, likes him so much.'

' Why cannot Corisande marry Carisbrooke,' said St. Aldegonde, pouting; ' he is a really good fellow, much better looking, and so far as land is concerned, which after all is the only thing, has as large an estate as the Duke.'

' Well, these things depend a little upon taste,' said Lady St. Aldegonde.

' No, no,' said St. Aldegonde; ' Corisande must marry Carisbrooke. Your father would not like my going to the Indian Archipelago and not returning for five years, perhaps never returning. Why should Corisande break up our society? Why are people so selfish? I never could go to Brentham again if the Duke of Brecon is always to be there, giving his opinion, and being what your mother calls "straightforward." I hate a straightforward fellow. As Pinto says, if every man were straightforward in his opinions, there would be no conversation. The fun of talk is to find out what a man really thinks, and then contrast it with the enormous lies he has been telling all dinner, and, perhaps, all his life.'

It was a favourable day for the Castle in the Air; enough but not too much sun, and a gentle breeze. Some pretty feet, not alone, were sauntering in the gardens, some pretty lips lingered in the rooms sipping tea; but the mass of the fair visitors, marvellously attired, were assembled at the scene of action, seated on chairs and in groups, which assumed something of the form of an amphitheatre. There were many gentlemen in attendance on them, or independent spectators of the sport. The field was large, not less than forty competitors, and comprising many of the best shots in England. The struggle, therefore, was long and ably maintained; but, as the end approached, it was evident that the contest would be between Bertram, Lothair, and the Duke of Brecon.

Lady St. Aldegonde and Lady Montairy were there and their unmarried sister. The married sisters were highly excited in favour of their brother, but Lady Corisande said nothing. At last Bertram missed a bird, or rather his bird, which he had hit, escaped, and fell beyond the enclosure. Lothair was more successful, and it seemed that it might be a tie between him and the Duke. His Grace, when called, advanced with confident composure, and apparently killed both his birds, when, at this moment, a dog rushed forward and chased one of the mortally struck pigeons. The blue-rock, which was content to die by the hand of a Duke, would not deign to be worried by a dog, and it frantically moved its expiring wings, scaled the paling, and died. So Lothair won the prize.

'Well,' said Lady Montairy to Lothair, 'as Bertram was not to win I am glad it was you.'

'And you will not congratulate me?' said Lothair to Lady Corisande.

She rather shook her head. 'A tournament of doves,' she said. 'I would rather see you all in the lists of Ashby.'

Lothair had to dine this day with one of the vanquished. This was Mr. Brancepeth, celebrated for his dinners, still

more for his guests. Mr. Brancepeth was a grave young
man. It was supposed that he was always meditating
over the arrangement of his menus, or the skilful means
by which he could assemble together the right persons to
partake of them. Mr. Brancepeth had attained the highest
celebrity in his peculiar career. To dine with Mr. Brancepeth was a social incident that was mentioned. Royalty
had consecrated his banquets, and a youth of note was
scarcely a graduate of society who had not been his guest.
There was one person however who, in this respect,
had not taken his degree, and, as always happens under
such circumstances, he was the individual on whom
Mr. Brancepeth was most desirous to confer it; and this
was St. Aldegonde. In vain Mr. Brancepeth had approached
him with vast cards of invitation to hecatombs, and with
insinuating little notes to dinners sans façon; proposals
which the presence of princes might almost construe into
a command, or the presence of some one even more attractive than princes must invest with irresistible charm. It
was all in vain. 'Not that I dislike Brancepeth,' said
St. Aldegonde; 'I rather like him : I like a man who can
do only one thing, but does that well. But then I hate
dinners.'

But the determined and the persevering need never
despair of gaining their object in this world. And this
very day, riding home from the Castle in the Air, Mr.
Brancepeth overtook St. Aldegonde, who was lounging
about on a rough Scandinavian cob, as dishevelled as himself, listless and groomless. After riding together for
twenty minutes, St. Aldegonde informed Mr. Brancepeth,
as was his general custom with his companions, that he
was bored to very extinction, and that he did not know
what he should do with himself for the rest of the day.
'If I could only get Pinto to go with me, I think I would
run down to the Star and Garter or perhaps to Hampton
Court.'

'You will not be able to get Pinto to-day,' said Mr. Brancepeth, 'for he dines with me.'

'What an unlucky fellow I am!' exclaimed St. Aldegonde, entirely to himself. 'I had made up my mind to dine with Pinto to-day.'

'And why should you not? Why not meet Pinto at my house?'

'Well, that is not in my way,' said St. Aldegonde, but not in a decided tone. 'You know I do not like strangers, and crowds of wine-glasses, and what is called all the delicacies of the season.'

'You will meet no one that you do not know and like. It is a little dinner I made for ——' and he mentioned Lothair.

'I like Lothair,' said St. Aldegonde, dreamily. 'He is a nice boy.'

'Well, you will have him and Pinto to yourself.'

The large fish languidly rose and swallowed the bait, and the exulting Mr. Brancepeth cantered off to Hill Street to give the necessary instructions.

Mr. Pinto was one of the marvels of English society; the most sought after of all its members, though no one could tell you exactly why. He was a little oily Portuguese, middle-aged, corpulent, and somewhat bald, with dark eyes of sympathy, not unmixed with humour. No one knew who he was, and in a country the most scrutinising as to personal details, no one enquired or cared to know. A quarter of a century ago an English noble had caught him in his travels, and brought him young to England, where he had always remained. From the favourite of an individual he had become the oracle of a circle, and then the idol of society. All this time his manner remained unchanged. He was never at any time either humble or pretentious. Instead of being a parasite, everybody flattered him; and instead of being a hanger-on of society, society hung on Pinto.

It must have been the combination of many pleasing qualities, rather than the possession of any commanding one, that created his influence. He certainly was not a wit, yet he was always gay, and always said things that made other people merry. His conversation was sparkling, interesting, and fluent, yet it was observed he never gave an opinion on any subject and never told an anecdote. Indeed, he would sometimes remark, when a man fell into his anecdotage it was a sign for him to retire from the world. And yet Pinto rarely opened his mouth without everybody being stricken with mirth. He had the art of viewing common things in a fanciful light, and the rare gift of raillery which flattered the self-love of those whom it seemed sportively not to spare. Sometimes those who had passed a fascinating evening with Pinto would try to remember on the morrow what he had said, and could recall nothing. He was not an intellectual Crœsus, but his pockets were full of sixpences.

One of the ingredients of his social spell was no doubt his manner, which was tranquil even when he was droll. He never laughed except with his eyes, and delivered himself of his most eccentric fancies in an unctuous style. He had a rare gift of mimicry, which he used with extreme reserve, and therefore was proportionately effective when displayed. Add to all this, a sweet voice, a soft hand, and a disposition both soft and sweet, like his own Azores. It was understood that Pinto was easy in his circumstances, though no one knew where these circumstances were. His equipage was worthy of his position, and in his little house in May Fair he sometimes gave a dinner to a fine lady, who was as proud of the event as the Queen of Sheba of her visit to Solomon the Great.

When St. Aldegonde arrived in Hill Street, and slouched into the saloon with as uncouth and graceless a general mien as a handsome and naturally graceful man could

contrive to present, his keen though listless glance at once
revealed to him that he was, as he described it at dinner
to Hugo Bohun, in a social jungle, in which there was a
great herd of animals that he particularly disliked, namely,
what he entitled 'swells.' The scowl on his distressed
countenance at first intimated a retreat; but after a survey,
courteous to his host and speaking kindly to Lothair as he
passed on, he made a rush to Mr. Pinto, and, cordially
embracing him, said, 'Mind we sit together.'

The dinner was not a failure, though an exception to the
polished ceremony of the normal Brancepeth banquet. The
host headed his table, with the Duke of Brecon on his
right and Lothair on his left hand, and 'swells' of calibre
in their vicinity; but St. Aldegonde sat far away, next to
Mr. Pinto, and Hugo Bohun on the other side of that
gentleman. Hugo Bohun loved swells, but he loved St.
Aldegonde more. The general conversation in the neighbourhood of Mr. Brancepeth did not flag: they talked of
the sport of the morning, and then, by association of ideas,
of every other sport. And then from the sports of England
they ranged to the sports of every other country. There
were several there who had caught salmon in Norway and
killed tigers in Bengal, and visited those countries only for
that purpose. And then they talked of horses, and then
they talked of women.

Lothair was rather silent; for in this society of ancients,
the youngest of whom was perhaps not less than five-and-
twenty, and some with nearly a lustre added to that
mature period, he felt the awkward modesty of a freshman.
The Duke of Brecon talked much, but never at length.
He decided everything, at least to his own satisfaction;
and if his opinion were challenged, remained unshaken,
and did not conceal it.

All this time a different scene was enacting at the other
end of the table. St. Aldegonde, with his back turned to

his other neighbour, hung upon the accents of Mr. Pinto,
and Hugo Bohun imitated St. Aldegonde. What Mr.
Pinto said or was saying was quite inaudible, for he always
spoke low, and in the present case he was invisible, like an
ortolan smothered in vineleaves; but every now and then
St. Aldegonde broke into a frightful shout, and Hugo
Bohun tittered immensely. Then St. Aldegonde, throwing
himself back in his chair, and talking to himself or the
ceiling, would exclaim, 'Best thing I ever heard,' while
Hugo nodded sympathy with a beaming smile.

The swells now and then paused in their conversation
and glanced at the scene of disturbance.

'They seem highly amused there,' said Mr. Brancepeth.
'I wish they would pass it on.'

'I think St. Aldegonde,' said the Duke of Brecon, 'is
the least conventional man of my acquaintance.'

Notwithstanding this stern sneer, a practised general
like Mr. Brancepeth felt he had won the day. All his
guests would disperse and tell the world that they had
dined with him and met St. Aldegonde, and to-morrow
there would be a blazoned paragraph in the journals com-
memorating the event, and written as if by a herald.
What did a little disturb his hospitable mind was that
St. Aldegonde literally tasted nothing. He did not care
so much for his occasionally leaning on the table with
both his elbows, but that he should pass by every dish was
distressing. So Mr. Brancepeth whispered to his own
valet, a fine gentleman, who stood by his master's chair
and attended on no one else except, when requisite, his
master's immediate neighbour, and desired him to suggest
to St. Aldegonde whether the side table might not provide,
under the difficulties, some sustenance. St. Aldegonde
seemed quite gratified by the attention, and said he should
like to have some cold meat. Now that was the only
thing the side table, bounteous as was its disposition,

could not provide. All the joints of the season were named in vain, and pies and preparations of many climes. But nothing would satisfy St. Aldegonde but cold meat.

'Well, now I shall begin my dinner,' he said to Pinto, when he was at length served. 'What surprises me most in you is your English. There is not a man who speaks such good English as you do.'

'English is an expressive language,' said Mr. Pinto, 'but not difficult to master. Its range is limited. It consists, as far as I can observe, of four words: "nice," "jolly," "charming," and "bore;" and some grammarians add "fond."'

When the guests rose and returned to the saloon, St. Aldegonde was in high spirits, and talked to every one, even to the Duke of Brecon, whom he considerately reminded of his defeat in the morning, adding that from what he had seen of his Grace's guns he had no opinion of them, and that he did not believe that breech-loaders suited pigeon-shooting.

Finally, when he bade farewell to his host, St. Aldegonde assured him that he 'never in his life made so good a dinner, and that Pinto had never been so rich.'

When the party broke up, the majority of the guests went, sooner or later, to a ball that was given this evening by Lady St. Jerome. Others, who never went to balls, looked forward with refined satisfaction to a night of unbroken tobacco. St. Aldegonde went to play whist at the house of a lady who lived out of town. 'I like the drive home,' he said; 'the morning air is so refreshing when one has lost one's money.'

A ball at St. Jerome House was a rare event, but one highly appreciated. It was a grand mansion, with a real suite of state apartments, including a genuine ball-room in the Venetian style, and lighted with chandeliers of rock crystal. Lady St. Jerome was a woman of taste and

splendour and romance, who could do justice to the scene
and occasion. Even Lord St. Jerome, quiet as he seemed,
in these matters was popular with young men. It was
known that Lord St. Jerome gave at his ball suppers the
same champagne that he gave at his dinners, and that was
of the highest class: in short, a patriot. We talk with
wondering execration of the great poisoners of past ages,
the Borgias, the inventor of aqua tofana, and the amiable
Marchioness de Brinvilliers; but Pinto was of opinion
that there were more social poisoners about in the present
day than in the darkest and the most demoralised periods,
and then none of them are punished; which is so strange,
he would add, as they are all found out.

Lady St. Jerome received Lothair, as Pinto said, with
extreme unction. She looked in his eyes, she retained his
hand, she said that what she had heard had made her so
happy. And then, when he was retiring, she beckoned
him back and said she must have some tea, and, taking his
arm, they walked away together. 'I have so much to tell
you,' she said, 'and everything is so interesting. I think
we are on the eve of great events. The Monsignore told
me your heart was with us. It must be. They are your
own thoughts, your own wishes. We are realising your
own ideal. I think next Sunday will be remembered as a
great day in English history; the commencement of a
movement that may save everything. The Monsignore, I
know, has told you all.'

Not exactly; the Oxford visit had deranged a little the
plans of the Monsignore, but he had partially communicated
the vast scheme. It seems there was a new society to be
instituted for the restoration of Christendom. The change
of name from Christendom to Europe had proved a failure
and a disastrous one. 'And what wonder?' said Lady
St. Jerome. 'Europe is not even a quarter of the globe, as
the philosophers pretended it was. There is already a

fifth division, and probably there will be many more as the philosophers announce it impossible.' The Cardinal was to inaugurate the institution on Sunday next at the Jesuits' Church by one of his celebrated sermons. It was to be a function of the highest class. All the faithful of consideration were to attend, but the attendance was not to be limited to the faithful. Every sincere adherent of Church principles who was in a state of prayer and preparation was solicited to be present and join in the holy and common work of restoring to the Divine Master his kingdom upon earth with its rightful name.

It was a brilliant ball. All the ' nice' people in London were there. All the young men who now will never go to balls were present. This was from respect to the high character of Lord St. Jerome. Clare Arundel looked divine, dressed in a wondrous white robe garlanded with violets, just arrived from Paris, a present from her godmother the Duchess of Lorrain-Schulenbourg. On her head a violet wreath, deep and radiant as her eyes, and which admirably contrasted with her dark golden brown hair.

Lothair danced with her and never admired her more. Her manner towards him was changed. It was attractive, even alluring. She smiled on him, she addressed him in tones of sympathy, even of tenderness. She seemed interested in all he was doing, she flattered him by a mode which is said to be irresistible to a man, by talking of himself. When the dance had finished he offered to attend her to the tea-room. She accepted the invitation even with cordiality.

' I think I must have some tea,' she said, ' and I like to go with my kinsman.'

Just before supper was announced, Lady St. Jerome told Lothair, to his surprise, that he was to attend Miss Arundel to the great ceremony. ' It is Clare's ball,' said

K

Lady St. Jerome, 'given in her honour, and you are to take care of her.'

'I am more than honoured,' said Lothair. 'But does Miss Arundel wish it? for, to tell you the truth, I thought I had rather abused her indulgence this evening.'

'Of course she wishes it,' said Lady St. Jerome. 'Who should lead her out on such an occasion, her own ball, than the nearest and dearest relation she has in the world except ourselves?'

Lothair made no reply to this unanswerable logic, but was as surprised as he was gratified. He recalled the hour when the kinship was at the best but coldly recognised, the inscrutable haughtiness, even distrust, with which Miss Arundel listened to the exposition of his views and feelings, and the contrast which her past mood presented to her present brilliant sympathy and cordial greeting. But he yielded to the magic of the flowing hour. Miss Arundel seemed indeed quite a changed being to-night, full of vivacity, fancy, feeling, almost fun. She was witty and humorous and joyous and fascinating. As he fed her with cates as delicate as her lips, and manufactured for her dainty beverages which would not outrage their purity, Lothair at last could not refrain from intimating his sense of her unusual but charming joyousness.

'No,' she said, turning round with animation, 'my natural disposition, always repressed because I have felt overwhelmed by the desolation of the world. But now I have hope; I have more than hope, I have joy. I feel sure this idea of the restoration of Christendom comes from Heaven. It has restored me to myself, and has given me a sense of happiness in this life which I never could contemplate. But what is the climax of my joy is, that you, after all my own, blood, and one in whose career I have ever felt the deepest interest, should be ordained to lay, as it were, the first stone of this temple of divine love.'

It was break of day when Lothair jumped into his brougham. 'Thank heavens,' he exclaimed, 'it is at last Friday!'

CHAPTER XXIX.

THERE is something very pleasant in a summer suburban ride in the valley of the Thames. London transforms itself into bustling Knightsbridge and airy Brompton brightly and gracefully lingers cheerfully in the long, miscellaneous, well-watered King's Road, and only says farewell when you come to an abounding river and a picturesque bridge. The boats were bright upon the waters when Lothair crossed it, and his dark chesnut barb, proud of its resplendent form, curvetted with joy when it reached a green common, studded occasionally with a group of pines and well-bedecked with gorse. After this he pursued the public road for a couple of miles until he observed on his left hand a gate on which was written 'private road,' and here he stopped. The gate was locked, but when Lothair assured the keeper that he was about to visit BELMONT, he was permitted to enter.

He entered a green and winding lane, fringed with tall elms and dim with fragrant shade, and after proceeding about half a mile came to a long low-built lodge with a thatched and shelving roof and surrounded by a rustic colonnade covered with honeysuckle. Passing through the gate at hand, he found himself in a road winding through gently undulating banks of exquisite turf studded with rare shrubs and occasionally rarer trees. Suddenly the confined scene expanded: wide lawns spread out before him, shadowed with the dark forms of many huge cedars and blazing with flower-beds of every hue. The house was also apparent, a stately mansion of hewn stone, with

K 2

wings and a portico of Corinthian columns, and backed by
deep woods.

This was BELMONT, built by a favourite Minister of State
to whom a grateful and gracious sovereign had granted a
slice of a royal park whereon to raise a palace and a garden
and find occasionally Tusculan repose.

The lady of the mansion was at home, and though
Lothair was quite prepared for this his heart beat. The inner
hall was of noble proportion, and there were ranged in it
many Roman busts and some ancient slabs and altars of
marble. These had been collected some century ago by
the Minister; but what immediately struck the eye of
Lothair were two statues by an American artist, and both
of fame, the Sibyl and the Cleopatra. He had heard of
these, but had never seen them, and could not refrain from
lingering a moment to gaze upon their mystical and fascinating beauty.

He proceeded through two spacious and lofty chambers,
of which it was evident the furniture was new. It was
luxurious and rich and full of taste, but there was no attempt to recall the past in the details: no cabinets and
clocks of French kings or tables of French queens, no
chairs of Venetian senators, no candelabra that had illumined Doges of Genoa, no ancient porcelain of rare
schools and ivory carvings and choice enamels. The walls
were hung with masterpieces of modern art, chiefly of the
French school, Ingres and Delaroche and Scheffer.

The last saloon led into a room of smaller dimensions
opening on the garden, and which Lothair at first thought
must be a fernery it seemed so full of choice and expanding specimens of that beautiful and multiform plant; but
when his eye had become a little accustomed to the scene
and to the order of the groups, he perceived they were
only the refreshing and profuse ornaments of a regularly
furnished and inhabited apartment. There was a table

covered with writing materials and books and some music. A chair before the table was so placed as if some one had only recently quitted it, a book being open but turned upon its face with an ivory cutter by its side. It would seem that the dweller in the chamber might not be far distant. The servant invited Lothair to be seated, and saying that Mrs. Campian must be in the garden, proceeded to inform his mistress of the arrival of a guest.

The room opened on a terrace adorned with statues and orange trees, and descending gently into a garden in the Italian style, in the centre of which was a marble fountain of many figures. The grounds were not extensive, but they were only separated from the royal park by a wire fence, so that the scene seemed alike rich and illimitable. On the boundary was a summerhouse in the shape of a classic temple, one of those pavilions of pleasure which nobles loved to raise in the last century.

As Lothair beheld the scene with gratification, the servant reappeared on the steps of the terrace and invited him to descend. Guiding him through the garden, the servant retired as Lothair recognised Mrs. Campian approaching them.

She gave her hand to Lothair and welcomed him cordially but with serenity. They mutually exchanged hopes that their return to town had been agreeable. Lothair could not refrain from expressing how pleased he was with Belmont.

'I am glad you approve of our hired home,' said Theodora; 'I think we were fortunate in finding one that suits our tastes and habits. We love pictures and statues and trees and flowers, and yet we love our friends, and our friends are people who live in cities.'

'I think I saw two statues to-day of which I have often heard,' said Lothair.

'The Sibyl and Cleopatra? Yes, Colonel Campian is

rather proud of possessing them. He collects only modern art, for which I believe there is a great future, though some of our friends think it is yet in its cradle.'

'I am very sorry to say,' said Lothair, 'that I know very little about art, or indeed anything else, but I admire what is beautiful. I know something about architecture, at least church architecture.'

'Well, religion has produced some of our noblest buildings,' said Theodora; 'there is no question of that; and as long as they are adapted to what takes place in them they are admirable. The fault I find in modern churches in this country is, that there is little relation between the ceremonies and the structure. Nobody seems now conscious that every true architectural form has a purpose. But I think the climax of confused ideas is capped when dissenting chapels are built like cathedrals.'

'Ah! to build a cathedral,' exclaimed Lothair, 'that is a great enterprise. I wish I might show you some day some drawings I have of a projected cathedral.'

'A projected cathedral!' said Theodora. 'Well, I must confess to you I never could comprehend the idea of a Protestant cathedral.'

'But I am not quite sure,' said Lothair blushing and agitated, 'that it will be a Protestant cathedral. I have not made up my mind about that.'

Theodora glanced at him, unobserved, with her wonderful grey eyes; a sort of supernatural light seemed to shoot from beneath their long dark lashes and read his inmost nature. They were all this time returning, as she had suggested, to the house. Rather suddenly she said, 'By the bye, as you are so fond of art, I ought to have asked you whether you would like to see a work by the sculptor of Cleopatra which arrived when we were at Oxford. We have placed it on a pedestal in the temple. It is the Genius of Freedom. I may say I was assist-

ing at its inauguration when your name was announced
to me.'

Lothair caught at this proposal, and they turned and
approached the temple. Some workmen were leaving the
building as they entered, and one or two lingered.

Upon a pedestal of porphyry rose the statue of a female
in marble. Though veiled with drapery which might have
become the Goddess of Modesty, admirable art permitted
the contour of the perfect form to be traced. The feet
were without sandals, and the undulating breadth of one
shoulder, where the drapery was festooned, remained uncovered. One expected with such a shape some divine
visage. That was not wanting; but humanity was asserted
in the transcendent brow, which beamed with sublime
thought and profound enthusiasm.

Some would have sighed that such beings could only be
pictured in a poet's or an artist's dream, but Lothair felt
that what he beheld with rapture was no ideal creation, and that he was in the presence of the inspiring
original.

'It is too like!' he murmured.

'It is the most successful recurrence to the true principles
of art in modern sculpture,' said a gentleman on his right
hand.

This person was a young man, though more than ten
years older than Lothair. His appearance was striking.
Above the middle height, his form, athletic though lithe
and symmetrical, was crowned by a countenance aquiline
but delicate, and from many circumstances of a remarkable
radiancy. The lustre of his complexion, the fire of his eye,
and his chesnut hair in profuse curls, contributed much
to this dazzling effect. A thick but small moustache did
not conceal his curved lip or the scornful pride of his distended nostril, and his beard, close but not long, did not
veil the singular beauty of his mouth. It was an arrogant

face, daring and vivacious, yet weighted with an expression of deep and haughty thought.

The costume of this gentleman was rich and picturesque. Such extravagance of form and colour is sometimes encountered in the adventurous toilette of a country house, but rarely experienced in what might still be looked upon as a morning visit in the metropolis.

'You know Mr. Phœbus?' asked a low clear voice, and turning round Lothair was presented to a person so famous that even Lothair had heard of him.

Mr. Phœbus was the most successful, not to say the most eminent, painter of the age. He was the descendant of a noble family of Gascony that had emigrated to England from France in the reign of Louis XIV. Unquestionably they had mixed their blood frequently during the interval and the vicissitudes of their various life; but in Gaston Phœbus nature, as is sometimes her wont, had chosen to reproduce exactly the original type. He was the Gascon noble of the sixteenth century, with all his brilliancy, bravery, and boastfulness, equally vain, arrogant, and eccentric, accomplished in all the daring or the graceful pursuits of man, yet nursed in the philosophy of our times.

'It is presumption in my talking about such things,' said Lothair; 'but might I venture to ask what you may consider the true principles of art?'

'Aryan principles,' said Mr. Phœbus; 'not merely the study of nature, but of beautiful nature; the art of design in a country inhabited by a firstrate race, and where the laws, the manners, the customs, are calculated to maintain the health and beauty of a firstrate race. In a greater or less degree, these conditions obtained from the age of Pericles to the age of Hadrian in pure Aryan communities, but Semitism began then to prevail, and ultimately triumphed. Semitism has destroyed art; it taught man to despise his own body, and the essence of art is to honour the human frame.'

'I am afraid I ought not to talk about such things,' said Lothair; 'but if by Semitism you mean religion, surely the Italian painters inspired by Semitism did something.'

'Great things,' said Mr. Phœbus; 'some of the greatest. Semitism gave them subjects, but the Renaissance gave them Aryan art, and it gave that art to a purely Aryan race. But Semitism rallied in the shape of the Reformation, and swept all away. When Leo the Tenth was Pope, popery was pagan; popery is now Christian and art is extinct.'

'I cannot enter into such controversies,' said Lothair. 'Every day I feel, more and more, I am extremely ignorant.'

'Do not regret it,' said Mr. Phœbus. 'What you call ignorance is your strength. By ignorance you mean a want of knowledge of books. Books are fatal; they are the curse of the human race. Nine-tenths of existing books are nonsense, and the clever books are the refutation of that nonsense. The greatest misfortune that ever befell man was the invention of printing. Printing has destroyed education. Art is a great thing, and Science is a great thing; but all that art and science can reveal can be taught by man and by his attributes: his voice, his hand, his eye. The essence of education is the education of the body. Beauty and health are the chief sources of happiness. Men should live in the air; their exercises should be regular, varied, scientific. To render his body strong and supple is the first duty of man. He should develope and completely master the whole muscular system. What I admire in the order to which you belong is that they do live in the air, that they excel in athletic sports; that they can only speak one language; and that they never read. This is not a complete education, but it is the highest education since the Greek.'

'What you say I feel encouraging,' said Lothair, repressing a smile, 'for I myself live very much in the air, and am fond of all sports; but I confess I am often ashamed of being so poor a linguist, and was seriously thinking that I ought to read.'

'No doubt every man should combine an intellectual with a physical training,' replied Mr. Phœbus; 'but the popular conception of the means is radically wrong. Youth should attend lectures on art and science by the most illustrious professors, and should converse together afterwards on what they have heard. They should learn to talk; it is a rare accomplishment, and extremely healthy. They should have music always at their meals. The theatre, entirely remodelled and reformed, and under a minister of state, should be an important element of education. I should not object to the recitation of lyric poetry. That is enough. I would not have a book in the house, or even see a newspaper.'

'These are Aryan principles?' said Lothair.

'They are,' said Mr. Phœbus; 'and of such principles, I believe, a great revival is at hand. We shall both live to see another Renaissance.'

'And our artist here,' said Lothair, pointing to the statue, 'you are of opinion that he is asserting these principles?'

'Yes; because he has produced the Aryan form by studying the Aryan form. Phidias never had a finer model, and he has not been unequal to it.

'I fancied,' said Lothair in a lower and enquiring tone, though Mrs. Campian had some time before glided out of the pavilion and was giving directions to the workmen, 'I fancied I had heard that Mrs. Campian was a Roman.'

'The Romans were Greeks,' said Mr. Phœbus, 'and in this instance the Phidian type came out. It has not been thrown away. I believe Theodora has inspired as many painters and sculptors as any Aryan goddess. I look upon her as such, for I know nothing more divine.'

'I fear the Phidian type is very rare,' said Lothair.

'In nature and in art there must always be surpassing instances,' said Mr. Phœbus. 'It is a law, and a wise one; but, depend upon it, so strong and perfect a type as the original Aryan must be yet abundant among the millions, and may be developed. But for this you want great changes in your laws. It is the first duty of a state to attend to the frame and health of the subject. The Spartans understood this. They permitted no marriage the probable consequences of which might be a feeble progeny; they even took measures to secure a vigorous one. The Romans doomed the deformed to immediate destruction. The union of the races concerns the welfare of the commonwealth much too nearly to be entrusted to individual arrangement. The fate of a nation will ultimately depend upon the strength and health of the population. Both France and England should look to this; they have cause. As for our mighty engines of war in the hands of a puny race, it will be the old story of the lower empire and the Greek fire. Laws should be passed to secure all this, and some day they will be. But nothing can be done until the Aryan races are extricated from Semitism.'

CHAPTER XXX.

LOTHAIR returned to town in a not altogether satisfactory state of mind. He was not serene or content. On the contrary, he was rather agitated and perplexed. He could not say he regretted his visit. He had seen her, and he had seen her to great advantage. He had seen much too that was pleasing, and had heard also many things that, if not pleasing, were certainly full of interest. And yet, when he cantered back over the common, the world somehow did not seem to him so bright and exhilarating as in the ambling morn. Was it because she was not alone? And yet why should he expect she should be alone? She had many friends, and she was as accessible to them as to himself. And yet a conversation with her, as in the gardens of Blenheim, would have been delightful, and he had rather counted on it. Nevertheless, it was a great thing to know men like Mr. Phœbus, and hear their views on the nature of things. Lothair was very young, and was more thoughtful than studious. His education hitherto had been, according to Mr. Phœbus, on the right principle, and chiefly in the open air; but he was intelligent and susceptible, and in the atmosphere of Oxford, now stirred with many thoughts, he had imbibed some particles of knowledge respecting the primæval races which had permitted him to follow the conversation of Mr. Phœbus not absolutely in a state of hopeless perplexity. He determined to confer with Father Coleman on the Aryan race and the genius of Semitism. As he returned through the park, he observed the Duchess and Lady Corisande in their barouche, resting for a moment in the shade, with Lord Carisbrooke on one side and the Duke of Brecon on the other.

As he was dressing for dinner, constantly brooding on one thought, the cause of his feeling of disappointment occurred to him. He had hoped in this visit to have established some basis of intimacy, and to have ascertained his prospect and his means of occasionally seeing her. But he had done nothing of the kind. He could not well call again at Belmont under a week, but even then Mr. Phœbus or some one else might be there. The world seemed dark. He wished he had never gone to Oxford. However a man may plan his life he is the creature of circumstances. The unforeseen happens and upsets everything. We are mere poppets.

He sat next to au agreeable woman at dinner, who gave him an interesting account of a new singer she had heard the night before at the Opera; a fair Scandinavian, fresh as a lily and sweet as a nightingale.

'I was resolved to go and hear her,' said the lady; 'my sister Feodore, at Paris, had written to me so much about her. Do you know, I have never been to the Opera for au age! That alone was quite a treat to me. I never go to the Opera, nor to the play, nor to anything else. Society has become so large and so exacting, that I have found out one never gets any amusement.'

'Do you know, I never was at the Opera,' said Lothair.

'I am not at all surprised; and when you go (which I suppose you will some day), what will most strike you is, that you will not see a single person you ever saw in your life.'

'Strange!'

'Yes; it shows what a mass of wealth and taste and refinement there is in this wonderful metropolis of ours, quite irrespective of the circles in which we move, and which we once thought entirely engrossed them.'

After the ladies had retired, Bertram, who dined at the same house, moved up to him; and Hugo Bohun came over and took the vacant seat on his other side.

'What have you been doing with yourself?' said Hugo. 'We have not seen you for a week.'

'I went down to Oxford about some horses,' said Lothair.

'Fancy going down to Oxford about some horses in the heart of the season,' said Hugo. 'I believe you are selling us, and that, as the "Scorpion" announces, you are going to be married.'

'To whom?' said Lothair.

'Ah! that is the point. It is a dark horse at present, and we want you to tell us.'

'Why do not you marry, Hugo?' said Bertram.

'I respect the institution,' said Hugo, 'which is admitting something in these days; and I have always thought that every woman should marry, and no man.'

'It makes a woman and it mars a man, you think?' said Lothair.

'But I do not exactly see how your view would work practically,' said Bertram.

'Well, my view is a social problem,' said Hugo, 'and social problems are the fashion at present. It would be solved through the exceptions, which prove the principle. In the first place, there are your swells who cannot avoid the halter: you are booked when you are born; and then there are moderate men like myself, who have their weak moments. I would not answer for myself if I could find an affectionate family with good shooting and firstrate claret.'

'There must be many families with such conditions,' said Lothair.

Hugo shook his head. 'You try. Sometimes the wine is good and the shooting bad; sometimes the reverse; sometimes both are excellent, but then the tempers and the manners are equally detestable.'

'I vote we three do something to-morrow,' said Bertram.

'What shall it be?' said Hugo.

'I vote we row down to Richmond at sunset and dine, and then drive our teams up by moonlight. What say you, Lothair?'

'I cannot, I am engaged. I am engaged to go to the Opera.'

'Fancy going to the Opera in this sweltering weather!' exclaimed Bertram.

'He must be going to be married,' said Hugo.

And yet on the following evening, though the weather was quite as sultry and he was not going to be married, to

the Opera Lothair went. While the agreeable lady the
day before was dilating at dinner on this once famous
entertainment, Lothair remembered that a certain person
went there every Saturday evening, and he resolved that
he should at least have the satisfaction of seeing her.

It was altogether a new scene for Lothair, and being
much affected by music he found the general influence so
fascinating that some little time elapsed before he was
sufficiently master of himself to recur to the principal
purpose of his presence. His box was on the first tier,
where he could observe very generally and yet himself be
sufficiently screened. As an astronomer surveys the starry
heavens until his searching sight reaches the desired planet,
so Lothair's scrutinising vision wandered till his eye at
length lighted on the wished-for orb. In the circle above
his own, opposite to him but nearer the stage, he recognised the Campians. She had a star upon her forehead, as
when he first met her some six months ago; it seemed an age.

Now what should he do? He was quite unlearned in
the social habits of an opera-house. He was not aware
that he had the privilege of paying the lady a visit in her
box, and had he been so, he was really so shy in little
things that he never could have summoned resolution to
open the door of his own box and request an attendant to
show him that of Mrs. Campian. He had contrived to get
to the Opera for the first time in his life, and the effort
seemed to have exhausted his social enterprise. So he remained still, with his glass fixed very constantly on Mrs.
Campian, and occasionally giving himself up to the scene.
The performance did not sustain the first impression.
There were rival prima-donnas, and they indulged in com-
petitive screams: the choruses were coarse, and the
orchestra much too noisy. But the audience were absorbed or enthusiastic. We may be a musical nation, but
our taste would seem to require some refinement.

There was a stir in Mrs. Campian's box; a gentleman entered and seated himself. Lothair concluded he was an invited guest, and envied him. In about a quarter of an hour the gentleman bowed and retired, and another person came in, and one whom Lothair recognised as a young man who had been sitting during the first act in a stall beneath him. The system of paying visits at the Opera then flashed upon his intelligence, as some discovery in science upon a painful observer. Why should he not pay a visit too? But how to do it? At last he was bold enough to open the door of his own box and go forth, but he could find no attendant, and some persons passing his open door, and nearly appropriating his lodge, in a fit of that nervous embarrassment which attends inexperience in little things, he secured his rights by returning baffled to his post.

There had been a change in Mrs. Campian's box in the interval. Colonel Campian had quitted it, and Mr. Phœbus occupied his place. Whether it were disappointment at his own failure or some other cause, Lothair felt annoyed. He was hot and cold by turns; felt awkward and blundering; fancied people were looking at him; that in some inexplicable sense he was ridiculous; wished he had never gone to the Opera.

As time, and considerable time, elapsed, he became even miserable. Mr. Phœbus never moved, and Mrs. Campian frequently conversed with him. More than one visitor had in the interval paid their respects to the lady, but Mr. Phœbus never moved. They did not stay, perhaps because Mr. Phœbus never moved.

Lothair never liked that fellow from the first. Sympathy and antipathy share our being as day and darkness share our lives. Lothair had felt an antipathy for Mr. Phœbus the moment he saw him. He had arrived at Belmont yesterday before Lothair, and he had outstayed him. These might be Aryan principles, but they were not the principles of good breeding.

Lothair determined to go home and never to come to the Opera again. He opened the door of his box with firmness, and slammed it with courage; he had quite lost his shyness, was indeed ready to run a muck with anyone who crossed him. The slamming of the door summoned a scudding attendant from a distant post, who with breathless devotion enquired whether Lothair wanted anything.

'Yes, I want you to show me the way to Mrs. Campian's box.'

'Tier above, No. 22,' said the boxkeeper.

'Ay, ay; but conduct me to it,' said Lothair, and he presented the man with an overpowering honorarium.

'Certainly, my Lord,' said the attendant.

'He knows me,' thought Lothair; but it was not so. When the British nation is at once grateful and enthusiastic, they always call you 'my Lord.'

But in his progress to 'No. 22, tier above,' all his valour evaporated, and when the box-door was opened he felt very much like a convict on the verge of execution; he changed colour, his legs tottered, his heart beat, and he made his bow with a confused vision. The serenity of Theodora somewhat reassured him, and he seated himself, and even saluted Mr. Phœbus.

The conversation was vapid and conventional: remarks about the Opera and its performers; even the heat of the weather was mentioned. Lothair had come, and he had nothing to say. Mrs. Campian seemed much interested in the performance; so, if he had had anything to say, there was no opportunity of expressing it. She had not appeared to be so engrossed with the music before his arrival. In the meantime that Phœbus would not move; a quarter of an hour elapsed, and that Phœbus would not move. Lothair could not stand it any longer; he rose and bowed.

'Are you going?' said Theodora. 'Colonel Campian will

L

be here in a moment; he will be quite grieved not to see
you.'

But Lothair was inflexible. 'Perhaps,' she added, 'we
may see you to-morrow night?'

'Never,' said Lothair to himself, as he clenched his teeth;
'my visit to Belmont was my first and my last. The dream
is over.'

He hurried to a club in which he had been recently
initiated, and of which the chief purpose is to prove to
mankind that night to a wise man has its resources as well
as gaudy day. Here striplings mature their minds in the
mysteries of whist, and stimulate their intelligence by
playing at stakes which would make their seniors look pale;
here matches are made, and odds are settled, and the cares
or enterprises of life are soothed or stimulated by fragrant
cheroots or beakers of Badminton. Here, in the society of
the listless and freakish St. Aldegonde, and Hugo Bohun,
and Bertram, and other congenial spirits, Lothair consigned
to oblivion the rival churches of Christendom, the Aryan
race, and the genius of Semitism.

It was an hour past dawn when he strolled home. London is often beautiful in summer at that hour, the architectural lines clear and defined in the smokeless atmosphere,
and ever and anon a fragrant gale from gardened balconies
wafted in the blue air. Nothing is stirring except wagons
of strawberries and asparagus, and no one visible except a
policeman or a Member of Parliament returning from a
late division, where they have settled some great question
that need never have been asked. Eve has its spell of
calmness and consolation, but Dawn brings hope and joy.

But not to Lothair. Young, sanguine, and susceptible,
he had, for a moment, yielded to the excitement of the
recent scene, but with his senses stilled by the morning air,
and free from the influence of Bertram's ready sympathy,
and Hugo Bohun's gay comments on human life, and all

the wild and amusing caprice, and during wilfulness, and
grand affectation that distinguish and inspire a circle of
patrician youth, there came over him the consciousness
that to him something dark had occurred, something bitter
and disappointing and humiliating, and that the breaking
morn would not bring to him a day so bright and hopeful
as his former ones.

At first he fell into profound slumber: it was the inevitable result of the Badminton and the late hour. There
was a certain degree of physical exhaustion which commanded repose. But the slumber was not long, and his
first feeling, for it could not be called thought, was that
some great misfortune had occurred to him; and then
the thought following the feeling brought up the form of
the hated Phœbus. After that he had no real sleep, but a
sort of occasional and feverish doze with intervals of infinite
distress, waking always to a consciousness of inexpressible
mortification and despair.

About one o'clock, relinquishing all hope of real and refreshing slumber, he rang his bell, and his valet appearing informed him that Father Coleman had called, and the Monsignore had called, and that now the Cardinal's secretary had
just called, but the valet had announced that his lord was indisposed. There was also a letter from Lady St. Jerome.
This news brought a new train of feeling. Lothair remembered that this was the day of the great ecclesiastical
function, under the personal auspices of the Cardinal, at
which indeed Lothair had never positively promised to
assist, his presence at which he had sometimes thought
they pressed unreasonably, not to say even indelicately, but
at which he had perhaps led them, not without cause, to believe that he would be present. Of late the Monsignore
had assumed that Lothair had promised to attend it.

Why should he not? The world was all vanity. Never
did he feel more convinced than at this moment of the

L 2

truth of his conclusion, that if religion were a real thing,
man should live for it alone; but then came the question
of the Churches. He could not bring himself without a
pang to contemplate a secession from the Church of his
fathers. He took refuge in the wild but beautiful thought
of a reconciliation between Rome and England. If the
consecration of the whole of his fortune to that end could
assist in effecting the purpose, he would cheerfully make
the sacrifice. He would then go on a pilgrimage to the
Holy Sepulchre, and probably conclude his days in a her-
mitage on Mount Athos.

In the meantime he rose, and, invigorated by his bath,
his thoughts became in a slight degree more mundane.
They recurred to the events of the last few days of his life,
but in a spirit of self-reproach and of conscious vanity and
weakness. Why, he had not known her a week! This
was Sunday morning, and last Sunday he had attended St.
Mary's and offered up his earnest supplications for the unity
of Christendom. That was then his sovereign hope and
thought. Singular that a casual acquaintance with a
stranger, a look, a glance, a word, a nothing, should have
so disturbed his spirit and distracted his mind.

And yet ——

And then he fell into an easy-chair, with a hairbrush in
either hand, and conjured up in reverie all that had passed
since that wondrous morn when he addressed her by the
roadside, until the last dark hour when they parted, and
for ever. There was not a word she had uttered to him, or
to anyone else, that he did not recall; not a glance, not a
gesture; her dress, her countenance, her voice, her hair.
And what scenes had all this passed in! What refined
and stately loveliness! Blenheim, and Oxford, and Belmont! They became her. Ah! why could not life con-
sist of the perpetual society of such delightful people in
such delightful places?

His valet entered and informed him that the Monsignore had returned, and would not be denied. Lothair roused himself from his delicious reverie, and his countenance became anxious and disquieted. He would have struggled against the intrusion, and was murmuring resistance to his hopeless attendant, who shook his head, when the Monsignore glided into the room without permission, as the valet disappeared.

It was a wonderful performance: the Monsignore had at the same time to make a reconnaissance and to take up a position, to find out what Lothair intended to do, and yet to act and speak as if he was acquainted with those intentions, and was not only aware of, but approved them. He seemed hurried and yet tranquil, almost breathless with solicitude and yet conscious of some satisfactory consummation. His tones were at all times hushed, but to-day he spoke in a whisper, though a whisper of emphasis, and the dark eyes of his delicate aristocratic visage peered into Lothair, even when he was making a remark which seemed to require no scrutiny.

'It is one of the most important days for England that have happened in our time,' said the Monsignore. 'Lady St. Jerome thinks of nothing else. All our nobility will be there, the best blood in England, and some others who sympathise with the unity of the Church, the real question. Nothing has ever gratified the Cardinal more than your intended presence. He sent to you this morning. He would have called himself, but he has much to go through to-day. His Eminence said to me: "It is exactly what I want. Whatever may be our differences, and they are really slight, what I want is to show to the world that the sons of the Church will unite for the cause of Divine truth. It is the only course that can save society." When Lady St. Jerome told him that you were coming this evening, his Eminence was so affected that ———'

'But I never said I was coming this evening,' said Lothair, rather dryly, and resolved to struggle, 'either to Lady St. Jerome or to anyone else. I said I would think of it.'

'But for a Christian to think of duty is to perform it,' said the Monsignore. 'To be ignorant of a duty is a sin, but to be aware of duty, and not to fulfil it, is heinous.'

'But is it a duty?' said Lothair, rather doggedly.

'What! to serve God and save society? Do you doubt it? Have you read the "Declaration of Geneva?" They have declared war against the Church, the State, and the domestic principle. All the great truths and laws on which the family reposes are denounced. Have you seen Garibaldi's letter? When it was read, and spoke of the religion of God being propagated throughout the world, there was a universal cry of "No, no! no religion!" But the religion of God was soon so explained as to allay all their fears. It is the religion of science. Instead of Adam, our ancestry is traced to the most grotesque of creatures; thought is phosphorus, the soul complex nerves, and our moral sense a secretion of sugar. Do you want these views in England? Rest assured they are coming. And how are we to contend against them? Only by Divine truth. And where is Divine truth? In the Church of Christ: in the gospel of order, peace, and purity.'

Lothair rose, and paced the room with his eyes on the ground.

'I wish I had been born in the middle ages,' he exclaimed, 'or on the shores of the Sea of Galilee, or in some other planet: anywhere, or at any time, but in this country and in this age!'

'That thought is not worthy of you, my Lord,' said Catesby. 'It is a great privilege to live in this country and in this age. It is a great privilege, in the mighty contest between the good and the evil principle, to combat for the righteous. They stand face to face now, as they have stood before. There is Christianity which, by revealing the truth, has limited the license of human reason; there is that human reason which resists revelation as a bondage, which insists upon being atheistical, or polytheistical, or pantheistical; which looks upon the requirements of obedience, justice, truth, and purity, as limitations of human freedom. It is to the Church that God has committed the custody and execution of His truth and law. The Church, as witness, teacher, and judge, contradicts and offends the spirit of license to the quick. This is why it is hated; this is why it is to be destroyed, and why they are preparing a future of rebellion, tyranny, falsehood, and degrading debauchery. The Church alone can save us, and you are asked to supplicate the Almighty to-night, under circumstances of deep hope, to favour the union of churchmen, and save the human race from the impending deluge.'

Lothair threw himself again into his seat and sighed. 'I am rather indisposed to-day, my dear Monsignore, which is unusual with me, and scarcely equal to such a theme, doubtless of the deepest interest to me and to all. I myself wish, as you well know, that all mankind were praying under the same roof. I shall continue in seclusion this morning. Perhaps you will permit me to think over what you have said with so much beauty and force.'

'I had forgotten that I had a letter to deliver to you,' said Catesby; and he drew from his breast-pocket a note which he handed to Lothair, who opened it quite unconscious of the piercing and even excited observation of his companion.

Lothair read the letter with a changing countenance, and then he read it again and blushed deeply. The letter was from Miss Arundel. After a slight pause, without looking up, he said, 'Nine o'clock is the hour, I believe.'

'Yes,' said the Monsignore rather eagerly, 'but were I

you, I would be earlier than that. I would order my carriage at eight. If you will permit me, I will order it for you. You are not quite well. It will save you some little trouble, people coming into the room and all that, and the Cardinal will be there by eight o'clock.

'Thank you,' said Lothair; 'have the kindness then, my dear Monsignore, to order my brougham for me at half-past eight, and just say I can see no one. Adieu!'

And the priest disappeared.

Lothair remained the whole morning in a most troubled state, pacing his rooms, leaning sometimes with his arm upon the mantelpiece and his face buried in his arm, and often he sighed. About half-past five he rung for his valet and dressed, and in another hour he broke his fast: a little soup, a cutlet, and a glass or two of claret. And then he looked at his watch; and he looked at his watch every five minutes for the next hour.

He was in deep reverie when the servant announced that his carriage was ready. He started as from a dream, then pressed his hand to his eyes, and kept it there for some moments, and then, exclaiming 'Jacta est alea,' he descended the stairs.

'Where to, my Lord?' enquired the servant when he had entered the carriage.

Lothair seemed to hesitate, and then he said, 'to Belmont.'

CHAPTER XXXI.

'BELMONT is the only house I know that is properly lighted,' said Mr. Phœbus, and he looked with complacent criticism round the brilliant saloons. 'I would not visit anyone who had gas in his house; but even in palaces I find lamps; it is too dreadful. When they came here first there was an

immense chandelier suspended in each of these rooms,
pulling down the ceilings, dwarfing the apartments, leaving
the guests all in darkness, and throwing all the light on
the roof. The chandelier is the great abomination of furniture; it makes a noble apartment look small. And then
they say you cannot light rooms without chandeliers!
Look at these: need anything be more brilliant? And all
the light in the right place: on those who are in the chamber. All light should come from the side of a room, and
if you choose to have candelabra like these you can always
secure sufficient.'

Theodora was seated on a sofa in conversation with a
lady of distinguished mien and with the countenance of a
Roman empress. There were various groups in the room,
standing or seated. Colonel Campian was attending a lady
to the piano where a celebrity presided, a gentleman with
cropped head and a long black beard. The lady was of
extraordinary beauty; one of those faces one encounters in
Asia Minor, rich, glowing, with dark fringed eyes of tremu-
lous lustre; a figure scarcely less striking, of voluptuous
symmetry. Her toilette was exquisite, perhaps a little too
splendid for the occasion, but abstractedly of fine taste,
and she held, as she sang, a vast bouquet entirely of white
stove flowers. The voice was as sweet as the stephanotis,
and the execution faultless. It seemed the perfection of
chamber-singing: no shrieks and no screams, none of those
agonising experiments which result from the fatal competition of rival prima-donnas.

She was singing when Lothair was ushered in. Theodora rose and greeted him with friendliness. Her glance
was that of gratification at his arrival, but the performance
prevented any conversation save a few kind remarks inter-
changed in a hushed tone. Colonel Campian came up: he
seemed quite delighted at renewing his acquaintance with
Lothair, and began to talk rather too loudly, which made

some of the gentlemen near the piano turn round with
glances of wondering reproach. This embarrassed his
newly-arrived guest, who in his distress caught the bow of
a lady who recognised him, and whom he instantly remembered as Mrs. Putney Giles. There was a vacant chair by
her side, and he was glad to occupy it.

'Who is that lady?' enquired Lothair of his companion
when the singing ceased.

'That is Madame Phœbus,' said Mrs. Giles.

'Madame Phœbus!' exclaimed Lothair, with an unconscious feeling of some relief. 'She is a very beautiful
woman. Who was she?'

'She is a Cantacuzene, a daughter of the famous Greek
merchant. The Cantacuzenes, you know, are great people,
descendants of the Greek Emperors. Her uncle is prince of
Samos. Mr. Cantacuzene was very much opposed to the
match, but I think quite wrong. Mr. Phœbus is a most
distinguished man, and the alliance is of the happiest.
Never was such mutual devotion.'

'I am not surprised,' said Lothair, wonderfully relieved.

'Her sister Euphrosyne is in the room,' continued Mrs.
Giles, 'the most extraordinary resemblance to her. There
is just the difference between the matron and the maiden;
that is all. They are nearly of the same age, and before
the marriage might have been mistaken for each other.
The most charming thing in the world is to hear the two
sisters sing together. I hope they may to-night. I know
the family very well. It was Mrs. Cantacuzene who introduced me to Theodora. You know it is quite en règle to
call her Theodora. All the men call her Theodora; "the
divine Theodora" is, I believe, the right thing.'

'And do you call her Theodora?' asked Lothair, rather
dryly.

'Why, no,' said Mrs. Giles, a little confused. 'We are

not intimate, at least not very. Mrs. Campian has been at
my house, and I have been here two or three times; not so
often as I could wish, for Mr. Giles, you see, does not like
servants and horses to be used on Sundays, and no more
do I, and on week days he is too much engaged or too tired
to come out this distance; so you see——'

The singing had ceased, and Theodora approached them.
Addressing Lothair, she said, 'The Princess of Tivoli wishes
that you should be presented to her.'

The Princess of Tivoli was a Roman dame of one of the
most illustrious houses, but who now lived at Paris. She
had in her time taken an active part in Italian politics, and
had sacrificed to the cause to which she was devoted the
larger part of a large fortune. What had been spared, however, permitted her to live in the French capital with
elegance, if not with splendour; and her saloon was the
gathering roof, in Paris, of almost everyone who was celebrated for genius or accomplishments. Though reputed to
be haughty and capricious, she entertained for Theodora an
even passionate friendship, and now visited England only to
see her.

'Madame Campian has been telling me of all the kind
things you did for her at Oxford,' said the Princess. 'Some
day you must show me Oxford, but it must be next year.
I very much admire the free University life. Tell me now,
at Oxford you still have the Protestant religion?'

Lothair ventured to bow assent.

'Ah! that is well,' continued the Princess. 'I advise
you to keep it. If we had only had the Protestant religion
in Italy, things would have been very different. You are
fortunate in this country in having the Protestant religion
and a real nobility. Tell me now, in your constitution, if
the father sits in the upper chamber, the son sits in the lower
house; that I know: but is there any majorat attached to
his seat?'

'Not at present.'

'You sit in the lower house of course?'

'I am not old enough to sit in either house,' said Lothair, 'but when I am of age, which I shall be when I have the honour of showing Oxford to your Highness, I must sit in the upper house, for I have not the blessing of a living father.'

'Ah! that is a great thing in your country,' exclaimed the Princess, 'a man being his own master at so early an age.'

'I thought it was a "heritage of woe,"' said Lothair.

'No, no,' said the Princess; 'the only tolerable thing in life is action, and action is feeble without youth. What if you do not obtain your immediate object?—you always think you will, and the detail of the adventure is full of rapture. And thus it is the blunders of youth are preferable to the triumphs of manhood, or the successes of old age.'

'Well, it will be a consolation for me to remember this when I am in a scrape,' said Lothair.

'Oh! you have many, many scrapes awaiting you,' said the Princess. 'You may look forward to at least ten years of blunders: that is, illusions; that is, happiness. Fortunate young man!'

Theodora had, without appearing to intend it, relinquished her seat to Lothair, who continued his conversation with the Princess, whom he liked, but who, he was sorry to hear, was about to leave England, and immediately: that very night. 'Yes,' she said, 'it is my last act of devotion. You know in my country we have saints and shrines. All Italians, they say, are fond, are superstitious; my pilgrimage is to Theodora. I must come and worship her once a year.'

A gentleman bowed lowly to the Princess, who returned

his salute with pleased alacrity. 'Do you know who that is?' said the Princess to Lothair. 'That is Baron Gozelius, one of our great reputations. He must have just arrived. I will present you to him: it is always agreeable to know a great man,' she added; 'at least Goethe says so!'

The philosopher, at her invitation, took a chair opposite the sofa. Though a profound man, he had all the vivacity and passion which are generally supposed to be peculiar to the superficial. He had remarkable conversational power, which he never spared. Lothair was captivated by his eloquence, his striking observations, his warmth, and the flashing of his southern eye.

'Baron Gozelius agrees with your celebrated pastor, Dr Cumming,' said Theodora, with a tinge of demure sarcasm, 'and believes that the end of the world is at hand.

'And for the same reasons?' enquired Lothair.

'Not exactly,' said Theodora, 'but in this instance science and revelation have arrived at the same result, and that is what all desire.'

'All that I said was,' said Gozelius, 'that the action of the sun had become so irregular that I thought the chances were in favour of the destruction of our planet. At least, if I were a public office, I would not insure it.'

'Yet the risk would not be very great under those circumstances,' said Theodora.

'The destruction of this world is foretold,' said Lothair; 'the stars are to fall from the sky; but while I credit, I cannot bring my mind to comprehend, such a catastrophe.'

'I have seen a world created and a world destroyed,' said Gozelius. 'The last was flickering ten years, and it went out as I was watching it.'

'And the first?' enquired Lothair anxiously.

'Disturbed space for half a century; a great pregnancy.

William Herschel told me it would come when I was a boy,
and I cruised for it through two-thirds of my life. It came
at last, and it repaid me.'

There was a stir. Euphrosyne was going to sing with
her sister. They swept by Lothair in their progress to the
instrument, like the passage of sultanas to some kiosk on
the Bosphorus. It seemed to him that he had never beheld anything so resplendent. The air was perfumed by
their movement and the rustling of their wondrous robes.
'They must be of the Aryan race,' thought Lothair,
'though not of the Phidian type.' They sang a Greek air,
and their sweet and touching voices blended with exquisite
harmony. Everyone was silent in the room, because everyone was entranced. Then they gave their friends some
patriotic lay which required a chorus, the sisters in turn
singing a stanza. Mr. Phœbus arranged the chorus in a
moment, and there clustered round the piano a number of
gentlemen almost as good-looking and picturesque as himself. Then, while Madame Phœbus was singing, Euphrosyne
suddenly and with quickness moved away and approached
Theodora, and whispered something to her, but Theodora
slightly shook her head and seemed to decline.

Euphrosyne regained the piano, whispered something to
Colonel Campian, who was one of the chorus, and then
commenced her own part. Colonel Campian crossed the
room and spoke to Theodora, who instantly, without the
slightest demur, joined her friends. Lothair felt agitated,
as he could not doubt Theodora was going to sing. And
so it was; when Euphrosyne had finished, and the chorus
she had inspired had died away, there rose a deep contralto
sound, which, though without effort, seemed to Lothair the
most thrilling tone he had ever listened to. Deeper and
richer, and richer and deeper, it seemed to become, as it
wound with exquisite facility through a symphony of delicious sound, until it ended in a passionate burst, which

made Lothair's heart beat so tumultuously that for a moment he thought he should be overpowered.

'I never heard anything so fine in my life,' said Lothair to the French philosopher.

'Ah! if you had heard that woman sing the Marseillaise, as I did once, to three thousand people, then you would know what was fine. Not one of us who would not have died on the spot for her!'

The concert was over. The Princess of Tivoli had risen to say farewell. She stood apart with Theodora, holding both her hands, and speaking with earnestness. Then she pressed her lips to Theodora's forehead and said, 'Adieu, my best beloved; the spring will return.'

The Princess had disappeared, and Madame Phœbus came up to say good night to her hostess.

'It is such a delicious night,' said Theodora, 'that I have ordered our strawberries and cream on the terrace. You must not go.'

And so she invited them all to the terrace. There was not a breath of air, the garden was flooded with moonlight in which the fountain glittered, and the atmosphere was as sweet as it was warm.

'I think the moon will melt the ice to-night,' said Theodora as she led Madame Phœbus to a table covered with that innocent refreshment in many forms, and pyramids of strawberries, and gentle drinks which the fancy of America could alone devise.

'I wonder we did not pass the whole evening on the terrace,' said Lothair

'One must sing in a room,' said Euphrosyne, 'or the nightingales would eclipse us.'

Lothair looked quickly at the speaker, and caught the glance of a peculiar countenance: mockery blended with Ionian splendour.

'I think strawberries and cream the most popular of all

food,' said Madame Phœbus, as some touched her beautiful
lips.

'Yes; and one is not ashamed of eating it,' said Theodora.

Soon there was that stir which precedes the breaking up
of an assembly. Mrs. Giles and some others had to return
to town. Madame Phœbus and Euphrosyne were near
neighbours at Roehampton, but their carriage had been for
some time waiting. Mr. Phœbus did not accompany them.
He chose to walk home on such a night, and descended
into the garden with his remaining friends.

'They are going to smoke,' said Theodora to Lothair.
'Is it your habit?'

'Not yet.'

'I do not dislike it in the air and at a distance; but I
banish them the terrace. I think smoking must be a great
consolation to a soldier;' and as she spoke, she moved,
and, without formally inviting him, he found himself walking by her side.

Rather abruptly he said, 'You wore last night at the
Opera the same ornament as on the first time I had the
pleasure of meeting you.'

She looked at him with a smile, and a little surprised.
'My solitary trinket; I fear you will never see any other.'

'But you do not despise trinkets?' said Lothair.

'Oh! no, they are very well. Once I was decked with
jewels and ropes of pearls, like Titian's Queen of Cyprus.
I sometimes regret my pearls. There is a reserve about
pearls which I like, something soft and dim. But they
are all gone, and I ought not to regret them, for they went
in a good cause. I kept the star, because it was given to
me by a hero, and once we flattered ourselves it was a
symbol.'

'I wish I were a hero,' said Lothair.

'You may yet prove one.'

'And if I do, may I give you a star?'

'If it be symbolical.'

'But of what?'

'Of an heroic purpose.'

'But what is an heroic purpose?' exclaimed Lothair. 'Instead of being here to-night, I ought perhaps to have been present at a religious function of the highest and deepest import, which might have influenced my destiny and led to something heroic. But my mind is uncertain and unsettled. I speak to you without reserve, for my heart always entirely opens to you, and I have a sort of unlimited confidence in your judgment. Besides, I have never forgotten what you said at Oxford about religion: that you could not conceive society without religion. It is what I feel myself, and most strongly; and yet there never was a period when religion was so assailed. There is no doubt the Atheists are bolder, are more completely organised, both as to intellectual and even physical force, than ever was known. I have heard that from the highest authority. For my own part, I think I am prepared to die for Divine truth. I have examined myself severely, but I do not think I should falter. Indeed, can there be for man a nobler duty than to be the champion of God? But then the question of the Churches interferes. If there were only one Church, I could see my way. Without a Church there can be no true religion, because otherwise you have no security for the truth. I am a member of the Church of England, and when I was at Oxford I thought the Anglican view might be sustained. But of late I have given my mind deeply to these matters, for after all they are the only matters a man should think of; and I confess to you the claim of Rome to orthodoxy seems to me irresistible'

'You make no distinction, then, between religion and orthodoxy,' said Theodora.

'Certainly I make no difference.'

M

'And yet what is orthodox at Dover is not orthodox at Calais or Ostend. I should be sorry to think that, because there was no orthodoxy in Belgium or France, there was no religion.'

'Yes,' said Lothair, 'I think I see what you mean.'

'Then again, if we go farther,' continued Theodora, 'there is the whole of the East; that certainly is not orthodox according to your views: you may not agree with all or any of their opinions, but you could scarcely maintain that, as communities, they are irreligious.'

'Well, you could not certainly,' said Lothair.

'So you see,' said Theodora, 'what is called orthodoxy has very little to do with religion; and a person may be very religious without holding the same dogmas as yourself, or, as some think, without holding any.' .

'According to you, then,' said Lothair, 'the Anglican view might be maintained.'

'I do not know what the Anglican view is,' said Theodora. 'I do not belong to the Roman or to the Anglican Church.'

'And yet you are very religious,' said Lothair.

'I hope so; I try to be so; and when I fail in any duty, it is not the fault of my religion. I never deceive myself into that; I know it is my own fault.'

There was a pause; but they walked on. The soft splendour of the scene and all its accessories, the moonlight, and the fragrance, and the falling waters, wonderfully bewitched the spirit of the young Lothair.

'There is nothing I would not tell you,' he suddenly exclaimed, turning to Theodora, 'and sometimes I think there is nothing you would not tell me. Tell me then, I entreat you, what is your religion?'

'The true religion, I think,' said Theodora. 'I worship in a church where I believe God dwells, and dwells for my guidance and my good: my conscience.'

'Your conscience may be divine,' said Lothair, 'and I believe it is; but the consciences of other persons are not divine, and what is to guide them, and what is to prevent or to mitigate the evil they would perpetrate?'

'I have never heard from priests,' said Theodora, 'any truth which my conscience had not revealed to me. They use different language from what I use, but I find after a time that we mean the same thing. What I call time they call eternity; when they describe heaven, they give a picture of earth; and beings whom they style divine they invest with all the attributes of humanity.'

'And yet is it not true,' said Lothair, 'that ——'

But at this moment there were the sounds of merriment and of approaching footsteps; the form of Mr. Phœbus appeared ascending the steps of the terrace, followed by others. The smokers had fulfilled their task. There were farewells, and bows, and good-nights. Lothair had to retire with the others, and as he threw himself into his brougham he exclaimed, 'I perceive that life is not so simple an affair as I once supposed.'

CHAPTER XXXII.

WHEN the stranger, who had proved so opportune an ally to Lothair at the Fenian meeting, separated from his companion, he proceeded in the direction of Pentonville, and, after pursuing his way through a number of obscure streets, but quiet, decent, and monotonous, he stopped at a small house in a row of many residences, all of them in form, size, colour, and general character so identical, that the number on the door could alone assure the visitor that he was not in error when he sounded the knocker.

'Ah! is it you, Captain Bruges?' said the smiling and

blushing maiden who answered to his summons. 'We have not seen you for a long time.'

'Well, you look as kind and as pretty as ever, Jenny,' said the Captain; 'and how is my friend?'

'Well,' said the damsel, and she shrugged her shoulders, 'he mopes. I'm very glad you have come back, Captain, for he sees very few now, and is always writing. I cannot bear that writing; if he would only go and take a good walk, I am sure he would be better.'

'There is something in that,' said Captain Bruges. 'And is he at home, and will he see me?'

'Oh! he is always at home to you, Captain; but I will just run up and tell him you are here. You know it is long since we have seen you, Captain; coming on half a year, I think.'

'Time flies, Jenny. Go, my good girl, and I will wait below.'

'In the parlour, if you please, Captain Bruges. It is to let now. It is more than a month since the Doctor left us. That was a loss, for as long as the Doctor was here, he always had some one to speak with.'

So Captain Bruges entered the little dining-room, with its mahogany table, and half-a-dozen chairs, and cellaret, and over the fireplace a portrait of Garibaldi, which had been left as a legacy to the landlady by her late lodger, Dr. Tresorio.

The Captain threw a quick glance at the print, and then falling into reverie, with his hands crossed behind him, paced the little chamber, and was soon lost in thoughts which made him unconscious how long had elapsed when the maiden summoned him.

Following her, and ascending the staircase, he was ushered into the front room of the first floor, and there came forward to meet him a man rather below the middle height, but of a symmetrical and imposing mien. His face was grave, not to say sad; thought, not time, had partially silvered the clustering of his raven hair; but intellectual power reigned in his wide brow, while determination was the character of the rest of his countenance under great control, yet apparently, from the dark flashing of his eye, not incompatible with fanaticism.

'General,' he exclaimed, 'your presence always reanimates me. I shall at least have some news on which I can rely. Your visit is sudden; sudden things are often happy ones. Is there anything stirring in the promised land? Speak, speak! You have a thousand things to say, and I have a thousand ears.'

'My dear Mirandola,' replied the visitor, 'I will take leave to call into council a friend whose presence is always profitable.'

So saying, he took out a cigar-case, and offered it to his companion.

'We have smoked together in palaces,' said Mirandola, accepting the proffer with a delicate white hand.

'But not these cigars,' replied the General. 'They are superb, my only reward for all my transatlantic work, and sometimes I think a sufficient one.'

'And Jenny shall give us a capital cup of coffee,' said Mirandola; 'it is the only hospitality that I can offer my friends. Give me a light, my General; and now, how are things?'

'Well, at the first glance, very bad; the French have left Rome, and we are not in it.'

'Well, that is an infamy not of to-day or yesterday,' replied Mirandola, 'though not less an infamy. We talked over this six months ago, when you were over here about something else, and from that moment unto the present I have with unceasing effort laboured to erase this stigma from the human consciousness, but with no success. Men are changed; public spirit is extinct; the deeds of '48 are

to the present generation as incomprehensible as the Punic
wars or the feats of Marius against the Cimbri. What we
want are the most natural things in the world, and easy of
attainment because they are natural. We want our metropolis, our native frontiers, and true liberty. Instead of
these we have compromises, conventions, provincial jealousies, and French prefects. It is disgusting, heartrending;
sometimes I fear my own energies are waning. My health
is wretched; writing and speaking are decidedly bad for
me, and I pass my life in writing and speaking. Towards
evening I feel utterly exhausted, and am sometimes, which
I thought I never could be, the victim of despondency.
The loss of the Doctor was a severe blow, but they harried
him out of the place. The man of Paris would never rest
till he was gone. I was myself thinking of once more
trying Switzerland, but the obstacles are great; and, in
truth, I was at my darkest moment when Jenny brought
me the light of your name.'

The General, who had bivouacked on a group of small
chairs, his leg on one, his elbow on another, took his cigar
from his mouth and delivered himself of a volume of smoke,
and then said dryly, 'Things may not be so bad as they
seem, comrade. Your efforts have not been without fruit.
I have traced them in many quarters, and, indeed, it is
about their possible consequences that I have come over to
consult with you.'

'Idle words, I know, never escape those lips,' said
Mirandola; 'speak on.'

'Well,' said the General, 'you see that people are a
little exhausted by the efforts of last year; and it must be
confessed that no slight results were accomplished. The
freedom of Venice——'

'A French intrigue,' exclaimed Mirandola. 'The freedom of Venice is the price of the slavery of Rome. I
heard of it with disgust.'

'Well, we do not differ much on that head,' said the General. 'I am not a Roman as you are, but I view Rome, with reference to the object of my life, with feelings not less ardent and absorbing than yourself, who would wish to see it again the empress of the world. I am a soldier, and love war, and, left to myself, would care little perhaps for what form of government I combated, provided the army was constituted on the principles of fraternity and equality; but the passion of my life, to which I have sacrificed military position, and perhaps,' he added in a lower tone, 'perhaps even military fame, has been to destroy priestcraft, and, so long as the Pope rules in Rome, it will be supreme.'

'We have struck him down once,' said Mirandola.

'And I hope we shall again, and for ever,' said the General, 'and it is about that I would speak. You are in error in supposing that your friends do not sympathise with you, or that their answers are dilatory or evasive. There is much astir; the old spirit is not extinct, but the difficulties are greater than in former days when we had only the Austrians to encounter, and we cannot afford to make another failure.'

'There could be no failure if we were clear and determined. There must be a hundred thousand men who would die for our metropolis, our natural frontiers, and true liberty. The mass of the pseudo-Italian army must be with us. As for foreign interference its repetition seems to me impossible. The brotherhood in the different countries, if well guided, could alone prevent it. There should be at once a manifesto addressed to the peoples. They have become absorbed in money-grubbing and what they call industry. The external life of a nation is its most important one. A nation, as an individual, has duties to fulfil appointed by God and His moral law: the individual towards his family, his town, his country; the nation

towards the country of countries, humanity: the outward
world. I firmly believe that we fail and renounce the
religious and divine element of our life whenever we
betray or neglect those duties. The internal activity of a
nation is important and sacred because it prepares the instrument for its appointed task. It is mere egotism if it
converges towards itself, degrading and doomed to expia-
tion; as will be the fate of this country in which we now
dwell,' added Mirandola, in a hushed voice. 'England had
a mission: it had belief, and it had power. It announced
itself the representative of religious, commercial, and political freedom, and yet, when it came to action, it allowed
Denmark to be crushed by Austria and Prussia, and, in
the most nefarious transaction of modern times, uttered
the approving shriek of "Perish Savoy!"'

'My dear Mirandola,' said the General, trimming his
cigar, ' there is no living man who appreciates your genius
and your worth more than myself; perhaps I might say
there is no living man who has had equal opportunities of
estimating them. You formed the mind of our country;
you kindled and kept alive the sacred flame when all was
gloom, and all were without heart. Such prodigious devotion, so much resource and pertinacity and patience, such
unbroken spirit, were never before exhibited by man, and,
whatever may be said by your enemies, I know that in the
greatest hour of action you proved equal to it; and yet at
this moment, when your friends are again stirring, and
there is a hope of spring, I am bound to tell you that there
are only two persons in the world who can effect the
revolution, and you are not one of them.'

'I am ardent, my General, perhaps too sanguine, but I
have no self-love, at least none when the interests of the
great cause are at stake. Tell me then their names, and
count, if required, on my co-operation.'

'Garibaldi and Mary-Anne.'

'A Pulchinello and a Bayadere!' exclaimed Mirandola, and, springing from his seat, he impatiently paced the room.

'And yet,' continued the General calmly, 'there is no manner of doubt that Garibaldi is the only name that could collect ten thousand men at any given point in Italy; while in France, though her influence is mythical, the name of Mary-Anne is a name of magic. Though never mentioned, it is never forgotten. And the slightest allusion to it among the initiated will open every heart. There are more secret societies in France at this moment than at any period since '85, though you hear nothing of them; and they believe in Mary-Anne, and in nothing else.'

'You have been at Caprera?' said Mirandola

'I have been at Caprera.'

'And what did he say?'

'He will do nothing without the sanction of the Savoyard.'

'He wants to get wounded in his other foot,' said Mirandola, with savage sarcasm. 'Will he never weary of being betrayed?'

'I found him calm and sanguine,' said the General.

'What of the woman?'

'Garibaldi will not move without the Savoyard, and Mary-Anne will not move without Garibaldi; that is the situation.'

'Have you seen her?'

'Not yet; I have been to Caprera, and I have come over to see her and you. Italy is ready for the move, and is only waiting for the great man. He will not act without the Savoyard; he believes in him. I will not be sceptical. There are difficulties enough without imagining any. We have no money, and all our sources of supply are drained; but we have the inspiration of a sacred cause, we have you; we may gain others, and, at any rate, the French are no longer at Rome.'

CHAPTER XXXIII.

'THE Goodwood Cup, my Lord; the Doncaster. This pair
of flagons for his Highness the Khedive, something quite
new. Yes, parcel-gilt, the only style now; it gives relief
to design : yes, by Monti, a great man, hardly inferior to
Flaxman, if at all. Flaxman worked for Rundell and
Bridge in the old days, one of the principal causes of their
success. Your Lordship's gold service was supplied by
Rundell and Bridge. Very fine service indeed, much by
Flaxman : nothing of that kind seen now.'

'I never did see it,' said Lothair. He was replying to
Mr. Ruby, a celebrated jeweller and goldsmith, in a celebrated street, who had saluted him when he had entered
the shop, and called the attention of Lothair to a group of
treasures of art.

'Strange,' said Mr. Ruby, smiling. 'It is in the next
room, if your Lordship would like to see it. I think your
Lordship should see your gold service. Mr. Putney Giles
ordered it here to be examined and put in order.'

'I should like to see it very much,' said Lothair, 'though
I came to speak to you about something else.'

And so Lothair, following Mr. Ruby into an inner apartment, had the gratification, for the first time, of seeing his
own service of gold plate laid out in completeness, and
which had been for some time exhibited to the daily admiration of that favoured portion of the English people who
frequent the brilliant and glowing counters of Mr. Ruby.

Not that Lothair was embarrassed by their presence at
this moment. The hour of their arrival had not yet come.
Business had not long commenced when Lothair entered
the shop, somewhat to the surprise of its master. Those

who know Bond Street only in the blaze of fashionable
hours can form but an imperfect conception of its matutinal
charm, when it is still shady and fresh, when there are no
carriages, rarely a cart, and passers-by gliding about
on real business. One feels as in some continental city.
Then there are time and opportunity to look at the shops;
and there is no street in the world that can furnish such a
collection, filled with so many objects of beauty, curiosity,
and interest. The jewellers and goldsmiths and dealers in
rare furniture; porcelain, and cabinets, and French pictures; have long fixed upon Bond Street as their favourite
quarter, and are not chary of displaying their treasures;
though it may be a question whether some of the magazines
of fancy food, delicacies culled from all the climes and
regions of the globe, particularly at the matin hour, may
not, in their picturesque variety, be the most attractive.
The palm, perhaps, would be given to the fishmongers,
with their exuberant exhibitions, grouped with skill,
startling often with strange forms, dazzling with prismatic
tints, and breathing the invigorating redolence of the sea.

'Well, I like the service,' said Lothair, 'and am glad, as
you tell me, that its fashion has come round again, because
there will now be no necessity for ordering a new one. I
do not myself much care for plate. I like flowers and porcelain on a table, and I like to see the guests. However, I
suppose it is all right, and I must use it. It was not about
plate that I called; I wanted to speak to you about pearls.'

'Ah!' said Mr. Ruby, and his face brightened; and
ushering Lothair to some glass cases, he at the same time
provided his customer with a seat.

'Something like that?' said Mr. Ruby, who by this time
had slid into his proper side of the counter, and was un-
locking the glass cases; 'something like that?' and he
placed before Lothair a string of pretty pearls with a
diamond clasp. 'With the earrings, twenty-five hundred,'

he added; and then, observing that Lothair did not seem enchanted, he said, ' This is something quite new,' and he carelessly pushed towards Lothair a magnificent necklace of turquoises and brilliants.

It was impossible not to admire it, the arrangement was so novel and yet of such good taste; but though its price was double that of the pearl necklace, Mr. Ruby did not seem to wish to force attention to it, for he put in Lothair's hands almost immediately the finest emerald necklace in the world, and set in a style that was perfectly ravishing.

' The setting is from the Campana collection,' said Mr. Ruby. ' They certainly understood things in those days, but I can say that, so far as mere workmanship is concerned, this quite equals them. I have made one for the Empress. Here is a black pearl, very rare, pear shape, and set in Golconda diamonds, two thousand guineas; it might be suspended to a necklace, or worn as a locket. This is pretty,' and he offered to Lothair a gigantic sapphire in brilliants and in the form of a bracelet.

' The finest sapphire I know is in this ring,' added Mr. Ruby, and he introduced his visitor to a tray of precious rings. ' I have a pearl bracelet here that your Lordship might like to see,' and he placed before Lothair a case of fifty bracelets, vying with each other in splendour.

' But what I want,' said Lothair, ' are pearls.'

' I understand,' said Mr. Ruby. ' This is a curious thing,' and he took out a paper packet. ' There!' he said, opening it and throwing it before Lothair so carelessly that some of the stones ran over the glass covering of the counter. ' There, that is a thing not to be seen every day, a packet of diamonds, bought of an Indian prince, and sent by us to be cut and polished at Amsterdam (nothing can be done in that way except there), and just returned; nothing very remarkable as to size, but all of high quality: some fine stones; that for example,' and he touched one with the

long nail of his little finger; 'that is worth seven hundred
guineas, the whole packet worth perhaps ten thousand
pounds.'

'Very interesting,' said Lothair, 'but what I want are
pearls. That necklace which you have shown me is like
the necklace of a doll. I want pearls, such as you see
them in Italian pictures, Titians and Giorgiones, such as a
Queen of Cyprus would wear. I want ropes of pearls.'

'Ah!' said Mr. Ruby, 'I know what your Lordship
means. Lady Bideford had something of that kind. She
very much deceived us: always told us her necklace must
be sold at her death, and she had very bad health. We
waited, but when she went, poor lady, it was claimed by
the heir, and is in Chancery at this very moment. The
Justinianis have ropes of pearls; Madame Justiniani of
Paris, I have been told, gives a rope to every one of her
children when they marry; but there is no expectation of
a Justiniani parting with anything. Pearls are troublesome property, my Lord. They require great care; they
want both air and exercise; they must be worn frequently;
you cannot lock them up. The Duchess of Havant has the
finest pearls in this country, and I told her Grace, "Wear
them whenever you can, wear them at breakfast;" and
her Grace follows my advice, she does wear them at breakfast. I go down to Havant Castle every year to see her
Grace's pearls, and I wipe every one of them myself, and
let them lie on a sunny bank in the garden, in a westerly
wind, for hours and days together. Their complexion
would have been ruined had it not been for this treatment.
Pearls are like girls, my Lord, they require quite as much
attention.'

'Then you cannot give me what I want?' said Lothair.

'Well, I can, and I cannot,' said Mr. Ruby. 'I am in a
difficulty. I have in this house exactly what your Lordship requires, but I have offered them to Lord Topaz, and

I have not received his answer. We have instructions to
inform his Lordship of every very precious jewel that we obtain, and give him the preference as a purchaser. Nevertheless there is no one I could more desire to oblige than your
Lordship; your Lordship has every claim upon us, and I
should be truly glad to find these pearls in your Lordship's
possession if I could only see my way. Perhaps your
Lordship would like to look at them?'

'Certainly, but pray do not leave me here alone with all
these treasures,' said Lothair, as Mr. Ruby was quitting
the apartment.

'Oh! my Lord, with you!'

'Yes, that is all very well; but if anything is missed
hereafter, it will always be remembered that these jewels
were in my possession, and I was alone. I highly object
to it.' But Mr. Ruby had vanished, and did not immediately reappear. In the meantime it was impossible for
Lothair to move: he was alone and surrounded with
precious necklaces, and glittering rings, and gorgeous
bracelets, with loose diamonds running over the counter.
It was not a kind or an amount of property that Lothair,
relinquishing the trust, could satisfactorily deliver to a
shopman. The shopman, however honest, might be suddenly tempted by Satan, and take the next train to Liver-
pool. He felt therefore relieved when Mr. Ruby re-
entered the room, breathless, with a velvet casket. 'I beg
pardon, my Lord, a thousand pardons, but I thought I
would just run over to Lord Topaz, only in the square
close by. His Lordship is at Madrid, the only city one
cannot depend on communications with by telegraph.
Spaniards strange people, very prejudiced, take all sorts of
fancies in their head. Besides, Lord Topaz has more
pearls than he can know what to do with, and I should
like your Lordship to see these,' and he opened the casket.

'Exactly what I want,' exclaimed Lothair; 'these must

be the very pearls the Queen of Cyprus wore. What is their price?'

'They are from Genoa and belonged to a Doge,' said Mr. Ruby; 'your Lordship shall have them for the sum we gave for them. There shall be no profit on the transaction, and we shall be proud of it. We gave for them four thousand guineas.'

'I will take them with me,' said Lothair, who was afraid, if he left them behind, Lord Topaz might arrive in the interval.

CHAPTER XXXIV.

LOTHAIR had returned home from his last visit to Belmont agitated by many thoughts, but, generally speaking, deeply musing over its mistress. Considerable speculation on religion, the Churches, the solar system, the cosmical order, the purpose of creation, and the destiny of man, was maintained in his too rapid progress from Roehampton to his Belgravian hotel; but the association of ideas always terminated the consideration of every topic by a wondering and deeply interesting enquiry when he should see her again. And here, in order to simplify this narrative, we will at once chronicle the solution of this grave question. On the afternoon of the next day, Lothair mounted his horse with the intention of calling on Lady St. Jerome, and perhaps some other persons, but it is curious to observe that he soon found himself on the road to Roehampton, where he was in due time paying a visit to Theodora. But what is more remarkable is that the same result occurred every day afterwards. Regularly every day he paid a visit to Belmont. Nor was this all; very often he paid two visits, for he remembered that in the evening

Theodora was always at home. Lothair used to hurry to
town from his morning visit, dine at some great house,
which satisfied the demands of society, and then drive down
to Rochampton. The guests of the evening saloon, when
they witnessed the high ceremony of Lothair's manner,
which was natural to him, when he entered, and the welcome of Theodora, could hardly believe that a few hours
only had elapsed since their separation.

And what was the manner of Theodora to him when they
were alone ? Precisely as before. She never seemed in the
least surprised that he called on her every day, or even twice
a day. Sometimes she was alone, frequently she had companions, but she was always the same, always appeared
gratified at his arrival, and always extended to him the
same welcome, graceful and genial, but without a spark of
coquetry. Yet she did not affect to conceal that she took a
certain interest in him, because she was careful to introduce
him to distinguished men, and would say, ' You should
know him ; he is master of such a subject. You will hear
things that you ought to know.' But all this in a sincere
and straightforward manner. Theodora had not the
slightest affectation ; she was always natural, though a
little reserved. But this reserve appeared to be the result
of modesty rather than of any desire of concealment. When
they were alone, though always calm, she would talk with
freedom and vivacity, but in the presence of others she
rather led to their display, and encouraged them, often
with a certain degree of adroit simplicity, to descant on
topics which interested them, or of which they were competent to treat. Alone with Lothair, and they were often
alone, though she herself never obtruded the serious subjects
round which he was always fluttering, she never avoided
them, and without involving herself in elaborate arguments,
or degenerating into conversational controversy, she had a
habit of asking a question, or expressing a sentiment, which
greatly affected his feelings or perplexed his opinions.

Had not the season been long waning, this change in the life of Lothair must have been noticed, and its cause ultimately discovered. But the social critics cease to be observant towards the end of July. All the world then are thinking of themselves, and have no time to speculate on the fate and fortunes of their neighbours. The campaign is too near its close; the balance of the season must soon be struck, the great book of society made. In a few weeks, even in a few days, what long and subtle plans shattered or triumphant! what prizes gained or missed! what baffled hopes, and what broken hearts! The baffled hopes must go to Cowes, and the broken hearts to Baden. There were some great ladies who did remark that Lothair was seldom seen at balls; and Hugo Bohun, who had been staying at his aunt Lady Gertrude's villa for change of air, did say to Bertram that he had met Lothair twice on Barnes Common, and asked Bertram if he knew the reason why. But the fact that Lothair was cruising in waters which their craft never entered combined with the lateness of the season to baffle all the ingenuity of Hugo Bohun, though he generally found out everything.

The great difficulty which Lothair had to apprehend was with his Roman Catholic friends. The system of the Monsignori was never to let him be out of sight, and his absence from the critical function had not only disappointed but alarmed them. But the Jesuits are wise men; they never lose their temper. They know when to avoid scenes as well as when to make them. Monsignore Catesby called on Lothair as frequently as before, and never made the slightest allusion to the miscarriage of their expectations. Strange to say, the innocent Lothair, naturally so straightforward and so honourable, found himself instinctively, almost it might be said unconsciously, defending himself against his invaders with some of their own weapons. He still talked about building his cathedral, of which, not

N

contented with more plans, he even gave orders that a model should be made, and he still received statements on points of faith from Father Coleman, on which he made marginal notes and queries. Monsignore Catesby was not altogether satisfied. He was suspicious of some disturbing cause, but at present it baffled him. Their hopes, however, were high; and they had cause to be sanguine. In a month's time or so, Lothair would be in the country to celebrate his majority; his guardian the Cardinal was to be his guest; the St. Jeromes were invited, Monsignore Catesby himself. Here would be opportunity and actors to avail themselves of it.

It was a very few days after the first evening visit of Lothair to Belmont that he found himself one morning alone with Theodora. She was in her bowery boudoir, copying some music for Madame Phœbus, at least in the intervals of conversation. That had not been of a grave character, but the contrary, when Lothair rather abruptly said, 'Do you agree, Mrs. Campian, with what Mr. Phœbus said the other night, that the greatest pain must be the sense of death?'

'Then mankind is generally spared the greatest pain,' she replied, 'for I apprehend few people are sensible of death, unless indeed,' she added, 'it be on the field of battle; and there, I am sure, it cannot be painful.'

'Not on the field of battle?' asked Lothair, inducing her to proceed.

'Well, I should think for all, on the field of battle, there must be a degree of excitement, and of sympathetic excitement, scarcely compatible with overwhelming suffering; but if death were encountered there for a great cause, I should rather associate it with rapture than pain.'

'But still a good number of persons must die in their beds and be conscious,' said Lothair.

'It may be, though I should doubt it. The witnesses of

such a demise are never impartial. All I have loved and lost have died upon the field of battle; and those who have suffered pain have been those whom they have left behind; and that pain,' she added with some emotion, 'may perhaps deserve the description of Mr. Phœbus.'

Lothair would not pursue the subject, and there was rather an awkward pause. Theodora herself broke it, and in a lighter vein, though recurring to the same theme, she said with a slight smile, 'I am scarcely a competent person to consult upon this subject, for, to be candid with you, I do not myself believe in death. There is a change, and doubtless a great one, painful it may be, certainly very perplexing, but I have a profound conviction of my immortality, and I do not believe that I shall rest in my grave in sæcula sæculorum, only to be convinced of it by the last trump.'

'I hope you will not leave this world before I do,' said Lothair; 'but if that sorrow be reserved for me, promise that to me, if only once, you will reappear.'

'I doubt whether the departed have that power,' said Theodora, 'or else I think my heroes would have revisited me. I lost a father more magnificent than Jove, and two brothers brighter than Apollo, and all of them passionately loved me, and yet they have not come; but I shall see them, and perhaps soon. So you see, my dear Lord,' speaking more briskly, and rising rather suddenly from her seat, 'that for my part I think it best to arrange all that concerns one in this world while one inhabits it; and this reminds me that I have a little business to fulfil in which you can help me,' and she opened a cabinet and took out a flat antique case, and then said, resuming her seat at her table, 'Some one, and anonymously, has made me a magnificent present; some strings of costly pearls. I am greatly embarrassed with them, for I never wear pearls or anything else, and I never wish to accept presents. To return them to an unknown is out of my power, but it is

not impossible that I may some day become acquainted
with the donor. I wish them to be kept in safety, and
therefore not by myself, for my life is subject to too great
vicissitudes. I have therefore placed them in this case,
which I shall now seal and entrust them to your care, as a
friend in whom I have entire confidence. See,' she said,
lighting a match, and opening the case, ' here are the pearls,
are they not superb ? and here is a note which will tell you
what to do with them in case of my absence, when you
open the case, which will not be for a year from this day.
There, it is locked. I have directed it to you, and I will
seal it with my father's seal.'

Lothair was about to speak. ' Do not say a word,' she
said ; ' this seal is a religious ceremony with me.' She
was some little time fulfilling it, so that the impression
might be deep and clear. She looked at it earnestly while
the wax was cooling, and then she said, ' I deliver the
custody of this to a friend whom I entirely trust. Adieu !'
and she disappeared.

The amazed Lothair glanced at the seal. It was a single
word, ' ROMA,' and then, utterly mystified, he returned to
town with his own present.

CHAPTER XXXV.

MR. PHŒBUS had just finished a picture which he had
painted for the Emperor of Russia. It was to depart immediately from England for its northern home, except that
his Imperial Majesty had consented that it should be exhibited for a brief space to the people of England. This
was a condition which Mr. Phœbus had made in the interests of art, and as a due homage alike to his own
patriotism and celebrity.

There was to be a private inspection of the picture at
the studio of the artist, and Mr. Phœbus had invited Lothair
to attend it. Our friend had accordingly, on the appointed
day, driven down to Belmont, and then walked to the residence of Mr. Phœbus with Colonel Campian and his wife.
It was a short and pretty walk, entirely through the royal
park, which the occupiers of Belmont had the traditionary
privilege thus to use.

The residence of Mr. Phœbus was convenient and agreeable, and in situation not unlike that of Belmont, being
sylvan and sequestered. He had himself erected a fine
studio, and added it to the original building. The flower
garden was bright and curious, and on the lawn was a
tent of many colours designed by himself, and which
might have suited some splendid field of chivalry. Upon
gilt and painted perches also there were paroquets and
macaws.

Lothair on his arrival found many guests assembled,
chiefly on the lawn. Mr Phœbus was highly esteemed,
and had distinguished and eminent friends, whose constant
courtesies the present occasion allowed him elegantly to
acknowledge. There was a polished and grey-headed noble
who was the head of the patrons of art in England, whose
nod of approbation sometimes made the fortune of a young
artist, and whose purchase of pictures for the nation even
the furious cognoscenti of the House of Commons dared
not question. Some of the finest works of Mr. Phœbus
were to be found in his gallery; but his Lordship admired
Madame Phœbus even more than her husband's works, and
Euphrosyne as much as her sister. It was sometimes
thought, among their friends, that this young lady had
only to decide in order to share the widowed coronet; but
Euphrosyne laughed at everything, even her adorers; and
while her witching mockery only rendered them more
fascinated, it often prevented critical declarations.

And Lady Beatrice was there, herself an artist, and full of æsthetical enthusiasm. Her hands were beautiful, and she passed her life in modelling them. And Cocrope was there, a rich old bachelor, with, it was supposed, the finest collection of modern pictures extant. His theory was, that a man could not do a wiser thing than invest the whole of his fortune in such securities, and it delighted him to tell his numerous nephews and nieces that he should, in all probability, leave his collection to the nation.

Clorinda, whose palace was always open to genius, and who delighted in the society of men who had discovered planets, excavated primæval mounds, painted pictures on new principles, or composed immortal poems which no human being could either scan or construe, but which she recognised as 'subtle' and full of secret melody, came leaning on the arm of a celebrated plenipotentiary, and beaming with sympathy on every subject, and with the consciousness of her universal charms.

And the accomplished Sir Francis was there, and several R.A.s of eminence, for Phœbus was a true artist and loved the brotherhood, and always placed them in the post of honour.

No language can describe the fascinating costume of Madame Phœbus and her glittering sister. 'They are habited as sylvans,' the great artist deigned to observe, if any of his guests could not refrain from admiring the dresses which he had himself devised. As for the venerable patron of art in Britain, he smiled when he met the lady of the house, and sighed when he glanced at Euphrosyne; but the first gave him a beautiful flower, and the other fastened it in his buttonhole. He looked like a victim bedecked by the priestesses of some old fane of Hellenic loveliness, and proud of his impending fate. What could the Psalmist mean in the immortal passage? Threescore and ten, at the present day, is the period of romantic passions. As for our enamoured sexagenarians, they avenge the theories of our cold-hearted youth.

Mr. Phœbus was an eminent host. It delighted him to see people pleased, and pleased under his influence. He had a belief, not without foundation, that everything was done better under his roof than under that of any other person. The banquet in the air on the present occasion could only be done justice to by the courtly painters of the reign of Louis XV. Vanloo, and Watteau, and Lancré would have caught the graceful groups, and the well-arranged colours, and the faces, some pretty, some a little affected; the ladies on fantastic chairs of wicker-work, gilt and curiously painted; the gentlemen, reclining on the turf, or bending behind them with watchful care. The little tables, all different, the soups in delicate cups of Sèvres, the wines in golden glass of Venice, the ortolans, the Italian confectionary, the bright bouquets, were worthy of the soft and invisible music that resounded from the pavilion, only varied by the coquetish scream of some macaw, jealous amid all this novelty and excitement of not being noticed.

'It is a scene of enchantment,' whispered the chief patron of British art to Madame Phœbus.

'I always think luncheon in the air rather jolly,' said Madame Phœbus.

'It is perfect romance!' murmured the chief patron of British art to Euphrosyne.

'With a due admixture of reality,' she said, helping him to an enormous truffle, which she extracted from its napkin. 'You know you must eat it with butter.'

Lothair was glad to observe that, though in refined society, none were present with whom he had any previous acquaintance, for he had an instinctive feeling that if Hugo Bohun had been there, or Bertram, or the Duke of Brecon, or any ladies with whom he was familiarly acquainted, he would scarcely have been able to avail himself of the society of Theodora with the perfect freedom which he now enjoyed. They would all have been asking who she was, where she came from, how long Lothair had known her: all those questions, kind and neighbourly, which under such circumstances occur. He was in a distinguished circle, but one different from that in which he lived. He sat next to Theodora, and Mr. Phœbus constantly hovered about them, ever doing something very graceful, or saying something very bright. Then he would whisper a word to the great Clorinda, who flashed intelligence from her celebrated eyes, and then he made a suggestion to the æsthetical Lady Beatrice, who immediately fell into enthusiasm and eloquence, and took the opportunity of displaying her celebrated hands.

The time had now arrived when they were to repair to the studio and view the picture. A curtain was over it, and then a silken rope across the chamber, and then some chairs. The subject of the picture was Hero and Leander, chosen by the heir of all the Russias himself, during a late visit to England.

'A fascinating subject,' said old Cecrops to Mr. Phœbus, 'but not a very original one.'

'The originality of a subject is in its treatment,' was the reply.

The theme, in the present instance, was certainly not conventionally treated. When the curtain was withdrawn, they beheld a figure of life-like size, exhibiting in undisguised completeness the perfection of the female form, and yet the painter had so skilfully availed himself of the shadowy and mystic hour and of some gauze-like drapery, which veiled without concealing his design, that the chastest eye might gaze on his heroine with impunity. The splendour of her upstretched arms held high the beacon light, which threw a glare upon the sublime anxiety of her countenance, while all the tumult of the Hellespont, the

waves, the scudding sky, the opposite shore revealed by a
blood-red flash, were touched by the hand of a master who
had never failed.

The applause was a genuine verdict, and the company
after a time began to disperse about the house and gardens.
A small circle remained, and passing the silken rope,
approached and narrowly scrutinised the picture. Among
these were Theodora and Lothair, the chief patron of
British art, an R.A. or two, Clorinda, and Lady Beatrice.

Mr. Phœbus, who left the studio but had now returned,
did not disturb them. After awhile he approached the
group. His air was elate, and was redeemed only from
arrogance by the intellect of his brow. The circle started
a little as they heard his voice, for they had been unaware
of his presence.

'To-morrow,' he said, 'the critics will commence. You
know who the critics are? The men who have failed in
literature and art.'

CHAPTER XXXVI.

THE lodge-gate of Belmont was opening as Lothair one
morning approached it; a Hansom cab came forth, and in
it was a person whose countenance was strongly marked
on the memory of Lothair. It was that of his unknown
friend at the Fenian meeting. Lothair instantly recognised
and cordially saluted him, and his greeting, though hurriedly, was not ungraciously returned; but the vehicle did
not stop. Lothair called to the driver to halt, but the
driver on the contrary stimulated his steed, and in the
winding lane was soon out of sight.

Theodora was not immediately visible. She was neither
in her usual apartment nor in her garden; but it was only

perhaps because Lothair was so full of his own impressions from his recent encounter at the lodge, that he did not observe that the demeanour of Mrs. Campian when she appeared was hardly marked by her habitual serenity. She entered the room hurriedly, and spoke with quickness.

'Pray,' exclaimed Lothair, rather eagerly, 'do tell me the name of the gentleman who has just called here.'

Theodora changed colour, looked distressed, and was silent; unobserved however by Lothair, who, absorbed by his own highly excited curiosity, proceeded to explain why he presumed to press for the information. 'I am under great obligations to that person; I am not sure I may not say I owe him my life, but certainly an extrication from great danger and very embarrassing danger too. I never saw him but once, and he would not give me his name, and scarcely would accept my thanks. I wanted to stop his cab to-day, but it was impossible. He literally galloped off.'

'He is a foreigner,' said Mrs. Campian, who had recovered herself; 'he was a particular friend of my dear father; and when he visits England, which he does occasionally, he calls to see us.'

'Ah!' said Lothair, 'I hope I shall soon have an opportunity of expressing to him my gratitude.'

'It was so like him not to give his name and to shrink from thanks,' said Mrs. Campian. 'He never enters society, and makes no acquaintances.'

'I am sorry for that,' said Lothair, 'for it is not only that he served me, but I was much taken with him, and felt that he was a person I should like to cultivate.'

'Yes, Captain Bruges is a remarkable man,' said Theodora; 'he is not one to be forgotten.'

'Captain Bruges. That then is his name?'

'He is known by the name of Captain Bruges,' said Theodora, and she hesitated; and then speaking more quickly she added, 'I cannot sanction, I cannot bear, any deception between you and this roof. Bruges is not his real name, nor is the title he assumes his real rank. He is not to be known, and not to be spoken of. He is one, and one of the most eminent, of the great family of sufferers in this world, but sufferers for a divine cause. I myself have been direly stricken in this struggle. When I remember the departed, it is not always easy to bear the thought. I keep it at the bottom of my heart; but this visit to-day has too terribly revived everything. It is well that you only are here to witness my suffering, but you will not have to witness it again, for we will never again speak of these matters.'

Lothair was much touched: his good heart and his good taste alike dissuaded him from attempting commonplace consolation. He ventured to take her hand and pressed it to his lips. 'Dear lady!' he murmured, and he led her to a seat. 'I fear my foolish tattle has added to pain which I would gladly bear for you.'

They talked about nothings: about a new horse which Colonel Campian had just purchased, and which he wanted to show to Lothair; an old opera revived, but which sounded rather flat; something amusing that somebody had said, and something absurd which somebody had done. And then, when the ruffled feeling had been quite composed, and all had been brought back to the tenor of their usual pleasant life, Lothair said suddenly and rather gaily, 'And now, dearest lady, I have a favour to ask. You know my majority is to be achieved and to be celebrated next month. I hope that yourself and Colonel Campian will honour me by being my guests.'

Theodora did not at all look like a lady who had received a social attention of the most distinguished class. She looked embarrassed, and began to murmur something about Colonel Campian, and their never going into society.

'Colonel Campian is going to Scotland, and you are going with him,' said Lothair. 'I know it, for he told me so, and said he could manage the visit to me, if you approved it, quite well. In fact it will fit in with his Scotch visit.'

'There was some talk once about Scotland,' said Theodora, 'but that was a long time ago. Many things have happened since then. I do not think the Scotch visit is by any means so settled as you think.'

'But however that may be decided,' said Lothair, 'there can be no reason why you should not come to me.'

'It is presumptuous in me, a foreigner, to speak of such matters,' said Theodora; 'but I fancy that, in such celebrations as you contemplate, there is, or there should be, some qualification of blood or family connection for becoming your guests. We should be there quite strangers, and in everybody's way, checking the local and domestic abandon which I should suppose is one of the charms of such meetings.'

'I have few relations and scarcely a connection,' said Lothair, rather moodily. 'I can only ask friends to celebrate my majority, and there are no friends whom I so much regard as those who live at Belmont.'

'It is very kind of you to say that, and to feel it; and I know that you would not say it if you did not feel it,' replied Theodora. 'But still, I think it would be better that we should come to see you at a time when you are less engaged; perhaps you will take Colonel Campian down some day and give him some shooting.'

'All I can say is that, if you do not come, it will be the darkest, instead of the brightest, week in my life,' said Lothair. 'In short, I feel I could not get through the business, I should be so mortified. I cannot restrain my feelings or arrange my countenance. Unless you come, the whole affair will be a complete failure, and worse than a failure.'

'Well, I will speak to Colonel Campian about it,' said Theodora, but with little animation.

'We will both speak to him about it now,' said Lothair, for the Colonel at that moment entered the room and greeted Lothair, as was his custom, cordially.

'We are settling the visit to Muriel,' said Lothair; 'I want to induce Mrs. Campian to come down a day or two before the rest, so that we may have the benefit of her counsel.'

CHAPTER XXXVII.

MURIEL TOWERS crowned a wooded steep, part of a wild and winding and sylvan valley at the bottom of which rushed a foaming stream. On the other side of the castle the scene, though extensive, was not less striking, and was essentially romantic. A vast park spread in all directions beyond the limit of the eye, and with much variety of character, ornate near the mansion, and choicely timbered; in other parts glens and spreading dells, masses of black pines and savage woods; everywhere, sometimes glittering and sometimes sullen, glimpses of the largest natural lake that inland England boasts, MURIEL MERE, and in the extreme distance moors, and the first crest of mountains. The park, too, was full of life, for there were not only herds of red and fallow deer, but, in its more secret haunts, wandered a race of wild cattle, extremely savage, white and dove-coloured, and said to be of the time of the Romans.

It was not without emotion that Lothair beheld the chief seat of his race. It was not the first time he had visited it. He had a clear and painful recollection of a brief, hurried, unkind glimpse caught of it in his very earliest boyhood.

His uncle had taken him there by some inconvenient cross-railroad, to avail themselves of which they had risen in the dark on a March morning, and in an east wind. When they arrived at their station they had hired an open fly drawn by a single horse, and when they had thus at last reached the uninhabited Towers, they entered by the offices, where Lothair was placed in the steward's room, by a smoky fire, given something to eat, and told that he might walk about and amuse himself, provided he did not go out of sight of the castle, while his uncle and the steward mounted their horses and rode over the estate; leaving Lothair for hours without companions, and returning just in time, in a shivering twilight, to clutch him up, as it were, by the nape of the neck, twist him back again into the one-horse fly, and regain the railroad; his uncle praising himself the whole time for the satisfactory and business-like manner in which he had planned and completed the expedition.

What a contrast to present circumstances! Although Lothair had wished, and thought he had secured, that his arrival at Muriel should be quite private and even unknown, and that all ceremonies and celebrations should be postponed for a few days, during which he hoped to become a little more familiar with his home, the secret could not be kept, and the county would not tolerate this reserve. He was met at the station by five hundred horsemen all well mounted, and some of them gentlemen of high degree, who insisted upon accompanying him to his gates. His carriage passed under triumphal arches, and choirs of enthusiastic children, waving parochial banners, hymned his auspicious approach.

At the park-gates his cavalcade quitted him with that delicacy of feeling which always distinguishes Englishmen, however rough their habit. As their attendance was self-invited, they would not intrude upon his home.

'Your Lordship will have enough to do to-day without being troubled with us,' said their leader as he shook hands with Lothair.

But Lothair would not part with them thus. With the inspiring recollection of his speech at the Fenian meeting, Lothair was not afraid of rising in his barouche and addressing them. What he said was said very well, and it was addressed to a people who, though the shyest in the world, have a passion for public speaking, than which no achievement more tests reserve. It was something to be a great peer and a great proprietor, and to be young and singularly well-favoured; but to be able to make a speech, and such a good one, such cordial words in so strong and musical a voice: all felt at once they were in the presence of the natural leader of the county. The enthusiasm of the hunting-field burst forth. They gave him three ringing cheers, and jostled their horses forward that they might grasp his hand.

The park-gates were open, and the postilions dashed along through scenes of loveliness on which Lothair would fain have lingered, but he consoled himself with the recollection that he should probably have an opportunity of seeing them again. Sometimes his carriage seemed in the heart of an ancient forest; sometimes the deer, startled at his approach, were scudding over expanding lawns; then his course wound by the margin of a sinuous lake with green islands and golden gondolas; and then, after advancing through stately avenues, he arrived at mighty gates of wondrous workmanship, that once had been the boast of a celebrated convent on the Danube, but which, in the days of revolutions, had reached England, and had been obtained by the grandfather of Lothair to guard the choice demesne that was the vicinage of his castle.

When we remember that Lothair, notwithstanding his rank and vast wealth, had never, from the nature of things,

been the master of an establishment, it must be admitted
that the present occasion was a little trying for his nerves.
The whole household of the Towers were arrayed and
arranged in groups on the steps of the chief entrance.
The steward of the estate, who had been one of the
cavalcade, had galloped on before, and he was of course the
leading spirit, and extended his arm to his Lord as Lothair
descended from his carriage. The house-steward, the chief
butler, the head-gardener, the chief of the kitchen, the
head-keeper, the head-forester, and grooms of the stud and
of the chambers, formed one group behind the housekeeper,
a grave and distinguished-looking female, who curtseyed
like the old court; half a dozen powdered gentlemen,
glowing in crimson liveries, indicated the presence of my
Lord's footmen; while the rest of the household, considerable in numbers, were arranged in two groups, according to their sex, and at a respectful distance.

What struck Lothair (who was always thinking, and
who had no inconsiderable fund of humour in his sweet
and innocent nature) was the wonderful circumstance that,
after so long an interval of neglect and abeyance, he should
find himself the master of so complete and consummate a
household.

'Castles and parks,' he thought, 'I had a right to count
on, and, perhaps, even pictures, but how I came to possess
such a work of art as my groom of the chambers, who
seems as respectfully haughty and as calmly graceful as if
he were at Brentham itself, and whose coat must have been
made in Savile Row, quite bewilders me.'

But Lothair, though he appreciated Putney Giles, had
not yet formed a full conception of the resources and all
accomplished providence of that wondrous man, acting
under the inspiration of the consummate Apollonia.

Passing through the entrance hall, a lofty chamber
though otherwise of moderate dimensions Lothair was

ushered into his armoury, a gallery two hundred feet long,
with suits of complete mail ranged on each side, and the
walls otherwise covered with rare and curious weapons.
It was impossible, even for the master of this collection, to
suppress the delight and the surprise with which he beheld
the scene. We must remember, in his excuse, that he
beheld it for the first time.

The armoury led to a large and lofty octagonal chamber,
highly decorated, in the centre of which was the tomb of
Lothair's grandfather. He had raised it in his lifetime.
The tomb was of alabaster surrounded by a railing of pure
gold, and crowned with a recumbent figure of the deceased
in his coronet; a fanciful man, who lived in solitude,
building castles and making gardens.

What charmed Lothair most as he proceeded were the
number of courts and quadrangles in the castle, all of
bright and fantastic architecture, and each of which was a
garden, glowing with brilliant colours, and gay with the
voice of fountains or the forms of gorgeous birds. Our
young friend did not soon weary in his progress; even the
suggestions of the steward, that his Lordship's luncheon
was at command, did not restrain him. Ball-rooms, and
baronial halls, and long libraries with curiously stained
windows, and suites of dazzling saloons where he beheld
the original portraits of his parents of which he had miniatures; he saw them all, and was pleased and interested.
But what most struck and even astonished him was the
habitable air which pervaded the whole of this enormous
structure; too rare even when families habitually reside in
such dwellings; but almost inconceivable, when it was to
be remembered that more than a generation had passed
without a human being living in these splendid chambers,
scarcely a human word being spoken in them. There was
not a refinement of modern furniture that was wanting;

o

even the tables were covered with the choicest publications
of the day.

'Mr. Putney Giles proposes to arrive. here to-morrow,'
said the steward. 'He thought your Lordship would like
to be a day or two alone.'

'He is the most sensible man I know,' said Lothair; 'he
always does the right thing. I think I will have my
luncheon now, Mr. Harvey, and I will go over the cellars
to-morrow.'

CHAPTER XXXVIII.

YES; Lothair wished to be alone. He had naturally a
love of solitude, but the events of the last few hours lent
an additional inducement to meditation. He was impressed
in a manner and degree not before experienced with the
greatness of his inheritance. His worldly position, until
to-day, had been an abstraction. After all he had only
been one of a crowd, which he resembled. But the sight
of this proud and abounding territory, and the unexpected
encounter with his neighbours, brought to him a sense of
power and of responsibility. He shrank from neither.
The world seemed opening to him with all its delights, and
with him duty was one. He was also sensible of the beautiful, and the surrounding forms of nature and art charmed
him. Let us not forget that extreme youth and perfect health
were ingredients not wanting in the spell any more than
power or wealth. Was it then complete? Not without
the influence of woman.

To that gentle yet mystical sway the spirit of Lothair
had yielded. What was the precise character of his feelings to Theodora, what were his hopes or views, he had
hitherto had neither the time nor the inclination to make

certain. The present was so delightful, and the enjoyment of her society had been so constant and complete, that he had ever driven the future from his consideration. Had the conduct of Theodora been different, had she deigned to practise on his affections, appealed to his sensibility, stimulated or piqued his vanity, it might have been otherwise. In the distraction of his heart, or the disturbance of his temper, he might have arrived at conclusions, and even expressed them, incompatible with the exquisite and even sublime friendship, which had so strangely and beautifully arisen, like a palace in a dream, and absorbed his being. Although their acquaintance could hardly be numbered by months, there was no living person of whom he had seen so much, or to whom he had opened his heart and mind with such profuse ingenuousness. Nor on her part, though apparently shrinking from egotism, had there ever been any intellectual reserve. On the contrary, although never authoritative, and even when touching on her convictions, suggesting rather than dictating them, Lothair could not but feel that during the happy period he had passed in her society, not only his taste had refined but his mind had considerably opened; his views had become larger, his sympathies had expanded; he considered with charity things and even persons from whom a year ago he would have recoiled with alarm or aversion.

The time during which Theodora had been his companion was the happiest period of his life. It was more than that; he could conceive no felicity greater, and all that he desired was that it should endure. Since they first met, scarcely four and twenty hours had passed without his being in her presence; and now, notwithstanding the novelty and the variety of the objects around him, and the vast, and urgent, and personal interest which they involved, he felt a want which meeting her, or the daily prospect of meeting her, could alone supply. Her voice lingered in his ear; he gazed upon a countenance invisible to others; and he scarcely saw or did anything without almost unconsciously associating with it her opinion or approbation.

Well, then, the spell was complete. The fitfulness or melancholy which so often are the doom of youth, however otherwise favoured, who do not love, were not the condition, capricious or desponding, of Lothair. In him combined all the accidents and feelings which enchant existence.

He had been rambling in the solitudes of his park, and had thrown himself on the green shadow of a stately tree, his cheek resting on his arm, and lost in reverie amid the deep and sultry silence. Wealthy and young, noble and full of noble thoughts, with the inspiration of health, surrounded by the beautiful, and his heart softened by feelings as exquisite, Lothair, nevertheless, could not refrain from pondering over the mystery of that life which seemed destined to bring to him only delight.

'Life would be perfect,' he at length exclaimed, 'if it would only last.' But it will not last; and what then? He could not reconcile interest in this life with the conviction of another, and an eternal one. It seemed to him that, with such a conviction, man could have only one thought and one occupation, the future, and preparation for it. With such a conviction, what they called reality appeared to him more vain and nebulous than the scenes and sights of sleep. And he had that conviction; at least he had it once. Had he it now? Yes; he had it now, but modified perhaps; in detail. He was not so confident as he was a few months ago, that he could be ushered by a Jesuit from his deathbed to the society of St. Michael and all the Angels. There might be long processes of initiation, intermediate states of higher probation and refinement.

There might be a horrible and apathetic pause. When millions of ages appeared to be necessary to mature the crust of a rather insignificant planet, it might be presumption in man to assume that his soul, though immortal, was to reach its final destination, regardless of all the influences of space and time.

And the philosophers and distinguished men of science with whom of late he had frequently enjoyed the opportunity of becoming acquainted, what were their views? They differed among themselves : did any of them agree with him? How they accounted for everything except the only point on which man requires revelation! Chance, necessity, atomic theories, nebular hypotheses, development, evolution, the origin of worlds, human ancestry; here were high topics on none of which was there lack of argument; and, in a certain sense, of evidence; and what then? There must be design. The reasoning and the research of all philosophy could not be valid against that conviction. If there were no design, why, it would all be nonsense; and he could not believe in nonsense. And if there were design, there must be intelligence; and if intelligence, pure intelligence; and pure intelligence was inconsistent with any disposition but perfect good. But between the all-wise and the all-benevolent and man, according to the new philosophers, no relations were to be any longer acknowledged. They renounce in despair the possibility of bringing man into connexion with that First Cause which they can neither explain nor deny. But man requires that there shall be direct relations between the created and the Creator; and that in those relations he should find a solution of the perplexities of existence. The brain that teems with illimitable thought will never recognise as his creator any power of nature, however irresistible, that is not gifted with consciousness. Atheism may be consistent with fine taste, and fine taste under certain conditions may for a time regulate a polished society; but ethics with atheism are impossible; and without ethics no human order can be strong or permanent.

The Church comes forward, and, without equivocation, offers to establish direct relations between God and man. Philosophy denies its title, and disputes its power. Why? Because they are founded on the supernatural. What is the supernatural? Can there be anything more miraculous than the existence of man and the world? anything more literally supernatural than the origin of things? The Church explains what no one else pretends to explain, and which, everyone agrees, it is of first moment should be made clear.

The clouds of a summer eve were glowing in the creative and flickering blaze of the vanished sun, that had passed like a monarch from the admiring sight, yet left his pomp behind. The golden and umber vapours fell into forms that to the eye of the musing Lothair depicted the objects of his frequent meditation. There seemed to rise in the horizon the dome and campaniles and lofty aisles of some celestial fane, such as he had often more than dreamed of raising to the revealed author of life and death. Altars arose and sacred shrines, and delicate chantries and fretted spires; now the flashing phantom of heavenly choirs, and then the dim response of cowled and earthly cenobites:

These are black Vesper's pageants!

CHAPTER XXXIX.

LOTHAIR was quite glad to see Mr. Putney Giles. That gentleman indeed was an universal favourite. He was intelligent, acquainted with everything except theology and metaphysics, liked to oblige, a little to patronise, never made difficulties, and always overcame them. His bright blue eye, open forehead, and sunny face indicated a man full of resource, and with a temper of natural sweetness.

The lawyer and his noble client had a great deal of business to transact. Lothair was to know his position in detail preparatory to releasing his guardians from their responsibilities, and assuming the management of his own affairs. Mr. Putney Giles was a first-rate man of business. With all his pleasant, easy manner he was precise and methodical, and was not content that his client should be less master of his own affairs than his lawyer. The mornings passed over a table covered with despatch-boxes and piles of ticketed and banded papers, and then they looked after the workmen who were preparing for the impending festivals, or rode over the estate.

'That is our weak point,' said Mr. Putney Giles, pointing to a distant part of the valley. 'We ought to have both sides of the valley. Your Lordship will have to consider whether you can devote the 200,000*l.* of the second and extinct trust to a better purpose than in obtaining that estate.'

Lothair had always destined that particular sum for the cathedral, the raising of which was to have been the first achievement of his majority; but he did not reply.

In a few days the guests began to arrive, but gradually. The Duke and Duchess and Lady Corisande came the first,

and were one day alone with Lothair, for Mr. Putney Giles
had departed to fetch Apollonia.

Lothair was unaffectedly gratified at not only receiving
his friends at his own castle, but under these circumstances
of intimacy. They had been the first persons who had
been kind to him, and he really loved the whole family.
They arrived rather late, but he would show them to their
rooms, and they were choice ones, himself, and then they
dined together in the small green dining-room. Nothing
could be more graceful or more cordial than the whole
affair. The Duchess seemed to beam with affectionate
pleasure as Lothair fulfilled his duties as their host; the
Duke praised the claret, and he seldom praised anything;
while Lady Corisande only regretted that the impending
twilight had prevented her from seeing the beautiful country, and expressed lively interest in the morrow's inspection of the castle and domain. Sometimes her eyes met
those of Lothair, and she was so happy that she unconsciously smiled.

'And to-morrow,' said Lothair, 'I am delighted to say,
we shall have to ourselves; at least all the morning. We
will see the castle first, and then, after luncheon, we will
drive about everywhere.'

'Everywhere,' said Corisande.

'It was very nice your asking us first, and alone,' said
the Duchess.

'It was very nice you coming, dear Duchess,' said
Lothair, 'and most kind, as you ever are to me.'

'Duke of Brecon is coming to you on Thursday,' said
the Duke; 'he told me so at White's.'

'Perhaps you would like to know, Duchess, whom you
are going to meet,' said Lothair.

'I should much like to hear. Pray tell us.'

'It is a rather formidable array,' said Lothair, and he
took out a paper. 'First, there are all the notables of the

county. 1 do not know any of them personally, so I wrote to each of them a letter, as well as sending them a formal invitation. I thought that was right.'

'Quite right,' said the Duchess. 'Nothing could be more proper.'

'Well, the first person, of course, is the Lord Lieutenant. He is coming.'

'By the bye, let me see, who is your lord lieutenant?' said the Duke.

'Lord Agramont.'

'To be sure. I was at college with him, a very good fellow; but I have never met him since, except once at Boodle's; and I never saw a man so red and grey, and I remember him such a good-looking fellow! He must have lived immensely in the country, and never thought of his person,' said the Duke in a tone of pity, and playing with his moustache.

'Is there a Lady Agramont?' enquired the Duchess.

'Oh yes! and she also honours me with her presence,' said Lothair.

'And who was Lady Agramont?'

'Oh! his cousin,' said the Duke. 'The Agramonts always marry their cousins. His father did the same thing. They are so shy. It is a family that never was in society and never will be. I was at Agramont Castle once when I was at college, and I never shall forget it. We used to sit down forty or fifty every day to dinner, entirely maiden aunts and clergymen, and that sort of thing. However, I shall be truly glad to see Agramont again, for, notwithstanding all these disadvantages, he is a thoroughly good fellow.'

'Then there is the High Sheriff,' continued Lothair; 'and both the county members and their wives; and Mrs. High Sheriff too. I believe there is some tremendous question respecting the precedency of this lady. There is

no doubt that, in the county, the High Sheriff takes
precedence of everyone, even of the Lord Lieutenant; but
how about his wife? Perhaps your Grace could aid me?
Mr. Putney Giles said he would write about it to the
Heralds' College.'

'I should give her the benefit of any doubt,' said the
Duchess.

'And then our Bishop is coming,' said Lothair.

'Oh! I am so glad you have asked the Bishop,' said
Lady Corisande.

'There could be no doubt about it,' said Lothair. 'I do
not know how his Lordship will get on with one of my
guardians, the Cardinal; but his Eminence is not here in a
priestly character; and, as for that, there is less chance of
his differing with the Cardinal than with my other guardian,
Lord Culloden, who is a member of the Free Kirk.'

'Is Lord Culloden coming?' said the Duchess.

'Yes, and with two daughters, Flora and Grizell. I
remember my cousins, good-natured little girls, but Mr.
Putney Giles tells me that the shortest is six feet high.'

'I think we shall have a very amusing party,' said the
Duchess.

'You know all the others,' said Lothair. 'No, by the
bye, there is the Dean of my college coming, and Monsignore Catesby, a great friend of the St. Jeromes.'

Lady Corisande looked grave.

'The St. Jeromes will be here to-morrow,' continued
Lothair, 'and the Montairys and the St. Aldegondes. I
have half an idea that Bertram and Carisbrooke and Hugo
Bohun will be here to-night; Duke of Brecon on Thursday.
And that, I think, is all, except an American lady and
gentleman, whom I think you will like; great friends of
mine: I knew them this year at Oxford, and they were
very kind to me. He is a man of considerable fortune;
they have lived at Paris a good deal.'

'I have known Americans who lived at Paris,' said the Duke; 'very good sort of people, and no end of money some of them.'

'I believe Colonel Campian has large estates in the South,' said Lothair; 'but, though really I have no right to speak of his affairs, he must have suffered very much.'

'Well, he has the consolation of suffering in a good cause,' said the Duke. 'I shall be happy to make his acquaintance. I look upon an American gentleman with large estates in the South as a real aristocrat; and whether he gets his rents, or whatever his returns may be, or not, I should always treat him with respect.'

'I have heard the American women are very pretty,' said Lady Corisande.

'Mrs. Campian is very distinguished,' said Lothair; 'but I think she was an Italian.'

'They promise to be an interesting addition to our party,' said the Duchess, and she rose.

CHAPTER XL.

THERE never was anything so successful as the arrangements of the next day. After breakfast they inspected the castle, and in the easiest manner, without form and without hurry, resting occasionally in a gallery or a saloon, never examining a cabinet, and only looking at a picture now and then. Generally speaking, nothing is more fatiguing than the survey of a great house, but this enterprise was conducted with so much tact and consideration, and much which they had to see was so beautiful and novel, that everyone was interested, and remained quite fresh for their subsequent exertions. 'And then the Duke is so much amused,' said the Duchess to her daughter, delighted

at the unusual excitement of the handsome, but somewhat
too serene, partner of her life.

After luncheon they visited the gardens, which had been
formed in a sylvan valley enclosed with gilded gates. The
creator of this paradise had been favoured by nature, and
had availed himself of this opportunity. The contrast
between the parterres blazing with colour and the sylvan
background, the undulating paths over romantic heights,
the fanes and the fountains, the glittering statues, and the
Babylonian terraces, formed a whole much of which was
beautiful, and all of which was striking and singular.

'Perhaps too many temples,' said Lothair, 'but this ancestor of mine had some imagination.'

A carriage met them on the other side of the valley, and
then they soon entered the park.

'I am almost as much a stranger here as yourself, dear
Duchess,' said Lothair; 'but I have seen some parts which
I think will please you.' And they commenced a drive of
varying, but unceasing, beauty.

'I hope I shall see the wild cattle,' said Lady Corisande.

Lady Corisande saw the wild cattle, and many other
things which gratified and charmed her. It was a long drive,
even of hours, and yet no one was for a moment wearied.

'What a delightful day!' Lady Corisande exclaimed in
her mother's dressing-room. 'I have never seen any place
so beautiful.'

'I agree with you,' said the Duchess; 'but what pleases
me most are his manners. They were always kind and
natural, but they are so polished, so exactly what they
ought to be; and he always says the right thing. I never
knew anyone who had so matured.'

'Yes; it is very little more than a year since he came
to us at Brentham,' said Lady Corisande thoughtfully.
'Certainly he has greatly changed. I remember he could
hardly open his lips; and now I think him very agreeable.'

'He is more than that,' said the Duchess, 'he is interesting.'

'Yes,' said Lady Corisande; 'he is interesting.'

'What delights me,' said the Duchess, 'is to see his enjoyment of his position. He seems to take such an interest in everything. It makes me happy to see him so happy.'

'Well, I hardly know,' said Lady Corisande, 'about that. There is something occasionally about his expression which I should hardly describe as indicative of happiness or content. It would be ungrateful to describe one as *distrait*, who seems to watch all one's wants, and hangs on every word; and yet, especially as we returned, and when we were all of us a little silent, there was a remarkable abstraction about him ; I caught it once or twice before, earlier in the day ; his mind seemed in another place, and anxiously.'

'He has a great deal to think of,' said the Duchess.

'I fear it is that dreadful Monsignore Catesby,' said Lady Corisande with a sigh.

CHAPTER XLI.

THE arrival of the guests was arranged with judgment. The personal friends came first; the formal visitors were invited only for the day before the public ceremonies commenced. No more dinners in small green dining-rooms. While the Duchess was dressing, Bertha St. Aldegonde and Victoria Montairy, who had just arrived, came in to give her a rapid embrace while their own toilettes were unpacking.

'Granville has come, mamma; I did not think that he would till the last moment. He said he was so afraid of being bored. There is a large party by this train; the St. Jeromes, Bertram, Mr. Bohun, Lord Carisbrooke, and some others we do not know.'

The Cardinal had been expected to-day, but he had telegraphed that his arrival must be postponed in consequence of business until the morrow, which day had been previously fixed for the arrival of his fellow guardian and trustee, the Earl of Culloden, and his daughters, the Ladies Flora and Grizell Falkirk. Monsignore Catesby had, however, arrived by this train, and the persons 'whom they did not know,' the Campians.

Lothair waited on Colonel Campian immediately and welcomed him, but he did not see Theodora. Still he had enquired after her, and left her a message, and hoped that she would take some tea; and thus, as he flattered himself, broken a little the strangeness of their meeting under his roof; but, notwithstanding all this, when she really entered the drawing-room he was seized with such a palpitation of the heart that for a moment he thought he should be unequal to the situation. But the serenity of Theodora reassured him. The Campians came in late, and all eyes were upon them. Lothair presented Theodora to the Duchess, who being prepared for the occasion, said exactly the right thing in the best manner, and invited Mrs. Campian to sit by her, and then Theodora being launched, Lothair whispered something to the Duke, who nodded, and the Colonel was introduced to his Grace. The Duke, always polite but generally cold, was more than courteous; he was cordial; he seemed to enjoy the opportunity of expressing his high consideration for a gentleman of the Southern States.

So the first step was over; Lothair recovered himself; the palpitation subsided; and the world still went on. The Campians had made a good start, and the favourable impression hourly increased. At dinner Theodora sat between Lord St. Jerome and Bertram, and talked more to the middle-aged peer than to the distinguished youth, who would willingly have engrossed her attention. All mothers

admire such discretion, especially in a young and beautiful
married woman, so the verdict of the evening among the
great ladies was, that Theodora was distinguished, and that
all she said or did was in good taste. On the plea of her
being a foreigner, she was at once admitted into a certain
degree of social intimacy. Had she had the misfortune of
being native-born and had flirted with Bertram, she would
probably, particularly with so much beauty, have been
looked upon as 'a horrid woman,' and have been relegated
for amusement, during her visit, to the attentions of the
dark sex. But, strange to say, the social success of Colonel
Campian was not less eminent than that of his distinguished wife. The character which the Duke gave of
him commanded universal sympathy. 'You know he is a
gentleman,' said the Duke; 'he is not a Yankee. People
make the greatest mistakes about these things. He is a
gentleman of the South; they have no property but land;
and I am told his territory was immense. He always
lived at Paris and in the highest style, disgusted of course
with his own country. It is not unlikely he may have lost
his estates now; but that makes no difference to me. I
shall treat him and all Southern gentlemen, as our fathers
treated the emigrant nobility of France.'

'Hugo,' said St. Aldegonde to Mr. Bohun, 'I wish you
would tell Bertha to come to me. I want her. She is
talking to a lot of women at the other end of the room,
and, if I go to her, I am afraid they will get hold of me.'

The future Duchess, who lived only to humour her lord,
was at his side in an instant. 'You wanted me, Granville?'

'Yes; you know I was afraid, Bertha, I should be bored
here. I am not bored. I like this American fellow. He
understands the only two subjects which interest me;
horses and tobacco.'

'I am charmed, Granville, that you are not bored. I

told mamma that you were very much afraid you would be.'

'Yes; but I tell you what, Bertha, I cannot stand any of the ceremonies. I shall go before they begin. Why cannot Lothair be content with receiving his friends in a quiet way? It is all humbug about the county. If he wants to do something for the county, he can build a wing to the infirmary, or something of that sort, and not bore us with speeches and fireworks. It is a sort of thing I cannot stand.'

And you shall not, dear Granville. The moment you are bored, you shall go. Only you are not bored at present.'

'Not at present; but I expected to be.'

'Yes; so I told mamma; but that makes the present more delightful.'

The St. Jeromes were going to Italy and immediately. Their departure had only been postponed in order that they might be present at the majority of Lothair. Miss Arundel had at length succeeded in her great object. They were to pass the winter at Rome. Lord St. Jerome was quite pleased at having made the acquaintance at dinner of a Roman lady, who spoke English so perfectly; and Lady St. Jerome, who in consequence fastened upon Theodora, was getting into ecstasies, which would have been embarrassing had not her new acquaintance skilfully checked her.

'We must be satisfied that we both admire Rome,' said Mrs. Campian, 'though we admire it for different reasons. Although a Roman, I am not a Roman Catholic; and Colonel Campian's views on Italian affairs generally would, I fear, not entirely agree with Lord St. Jerome's.'

'Naturally,' said Lady St. Jerome gracefully dropping the subject, and remembering that Colonel Campian was a citizen of the United States, which accounted in her apprehension for his peculiar opinions.

Lothair, who had been watching his opportunity the

whole evening, approached Theodora. He meant to have expressed his hope that she was not wearied by her journey, but instead of that he said, 'Your presence here makes me inexpressibly happy.'

'I think everybody seems happy to be your guest,' she replied, parrying, as was her custom, with a slight kind smile, and a low, sweet, unembarrassed voice, any personal allusion from Lothair of unusual energy or ardour.

'I wanted to meet you at the station to-day,' he continued, 'but there were so many people coming, that——' and he hesitated.

'It would really have been more embarrassing to us than to yourself,' she said. 'Nothing could be better than all the arrangements.'

'I sent my own brougham for you,' said Lothair. 'I hope there was no mistake about it.'

'None: your servant gave us your kind message; and as for the carriage it was too delightful. Colonel Campian was so pleased with it, that he has promised to give me one, with your permission, exactly the same.'

'I wish you would accept the one you used to-day.'

'You are too magnificent; you really must try to forget, with us, that you are the lord of Muriel Towers. But I will willingly use your carriages as much as you please, for I caught glimpses of beauty to-day in our progress from the station that made me anxious to explore your delightful domain.'

There was a slight burst of merriment from a distant part of the room, and everybody looked around. Colonel Campian had been telling a story to a group formed of the Duke, St. Aldegonde, and Mr. Bohun.

'Best story I ever heard in my life,' exclaimed St. Aldegonde, who prided himself when he did laugh, which was rare, on laughing loud. But even the Duke tittered, and Hugo Bohun smiled.

P

'I am glad to see the Colonel get on so well with everyone,' said Lothair; 'I was afraid he might have been bored.'

'He does not know what that means,' said Theodora; 'and he is so natural and so sweet-tempered, and so intelligent, that it seems to me he always is popular.'

'Do you think that will be a match?' said Monsignore Catesby to Miss Arundel.

'Well, I rather believe in the Duke of Brecon,' she replied. They were referring to Lord Carisbrooke who appeared to be devoted to Lady Corisande. 'Do you admire the American lady?'

'Who is an Italian, they tell me, though she does not look like one. What do you think of her?' said the Monsignore, evading, as was his custom, a direct reply.

'Well, I think she is very distinguished: unusual. I wonder where our host became acquainted with them? Do you know?'

'Not yet; but I dare say Mr. Bohun can tell us;' and he addressed that gentleman accordingly as he was passing by.

'Not the most remote idea,' said Mr. Bohun. 'You know the Colonel is not a Yankee; he is a tremendous swell. The Duke says with more land than he has.'

'He seems an agreeable person,' said Miss Arundel.

'Well, he tells anecdotes; he has just been telling one; Granville likes anecdotes; they amuse him, and he likes to be amused: that is all he cares about. I hate anecdotes, and I always get away when conversation falls into what Pinto calls its anecdotage.'

'You do not like to be amused?'

'Not too much; I like to be interested.'

'Well,' said Miss Arundel, 'so long as a person can talk agreeably, I am satisfied. I think to talk well a rare gift; quite as rare as singing: and yet you expect everyone to be able to talk, and very few to be able to sing.'

'There are amusing people who do not interest,' said the Monsignore, 'and interesting people who do not amuse. What I like is an agreeable person.'

'My idea of an agreeable person,' said Hugo Bohun, 'is a person who agrees with me.'

'Talking of singing, something is going to happen,' said Miss Arundel.

A note was heard; a celebrated professor had entered the room and was seated at the piano which he had just touched. There was a general and unconscious hush, and the countenance of Lord St. Aldegonde wore a rueful expression. But affairs turned out better than could be anticipated. A young and pretty girl, dressed in white with a gigantic sash of dazzling beauty, played upon the violin with a grace, and sentiment, and marvellous skill, and passionate expression, worthy of St. Cecilia. She was a Hungarian lady, and this was her English début. Everybody praised her, and everybody was pleased; and Lord St. Aldegonde, instead of being bored, took a wondrous rose out of his buttonhole and presented it to her.

The performance only lasted half an hour, and then the ladies began to think of their bowers. Lady St. Aldegonde, before she quitted the room, was in earnest conversation with her lord.

'I have arranged all that you wished, Granville,' she said, speaking rapidly and holding a candlestick. 'We are to see the castle to-morrow, and the gardens and the parks and everything else, but you are not to be bored at all, and not to lose your shooting. The moors are sixteen miles off, but our host says, with an omnibus and a good team (and he will give you a first-rate one), you can do it in an hour and ten minutes, certainly an hour and a quarter; and you are to make your own party in the smoking-room to-night, and take a capital luncheon with you.'

P 2

'All right: I shall ask the Yankee; and I should like to take that Hungarian girl too, if she would only fiddle to us at luncheon.'

CHAPTER XLII.

NEXT day the Cardinal, with his secretary and his chaplain, arrived. Monsignore Catesby received his Eminence at the station, and knelt and kissed his hand as he stepped from the carriage. The Monsignore had wonderfully manœuvred that the whole of the household should have been marshalled to receive this Prince of the Church, and perhaps have performed the same ceremony: no religious recognition, he assured them, in the least degree involved, only an act of not unusual respect to a foreign Prince; but considering that the Bishop of the diocese and his suite were that day expected, to say nothing of the Presbyterian guardian probably arriving by the same train, Lothair would not be persuaded to sanction any ceremony whatever. Lady St. Jerome and Miss Arundel, however, did their best to compensate for this omission with reverences which a posture master might have envied, and certainly would not have surpassed. They seemed to sink into the earth, and then slowly and supernaturally to emerge. The Bishop had been at college with the Cardinal and intimate with him, though they now met for the first time since his secession: a not uninteresting rencounter. The Bishop was high-church, and would not himself have made a bad cardinal, being polished and plausible, well-lettered, yet quite a man of the world. He was fond of society, and justified his taste in this respect by the flattering belief that by his presence he was extending the power of the Church; certainly favouring an ambition which could not be described as being moderate. The Bishop had no abstract prejudice against gentlemen who wore red hats, and under ordinary circumstances would have welcomed his brother churchman with unaffected cordiality, not to say sympathy; but in the present instance, however gracious his mien and honeyed his expressions, he only looked upon the Cardinal as a dangerous rival, intent upon clutching from his fold the most precious of his flock, and he had long looked to this occasion as the one which might decide the spiritual welfare and career of Lothair. The odds were not to be despised. There were two Monsignores in the room besides the Cardinal, but the Bishop was a man of contrivance and resolution, not easily disheartened or defeated. Nor was he without allies. He did not count much on the University don, who was to arrive on the morrow in the shape of the head of an Oxford house, though he was a don of magnitude. This eminent personage had already let Lothair slip from his influence. But the Bishop had a subtle counsellor in his chaplain, who wore as good a cassock as any Monsignore, and he brought with him also a trusty archdeacon in a purple coat, whose countenance was quite entitled to a place in the Acta Sanctorum.

It was amusing to observe the elaborate courtesy and more than Christian kindness which the rival prelates and their official followers extended to each other. But under all this unction on both sides were unceasing observation, and a vigilance that never flagged; and on both sides there was an uneasy but irresistible conviction that they were on the eve of one of the decisive battles of the social world. Lord Culloden also at length appeared with his daughters, Ladies Flora and Grizell. They were quite as tall as Mr. Putney Giles had reported, but very pretty, with radiant complexions, sunny blue eyes, and flaxen locks. Their dimples and white shoulders and small feet and hands were much admired. Mr. Giles also returned with Apollonia; and at length also appeared the rival of Lord Carisbrooke, his Grace of Brecon.

Lothair had passed a happy morning, for he had contrived, without difficulty, to be the companion of Theodora during the greater part of it. As the Duchess and Lady Corisande had already inspected the castle, they disappeared after breakfast to write letters; and when the after-luncheon expedition took place, Lothair allotted them to the care of Lord Carisbrooke, and himself became the companion of Lady St. Jerome and Theodora.

Notwithstanding all his efforts in the smoking-room, St. Aldegonde had only been able to induce Colonel Campian to be his companion in the shooting expedition, and the Colonel fell into the lure only through his carelessness and good-nature. He much doubted the discretion of his decision as he listened to Lord St. Aldegonde's reasons for the expedition in their rapid journey to the moors.

'I do not suppose,' he said, 'we shall have any good sport; but when you are in Scotland and come to me, as I hope you will, I will give you something you will like. But it is a great thing to get off seeing the Towers, and the gardens, and all that sort of thing. Nothing bores me so much as going over a man's house. Besides, we get rid of the women.'

The meeting between the two guardians did not promise to be as pleasant as that between the Bishop and the Cardinal, but the crusty Lord Culloden was scarcely a match for the social dexterity of his Eminence. The Cardinal, crossing the room, with winning ceremony approached and addressed his colleague.

'We can have no more controversies, my Lord, for our reign is over;' and he extended a delicate hand, which the surprised peer touched with a huge finger.

'Yes; it all depends on himself now,' replied Lord Culloden with a grim smile; 'and I hope he will not make a fool of himself.'

'What have you got for us to-night?' enquired Lothair

of Mr. Giles, as the gentleman rose from the dining table.

Mr. Giles said he would consult his wife, but Lothair observing he would himself undertake that office, when he entered the saloon addressed Apollonia. Nothing could be more skilful than the manner in which Mrs. Giles in this party assumed precisely the position which equally became her and suited her own views; at the same time the somewhat humble friend, but the trusted counsellor, of the Towers, she disarmed envy and conciliated consideration. Never obtrusive, yet always prompt and prepared with unfailing resource, and gifted apparently with universal talents, she soon became the recognised medium by which everything was suggested or arranged; and before eight and forty hours had passed she was described by Duchesses and their daughters as that 'dear Mrs. Giles.'

'Monsieur Raphael and his sister came down in the train with us,' said Mrs. Giles to Lothair; 'the rest of the troupe will not be here until to-morrow; but they told me they could give you a perfect proverbe if your Lordship would like it; and the Spanish conjuror is here; but I rather think, from what I gather, that the young ladies would like a dance.'

'I do not much fancy acting the moment these great churchmen have arrived, and with Cardinals and Bishops I would rather not have dances the first night. I almost wish we had kept the Hungarian lady for this evening.'

'Shall I send for her? she is ready.'

'The repetition would be too soon, and would show a great poverty of resources,' said Lothair smiling; 'what we want is some singing.'

'Mardoni ought to have been here to-day,' said Mrs. Giles; 'but he never keeps his engagements.'

'I think our amateur materials are rather rich,' said Lothair.

'There is Mrs. Campian,' said Apollonia in a low voice, but Lothair shook his head.

'But perhaps if others set her the example,' he added after a pause; 'Lady Corisande is firstrate, and all her sisters sing; I will go and consult the Duchess.'

There was soon a stir in the room. Lady St. Aldegonde and her sisters approached the piano at which was seated the eminent professor. A note was heard, and there was silence. The execution was exquisite; and indeed there are few things more dainty than the blended voices of three women. No one seemed to appreciate the performance more than Mrs. Campian, who, greatly attracted by what was taking place, turned a careless ear even to the honeyed sentences of no less a personage than the Lord Bishop.

After an interval Lady Corisande was handed to the piano by Lothair. She was in fine voice and sang with wonderful effect. Mrs. Campian, who seemed much interested, softly rose and stole to the outward circle of the group which had gathered round the instrument. When the sounds had ceased, amid the general applause her voice of admiration was heard. The Duchess approached her, evidently prompted by the general wish, and expressed her hope that Mrs. Campian would now favour them. It was not becoming to refuse when others had contributed so freely to the general entertainment, but Theodora was anxious not to place herself in competition with those who had preceded her. Looking over a volume of music she suggested to Lady Corisande a duet in which the peculiarities of their two voices, which in character were quite different, one being a soprano and the other a contralto, might be displayed. And very seldom in a private chamber had anything of so high a class been heard. Not a lip moved except those of the singers, so complete was the fascination, till the conclusion elicited a burst of irresistible applause.

'In imagination I am throwing endless bouquets,' said Hugo Bohun.

'I wish we could induce her to give us a recitation from Alfieri,' said Mrs. Putney Giles in a whisper to Lady St. Aldegonda. 'I heard it once: it was the finest thing I ever listened to.'

'But cannot we?' said Lady St. Aldegonde.

Apollonia shook her head. 'She is extremely reserved. I am quite surprised that she sang; but she could not well refuse after your Ladyship and your sisters had been so kind.'

'But if the Lord of the Towers asks her,' suggested Lady St. Aldegonde.

'No, no,' said Mrs. Giles, 'that would not do; nor would he. He knows she dislikes it. A word from Colonel Campian and the thing would be settled; but it is rather absurd to invoke the authority of a husband for so light a matter.'

'I should like so much to hear her,' said Lady St. Aldegonde. 'I think I will ask her myself. I will go and speak to mamma.'

There was much whispering and consulting in the room, but unnoticed, as general conversation had now been resumed. The Duchess sent for Lothair and conferred with him; but Lothair seemed to shake his head. Then her Grace rose and approached Colonel Campian, who was talking to Lord Culloden, and then the Duchess and Lady St. Aldegonde went to Mrs. Campian. Then, after a short time, Lady St. Aldegonde rose and fetched Lothair.

'Her Grace tells me,' said Theodora, 'that Colonel Campian wishes me to give a recitation. I cannot believe that such a performance can ever be generally interesting, especially in a foreign language, and I confess that I would rather not exhibit. But I do not like to be churlish when all are so amiable and compliant, and the Duchess tells me

that it cannot well be postponed, for this is the last quiet
night we shall have. What I want is a screen, and I must
be a moment alone, before I venture on these enterprises. I
require it to create the ideal presence.'

Lothair and Bertram arranged the screen, the Duchess
and Lady St. Aldegonde glided about, and tranquilly intimated what was going to occur, so that, without effort,
there was in a moment complete silence and general expectation. Almost unnoticed Mrs. Campian had disappeared,
whispering a word as she passed to the eminent conductor,
who was still seated at the piano. The company had
almost unconsciously grouped themselves in the form of
a theatre, the gentlemen generally standing behind the
ladies who were seated. There were some bars of solemn
music, and then to an audience not less nervous than herself, Theodora came forward as Electra in that beautiful
appeal to Clytemnestra, where she veils her mother's guilt
even while she intimates her more than terrible suspicion
of its existence, and makes one last desperate appeal of
pathetic duty in order to save her parent and her fated
house :

> O amata madre,
> Che fai ? Non credo io, no, che ardente fiamma
> Il cor ti avvampi.

The ineffable grace of her action, simple without redun-
dancy, her exquisite elocution, her deep yet controlled passion, and the magic of a voice thrilling even in a whisper,
this form of Phidias with the genius of Sophocles, entirely
enraptured a fastidious audience. When she ceased, there
was an outburst of profound and unaffected appreciation ;
and Lord St. Aldegonde, who had listened in a sort of
ecstasy, rushed forward, with a countenance as serious as
the theme, to offer his thanks and express his admiration.

And then they gathered round her, all these charming
women and some of these admiring men, as she would have

resumed her seat, and entreated her once more, only once more, to favour them. She caught the adoring glance of the Lord of the Towers, and her eyes seemed to enquire what she should do. 'There will be many strangers here to-morrow,' said Lothair, 'and next week all the world. This is a delight only for the initiated,' and he entreated her to gratify them.

'It shall be Alfieri's ode to America then,' said Theodora, 'if you please.'

'She is a Roman I believe,' said Lady St. Jerome to his Eminence, 'but not, alas! a child of the Church. Indeed I fear her views generally are advanced,' and she shook her head.

'At present,' said the Cardinal, 'this roof and this visit may influence her. I should like to see such powers engaged in the cause of God.'

The Cardinal was an entire believer in female influence, and a considerable believer in his influence over females; and he had good cause for his convictions. The catalogue of his proselytes was numerous and distinguished. He had not only converted a duchess and several countesses, but he had gathered into his fold a real Mary Magdalen. In the height of her beauty and her fame, the most distinguished member of the demi-monde had suddenly thrown up her golden whip and jingling reins, and cast herself at the feet of the Cardinal. He had a right, therefore, to be confident; and while his exquisite taste and consummate cultivation rendered it impossible that he should not have been deeply gratified by the performance of Theodora, he was really the whole time considering the best means by which such charms and powers could be enlisted in the cause of the Church.

After the ladies had retired, the gentlemen talked for a few minutes over the interesting occurrence of the evening.

'Do you know,' said the Bishop to the Duke and some surrounding auditors, 'fine as was the Electra, I preferred the ode to the tragedy. There was a tumult of her brow, especially in the address to Liberty, that was sublime— quite a Mœnad look.'

'What do you think of it, Carry?' said St. Aldegonde to Lord Carisbrooke.

'Brecon says she puts him in mind of Ristori.'

'She is not in the least like Ristori, or anyone else,' said St. Aldegonde. 'I never heard, I never saw anyone like her. I'll tell you what: you must take care what you say about her in the smoking-room, for her husband will be there, and an excellent fellow too. We went together to the moors this morning, and he did not bore me in the least. Only, if I had known as much about his wife as I do now, I would have stayed at home, and passed my morning with the women.'

CHAPTER XLIII.

St. ALDEGONDE loved to preside over the mysteries of the smoking-room. There, enveloped in his Egyptian robe, occasionally blurting out some careless or headstrong paradox to provoke discussion among others, which would amuse himself, rioting in a Rabelaisian anecdote, and listening with critical delight to endless memoirs of horses and prima-donnas, St. Aldegonde was never bored. Sometimes, too, when he could get hold of an eminent traveller, or some individual distinguished for special knowledge, St. Aldegonde would draw him out with skill, himself displaying an acquaintance with the particular topic which often surprised his habitual companions, for St. Aldegonde professed never to read; but he had no ordinary abilities,

and an original turn of mind and habit of life, which threw
him in the way of unusual persons of all classes, from
whom he imbibed or extracted a vast variety of queer,
always amusing, and not altogether useless, information.

'Lothair has only one weakness,' he said to Colonel
Campian as the ladies disappeared; 'he does not smoke.
Carry, you will come?'

'Well, I do not think I shall to-night,' said Lord Carisbrooke. Lady Corisande, it appears, particularly disapproved of smoking.

'Hum!' said St. Aldegonde; 'Duke of Brecon I know
will come, and Hugo and Bertram. My brother Montairy
would give his ears to come, but is afraid of his wife; and
then there is the Monsignore, a most capital fellow, who
knows everything.'

There were other gatherings before the midnight bell
struck at the Towers which discussed important affairs,
though they might not sit so late as the smoking party.
Lady St. Aldegonde had a reception in her room as well as
her lord. There the silent observation of the evening
found avenging expression in sparkling criticism; and the
summer lightning, though it generally blazed with harm-
less brilliancy, occasionally assumed a more arrowy character. The gentlemen of the smoking-room have it not all
their own way quite so much as they think. If, indeed, a
new school of Athens were to be pictured, the sages and
the students might be represented in exquisite dressing-
gowns, with slippers rarer than the lost one of Cinderella,
and brandishing beautiful brushes over tresses still more
fair. Then is the time when characters are never more
finely drawn, or difficult social questions more accurately
solved; knowledge without reasoning, and truth without
logic: the triumph of intuition! But we must not pro-
fane the mysteries of Bona Dea.

The Archdeacon and the Chaplain had also been in

council with the Bishop in his dressing-room, who, while
he dismissed them with his benison, repeated his apparently satisfactory assurance, that something would
happen 'the first thing after breakfast.'

Lothair did not smoke, but he did not sleep. He was
absorbed by the thought of Theodora. He could not but
be conscious, and so far he was pleased by the consciousness, that she was as fascinating to others as to himself.
What then? Even with the splendid novelty of his
majestic home, and all the excitement of such an incident
in his life, and the immediate prospect of their again meeting, he had felt, and even acutely, their separation. Whether it were the admiration of her by others which proved
his own just appreciation, or whether it were the unob-
trusive display of exquisite accomplishments, which with
all their intimacy she had never forced on his notice;
whatever the cause, her hold upon his heart and life, powerful as it was before, had strengthened. Lothair could
not conceive existence tolerable without her constant presence; and with her constant presence existence would be
rapture. It had come to that. All his musings, all his
profound investigation and high resolve, all his sublime
speculations on God and man, and life and immortality,
and the origin of things, and religious truth, ended in an
engrossing state of feeling, which could be denoted in that
form and in no other.

What then was his future? It seemed dark and distressing. Her constant presence his only happiness; her
constant presence impossible. He seemed on an abyss.

In eight and forty hours or so one of the chief provinces
of England would be blazing with the celebration of his
legal accession to his high estate. If anyone in the Queen's
dominions had to be fixed upon as the most fortunate and
happiest of her subjects, it might well be Lothair. If
happiness depend on lofty station, his ancient and here-

ditary rank was of the highest; if, as there seems no
doubt, the chief source of felicity in this country is wealth,
his vast possessions and accumulated treasure could not
easily be rivalled, while he had a matchless advantage over
those who pass, or waste, their grey and withered lives in
acquiring millions, in his consummate and healthy youth.
He had bright abilities, and a brighter heart. And yet the
unknown truth was, that this favoured being, on the eve of
this critical event, was pacing his chamber agitated and
infinitely disquieted, and struggling with circumstances
and feelings over which alike he seemed to have no control,
and which seemed to have been evoked without the exercise
of his own will, or that of any other person.

'I do not think I can blame myself,' he said; 'and I am
sure I cannot blame her. And yet ——'

He opened his window and looked upon the moonlit
garden, which filled the fanciful quadrangle. The light of
the fountain seemed to fascinate his eye, and the music of
its fall soothed him into reverie. The distressful images
that had gathered round his heart gradually vanished, and
all that remained to him was the reality of his happiness.
Her beauty and her grace, the sweet stillness of her
searching intellect, and the refined pathos of her disposition only occurred to him, and he dwelt on them with spell-
bound joy.

The great clock of the Towers sounded two.

'Ah!' said Lothair, 'I must try to sleep. I have got to
see the Bishop to-morrow morning. I wonder what he
wants.'

CHAPTER XLIV.

THE Bishop was particularly playful on the morrow at breakfast. Though his face beamed with Christian kindness, there was a twinkle in his eye which seemed not entirely superior to mundane self-complacency, even to a sense of earthly merriment. His seraphic raillery elicited sympathetic applause from the ladies, especially from the daughters of the house of Brentham, who laughed occasionally even before his angelic jokes were well launched. His lambent flashes sometimes even played over the Cardinal, whose cerulean armour, nevertheless, remained always unscathed. Monsignore Chidioch, however, who would once unnecessarily rush to the aid of his chief, was tumbled over by the Bishop with relentless gaiety, to the infinite delight of Lady Corisande, who only wished it had been that dreadful Monsignore Catesby. But, though less demonstrative, apparently not the least devout of his Lordship's votaries were the Lady Flora and the Lady Grizell. These young gentlewomen, though apparently gifted with appetites becoming their ample but far from graceless forms, contrived to satisfy all the wants of nature without taking their charmed vision for a moment off the prelate, or losing a word which escaped his consecrated lips. Sometimes even they ventured to smile, and then they looked at their father and sighed. It was evident, notwithstanding their appetites and their splendid complexions, which would have become the Aurora of Guido, that these young ladies had some secret sorrow which required a confidante. Their visit to Muriel Towers was their introduction to society, for the eldest had only just attained sweet seventeen. Young ladies under these circumstances always fall in love, but with their own sex. Lady Flora and Lady Grizell both

fell in love with Lady Corisande, and before the morning
had passed away she had become their friend and counsellor,
and the object of their devoted adoration. It seems that
their secret sorrow had its origin in that mysterious religious sentiment which agitates or affects every class and
condition of man, and which creates or destroys states,
though philosophers are daily assuring us 'that there is
nothing in it.' The daughters of the Earl of Culloden
could not stand any longer the Free Kirk, of which their
austere parent was a fiery votary. It seems that they had
been secretly converted to the Episcopal Church of Scotland by a governess, who pretended to be a daughter of the
Covenant, but who was really a niece of the Primus, and,
as Lord Culloden acutely observed, when he ignominiously
dismissed her, 'a Jesuit in disguise.' From that moment
there had been no peace in his house. His handsome and
gigantic daughters, who had hitherto been all meekness,
and who had obeyed him as they would a tyrant father of
the feudal ages, were resolute, and would not compromise
their souls. They humbly expressed their desire to enter
a convent, or to become at least sisters of mercy. Lord
Culloden raged and raved, and delivered himself of cynical
taunts, but to no purpose. The principle that forms free
kirks is a strong principle, and takes many forms, which
the social Polyphemes, who have only one eye, cannot perceive. In his desperate confusion, he thought that change
of scene might be a diversion when things were at the
worst, and this was the reason that he had, contrary to his
original intention, accepted the invitation of his ward.

Lady Corisande was exactly the guide the girls required.
They sate on each side of her, each holding her hand, which
they frequently pressed to their lips. As her form was
slight, though of perfect grace and symmetry, the contrast
between herself and her worshippers was rather startling;
but her noble brow, full of thought and purpose, the firm-

Q

ness of her chiselled lip, and the rich fire of her glance,
vindicated her post as the leading spirit.

They breakfasted in a room which opened on a gallery,
and at the other end of the gallery was an apartment
similar to the breakfast-room, which was the male morning-
room, and where the world could find the newspapers, or
join in half an hour's talk over the intended arrangements
of the day. When the breakfast-party broke up, the
Bishop approached Lothair, and looked at him earnestly.

'I am at your Lordship's service,' said Lothair, and they
quitted the breakfast-room together. Halfway down the
gallery they met Monsignore Catesby, who had in his hand
a number, just arrived, of a newspaper which was esteemed
an Ultramontane organ. He bowed as he passed them,
with an air of some exultation, and the Bishop and he
exchanged significant smiles, which, however, meant
different things. Quitting the gallery, Lothair led the way
to his private apartments; and, opening the door, ushered
in the Bishop.

Now what was contained in the Ultramontane organ
which apparently occasioned so much satisfaction to Monsignore Catesby? A deftly drawn-up announcement of
some important arrangements which had been deeply
planned. The announcement would be repeated in all the
daily papers, which were hourly expected. The world was
informed that his Eminence, Cardinal Grandison, now on a
visit at Muriel Towers to his ward, Lothair, would celebrate High Mass on the ensuing Sunday in the city which
was the episcopal capital of the Bishop's see, and afterwards preach on the present state of the Church of Christ.
As the Bishop must be absent from his cathedral that day,
and had promised to preach in the chapel at Muriel, there
was something dexterous in thus turning his Lordship's
flank, and desolating his diocese when he was not present
to guard it from the fiery dragon. It was also remarked

that there would be an unusual gathering of the Catholic
aristocracy for the occasion. The rate of lodgings in the
city had risen in consequence. At the end of the paragraph it was distinctly contradicted that Lothair had
entered the Catholic Church. Such a statement was declared to be 'premature,' as his guardian the Cardinal
would never sanction his taking such a step until he was
the master of his own actions; the general impression left
by the whole paragraph being, that the world was not to
be astonished if the first step of Lothair, on accomplishing
his majority, was to pursue the very course which was now
daintily described as premature.

At luncheon the whole party were again assembled.
The newspapers had arrived in the interval and had been
digested. Every one was aware of the Popish plot, as
Hugo Bohun called it. The Bishop, however, looked
serene and, if not as elate as in the morning, calm and
content. He sate by the Duchess, and spoke to her in a
low voice and with seriousness. The Monsignori watched
every expression.

When the Duchess rose the Bishop accompanied her into
the recess of a window, and she said, 'You may depend
upon me; I cannot answer for the Duke. It is not the
early rising; he always rises early in the country, but he
likes to read his letters before he dresses, and that sort of
thing. I think you had better speak to Lady Corisande
yourself.'

What had taken place at the interview of the Bishop with
Lothair, and what had elicited from the Duchess an assurance that the prelate might depend upon her, generally transpired, in consequence of some confidential communications,
in the course of the afternoon. It appeared that the Right
Reverend Lord had impressed, and successfully, on Lothair
the paramount duty of commencing the day of his majority
by assisting in an early celebration of the most sacred rite

q 2

of the Church. This, in the estimation of the Bishop, though he had not directly alluded to the subject in the interview, but had urged the act on higher grounds, would be a triumphant answer to the insidious and calumnious paragraphs which had circulated during the last six months, and an authentic testimony that Lothair was not going to quit the Church of his fathers.

This announcement, however, produced consternation in the opposite camp. It seemed to more than neutralise the anticipated effect of the programme, and the deftly-conceived paragraph. Monsignore Catesby went about whispering that he feared Lothair was going to overdo it; and considering what he had to go through on Monday, if it were only for considerations of health, an early celebration was inexpedient. He tried the Duchess, about whom he was beginning to hover a good deal, as he fancied she was of an impressionable disposition, and gave some promise of results; but here the ground had been too forcibly preoccupied: then he flew to Lady St. Aldegonde, but he had the mortification of learning from her lips that she herself contemplated being a communicant at the same time. Lady Corisande had been before him. All the energies of that young lady were put forth in order that Lothair should be countenanced on this solemn occasion. She conveyed to the Bishop before dinner the results of her exertions.

'You may count on Alberta St. Aldegonde and Victoria Montairy, and, I think, Lord Montairy also, if she presses him, which she has promised to do. Bertram must kneel by his friend at such a time. I think Lord Carisbrooke may: Duke of Brecon I can say nothing about at present.'

'Lord St. Aldegonde?' said the Bishop.

Lady Corisande shook her head.

There had been a conclave in the Bishop's room before dinner, in which the interview of the morning was discussed.

'It was successful; scarcely satisfactory,' said the Bishop. 'He is a very clever fellow, and knows a great deal. They have got hold of him, and he has all the arguments at his fingers' ends. When I came to the point he began to demur; I saw what was passing through his mind, and I said at once, "Your views are high: so are mine: so are those of the Church. It is a sacrifice, undoubtedly, in a certain sense. No sound theologian would maintain the simplicity of the elements; but that does not involve the coarse interpretation of the dark ages."'

'Good, good,' said the Archdeacon; 'and what is it your Lordship did not exactly like?'

'He fenced too much; and he said more than once, and in a manner I did not like, that, whatever were his views as to the Church, he thought he could on the whole conscientiously partake of this rite as administered by the Church of England.'

'Everything depends on this celebration,' said the Chaplain; 'after that his doubts and difficulties will disperse.'

'We must do our best that he may be well supported,' said the Archdeacon.

'No fear of that,' said the Bishop. 'I have spoken to some of our friends. We may depend on the Duchess and her daughters, all admirable women; and they will do what they can with others. It will be a busy day, but I have expressed my hope that the heads of the household may be able to attend. But the county notables arrive to-day, and I shall make it a point with them, especially the Lord Lieutenant.'

'It should be known,' said the Chaplain. 'I will send a memorandum to the "Guardian."'

'And "John Bull,"' said the Bishop.

The Lord Lieutenant and Lady Agramont, and their daughter, Lady Ida Alice, arrived to-day; and the High Sheriff, a manufacturer, a great liberal who delighted in poers, but whose otherwise perfect felicity to-day was a little marred and lessened by the haunting and restless fear that Lothair was not duly aware that he took precedence of the Lord Lieutenant. Then there were Sir Hamlet Clotworthy, the master of the hounds, and a capital man of business; and the honourable Lady Clotworthy, a haughty dame who ruled her circle with tremendous airs and graces, but who was a little subdued in the empyrean of Muriel Towers. The other county member, Mr. Ardenne, was a refined gentleman and loved the arts. He had an ancient pedigree, and knew everybody else's, which was not always pleasant. What he most prided himself on was being the hereditary owner of a real deer park; the only one, he asserted, in the county. Other persons had parks which had deer in them, but that was quite a different thing. His wife was a pretty woman, and the inspiring genius of archæological societies, who loved their annual luncheon in her Tudor Halls, and illustrated by their researches the deeds and dwellings of her husband's ancient race.

The clergy of the various parishes on the estate all dined at the Towers to-day, in order to pay their respects to their Bishop. 'Lothair's œcumenical council,' said Hugo Bohun, as he entered the crowded room, and looked around him with an air of not ungraceful impertinence. Among the clergy was Mr. Smylie, the brother of Apollonia.

A few years ago, Mr. Putney Giles had not unreasonably availed himself of the position which he so usefully and so honourably filled, to recommend this gentleman to the guardians of Lothair to fill a vacant benefice. The Reverend Dionysius Smylie had distinguished himself at Trinity College, Dublin, and had gained a Hebrew scholarship there; after that he had written a work on the Revelation, which clearly settled the long-controverted point whether Rome in the great apocalypse was signified by Babylon. The Bishop shrugged his shoulders when he received Mr. Smylie's papers, the examining Chaplain sighed, and the Archdeacon groaned. But man is proverbially shortsighted. The doctrine of evolution affords no instances so striking as those of sacerdotal development. Placed under the favouring conditions of clime and soil, the real character of the Rev. Dionysius Smylie gradually, but powerfully, developed itself. Where he now ministered, he was attended by acolytes, and incensed by thurifers. The shoulders of a fellow-countryman were alone equal to the burden of the enormous cross which preceded him; while his ecclesiastical wardrobe furnished him with many coloured garments, suited to every season of the year, and every festival of the Church.

At first there was indignation, and rumours or prophecies that we should soon have another case of perversion, and that Mr. Smylie was going over to Rome; but these superficial commentators misapprehended the vigorous vanity of the man. 'Rome may come to me,' said Mr. Smylie, 'and it is perhaps the best thing it could do. This is the real Church without Romish error.'

The Bishop and his reverend staff, who were at first so much annoyed at the preferment of Mr. Smylie, had now, with respect to him, only one duty, and that was to restrain his exuberant priestliness; but they fulfilled that duty in a kindly and charitable spirit; and when the Rev. Dionysius Smylie was appointed chaplain to Lothair, the Bishop did not shrug his shoulders, the Chaplain did not sigh, nor the Archdeacon groan.

The party was so considerable to-day that they dined in the great hall. When it was announced to Lothair that his Lordship's dinner was served, and he offered his arm to his destined companion, he looked around, and then, in an audible voice, and with a stateliness becoming such an incident, called upon the High Sheriff to lead the Duchess to the table. Although that eminent personage had been thinking of nothing else for days, and during the last half-hour had felt as a man feels, and can only feel, who knows that some public function is momentarily about to fall to his perilous discharge, he was taken quite aback, changed colour, and lost his head. But the band of Lothair, who were waiting at the door of the apartment to precede the procession to the hall, striking up at this moment 'The Roast Beef of Old England,' reanimated his heart; and following Lothair, and preceding all the other guests down the gallery, and through many chambers, he experienced the proudest moment of a life of struggle, ingenuity, vicissitude, and success.

CHAPTER XLV.

UNDER all this flowing festivity there was already a current of struggle and party passion. Serious thoughts and some anxiety occupied the minds of several of the guests, amid the variety of proffered dishes and sparkling wines, and the subdued strains of delicate music. This disquietude did not touch Lothair. He was happy to find himself in his ancestral hall, surrounded by many whom he respected and by some whom he loved. He was an excellent host, which no one can be who does not combine a good heart with high breeding.

Theodora was rather far from him, but he could catch her grave, sweet countenance at an angle of the table, as she bowed her head to Mr. Ardenne, the county member, who was evidently initiating her in all the mysteries of deer parks. The Cardinal sate near him, winning over, though without apparent effort, the somewhat prejudiced Lady Agramont. His Eminence could converse with more facility than others, for he dined off biscuits and drank only water. Lord Cullodon had taken out Lady St. Jerome,

who expended on him all the resources of her impassioned
tittle-tattle, extracting only grim smiles; and Lady Corisande had fallen to the happy lot of the Duke of Brecon; according to the fine perception of Clare Arundel (and women
are very quick in these discoveries) the winning horse.   St.
Aldegonde had managed to tumble in between Lady Flora
and Lady Grizell, and seemed immensely amused.

The Duke enquired of Lothair how many he could dine
in his hall.

'We must dine more than two hundred on Monday,' he
replied.

'And now, I should think, we have only a third of that
number,' said his Grace.   'It will be a tight fit.'

'Mr. Putney Giles has had a drawing made, and every
seat apportioned.   We shall just do it.'

'I fear you will have too busy a day on Monday,' said
the Cardinal, who had caught up the conversation.

'Well, you know, sir, I do not sit up smoking with Lord
St. Aldegonde.'

After dinner, Lady Corisande seated herself by Mrs.
Campian.   'You must have thought me very rude,' she
said, ' to have left you so suddenly at tea, when the Bishop
looked into the room; but he wanted me on a matter of
the greatest importance.   I must, therefore, ask your
pardon.   You naturally would not feel on this matter as
we all do, or most of us do,' she added with some hesitation; ' being, pardon me, a foreigner, and the question
involving national as well as religious feelings;' and then
somewhat harriedly, but with emotion, she detailed to
Theodora all that had occurred respecting the early celebration on Monday, and the opposition it was receiving
from the Cardinal and his friends.   It was a relief to Lady
Corisande thus to express all her feelings on a subject on
which she had been brooding the whole day.

'You mistake,' said Theodora quietly, when Lady Cori-

sande had finished. 'I am much interested in what you
tell me. I should deplore our friend falling under the influence of the Romish priesthood.'

'And yet there is danger of it,' said Lady Corisande,
'more than danger,' she added in a low but earnest voice.
'You do not know what a conspiracy is going on, and has
been going on for months to effect this end. I tremble.'

'That is the last thing I ever do,' said Theodora with a
faint sweet smile. 'I hope, but I never tremble.'

'You have seen the announcement in the newspapers to-
day?' said Lady Corisande.

'I think if they were certain of their prey they would be
more reserved,' said Theodora.

'There is something in that,' said Lady Corisande
musingly. 'You know not what a relief it is to me to
speak to you on this matter. Mamma agrees with me,
and so do my sisters; but still they may agree with me
because they are my mamma and my sisters; but I look
upon our nobility joining the Church of Rome as the
greatest calamity that has ever happened to England.
Irrespective of all religious considerations, on which I will
not presume to touch, it is an abnegation of patriotism;
and in this age, when all things are questioned, a love of
our country seems to me the one sentiment to cling to.'

'I know no higher sentiment,' said Theodora in a low
voice, and yet which sounded like the breathing of some
divine shrine, and her Athenian eye met the fiery glance of
Lady Corisande with an expression of noble sympathy.

'I am so glad that I spoke to you on this matter,' said
Lady Corisande, 'for there is something in you which
encourages me. As you say, if they were certain they
would be silent; and yet, from what I hear, their hopes
are high. You know,' she added in a whisper, 'that he
has absolutely engaged to raise a Popish Cathedral. My
brother, Bertram, has seen the model in his rooms.'

'I have known models that were never realised,' said Theodora.

'Ah! you are hopeful; you said you were hopeful. It is a beautiful disposition. It is not mine,' she added with a sigh.

'It should be,' said Theodora; 'you were not born to sigh. Sighs should be for those who have no country, like myself; not for the daughters of England, the beautiful daughters of proud England.'

'But you have your husband's country, and that is proud and great.'

'I have only one country, and it is not my husband's; and I have only one thought, and it is to see it free.'

'It is a noble one,' said Lady Corisande, 'as I am sure are all your thoughts. There are the gentlemen; I am sorry they have come. There,' she added, as Monsignore Catesby entered the room, 'there is his evil genius.'

'But you have baffled him,' said Theodora.

'Ah!' said Lady Corisande, with a long-drawn sigh. 'Their manœuvres never cease. However, I think Monday must be safe. Would you come?' she said, with a serious, searching glance, and in a kind of coaxing murmur.

'I should be an intruder, my dear lady,' said Theodora, declining the suggestion; 'but so far as hoping that our friend will never join the Church of Rome, you will have ever my ardent wishes.'

Theodora might have added her belief, for Lothair had never concealed from her a single thought or act of his life in this respect. She knew all and had weighed everything, and flattered herself that their frequent and unreserved conversations had not confirmed his belief in the infallibility of the Church of Rome, and perhaps of some other things.

It had been settled that there should be dancing this evening; all the young ladies had wished it. Lothair

danced with Lady Flora Falkirk, and her sister, Lady
Grizell, was in the same quadrille. They moved about
like young giraffes in an African forest, but looked bright
and happy. Lothair liked his cousins; their inexperience
and innocence, and the simplicity with which they exhibited and expressed their feelings, had in it something
bewitching. Then the rough remembrance of his old life
at Falkirk and its contrast with the present scene, had in
it something stimulating. They were his juniors by several
years, but they were always gentle and kind to him; and
sometimes it seemed he was the only person whom they
too had found kind and gentle. He called his cousin
too by her christian name, and he was amused, standing
by this beautiful giantess, and calling her Flora. There
were other amusing circumstances in the quadrille; not
the least, Lord St. Aldegonde dancing with Mrs. Campian.
The wonder of Lady St. Aldegonde was only equalled by
her delight.

The Lord Lieutenant was standing by the Duke in a
corner of the saloon, observing not with dissatisfaction his
daughter, Lady Ida Alice, dancing with Lothair.

'Do you know this is the first time I ever had the
honour of meeting a Cardinal?' he said.

'And we never expected that it would happen to either
of us in this country when we were at Christchurch together,' replied the Duke.

'Well, I hope everything is for the best,' said Lord
Agramont. 'We are to have all these gentlemen in our
good city of Grandchester to-morrow.'

'So I understand.'

'You read that paragraph in the newspapers? Do you
think there is anything in it?'

'About our friend? It would be a great misfortune.'

'The Bishop says there is nothing in it,' said the Lord
Lieutenant.

'Well, he ought to know. I understand he has had some serious conversation recently with our friend?'

'Yes; he has spoken to me about it. Are you going to attend the early celebration to-morrow? It is not much to my taste; a little new-fangled, I think; but I shall go, as they say it will do good.'

'I am glad of that; it is well that he should be impressed at this moment with the importance and opinion of his county.'

'Do you know I never saw him before,' said the Lord Lieutenant. 'He is winning.'

'I know no youth,' said the Duke, '(I would not except my own son, and Bertram has never given me an uneasy moment,) of whom I have a better opinion, both as to heart and head. I should deeply deplore his being smashed by a Jesuit.'

The dancing had ceased for a moment; there was a stir; Lord Carisbrooke was enlarging, with unusual animation, to an interested group about a new dance at Paris: the new dance. Could they not have it here? Unfortunately he did not know its name, and could not describe its figure; but it was something new; quite new; they have got it at Paris. Princess Metternich dances it. He danced it with her, and she taught it him; only he never could explain anything, and indeed never did exactly make it out. 'But you dance it with a shawl, and then two ladies hold the shawl, and the cavaliers pass under it. In fact it is the only thing; it is the new dance at Paris.'

What a pity that anything so delightful should be so indefinite and perplexing, and indeed impossible, which rendered it still more desirable! If Lord Carisbrooke only could have remembered its name, or a single step in its figure; it was so tantalising!

'Do not you think so?' said Hugo Bohun to Mrs. Campian, who was sitting apart listening to Lord St.

Aldegonde's account of his travels in the United States,
which he was very sorry he ever quitted. And then they
enquired to what Mr. Bohun referred, and then he told
them all that had been said.

'I know what he means,' said Mrs. Campian. 'It is
not a French dance; it is a Moorish dance.'

'That woman knows everything, Hugo,' said Lord St.
Aldegonde in a solemn whisper. And then he called to
his wife. 'Bertha, Mrs. Campian will tell you all about
this dance that Carisbrooke is making such a mull of.
Now look here, Bertha; you must get the Campians to
come to us as soon as possible. They are going to Scotland from this place, and there is no reason, if you manage
it well, why they should not come on to us at once. Now
exert yourself.'

'I will do all I can, Granville.'

'It is not French, it is Moorish; it is called the Tangerine,' said Theodora to her surrounding votaries. 'You
begin with a circle.'

'But how are we to dance without the music?' said
Lady Montairy.

'Ah! I wish I had known this,' said Theodora, 'before
dinner, and I think I could have dotted down something
that would have helped us. But let me see,' and she went
up to the eminent professor, with whom she was well
acquainted, and said, 'Signor Ricci, it begins so,' and she
hummed divinely a fantastic air, which, after a few
moments' musing, he reproduced; 'and then it goes off
into what they call in Spain a saraband. Is there a shawl
in the room?'

'My mother has always a shawl in reserve,' said Bertram, 'particularly when she pays visits to houses where
there are galleries;' and he brought back a mantle of
Cashmere.

'Now, Signor Ricci,' said Mrs. Campian, and she again

hummed an air, and moved forward at the same time with brilliant grace, waving at the end the shawl.

The expression of her countenance, looking round to Signor Ricci, as she was moving on to see whether he had caught her idea, fascinated Lothair.

'It is exactly what I told you,' said Lord Carisbrooke, 'and, I can assure you, it is the only dance now. I am very glad I remembered it.'

'I see it all,' said Signor Ricci, as Theodora rapidly detailed to him the rest of the figure. 'And at any rate it will be the Tangerine with variations.'

'Let me have the honour of being your partner in this great enterprise,' said Lothair; 'you are the inspiration of Muriel.'

'Oh! I am very glad I can do anything, however slight, to please you and your friends. I like them all; but particularly Lady Corisande.'

A new dance in a country house is a festival of frolic grace. The incomplete knowledge and the imperfect execution are themselves causes of merry excitement, in their contrast with the unimpassioned routine and almost unconscious practice of traditionary performances. And gay and frequent were the bursts of laughter from the bright and airy band who were proud to be the scholars of Theodora. The least successful among them was perhaps Lord Carisbrooke.

'Princess Metternich must have taught you wrong, Carisbrooke,' said Hugo Bohun.

They ended with a waltz, Lothair dancing with Miss Arundel. She accepted his offer to take some tea on its conclusion. While they were standing at the table, a little withdrawn from others, and he holding a sugar basin, she said in a low voice, looking on her cup and not at him, 'The Cardinal is vexed about the early celebration; he says it should have been at midnight.'

' I am sorry he is vexed,' said Lothair.

' He was going to speak to you himself,' continued Miss
Arundel; ' but he felt a delicacy about it. He had thought
that your common feelings respecting the Church might
have induced you, if not to consult, at least to converse,
with him on the subject; I mean as your guardian.'

' It might have been perhaps as well,' said Lothair;
' but I also feel a delicacy on these matters.'

' There ought to be none on such matters,' continued
Miss Arundel, ' when everything is at stake.'

' I do not see that I could have taken any other course
than I have done,' said Lothair. ' It can hardly be wrong.
The Bishop's church views are sound.'

' Sound! ' said Miss Arundel; ' moonshine instead of
sunshine.'

' Moonshine would rather suit a midnight than a morning celebration,' said Lothair; ' would it not ? '

' A fair repartee, but we are dealing with a question that
cannot be settled by jests. See,' she said with great
seriousness, putting down her cup and taking again his
offered arm, ' you think you are only complying with
a form befitting your position and the occasion. You
deceive yourself. You are hampering your future freedom
by this step, and they know it. That is why it was
planned. It was not necessary; nothing can be necessary
so pregnant with evil. You might have made, you might
yet make, a thousand excuses. It is a rite which hardly
suits the levity of the hour, even with their feelings; but,
with your view of its real character, it is sacrilege. What
is occurring to-night might furnish you with scruples.'
And she looked up in his face.

' I think you take an exaggerated view of what I contemplate,' said Lothair. ' Even with your convictions it
may be an imperfect rite; but it never can be an injurious
one.'

'There can be no compromise on such matters,' said Miss Arundel. 'The Church knows nothing of imperfect rites. They are all perfect because they are all divine: any deviation from them is heresy, and fatal. My convictions on this subject are your convictions ; act up to them.'

'I am sure if thinking of these matters would guide a man right ——' said Lothair with a sigh, and he stopped.

'Human thought will never guide you ; and very justly, when you have for a guide Divine truth. You are now your own master ; go at once to its fountain-head ; go to Rome, and then all your perplexities will vanish, and for ever.'

'I do not see much prospect of my going to Rome,' said Lothair, 'at least at present.'

'Well,' said Miss Arundel ; 'in a few weeks I hope to be there ; and if so, I hope never to quit it.'

'Do not say that ; the future is always unknown.'

'Not yours,' said Miss Arundel. 'Whatever you think, you will go to Rome. Mark my words. I summon you to meet me at Rome.'

CHAPTER XLVI.

THERE can be little doubt, generally speaking, that it is more satisfactory to pass Sunday in the country than in town. There is something in the essential stillness of country life, which blends harmoniously with the ordinance of the most divine of our divine laws. It is pleasant too, when the congregation breaks up, to greet one's neighbours ; to say kind words to kind faces ; to hear some rural news profitable to learn, which sometimes enables you to do some good, and sometimes prevents others from doing some harm. A quiet domestic walk too in the

R

afternoon has its pleasures; and so numerous and so various
are the sources of interest in the country, that, though it
be Sunday, there is no reason why your walk should not
have an object.

But Sunday in the country, with your house full of
visitors, is too often an exception to this general truth.
It is a trial. Your guests cannot always be at church,
and, if they could, would not like it. There is nothing to
interest or amuse them: no sport; no castles or factories
to visit; no adventurous expeditions; no gay music in the
morn, and no light dance in the evening. There is always
danger of the day becoming a course of heavy meals and
stupid walks, for the external scene and all its teeming
circumstances, natural and human, though full of concern
to you, are to your visitors an insipid blank.

How did Sunday go off at Muriel Towers?

In the first place there was a special train, which at an
early hour took the Cardinal and his suite and the St.
Jerome family to Grandchester, where they were awaited
with profound expectation. But the Anglican portion of the
guests were not without their share of ecclesiastical and
spiritual excitement, for the Bishop was to preach this day
in the chapel of the Towers, a fine and capacious sanctuary
of florid Gothic, and his Lordship was a sacerdotal orator
of repute.

It had been announced that the breakfast hour was to be
somewhat earlier. The ladies in general were punctual, and
seemed conscious of some great event impending. The
ladies Flora and Grizell entered with, each in her hand, a
prayer-book of purple velvet adorned with a decided cross,
the gift of the Primus. Lord Culloden, at the request of
Lady Corisande, had consented to their hearing the Bishop,
which he would not do himself. He passed his morning in
finally examining the guardians' accounts, the investigation
of which he conducted and concluded during the rest of

the day with Mr. Putney Giles. Mrs. Campian did not leave her room. Lord St. Aldegonde came down late, and looked about him with an uneasy, ill-humoured air.

Whether from the absence of Theodora or from some other cause, he was brusk, ungracious, scowling, and silent, only nodding to the Bishop who benignly saluted him, refusing every dish that was offered, then getting up and helping himself at the side table, making a great noise with the carving instruments, and flouncing down his plate when he resumed his seat. Nor was his costume correct. All the other gentlemen, though their usual morning dresses were sufficiently fantastic (trunk hose of every form, stockings bright as paroquets, wondrous shirts, and velvet coats of every tint), habited themselves to-day, both as regards form and colour, in a style indicative of the subdued gravity of their feelings. Lord St. Aldegonde had on his shooting jacket of brown velvet and a pink shirt and no cravat, and his rich brown locks, always to a certain degree neglected, were peculiarly dishevelled.

Hugo Bohun, who was not afraid of him and was a high churchman, being in religion and in all other matters always on the side of the Duchesses, said, 'Well, St. Aldegonde, are you going to chapel in that dress?' But St. Aldegonde would not answer; he gave a snort and glanced at Hugo with the eye of a gladiator.

The meal was over. The Bishop was standing near the mantelpiece talking to the ladies, who were clustered round him; the Archdeacon and the Chaplain and some other clergy a little in the background; Lord St. Aldegonde, who, whether there were a fire or not, always stood with his back to the fireplace with his hands in his pockets, moved discourteously among them, assumed his usual position, and listened, as it were grimly, for a few moments to their talk; then he suddenly exclaimed in a loud voice, and with the groan of a rebellious Titan, 'How I hate Sunday!'

R 2

'Granville!' exclaimed Lady St. Aldegonde, turning pale. There was a general shudder.

'I mean in a country-house,' said Lord St. Aldegonde. 'Of course I mean in a country-house. I do not dislike it when alone, and I do not dislike it in London. But Sunday in a country-house is infernal.'

'I think it is now time for us to go,' said the Bishop, walking away with dignified reserve, and they all dispersed.

The service was choral and intoned; for although the Rev. Dionysius Smylie had not yet had time or opportunity, as was his intention, to form and train a choir from the household of the Towers, he had secured from his neighbouring parish and other sources external and effective aid in that respect. The parts of the service were skilfully distributed, and rarely were a greater number of priests enlisted in a more imposing manner. A good organ was well played; the singing, as usual, a little too noisy; there was an anthem and an introit, but no incense, which was forbidden by the Bishop; and though there were candles on the altar, they were not permitted to be lighted.

The sermon was most successful; the ladies returned with elate and animated faces, quite enthusiastic and almost forgetting in their satisfaction the terrible outrage of Lord St. Aldegonde. He himself had by this time repented of what he had done and recovered his temper, and greeted his wife with a voice and look which indicated to her practised senses the favourable change.

'Bertha,' he said, 'you know I did not mean anything personal to the Bishop in what I said. I do not like Bishops; I think there is no use in them; but I have no objection to him personally; I think him an agreeable man; not at all a bore. Just put it right, Bertha. But I tell you what, Bertha, I cannot go to church here. Lord Culloden does not go, and he is a very religious man. He is the man I most agree with on these matters. I am a free churchman, and there is an end of it. I cannot go this afternoon. I do not approve of the whole thing. It is altogether against my conscience. What I mean to do, if I can manage it, is to take a real long walk with the Campians.'

Mrs. Campian appeared at luncheon. The Bishop was attentive to her; even cordial. He was resolved she should not feel he was annoyed by her not having been a member of his congregation in the morning. Lady Corisande too had said to him, 'I wish so much you would talk to Mrs. Campian; she is a sweet, noble creature, and so clever! I feel that she might be brought to view things in the right light.'

'I never know,' said the Bishop, 'how to deal with these American ladies. I never can make out what they believe, or what they disbelieve. It is a sort of confusion between Mrs. Beecher Stowe and the Fifth Avenue congregation and Barnum,' he added with a twinkling eye.

The second service was late; the Dean preached. The lateness of the hour permitted the Lord Lieutenant and those guests who had arrived only the previous day to look over the castle, or ramble about the gardens. St. Aldegonde succeeded in his scheme of a real long walk with the Campians, which Lothair, bound to listen to the head of his college, was not permitted to share.

In the evening Signor Mardoni, who had arrived, and Madame Isola Bella favoured them with what they called sacred music; principally prayers from operas and a grand Stabat Mater.

Lord Culloden invited Lothair into a further saloon, where they might speak without disturbing the performers or the audience.

'I'll just take advantage, my dear boy,' said Lord Culloden, in a tone of unusual tenderness, and of Doric accent, 'of the absence of these gentlemen to have a little quiet

conversation with you. Though I have not seen so much
of you of late as in old days, I take a great interest in you,
no doubt of that, and I was very pleased to see how good-
natured you were to the girls. You have romped with
them when they were little ones. Now, in a few hours,
you will be master of a great inheritance, and I hope it
will profit ye. I have been over the accounts with Mr.
Giles, and I was pleased to hear that you had made yourself properly acquainted with them in detail. Never you
sign any paper without reading it first, and knowing well
what it means. You will have to sign a release to us if
you be satisfied, and that you may easily be. My poor
brother-in-law left you as large an income as may be found
on this side Trent, but I will be bound he would stare if
he saw the total of the whole of your rentroll, Lothair.
Your affairs have been well administered, though I say it
who ought not. But it is not my management only, or
principally, that has done it. It is the progress of the
country, and you owe the country a good deal, and you
should never forget you are born to be a protector of its
liberties, civil and religious. And if the country sticks to
free trade, and would enlarge its currency, and be firm to
the Protestant faith, it will, under Divine Providence, continue to progress.

‘And here, my boy, I'll just say a word, in no disagreeable manner, about your religious principles. There are a
great many stories about, and perhaps they are not true, and
I am sure I hope they are not. If Popery were only just
the sign of the cross, and music, and censer-pots, though I
think them all superstitious, I'd be free to leave them alone
if they would leave me. But Popery is a much deeper thing
than that, Lothair, and our fathers found it out. They
could not stand it, and we should be a craven crew to stand
it now. A man should be master in his own house. You
will be taking a wife some day; at least it is to be hoped

so; and how will you like one of these Monsignores to be walking into her bedroom, eh; and talking to her alone when he pleases, and where he pleases; and when you want to consult your wife, which a wise man should often do, to find there is another mind between hers and yours? There's my girls, they are just two young geese, and they have a hankering after Popery, having had a Jesuit in the house. I do not know what has come to the women. They are for going into a convent, and they are quite right in that, for if they be Papists they will not find a husband easily in Scotland, I ween.

'And as for you, my boy, they will be telling you that it is only just this and just that, and there's no great difference, and what not; but I tell you that if once you embrace the scarlet lady, you are a tainted corpse. You'll not be able to order your dinner without a priest, and they will ride your best horses without saying with your leave or by your leave.'

The concert in time ceased; there was a stir in the room; the Rev. Dionysius Smylie moved about mysteriously, and ultimately seemed to make an obeisance before the Bishop. It was time for prayers.

'Shall you go?' said Lord St. Aldegonde to Mrs. Campian, by whom he was sitting.

'I like to pray alone,' she answered.

'As for that,' said St. Aldegonde, 'I am not clear we ought to pray at all; either in public or private. It seems very arrogant in us to dictate to an all-wise Creator what we desire.'

'I believe in the efficacy of prayer,' said Theodora.

'And I believe in you,' said St. Aldegonde, after a momentary pause.

CHAPTER XLVII.

On the morrow, the early celebration in the chapel was numerously attended. The Duchess and her daughters, Lady Agramont, and Mrs. Ardenne were among the faithful; but what encouraged and gratified the Bishop was, that the laymen, on whom he less relied, were numerously represented. The Lord Lieutenant, Lord Carisbrooke, Lord Montairy, Bertram, and Hugo Bohun accompanied Lothair to the altar.

After the celebration, Lothair retired to his private apartments. It was arranged that he was to join his assembled friends at noon, when he would receive their congratulations, and some deputations from the county.

At noon, therefore, preparatively preceded by Mr. Putney Giles, whose thought was never asleep, and whose eye was on everything, the guardians, the Cardinal and the Earl of Culloden, waited on Lothair to accompany him to his assembled friends, and, as it were, launch him into the world.

They were assembled at one end of the chief gallery, and in a circle. Although the deputations would have to advance the whole length of the chamber, Lothair and his guardians entered from a side apartment. Even with this assistance he felt very nervous. There was no lack of feeling, and, among many, of deep feeling, on this occasion, but there was an equal and a genuine exhibition of ceremony.

The Lord Lieutenant was the first person who congratulated Lothair, though the High Sheriff had pushed forward for that purpose, but, in his awkward precipitation, he got involved with the train of the Honorable Lady Clotworthy,

who bestowed on him such a withering glance, that he felt
a routed man, and gave up the attempt. There were many
kind and some earnest words. Even St. Aldegonde acknowledged the genius of the occasion. He was grave,
graceful, and dignified, and addressing Lothair by his title
he said, 'that he hoped he would meet in life that happiness
which he felt confident he deserved.' Theodora said nothing, though her lips seemed once to move; but she retained for a moment Lothair's hand, and the expression of
her countenance touched his innermost heart. Lady Corisande beamed with dazzling beauty. Her countenance was
joyous, radiant; her mien imperial and triumphant. She
gave her hand with graceful alacrity to Lothair, and said in
a hushed tone, but every word of which reached his ear,
'One of the happiest hours of my life was eight o'clock this
morning.'

The Lord Lieutenant and the county members then retired to the other end of the gallery, and ushered in the
deputation of the magistracy of the county, congratulating
their new brother, for Lothair had just been appointed to
the bench, on his accession to his estates. The Lord Lieutenant himself read the address, to which Lothair replied
with a propriety all acknowledged. Then came the address
of the Mayor and Corporation of Grandchester, of which
city Lothair was hereditary high steward; and then that of
his tenantry, which was cordial and characteristic. And
here many were under the impression that this portion of
the proceedings would terminate; but it was not so. There
had been some whispering between the Bishop and the
Archdeacon, and the Rev. Dionysius Smylie had, after
conference with his superiors, twice left the chamber. It
seems that the clergy had thought fit to take this occasion
of congratulating Lothair on his great accession, and the
proportionate duties which it would fall on him to fulfil.
The Bishop approached Lothair and addressed him in a

whisper. Lothair seemed surprised and a little agitated, but apparently bowed assent. Then the Bishop and his staff proceeded to the end of the gallery and introduced a diocesan deputation, consisting of archdeacons and rural deans, who presented to Lothair a most uncompromising address, and begged his acceptance of a bible and prayer-book richly bound, and borne by the Rev. Dionysius Smylie on a cushion of velvet.

The habitual pallor of the Cardinal's countenance became unusually wan; the cheek of Clare Arundel was a crimson flush; Monsignore Catesby bit his lip; Theodora looked with curious seriousness as if she were observing the manners of a foreign country; St. Aldegonde snorted and pushed his hand through his hair, which had been arranged in unusual order. The great body of those present, unaware that this deputation was unexpected, were unmoved.

It was a trial for Lothair, and scarcely a fair one. He was not unequal to it, and what he said was esteemed at the moment by all parties as satisfactory; though the Arch-deacon in secret conclave afterwards observed, that he dwelt more on Religion than on the Church, and spoke of the Church of Christ and not of the Church of England. He thanked them for their present of volumes which all must reverence or respect.

While all this was taking place within the Towers, vast bodies of people were assembling without. Besides the notables of the county and his tenantry and their families, which drained all the neighbouring villages, Lothair had forwarded several thousand tickets to the Mayor and Cor-poration of Grandchester, for distribution among their fellow-townsmen, who were invited to dine at Muriel and partake of the festivities of the day, and trains were hourly arriving with their eager and happy guests. The gardens were at once open for their unrestricted pleasure, but at two o'clock, according to the custom of the county under

such circumstances, Lothair held what in fact was a levée,
or rather a drawing-room, when every person who possessed a ticket was permitted, and even invited and expected, to pass through the whole range of the state apartments of Muriel Towers, and at the same time pay their
respects to, and make the acquaintance of, their lord.

Lothair stood with his chief friends near him, the ladies
however seated, and everyone passed: farmers and towns-
men and honest folk down to the stokers of the trains
from Grandchester, with whose presence St. Aldegonde
was much pleased, and whom he carefully addressed as
they passed by.

After this great reception they all dined in pavilions in
the park: one thousand tenantry by themselves and at a
fixed hour; the miscellaneous multitude in a huge crimson
tent, very lofty, with many flags, and in which was served
a banquet that never stopped till sunset, so that in time all
might be satisfied; the notables and deputations, with
the guests in the house, lunched in the armoury. It was
a bright day, and there was unceasing music.

In the course of the afternoon, Lothair visited the
pavilions, where his health was proposed and pledged, in
the first by one of his tenants, and in the other by a work-
man, both orators of repute; and he addressed and thanked
his friends. This immense multitude, orderly and joyous,
roamed about the parks and gardens, or danced on a platform which the prescient experience of Mr. Giles had provided for them in a due locality, and whiled away the
pleasant hours, in expectation a little feverish of the impending fireworks, which, there was a rumour, were to be
on a scale and in a style of which neither Grandchester nor
the county had any tradition.

'I remember your words at Blenheim,' said Lothair to
Theodora. 'You cannot say the present party is founded
on the principle of exclusion.'

In the meantime, about six o'clock, Lothair dined in his
great hall with his two hundred guests at a banquet where
all the resources of nature and art seemed called upon to
contribute to its luxury and splendour. The ladies who
had never before dined at a public dinner were particularly
delighted. They were delighted by the speeches, though
they had very few; they were delighted by the national
anthem, all rising; particularly they were delighted by
'three times three and one cheer more,' and 'hip, hip.' It
seemed to their unpractised ears like a great naval battle,
or the end of the world, or anything else of unimaginable
excitement, tumult, and confusion.

The Lord Lieutenant proposed Lothair's health, and
dexterously made his comparative ignorance of the subject
the cause of his attempting a sketch of what he hoped
might be the character of the person whose health he proposed. Everyone intuitively felt the resemblance was just
and even complete, and Lothair confirmed their kind and
sanguine anticipations by his terse and well-considered
reply. His proposition of the ladies' healths was a signal
that the carriages were ready to take them, as arranged, to
Muriel Mere.

The sun had set in glory over the broad expanse of
waters still glowing in the dying beam; the people were
assembled in thousands on the borders of the lake, in the
centre of which was an island with a pavilion. Fanciful
barges and gondolas of various shapes and colours were
waiting for Lothair and his party, to carry them over to
the pavilion, where they found a repast which became the
hour and the scene: coffee and ices and whimsical drinks,
which sultanas would sip in Arabian tales. No sooner
were they seated than the sound of music was heard, distant, but now nearer, till there came floating on the lake,
until it rested before the pavilion, a gigantic shell, larger

than the building itself, but holding in its golden and opal seats Signor Mardoni and all his orchestra.

Then came a concert rare in itself, and ravishing in the rosy twilight; and in about half an hour, when the rosy twilight had subsided into a violet eve, and when the white moon that had only gleamed began to glitter, the colossal shell again moved on, and Lothair and his companions embarking once more in their gondolas, followed it in procession about the lake. He carried in his own barque the Duchess, Theodora, and the Lord Lieutenant, and was rowed by a crew in Venetian dresses. As he handed Theodora to her seat the impulse was irresistible: he pressed her hand to his lips.

Suddenly a rocket rose with a hissing rush from the pavilion. It was instantly responded to from every quarter of the lake. Then the island seemed on fire, and the scene of their late festivity became a brilliant palace, with pediments and columns and statues, bright in the blaze of coloured flame. For half an hour the sky seemed covered with blue lights and the bursting forms of many-coloured stars; golden fountains, like the eruption of a marine volcano, rose from different parts of the water; the statued palace on the island changed and became a forest glowing with green light; and finally a temple of cerulean tint, on which appeared in huge letters of prismatic colour the name of Lothair.

The people cheered, but even the voice of the people was overcome by troops of rockets rising from every quarter of the lake, and by the thunder of artillery. When the noise and the smoke had both subsided, the name of Lothair still legible on the temple but the letters quite white, it was perceived that on every height for fifty miles round they had fired a beacon.

CHAPTER XLVIII.

THE ball at Muriel which followed the concert on the lake was one of those balls which, it would seem, never would end. All the preliminary festivities, instead of exhausting the guests of Lothair, appeared only to have excited them, and rendered them more romantic and less tolerant of the routine of existence. They danced in the great gallery, which was brilliant and crowded, and they danced as they dance in a festive dream, with joy and the enthusiasm of gaiety. The fine ladies would sanction no exclusiveness. They did not confine their inspiring society, as is some-times too often the case, to the Brecons and the Bertrams and the Carisbrookes; they danced fully and freely with the youth of the county, and felt that in so doing they were honouring and gratifying their host.

At one o'clock they supped in the armoury, which was illuminated for the first time, and a banquet in a scene so picturesque and resplendent renovated not merely their physical energies. At four o'clock the Duchess and a few others quietly disappeared, but her daughters remained, and St. Aldegonde danced endless reels, which was a form in which he preferred to worship Terpsichore. Perceiving by an open window that it was dawn, he came up to Lothair and said, 'This is a case of breakfast.'

Happy and frolicsome suggestion! The invitations cir-culated, and it was soon known that they were all to gather at the matin meal.

'I am so sorry that her Grace has retired,' said Hugo Bohun to Lady St. Aldegonde, as he fed her with bread and butter, 'because she always likes early breakfasts in the country.'

The sun was shining as the guests of the house retired, and sank into couches from which it seemed they never could rise again; but, long after this, the shouts of servants and the scuffle of carriages intimated that the company in general were not so fortunate and expeditious in their retirement from the scene; and the fields were all busy, and even the towns awake, when the great body of the wearied but delighted wassailers returned from celebrating the majority of Lothair.

In the vast and statesmanlike programme of the festivities of the week, which had been prepared by Mr. and Mrs. Putney Giles, something of interest and importance had been appropriated to the morrow, but it was necessary to erase all this; and for a simple reason: no human being on the morrow morn even appeared; one might say, even stirred. After all the gay tumult in which even thousands had joined, Muriel Towers on the morrow presented a scene which only could have been equalled by the castle in the fairy tale inhabited by the Sleeping Beauty.

At length, about two hours after noon, bells began to sound which were not always answered. Then a languid household prepared a meal of which no one for a time partook, till at last a Monsignore appeared and a rival Anglican or two. Then St. Aldegonde came in with a troop of men who had been bathing in the mere, and called loudly for kidneys, which happened to be the only thing not at hand, as is always the case. St. Aldegonde always required kidneys when he had sate up all night and bathed. 'But the odd thing is,' he said, 'you never can get anything to eat in those houses. Their infernal cooks spoil everything. That is why I hate staying with Bertha's people in the north at the end of the year. What I want in November is a slice of cod and a beefsteak, and by Jove I never could get them; I was obliged to come to town. It is no joke to have to travel three hundred miles for a slice of cod and a beefsteak.'

Notwithstanding all this, however, such is the magic of custom, that by sunset civilisation had resumed its reign at Muriel Towers. The party were assembled before dinner in the saloon, and really looked as fresh and bright as if the exhausting and tumultuous yesterday had never happened. The dinner, too, notwithstanding the criticism of St. Aldegonde, was first-rate, and pleased palates not so simply fastidious as his own. The Bishop and his suite were to depart on the morrow, but the Cardinal was to remain. His Eminence talked much to Mrs. Campian, by whom, from the first, he was much struck. He was aware that she was born a Roman, and was not surprised that, having married a citizen of the United States, her sympathies were what are styled liberal; but this only stimulated his anxious resolution to accomplish her conversion, both religious and political. He recognised in her a being whose intelligence, imagination, and grandeur of character might be of invaluable service to the Church.

In the evening Monsieur Raphael and his sister, and their colleagues, gave a representation which was extremely well done. There was no theatre at Muriel, but Apollonia had felicitously arranged a contiguous saloon for the occasion, and, as everybody was at ease in an arm-chair, they all agreed it was preferable to a regular theatre.

On the morrow they were to lunch with the Mayor and Corporation of Grandchester and view some of the principal factories; on the next day the county gave a dinner to Lothair in their hall, the Lord Lieutenant in the chair; on Friday there was to be a ball at Grandchester given by the county and city united to celebrate the great local event. It was whispered that this was to be a considerable affair. There was not an hour of the week that was not appropriated to some festive ceremony.

It happened on the morning of Thursday, the Cardinal being alone with Lothair, transacting some lingering busi-noss connected with the guardianship, and on his legs as he spoke, that he said, 'We live in such a happy tumult here, my dear child, that I have never had an opportunity of speaking to you on one or two points which interest me and should not be uninteresting to you. I remember a pleasant morning-walk we had in the park at Vauxe, when we began a conversation which we never finished. What say you to a repetition of our stroll? 'Tis a lovely day, and I dare say we might escape by this window, and gain some green retreat without anyone disturbing us.'

'I am quite of your Eminence's mind,' said Lothair, taking up a wide-awake, 'and I will lead you where it is not likely we shall be disturbed.'

So winding their way through the pleasure-grounds, they entered by a wicket a part of the park where the sunny glades soon wandered among the tall fern and wild groves of venerable oaks.

'I sometimes feel,' said the Cardinal, 'that I may have been too punctilious in avoiding conversation with you on a subject the most interesting and important to man. But I felt a delicacy in exerting my influence as a guardian on a subject my relations to which, when your dear father appointed me to that office, were so different from those which now exist. But you are now your own master; I can use no control over you but that influence which the words of truth must always exercise over an ingenuous mind.'

His Eminence paused for a moment and looked at his companion; but Lothair remained silent, with his eyes fixed upon the ground.

'It has always been a source of satisfaction, I would even say consolation, to me,' resumed the Cardinal, 'to know you were a religious man; that your disposition was reverential, which is the highest order of temperament, and brings us nearest to the angels. But we live in times of difficulty and danger, extreme difficulty and danger; a

s

religious disposition may suffice for youth in the tranquil
hour, and he may find, in due season, his appointed resting-
place: but these are days of imminent peril; the soul requires a sanctuary. Is yours at hand?'

The Cardinal paused, and Lothair was obliged to meet a
direct appeal. He said then, after a momentary hesitation,
'When you last spoke to me, sir, on these grave matters,
I said I was in a state of great despondency. My situation
now is not so much despondent as perplexed.'

'And I wish you to tell me the nature of your perplexity,'
replied the Cardinal, 'for there is no anxious embarrassment of mind which Divine truth cannot disentangle and
allay.'

'Well,' said Lothair, 'I must say I am often perplexed
at the differences which obtrude themselves between Divine
truth and human knowledge.'

'These are inevitable,' said the Cardinal. 'Divine truth
being unchangeable, and human knowledge changing every
century; rather, I should say, every generation.'

'Perhaps, instead of human knowledge, I should have
said human progress,' rejoined Lothair.

'Exactly,' said the Cardinal; 'but what is progress?
Movement. But what if it be movement in the wrong
direction? What if it be a departure from Divine truth?'

'But I cannot understand why religion should be inconsistent with civilisation,' said Lothair.

'Religion is civilisation,' said the Cardinal; 'the highest:
it is a reclamation of man from savageness by the Almighty
What the world calls civilisation, as distinguished from
religion, is a retrograde movement, and will ultimately
lead us back to the barbarism from which we have escaped.
For instance, you talk of progress; what is the chief social
movement of all the countries that three centuries ago
separated from the unity of the Church of Christ? The
rejection of the sacrament of Christian matrimony. The

introduction of the law of divorce, which is, in fact, only a
middle term to the abolition of marriage. What does that
mean? The extinction of the home and the household on
which God has rested civilisation. If there be no home,
the child belongs to the state, not to the parent. The
state educates the child, and without religion, because the
state in a country of progress acknowledges no religion.
For every man is not only to think as he likes, but to write
and to speak as he likes, and to sow with both hands
broadcast where he will, errors, heresies, and blasphemies,
without any authority on earth to restrain the scattering
of this seed of universal desolation. And this system,
which would substitute for domestic sentiment and Divine
belief the unlimited and licentious action of human intellect and human will, is called progress. What is it but a
revolt against God!'

'I am sure I wish there were only one Church and one
religion,' said Lothair.

'There is only one Church and only one religion,' said
the Cardinal; 'all other forms and phrases are mere
phantasms, without root, or substance, or coherency.
Look at that unhappy Germany, once so proud of its
Reformation. What they call the leading journal tells us
to-day, that it is a question there whether four-fifths or
three-fourths of the population believe in Christianity.
Some portion of it has already gone back, I understand, to
NUMBER NIP. Look at this unfortunate land, divided, sub-
divided, parcelled out in infinite schism, with new oracles
every day, and each more distinguished for the narrowness
of his intellect or the loudness of his lungs; once the land
of saints and scholars, and people in pious pilgrimages, and
finding always solace and support in the divine offices of an
ever-present Church, which were a true though a faint
type of the beautiful future that awaited man. Why, only
three centuries of this rebellion against the Most High

s 2

have produced throughout the world, on the subject the
most important that man should possess a clear, firm faith,
an anarchy of opinion throwing out every monstrous and
fantastic form, from a caricature of the Greek philosophy
to a revival of Fetism.'

'It is a chaos,' said Lothair, with a sigh.

'From which I wish to save you,' said the Cardinal,
with some eagerness. 'This is not a time to hesitate.
You must be for God, or for Antichrist. The Church calls
upon her children.'

'I am not unfaithful to the Church,' said Lothair,
'which was the Church of my fathers.'

'The Church of England,' said the Cardinal. 'It was
mine. I think of it ever, with tenderness and pity. Parliament made the Church of England, and Parliament will
unmake the Church of England. The Church of England
is not the Church of the English. Its fate is sealed. It
will soon become a sect, and all sects are fantastic. It will
adopt new dogmas, or it will abjure old ones; anything to
distinguish it from the non-conforming herd in which,
nevertheless, it will be its fate to merge. The only con-
soling hope is that, when it falls, many of its children, by
the aid of the Blessed Virgin, may return to Christ.'

'What I regret, sir,' said Lothair, 'is that the Church of
Rome should have placed itself in antagonism with political
liberty. This adds to the difficulties which the religious
cause has to encounter; for it seems impossible to deny
that political freedom is now the sovereign passion of
communities.'

'I cannot admit,' replied the Cardinal, 'that the Church
is in antagonism with political freedom. On the contrary,
in my opinion, there can be no political freedom which is
not founded on Divine authority; otherwise it can be at the
best but a specious phantom of license inevitably terminating in anarchy. The rights and liberties of the people of

Ireland have no advocates except the Church; because there, political freedom is founded on Divine authority; but if you mean by political freedom the schemes of the illuminati and the freemasons which perpetually torture the Continent, all the dark conspiracies of the secret societies, there, I admit, the Church is in antagonism with such aspirations after liberty; those aspirations, in fact, are blasphemy and plunder; and if the Church were to be destroyed, Europe would be divided between the Atheist and the Communist.'

There was a pause; the conversation had unexpectedly arrived at a point where neither party cared to pursue it. Lothair felt he had said enough; the Cardinal was disappointed with what Lothair had said. His Eminence felt that his late ward was not in that ripe state of probation which he had fondly anticipated; but being a man not only of vivid perception, but also of fertile resource, while he seemed to close the present conversation, he almost immediately pursued his object by another combination of means. Noticing an effect of scenery which pleased him, reminded him of Styria, and so on, he suddenly said: 'You should travel.'

'Well, Bertram wants me to go to Egypt with him,' said Lothair.

'A most interesting country,' said the Cardinal, 'and well worth visiting. It is astonishing what a good guide old Herodotus still is in that land! But you should know something of Europe before you go there. Egypt is rather a land to end with. A young man should visit the chief capitals of Europe, especially the seats of learning and the arts. If my advice were asked by a young man who contemplated travelling on a proper scale, I should say begin with Rome. Almost all that Europe contains is derived from Rome. It is always best to go to the fountain-head, to study the original. The society too, there, is delightful:

I know none equal to it. That, if you please, is civilisation, pious and refined. And the people, all so gifted and so good, so kind, so orderly, so charitable, so truly virtuous. I believe the Roman people to be the best people that ever lived, and this too while the secret societies have their foreign agents in every quarter, trying to corrupt them, but always in vain. If an act of political violence occurs, you may be sure it is confined entirely to foreigners.'

'Our friends the St. Jeromes are going to Rome,' said Lothair.

'Well, and that would be pleasant for you. Think seriously of this, my dear young friend. I could be of some little service to you if you go to Rome, which, after all, every man ought to do. I could put you in the way of easily becoming acquainted with all the right people, who would take care that you saw Rome with profit and advantage.'

Just at this moment, in a winding glade, they were met abruptly by a third person. All seemed rather to start at the sudden rencounter; and then Lothair eagerly advanced and welcomed the stranger with a proffered hand.

'This is a most unexpected, but to me most agreeable, meeting,' he said. 'You must now be my guest.'

'That would be a great honour,' said the stranger, 'but one I cannot enjoy. I had to wait at the station a couple of hours or so for my train, and they told me if I strolled here I should find some pretty country. I have been so pleased with it, that I fear I have strolled too long, and I literally have not an instant at my command,' and he hurried away.

'Who is that person?' asked the Cardinal with some agitation.

'I have not the slightest idea,' said Lothair. 'All I know is, he once saved my life.'

'And all I know is,' said the Cardinal, 'he once threatened mine.'

'Strange!' said Lothair, and then he rapidly recounted to the Cardinal his adventure at the Fenian meeting.

'Strange!' echoed his Eminence.

CHAPTER XLIX.

MRS. CAMPIAN did not appear at luncheon, which was observed but not noticed. Afterwards, while Lothair was making some arrangements for the amusement of his guests, and contriving that they should fit in with the chief incident of the day, which was the banquet given to him by the county, and which it was settled the ladies were not to attend, the Colonel took him aside and said, 'I do not think that Theodora will care to go out to-day.'

'She is not unwell, I hope?'

'Not exactly; but she has had some news, some news of some friends, which has disturbed her. And if you will excuse me, I will request your permission not to attend the dinner to-day, which I had hoped to have had the honour of doing. But I think our plans must be changed a little. I almost think we shall not go to Scotland after all.'

'There is not the slightest necessity for your going to the dinner. You will have plenty to keep you in countenance at home. Lord St. Aldegonde is not going, nor I fancy any of them. I shall take the Duke with me and Lord Culloden, and if you do not go, I shall take Mr. Putney Giles. The Lord Lieutenant will meet us there. I am sorry about Mrs. Campian, because I know she is not over put out by little things. May I not see her in the course of the day? I should be very sorry that the day should pass over without seeing her.'

'Oh! I dare say she will see you in the course of the day, before you go.'

'When she likes. I shall not go out to-day; I shall keep in my rooms, always at her commands. Between ourselves I shall not be sorry to have a quiet morning and collect my ideas a little. Speech-making is a new thing for me. I wish you would tell me what to say to the county.'

Lothair had appropriated to the Campians one of the most convenient and complete apartments in the castle. It consisted of four chambers, one of them a saloon which had been fitted up for his mother when she married; a pretty saloon, hung with pale green silk, and portraits and scenes inlaid by Vanloo and Boucher. It was rather late in the afternoon when Lothair received a message from Theodora in reply to the wish that he had expressed of seeing her.

When he entered the room she was not seated, her countenance was serious. She advanced, and thanked him for wishing to see her, and regretted she could not receive him at an earlier hour. 'I fear it may have inconvenienced you,' she added; 'but my mind has been much disturbed, and too agitated for conversation.'

'Even now I may be an intruder?'

'No, it is past; on the contrary, I wish to speak to you; indeed, you are the only person with whom I could speak,' and she sate down.

Her countenance, which was unusually pale when he entered, became flushed. 'It is not a subject for the festive hour of your life,' she said, 'but I cannot resist my fate.'

'Your fate must always interest me,' murmured Lothair.

'Yes, but my fate is the fate of ages and of nations,' said Theodora, throwing up her head with that tumult of the brow which he had once before noticed. 'Amid the tortures of my spirit at this moment, not the least is that there is only one person I can appeal to, and he is one to whom I have no right to make that appeal.'

'If I be that person,' said Lothair, 'you have every right, for I am devoted to you.'

'Yes; but it is not personal devotion that is the qualification needed. It is not sympathy with me that would authorise such an appeal. It must be sympathy with a cause, and a cause for which I fear you do not, perhaps I should say you cannot, feel.'

'Why?' said Lothair.

'Why should you feel for my fallen country, who are the proudest citizen of the proudest of lands? Why should you feel for its debasing thraldom, you who, in the religious mystification of man, have at least the noble privilege of being a Protestant?'

'You speak of Rome?'

'Yes, of the only thought I have or ever had. I speak of that country which first impressed upon the world a general and enduring form of masculine virtue; the land of liberty, and law, and eloquence, and military genius, now garrisoned by monks and governed by a doting priest.'

'Everybody must be interested about Rome,' said Lothair. 'Rome is the country of the world, and even the doting priest you talk of boasts of two hundred millions of subjects.'

'If he were at Avignon again, I should not care for his boasts,' said Theodora. 'I do not grudge him his spiritual subjects; I am content to leave his superstition to Time. Time is no longer slow; his scythe mows quickly in this age. But when his debasing creeds are palmed off on man by the authority of our glorious Capitol, and the slavery of the human mind is schemed and carried on in the Forum, then, if there be real Roman blood left, and I thank my Creator there is much, it is time for it to mount and move,' and she rose and walked up and down the room.'

'You have had news from Rome?' said Lothair.

'I have had news from Rome,' she replied, speaking slowly in a deep voice. And there was a pause.

Then Lothair said, 'When you have alluded to these matters before, you never spoke of them in a sanguine spirit.'

'I have seen the cause triumph,' said Theodora; 'the sacred cause of truth, of justice, of national honour. I have sate at the feet of the triumvirate of the Roman Republic: men who for virtue, and genius, and warlike skill and valour, and every quality that exalts man, were never surpassed in the olden time; no, not by the Catos and the Scipios; and I have seen the blood of my own race poured like a rich vintage on the victorious Roman soil. My father fell, who in stature and in mien was a god; and, since then, my beautiful brothers, with shapes to enshrine in temples; and I have smiled amid the slaughter of my race, for I believed that Rome was free; and yet all this vanished. How then, when we talked, could I be sanguine?'

'And yet you are sanguine now?' said Lothair, with a scrutinising glance, and he rose and joined her, leaning slightly on the mantelpiece.

'There was only one event that could secure the success of our efforts,' said Theodora, 'and that event was so improbable that I had long rejected it from calculation. It has happened, and Rome calls upon me to act.'

'The Papalini are strong,' continued Theodora after a pause; 'they have been long preparing for the French evacuation; they have a considerable and disciplined force of Janissaries, a powerful artillery, the strong places of the city. The result of a rising under such circumstances might be more than doubtful; if unsuccessful, to us it would be disastrous. It is necessary that the Roman States should be invaded, and the Papal army must then quit their capital. We have no fear of them in the field. Yes,' she added with energy, 'we could sweep them from the face of the earth!'

'But the army of Italy,' said Lothair, 'will that be inert?'

'There it is,' said Theodora. 'That has been our stumbling-block. I have always known that if ever the French quitted Rome it would be on the understanding that the house of Savoy should inherit the noble office of securing our servitude. He in whom I alone confide would never credit this, but my information in this respect was authentic. However, it is no longer necessary to discuss the question. News has come, and in no uncertain shape, that whatever may have been the understanding, under no circumstances will the Italian army enter the Roman States. We must strike, therefore, and Rome will be free. But how am I to strike? We have neither money nor arms. We have only men. I can give them no more, because I have already given them everything except my life, which is always theirs. As for my husband, who, I may say, wedded me on the battle-field, so far as wealth was concerned he was then a prince among princes, and would pour forth his treasure and his life with equal eagerness. But things have changed since Aspromonte. The struggle in his own country has entirely deprived him of revenues as great as any forfeited by their Italian princelings. In fact it is only by a chance that he is independent. Had it not been for an excellent man, one of your great English merchants, who was his agent here and managed his affairs, we should have been penniless. His judicious investments of the superfluity of our income, which at the time my husband never even noticed, have secured for Colonel Campian the means of that decorous life which he appreciates, but no more. As for myself these considerations are nothing. I will not say I should be insensible to a refined life with refined com-

panions, if the spirit were content and the heart serene;
but I never could fully realise the abstract idea of what
they call wealth; I never could look upon it except as a
means to an end, and my end has generally been military
material. Perhaps the vicissitudes of my life have made
me insensible to what are called reverses of fortune, for
when a child I remember sleeping on the moonlit flags
of Paris, with no pillow except my tambourine, and I
remember it not without delight. Let us sit down. I feel
I am talking in an excited, injudicious, egotistical, rhap-
sodical manner. I thought I was calm and I meant to
have been clear. But the fact is I am ashamed of myself.
I am doing a wrong thing and in a wrong manner. But I
have had a sleepless night and a day of brooding thought.
I meant once to have asked you to help me, and now
I feel that you are the last person to whom I ought to
appeal.'

'In that you are in error,' said Lothair rising and
taking her hand with an expression of much gravity;
'I am the right person for you to appeal to, the only
person.'

'Nay,' said Theodora, and she shook her head.

'For I owe to you a debt that I never can repay,'
continued Lothair. 'Had it not been for you, I should
have remained what I was when we first met, a prejudiced,
narrow-minded being, with contracted sympathies and
false knowledge, wasting my life on obsolete trifles, and
utterly insensible to the privilege of living in this wondrous
age of change and progress. Why, had it not been for you
I should have at this very moment been lavishing my
fortune on an ecclesiastical toy, which I think of with a
blush. There may be, doubtless there are, opinions in
which we may not agree; but in our love of truth and
justice there is no difference, dearest lady. No; though
you must have felt that I am not, that no one could be,

insensible to your beauty and infinite charms, still it is your consummate character that has justly fascinated my thought and heart; and I have long resolved, were I permitted, to devote to you my fortune and my life.'

CHAPTER L.

THE month of September was considerably advanced, when a cab, evidently from its luggage fresh from the railway, entered the courtyard of Hexham House, of which the shuttered windows indicated the absence of its master, the Cardinal, then in Italy. But it was evident that the person who had arrived was expected, for before his servant could ring the hall bell the door opened, and a grave-looking domestic advanced with much deference, and awaited the presence of no less a personage than Monsignore Berwick.

'We have had a rough passage, good Clifford,' said the great man, alighting, 'but I see you duly received my telegram. You are always ready.'

'I hope my Lord will find it not uncomfortable,' said Clifford. 'I have prepared the little suite which you mentioned, and have been careful that there should be no outward sign of anyone having arrived.'

'And now,' said the Monsignore, stopping for a moment in the hall, 'here is a letter which must be instantly delivered and by a trusty hand,' and he gave it to Mr. Clifford, who, looking at the direction, nodded his head and said, 'By no one but myself. I will show my Lord to his rooms, and depart with this instantly.'

'And bring back a reply,' added the Monsignore.

The well-lit room, the cheerful fire, the judicious refection on a side table, were all circumstances which usually

would have been agreeable to a wearied traveller, but
Monsignore Berwick seemed little to regard them. Though
a man in general superior to care and master of thought,
his countenance was troubled and pensive even to de-
jection.

'Even the winds and waves are against us,' he exclaimed,
too restless to be seated, and walking up and down the
room with his arms behind his back. 'That such a struggle
should fall to my lot! Why was I not a minister in the
days of the Gregorys, the Innocents, even the Leos! But
this is craven. There should be inspiration in peril, and
the greatest where peril is extreme. I am a little upset
with travel and the voyage and those telegrams not being
answered. The good Clifford was wisely provident,' and
he approached the table and took one glass of wine. 'Good!
One must never despair in such a cause. And if the worse
happens, it has happened before: and what then? Suppose
Avignon over again, or even Gaeta, or even Paris? So
long as we never relinquish our title to the Eternal City we
shall be eternal. But then, some say, our enemies before
were the sovereigns; now it is the people. Is it so? True
we have vanquished kings and baffled emperors; but the
French Republic and the Roman Republic have alike
reigned and ruled in the Vatican, and where are they?
We have lost provinces, but we have also gained them.
We have twelve millions of subjects in the United States of
America, and they will increase like the sands of the sea.
Still it is a hideous thing to have come back, as it were, to
the days of the Constable of Bourbon, and to be contemplating the siege of the Holy See, and massacre and pillage
and ineffable horrors! The Papacy may survive such calamities, as it undoubtedly will, but I shall scarcely figure in
history if under my influence such visitations should accrue.
If I had only to deal with men I would not admit of failure;
but when your antagonists are human thoughts, represented

by invisible powers, there is something that might baffle a Machiavel and appal a Borgia.'

While he was meditating in this vein the door opened, and Mr. Clifford with some hasty action and speaking rapidly exclaimed,

'He said he would be here sooner than myself. His carriage was at the door. I drove back as fast as possible; and indeed I hear something now in the court,' and he disappeared.

It was only to usher in, almost immediately, a stately personage in an evening dress, and wearing a decoration of a high class, who saluted the Monsignore with great cordiality.

'I am engaged to dine with the Prussian Ambassador, who has been obliged to come to town to receive a prince of the blood who is visiting the dockyards here; but I thought you might be later than you expected, and I ordered my carriage to be in waiting, so that we have a good little hour, and I can come on to you again afterwards if that will not do.'

'A little hour with us is a long hour with other people,' said the Monsignore, 'because we are friends and can speak without windings. You are a true friend to the Holy See; you have proved it. We are in great trouble and need of aid.'

'I hear that things are not altogether as we could wish,' said the gentleman in an evening dress; 'but I hope, and should think, only annoyances.'

'Dangers,' said Berwick, 'and great.'

'How so?'

'Well, we have invasion threatening us without and insurrection within,' said Berwick. 'We might, though it is doubtful, successfully encounter one of these perils, but their united action must be fatal.'

'All this has come suddenly,' said the gentleman. 'In

the summer you had no fear, and our people wrote to us that we might be perfectly tranquil.'

'Just so,' said Berwick. 'If we had met a month ago I should have told you the same thing. A month ago the revolution seemed lifeless, penniless; without a future, without a resource. They had no money, no credit, no men. At present, quietly but regularly, they are assembling by thousands on our frontiers; they have to our knowledge received two large consignments of small arms, and apparently have unlimited credit with the trade, both in Birmingham and Liège; they have even artillery; everything is paid for in coin or in good bills; and, worst of all, they have a man, the most consummate soldier in Europe. I thought he was at New York, and was in hopes he would never have recrossed the Atlantic; but I know that he passed through Florence a fortnight ago, and I have seen a man who says he spoke to him at Narni.'

'The Italian government must stop all this,' said the gentleman.

'They do not stop it,' said Berwick. 'The government of his Holiness has made every representation to them: we have placed in their hands indubitable evidence of the illegal proceedings that are taking place and of the internal dangers we experience in consequence of their exterior movements. But they do nothing: it is even believed that the royal troops are joining the insurgents, and Garibaldi is spouting with impunity in every balcony of Florence.'

'You may depend upon it that our government is making strong representations to the government of Florence.'

'I come from Paris and elsewhere,' said Berwick with animation and perhaps a degree of impatience. 'I have seen everybody there, and I have heard everything. It is not representations that are wanted from your government; it is something of a different kind.'

'But if you have seen everybody at Paris and heard everything, how can I help you?'

'By acting upon the government here. A word from you to the English Minister would have great weight at this juncture. Queen Victoria is interested in the maintenance of the Papal throne. Her Catholic subjects are counted by millions. The influence of his Holiness has been hitherto exercised against the Fenians. France would interfere if she was sure the step would not be disapproved by England.'

'Interfere!' said the gentleman. 'Our return to Rome almost before we have paid our laundresses' bills in the Eternal City would be a diplomatic scandal.'

'A diplomatic scandal would be preferable to a European revolution.'

'Suppose we were to have both?' and the gentleman drew his chair near the fire.

'I am convinced that a want of firmness now,' said Berwick, 'would lead to inconceivable calamities for all of us.'

'Let us understand each other, my very dear friend Berwick,' said his companion, and he threw his arm over the back of his chair and looked the Roman full in his face. 'You say you have been at Paris and elsewhere, and have seen everybody and heard everything.'

'Yes, yes.'

'Something has happened to us also during the last month, and as unexpectedly as to yourselves.'

'The secret societies? Yes, he spoke to me on that very point, and fully. 'Tis strange, but is only, in my opinion, an additional argument in favour of crushing the evil influence.'

'Well, that he must decide. But the facts are startling. A month ago the secret societies in France were only a name; they existed only in the memory of the police, and almost as a tradition. At present we know that they are in complete organisation, and what is most strange is, that the prefects write they have information that the Mary-

Anne associations, which are essentially republican and are scattered about the provinces, are all revived and are astir. MARY-ANNE, as you know, was the red name for the Republic years ago, and there always was a sort of myth that these societies had been founded by a woman. Of course that is all nonsense, but they keep it up; it affects the public imagination, and my government has undoubted evidence that the word of command has gone round to all these societies that Mary-Anne has returned and will issue her orders, which must be obeyed.'

'The Church is stronger, and especially in the provinces, than the Mary-Anne societies,' said Berwick.

'I hope so,' said his friend; 'but you see, my dear Monsignore, the question with us is not so simple as you put it. The secret societies will not tolerate another Roman interference, to say nothing of the diplomatic hubbub, which we might, if necessary, defy; but what if, taking advantage of the general indignation, your new kingdom of Italy may seize the golden opportunity of making a popular reputation, and declare herself the champion of national independence against the interference of the foreigner? My friend, we tread on delicate ground.'

'If Rome falls, not an existing dynasty in Europe will survive five years,' said Berwick.

'It may be so,' said his companion, but with no expression of incredulity. 'You know how consistently and anxiously I have always laboured to support the authority of the Holy See, and to maintain its territorial position as the guarantee of its independence; but fate has decided against us. I cannot indulge in the belief that his Holiness will ever regain his lost provinces; a capital without a country is an apparent anomaly, which I fear will always embarrass us. We can treat the possession as the capital of Christendom, but, alas! all the world are not as good Christians as ourselves, and Christendom is a country no

longer marked out in the map of the world. I wish,'
continued the gentleman in a tone almost coaxing, 'I wish
we could devise some plan which, humanly speaking, would
secure to his Holiness the possession of his earthly throne
for ever.   I wish I could induce you to consider more
favourably that suggestion, that his Holiness should content himself with the ancient city, and, in possession of St.
Peter's and the Vatican, leave the rest of Rome to the
vulgar cares and the mundane anxieties of the transient
generation.   Yes,' he added with energy, 'if, my dear
Berwick, you could see your way to this, or something like
this, I think, even now and at once, I could venture to
undertake that the Emperor, my master, would soon put an
end to all these disturbances and dangers, and that——'

'Non possumus,' said Berwick, sternly stopping him,
'sooner than that Attila, the Constable of Bourbon, or the
blasphemous orgies of the Red Republic!   After all, it is
the Church against the secret societies.   They are the only
two strong things in Europe, and will survive kings, emperors, or parliaments.'

At this moment there was a tap at the door, and, bidden
to enter, Mr. Clifford presented himself with a sealed paper
for the gentleman in evening dress.   'Your secretary, sir,
brought this, which he said must be given you before you
went to the Ambassador.'

' 'Tis well,' said the gentleman, and he rose, and with a
countenance of some excitement read the paper, which contained a telegram; and then he said, 'This, I think, will
help us out of our immediate difficulties, my dear Monsignore.   Rattazzi has behaved like a man of sense, and has
arrested Garibaldi.   But you do not seem, my friend, as
pleased as I should have anticipated.'

' Garibaldi has been arrested before,' said Berwick

' Well, well, I am hopeful; but I must go to my dinner.
I will see you again to-morrow.'

                         T 2

CHAPTER LI.

THE continuous gathering of what, in popular language, were styled the Garibaldi Volunteers, on the southern border of the Papal territory in the autumn of 1867, was not the only or perhaps the greatest danger which then threatened the Holy See, though the one which most attracted its alarmed attention. The considerable numbers in which this assemblage was suddenly occurring; the fact that the son of the Liberator had already taken its command, and only as the precursor of his formidable sire; the accredited rumour that Ghirelli at the head of a purely Roman legion was daily expected to join the frontier force; that Nicotera was stirring in the old Neapolitan kingdom, while the Liberator himself at Florence and in other parts of Tuscany was even ostentatiously, certainly with impunity, preaching the new crusade and using all his irresistible influence with the populace to excite their sympathies and to stimulate their energy, might well justify the extreme apprehension of the court of Rome. And yet dangers at least equal, and almost as close, were at the same time preparing unnoticed and unknown.

In the mountainous range between Fiascone and Viterbo, contiguous to the sea, is a valley surrounded by chains of steep and barren hills, but which is watered by a torrent scarcely dry even in summer; so that the valley itself, which is not inconsiderable in its breadth, is never without verdure, while almost a forest of brushwood formed of shrubs, which in England we should consider rare, bounds the natural turf and ascends, sometimes to no inconsiderable height, the nearest hills.

Into this valley, towards the middle of September, there

defiled one afternoon, through a narrow pass, a band of about
fifty men, all armed, and conducting a cavalcade or rather
a caravan of mules laden with munitions of war and other
stores. When they had gained the centre of the valley, and
a general halt was accomplished, their commander, accompanied by one who was apparently an officer, surveyed all
the points of the locality ; and when their companions had
rested and refreshed themselves, they gave the necessary
orders for the preparation of a camp. The turf already
afforded a sufficient area for their present wants, but it was
announced that on the morrow they must commence clearing the brushwood. In the mean time one of the liveliest
scenes of military life soon rapidly developed itself: the
canvas houses were pitched, the sentries appointed, the
videttes established. The commissariat was limited to bread
and olives, and generally the running stream, varied sometimes by coffee and always consoled by tobacco.

On the third day, amidst their cheerful though by no
means light labours, a second caravan arrived, evidently
expected and heartily welcomed. Then in another eight-
and-forty hours, smaller bodies of men seemed to drop down
from the hills, generally without stores, but always armed.
Then men came from neighbouring islands in open boats,
and one morning a considerable detachment crossed the
water from Corsica. So that at the end of a week or ten
days there was an armed force of several hundred men in
this once silent valley, now a scene of constant stir and con-
tinual animation, for some one or something was always
arriving, and from every quarter ; men and arms and stores
crept in from every wild pass of the mountains and every
little rocky harbour of the coast.

About this time, while the officer in command was re-
viewing a considerable portion of the troops, the rest labouring in still clearing the brushwood and establishing the
many works incidental to a camp, half a dozen horsemen

were seen descending the mountain pass by which the
original body had entered the valley. A scout had preceded
them, and the troops with enthusiasm awaited the arrival of
that leader a message from whose magic name had summoned them to this secluded rendezvous from many a distant state and city. Unruffled, but with an inspiring fire
in his pleased keen eye, that General answered their devoted salute whom hitherto we have known by his travelling name of Captain Bruges.

It was only towards the end of the preceding month that
he had resolved to take the field; but the organisation of
the secret societies is so complete that he knew he could
always almost instantly secure the assembling of a picked
force in a particular place. The telegraph circulated its
mystic messages to every part of France and Italy and
Belgium, and to some old friends not so conveniently at
hand, but who he doubted not would arrive in due time for
action. He himself had employed the interval in forward-
ing all necessary supplies, and he had passed through
Florence in order that he might confer with the great
spirit of Italian movement and plan with him the impending campaign.

After he had passed in review the troops, the General,
with the officers of his staff who had accompanied him,
visited on foot every part of the camp. Several of the men
he recognised by name; to all of them he addressed some
inspiring word: a memory of combats in which they had
fought together, or happy allusions to adventures of romantic peril; some question which indicated that local knowledge which is magical for those who are away from
home; mixed with all this, sharp, clear enquiries as to the
business of the hour, which proved the master of detail,
severe in discipline but never deficient in sympathy for his
troops.

After sunset, enveloped in their cloaks, the General and

his companions, the party increased by the officers who had been in command previous to his arrival, smoked their cigars round the camp fire.

'Well, Sarano,' said the General, 'I will look over your muster-roll to-morrow, but I should suppose I may count on a thousand rifles or so. I want three, and we shall get them. The great man would have supplied them me at once, but I will not have boys. He must send those on to Menotti. I told him, "I am not a man of genius; I do not pretend to conquer kingdoms with boys. Give me old soldiers, men who have served a couple of campaigns, and been seasoned with four-and-twenty months of camp life, and I will not disgrace you or myself."'

'We have had no news from the other place for a long time,' said Sarano. 'How is it?'

'Well enough. They are in the mountains about Nerola, in a position not very unlike this; numerically strong, for Nicotera has joined them, and Ghirelli with the Roman Legion is at hand. They must be quiet till the great man joins them; I am told they are restless. There has been too much noise about the whole business. Had they been as mum as you have been, we should not have had all these representations from France and these threatened difficulties from that quarter. The Papalini would have complained and remonstrated, and Rattazzi could have conscientiously assured the people at Paris that they were dealing with exaggerations and bugbears; the very existence of the frontier force would have become a controversy, and while the newspapers were proving it was a myth we should have been in the Vatican.'

'And when shall we be there, General?'

'I do not want to move for a month. By that time I shall have two thousand five hundred or three thousand of my old comrades, and the great man will have put his boys in trim. Both bodies must leave their mountains at

the same time, join in the open country and march to
Rome.'

As the night advanced, several of the party rose and left
the camp fire, some to their tents, some to their duties.
Two of the staff remained with the General.

'I am disappointed and uneasy that we have not heard
from Paris,' said one of them.

'I am disappointed,' said the General, 'but not uneasy;
she never makes a mistake.'

'The risk was too great,' rejoined the speaker in a depressed tone.

'I do not see that,' said the General. 'What is the
risk? Who could possibly suspect the lady's maid of
the Princess of Tivoli! I am told that the Princess has
become quite a favourite at the Tuileries.'

'They say that the police is not so well informed as it
used to be; nevertheless, I confess I should be much happier
were she sitting round this camp fire.'

'Courage!' said the General. 'I do not believe in many
things, but I do believe in the divine Theodora. What say
you, Captain Muriel? I hope you are not offended by my
criticism of young soldiers. You are the youngest in our
band, but you have good military stuff in you, and will be
soon seasoned.'

'I feel I serve under a master of the art,' replied Lothair,
'and will not take the gloomy view of Colonel Campian
about our best friend, though I share all his disappointment. It seems to me that detection is impossible. I am
sure that I could not have recognised her when I handed
the Princess into her carriage.'

'The step was absolutely necessary,' said the General;
'no one could be trusted but herself, no other person has
the influence. All our danger is from France. The Italian
troops will never cross the frontier to attack us, rest
assured of that. I have proof of it. And it is most difficult,
almost impossible, for the French to return. There never

would have been an idea of such a step, if there had been a little more discretion at Florence, less of those manifestoes and speeches from balconies. But we must not criticise one who is above criticism. Without him we could do nothing, and when he stamps his foot men rise from the earth. I will go the rounds; come with me, Captain Muriel. Colonel, I order you to your tent: you are a veteran; the only one among us, at least on the staff, who was wounded at Aspromonte.'

CHAPTER LII.

THE life of Lothair had been so strange and exciting since he quitted Muriel Towers that he had found little time for that reflection in which he was once so prone to indulge. Perhaps he shrank from it. If he wanted an easy distraction from self-criticism (it may be a convenient refuge from the scruples, or even the pangs, of conscience), it was profusely supplied by the startling affairs of which he formed a part, the singular characters with whom he was placed in contact, the risk and responsibility which seemed suddenly to have encompassed him with their over-stimulating influence, and lastly, by the novelty of foreign travel, which even under ordinary circumstances has a tendency to rouse and stir up even ordinary men.

So long as Theodora was his companion in their councils and he was listening to her deep plans and daring suggestions, enforced by that calm enthusiasm which was not the least powerful of her commanding spells, it is not perhaps surprising that he should have yielded without an effort to her bewitching ascendency. But when they had separated, and she had embarked on that perilous enterprise of personally conferring with the chiefs of those secret societies of France which had been fancifully baptised by her

popular name and had nurtured her tradition as a religious
faith, it might have been supposed that Lothair, left to
himself, might have recurred to the earlier sentiments of
his youth. But he was not left to himself. He was left
with her injunctions, and the spirit of the oracle, though the
divinity was no longer visible, pervaded his mind and life.

Lothair was to accompany the General as one of his
aides-de-camp, and he was to meet Theodora again on
what was contemplated as the field of memorable actions.
Theodora had wisely calculated on the influence, beneficial
in her view, which the character of a man like the General
would exercise over Lothair. This consummate military
leader, though he had pursued a daring career and was a
man of strong convictions, was distinguished by an almost
unerring judgment and a mastery of method rarely surpassed. Though he was without imagination or sentiment,
there were occasions on which he had shown he was not
deficient in a becoming sympathy, and he had a rapid and
correct perception of character. He was a thoroughly
honest man, and in the course of a life of great trial and
vicissitude even envenomed foes had never impeached his
pure integrity. For the rest, he was unselfish, but severe
in discipline, inflexible and even ruthless in the fulfilment
of his purpose. A certain simplicity of speech and conduct,
and a disinterestedness which even in little things was
constantly exhibiting itself, gave to his character even
charm, and rendered personal intercourse with him highly
agreeable.

In the countless arrangements which had to be made,
Lothair was never wearied in recognising and admiring the
prescience and precision of his chief; and when the day
had died, and for a moment they had ceased from their
labours, or were travelling together, often through the
night, Lothair found in the conversation of his companion,
artless and unrestrained, a wonderful fund of knowledge

both of men and things, and that, too, in very different
climes and countries.

The camp in the Apennines was not favourable to useless
reverie. Lothair found unceasing and deeply interesting
occupation in his numerous and novel duties, and if his
thoughts for a moment wandered beyond the barren peaks
around him, they were attracted and engrossed by one subject, and that was, naturally, Theodora. From her they
had heard nothing since her departure, except a mysterious
though not discouraging telegram which was given to
them by Colonel Campian when he had joined them at
Florence. It was difficult not to feel anxious about her,
though the General would never admit the possibility of
her personal danger.

In this state of affairs, a week having elapsed since his
arrival at the camp, Lothair, who had been visiting the
outposts, was summoned one morning by an orderly to the
tent of the General. That personage was on his legs when
Lothair entered it, and was dictating to an officer writing
at a table.

'You ought to know my military secretary,' said the
General as Lothair entered, 'and therefore I will introduce
you.'

Lothair was commencing a suitable reverence of recognition as the secretary raised his head to receive it, when
he suddenly stopped, changed colour, and for a moment
seemed to lose himself, and then murmured, 'Is it possible?'

It was indeed Theodora: clothed in male attire she
seemed a stripling.

'Quite possible,' she said, 'and all is well. But I found
it a longer business than I had counted on. You see, there
are so many new persons who knew me only by tradition,
but with whom it was necessary I should personally confer.
And I had more difficulty, just now, in getting through
Florence than I had anticipated. The Papalini and the

French are both worrying our allies in that city about the
gathering on the southern frontier, and there is a sort of
examination, true or false I will not aver, of all who depart.
However, I managed to pass with some soldiers' wives who
were carrying fruit as far as Narni, and there I met an old
comrade of Aspromonte, who is a custom-officer now, but
true to the good cause, and he, and his daughter who is
with me, helped me through everything, and so I am with
my dear friends again.'

After some slight conversation in this vein Theodora
entered into a detailed narrative of her proceedings, and
gave to them her views of the condition of affairs.

'By one thing, above all others,' she said, 'I am impressed, and that is the unprecedented efforts which Rome
is making to obtain the return of the French.   There never
was such influence exercised, such distinct offers made,
such prospects intimated.   You may prepare yourself for
anything: a papal coronation, a family pontiff; I could
hardly say a king of Rome, though he has been reminded
of that royal fact.   Our friends have acted with equal
energy and with perfect temper.   The heads of the societies
have met in council, and resolved that if France will refuse
to interfere, no domestic disturbance shall be attempted
during this reign, and they have communicated this resolution to head-quarters.   He trusts them; he knows they
are honest men.   They did something like this before the
Italian war, when he hesitated about heading the army
from the fear of domestic revolution.   Anxious to secure
the freedom of Italy, they apprised him that if he personally
entered the field they would undertake to ensure tranquillity at home.   The engagement was scrupulously fulfilled.
When I left Paris all looked well, but affairs require the
utmost vigilance and courage.   It is a mighty struggle;
it is a struggle between the Church and the secret societies;
and it is a death struggle.'

CHAPTER LIII.

During the week that elapsed after the arrival of Theodora
at the camp, many recruits and considerable supplies of
military stores reached the valley. Theodora really acted
as secretary to the General, and her labours were not light.
Though Lothair was frequently in her presence, they were
never or rarely alone, and when they conversed together
her talk was of details. The scouts, too, had brought
information, which might have been expected, that their
rendezvous was no longer a secret at Rome. The garrison
of the neighbouring town of Viterbo had therefore been
increased, and there was even the commencement of an
entrenched camp in the vicinity of that place, to be garrisoned by a detachment of the legion of Antibes and other
good troops, so that any junction between the General and
Garibaldi, if contemplated, should not be easily effected.

In the meantime, the life of the camp was busy. The
daily drill and exercise of two thousand men was not a
slight affair, and the constant changes in orders which the
arrival of bodies of recruits occasioned rendered this primary
duty more difficult; the office of quartermaster required
the utmost resource and temper; the commissariat, which
from the nature of the country could depend little upon
forage, demanded extreme husbandry and forbearance. But
perhaps no labours were more severe than those of the
armourers, the clink of whose instruments resounded unceasingly in the valley. And yet such is the magic of
method, when directed by a master mind, that the whole
went on with the regularity and precision of machinery.
More than two thousand armed men, all of whom had been
accustomed to an irregular, some to a lawless life, were as

docile as children; animated, in general, by what they deemed a sacred cause, and led by a chief whom they universally alike adored and feared.

Among these wild warriors, Theodora, delicate and fragile, but with a mien of majesty, moved like the spirit of some other world, and was viewed by them with admiration not unmixed with awe. Veterans round the camp fire had told to the new recruits her deeds of prowess and devotion; how triumphantly she had charged at Voltorno, and how heroically she had borne their standard when they were betrayed at fatal Aspromonte.

The sun had sunk behind the mountains, but was still high in the western heaven, when a mounted lancer was observed descending a distant pass into the valley. The General and his staff had not long commenced their principal meal of the day, of which the disappearance of the sun behind the peak was the accustomed signal. This permitted them, without inconvenience, to take their simple repast in the open, but still warm, air. Theodora was seated between the General and her husband, and her eye was the first that caught the figure of the distant but descending stranger.

'What is that?' she asked.

The General immediately using his telescope, after a moment's examination, said:

'A lancer of the Royal Guard.'

All eyes were now fixed upon the movements of the horseman. He had descended the winding steep, and now was tracking the craggy path which led into the plain. As he reached the precinct of the camp he was challenged but not detained. Nearer and nearer he approached, and it was evident from his uniform that the conjecture of his character by the General was correct.

'A deserter from the Guard,' whispered Colonel Campian to Lothair.

The horseman was conducted by an officer to the presence of the commander. When that presence was reached the lancer, still silent, slowly lowered his tall weapon and offered the General the despatch which was fastened to the head of his spear.

Every eye was on the countenance of their chief as he perused the missive, but that countenance was always inscrutable. It was observed, however, that he read the paper twice. Looking up, the General said to the officer: 'See that the bearer is well quartered. This is for you,' he added in a low voice to Theodora, and he gave her an enclosure; 'read it quietly, and then come into my tent.'

Theodora read the letter, and quietly; though, without the preparatory hint, it might have been difficult to have concealed her emotion. Then, after a short pause, she rose, and the General, requesting his companions not to disturb themselves, joined her, and they proceeded in silence to his tent.

'He is arrested,' said the General when they had entered it, 'and taken to Alessandria, where he is a close prisoner. 'Tis a blow, but I am more grieved than surprised.'

This was the arrest of Garibaldi at Sinigaglia by the Italian Government, which had been communicated at Hexham House to Monsignore Berwick by his evening visitor.

'How will it affect operations in the field?' enquired Theodora.

'According to this despatch, in no degree. Our original plan is to be pursued, and acted upon the moment we are ready. That should be in a fortnight, or perhaps three weeks. Menotti is to take the command on the southern frontier. Well, it may prevent jealousies. I think I shall send Sarano there to reconnoitre; he is well both with Nicotera and Ghirelli, and may keep things straight.'

'But there are other affairs besides operations in the

field,' said Theodora, 'and scarcely less critical. Read
this,' and she gave him the enclosure, which ran in these
words:

'The General will tell thee what has happened. Have
no fear for that. All will go right. It will not alter our
plans a bunch of grapes. Be perfectly easy about this
country. No Italian soldier will ever cross the frontier
except to combat the French. Write that on thy heart.
Are other things as well? other places? My advices are
bad. All the prelates are on their knees to him, with
blessings on their lips and curses in their pockets. Arch-
bishop of Paris is as bad as any. Berwick is at Biarritz,
an inexhaustible intriguer; the only priest I fear. I hear
from one who never misled me that the Polhes brigade has
orders to be in readiness. The MARY-ANNE societies are
not strong enough for the situation; too local: he listens
to them, but he has given no pledge. We must go deeper.
'Tis an affair of "MADRE NATURA." Thou must see
Colonna.'

'Colonna is at Rome,' said the General, 'and cannot be
spared. He is acting President of the National Committee,
and has enough upon his hands.'

'I must see him,' said Theodora.

'I had hoped I had heard the last of the "Madre
Natura,"' said the General with an air of discontent.

'And the Neapolitans hope they have heard the last of
the eruptions of their mountain,' said Theodora; 'but the
necessities of things are sterner stuff than the hopes of
men.'

'Its last effort appalled and outraged Europe,' said the
General.

'Its last effort forced the French into Italy, and has
freed the country from the Alps to the Adriatic,' rejoined
Theodora.

'If the great man had only been as quiet as we have

been,' said the General, lighting a cigar, 'we might have been in Rome by this time.'

'If the great man had been quiet, we should not have had a volunteer in our valley,' said Theodora. 'My faith in him is implicit; he has been right in everything, and has never failed except when he has been betrayed. I see no hope for Rome except in his convictions and energy. I do not wish to die and feel I have devoted my life only to secure the triumph of Savoyards who have sold their own country, and of priests whose impostures have degraded mine.'

'Ah! those priests!' exclaimed the General. 'I really do not much care for anything else. They say the Savoyard is not a bad comrade, and at any rate he can charge like a soldier. But those priests! I fluttered them once! Why did I spare any? Why did I not burn down St. Peter's? I proposed it, but Mirandola, with his history and his love of art and all that old furniture, would reserve it for a temple of the true God and for the glory of Europe! Fine results we have accomplished! And now we are here, hardly knowing where we are, and, as it appears, hardly knowing what to do.'

'Not so, dear General,' said Theodora. 'Where we are is the threshold of Rome, and if we are wise we shall soon cross it. This arrest of our great friend is a misfortune, but not an irredeemable one. I thoroughly credit what he says about the Italian troops. Rest assured he knows what he is talking about: they will never cross the frontier against us. The danger is from another land. But there will be no peril if we are prompt and firm. Clear your mind of all these dark feelings about the MADRE NATURA. All that we require is that the most powerful and the most secret association in Europe should ratify what the local societies of France have already intimated. It will be enough. Send for Colonna, and leave the rest to me.'

U

CHAPTER LIV.

The 'Madre Natura' is the oldest, the most powerful, and the most occult of the secret societies of Italy. Its mythic origin reaches the era of paganism, and it is not impossible that it may have been founded by some of the despoiled professors of the ancient faith. As time advanced, the brotherhood assumed many outward forms, according to the varying spirit of the age: sometimes they were free-masons, sometimes they were soldiers, sometimes artists, sometimes men of letters. But whether their external representation were a lodge, a commandery, a studio, or an academy, their inward purpose was ever the same; and that was to cherish the memory, and, if possible, to secure the restoration, of the Roman republic, and to expel from the Aryan settlement of Romulus the creeds and sovereignty of what they styled the Semitic invasion.

The 'Madre Natura' have a tradition that one of the most celebrated of the Popes was admitted to their frater-nity as Cardinal dei Modici, and that when he ascended the throne, mainly through their labours, he was called upon to co-operate in the fulfilment of the great idea. An individual who in his youth has been the member of a secret society, and subsequently ascends a throne, may find himself in an embarrassing position. This, however, ac-cording to the tradition, which there is some documentary ground to accredit, was not the perplexing lot of his Holi-ness, Pope Leo X. His tastes and convictions were in entire unison with his early engagements, and it is believed that he took an early and no unwilling opportunity of sub-mitting to the conclave a proposition to consider whether it was not both expedient and practicable to return to the ancient faith, for which their temples had been originally erected.

The chief tenet of the society of 'MADRE NATURA' is denoted by its name. They could conceive nothing more benignant and more beautiful, more provident and more powerful, more essentially divine, than that system of creative order to which they owed their being, and in which it was their privilege to exist. But they differed from other schools of philosophy that have held this faith in this singular particular: they recognised the inability of the Latin race to pursue the worship of nature in an abstract spirit, and they desired to revive those exquisite personifications of the abounding qualities of the mighty mother which the Aryan genius had bequeathed to the admiration of man. Parthenope was again to rule at Naples instead of Januarius, and starveling saints and winking madonnas were to restore their usurped altars to the god of the silver bow and the radiant daughter of the foaming wave.

Although the society of 'MADRE NATURA' themselves accepted the allegorical interpretation which the Neo-Platonists had placed upon the Pagan creeds during the first ages of Christianity, they could not suppose that the populace could ever comprehend an exposition so refined, not to say so fanciful. They guarded, therefore, against the corruptions and abuses of the religion of nature by the entire abolition of the priestly order, and in the principle that every man should be his own priest they believed they had found the necessary security.

As it was evident that the arrest of Garibaldi could not be kept secret, the General thought it most prudent to be himself the herald of its occurrence, which he announced to the troops in a manner as little discouraging as he could devise. It was difficult to extenuate the consequences of so great a blow, but they were assured that it was not a

catastrophe, and would not in the slightest degree affect
the execution of the plans previously resolved on.   Two or
three days later some increase of confidence was occasioned
by the authentic intelligence that Garibaldi had been removed from his stern imprisonment at Alessandria, and
conveyed to his island-home, Caprera, though still a prisoner.

About this time, the General said to Lothair, 'My
secretary has occasion to go on an expedition.   I shall
send a small detachment of cavalry with her, and you will
be at its head.   She has requested that her husband should
have this office, but that is impossible; I cannot spare my
best officer.   It is your first command, and though I hope
it will involve no great difficulty, there is no command
that does not require courage and discretion.   The distance is not very great, and so long as you are in the
mountains you will probably be safe; but in leaving this
range and gaining the southern Apennines, which is your
point of arrival, you will have to cross the open country.
I do not hear the Papalini are in force there; I believe
they have concentrated themselves at Rome, and about
Viterbo.   If you meet any scouts and reconnoitring parties,
you will be able to give a good account of them, and
probably they will be as little anxious to encounter you as
you to meet them.   But we must be prepared for everything, and you may be threatened by the enemy in force;
in that case you will cross the Italian frontier, in the
immediate neighbourhood of which you will keep during
the passage of the open country, and surrender yourselves
and your arms to the authorities.   They will not be very
severe; but at whatever cost and whatever may be the
odds, Theodora must never be a prisoner to the Papalini.
You will depart to-morrow at dawn.'

There is nothing so animating, so invigorating alike to
body and soul, so truly delicious, as travelling among

mountains in the early hours of the day. The freshness
of nature falls upon a responsive frame, and the nobility of
the scene discards the petty thoughts that pester ordinary
life. So felt Captain Muriel, as with every military precaution he conducted his little troop and his precious
charge among the winding passes of the Apennines; at
first dim in the matin twilight, then soft with incipient
day, then coruscating with golden flashes. Sometimes
they descended from the austere heights into the sylvan
intricacies of chesnut forests, amid the rush of waters and
the fragrant stir of ancient trees; and then again ascending to lofty summits, ranges of interminable hills, grey or
green, expanded before them, with ever and anon a glimpse
of plains, and sometimes the splendour and the odour of
the sea.

Theodora rode a mule, which had been presented to the
General by some admirer. It was an animal of remarkable
beauty and intelligence, perfectly aware, apparently, of the
importance of its present trust, and proud of its rich
accoutrements, its padded saddle of crimson velvet, and its
silver bells. A couple of troopers formed the advanced
guard, and the same number at a certain distance furnished the rear. The body of the detachment, fifteen
strong, with the sumpter mules, generally followed Theodora, by whose side, whenever the way permitted, rode
their commander. Since he left England Lothair had
never been so much alone with Theodora. What struck
him most now, as indeed previously at the camp, was that
she never alluded to the past. For her there would seem
to be no Muriel Towers, no Belmont, no England. You
would have supposed that she had been born in the
Apennines and had never quitted them. All her conversation was details, political or military. Not that her manner
was changed to Lothair. It was not only as kind as
before but it was sometimes unusually and even unneces-

sarily tender, as if she reproached herself for the too frequent and too evident self-engrossment of her thoughts, and wished to intimate to him that though her brain were absorbed, her heart was still gentle and true.

Two hours after noon they halted in a green nook, near a beautiful cascade that descended in a mist down a sylvan cleft, and poured its pellucid stream, for their delightful use, into a natural basin of marble. The men picketed their horses, and their corporal, who was a man of the country and their guide, distributed their rations. All vied with each other in administering to the comfort and convenience of Theodora, and Lothair hovered about her as a bee about a flower; but she was silent, which he wished to impute to fatigue. But she said she was not at all fatigued, indeed quite fresh. Before they resumed their journey he could not refrain from observing on the beauty of their resting-place. She assented with a pleasing nod, and then resuming her accustomed abstraction she said: 'The more I think, the more I am convinced that the battle is not to be fought in this country, but in France.'

After one more ascent, and that comparatively a gentle one, it was evident that they were gradually emerging from the mountainous region. Their course since their halting lay through a spar of the chief chain they had hitherto pursued, and a little after sunset they arrived at a farm-house, which the corporal informed his Captain was the intended quarter of Theodora for the night, as the horses could proceed no farther without rest. At dawn they were to resume their way, and soon to cross the open country, where danger, if any, was to be anticipated.

The farmer was frightened when he was summoned from his house by a party of armed men; but having some good ducats given him in advance, and being assured they were all Christians, he took heart and laboured to do what they desired. Theodora duly found herself in becoming quar-tera, and a sentry was mounted at her residence. The troopers, who had been quite content to wrap themselves in their cloaks and pass the night in the air, were pleased to find no despicable accommodation in the out-buildings of the farm, and still more with the proffered vintage of their host. As for Lothair, he enveloped himself in his mantle and threw himself on a bed of sacks, with a truss of Indian corn for his pillow, and though he began by musing over Theodora, in a few minutes he was immersed in that profound and dreamless sleep which a life of action and mountain air combined can alone secure.

CHAPTER LV.

The open country extending from the Apennines to the very gates of Rome, and which they had now to cross, was in general a desert; a plain clothed with a coarse vegetation, and undulating with an interminable series of low and uncouth mounds, without any of the grace of form which always attends the disposition of nature. Nature had not created them. They were the offspring of man and time, and of their rival powers of destruction. Ages of civilisation were engulfed in this drear expanse. They were the tombs of empires and the sepulchres of contending races. The Campagna proper has at least the grace of aqueducts to break its monotony, and everywhere the cerulean spell of distance; but in this grim solitude antiquity has left only the memory of its violence and crimes, and nothing is beautiful except the sky.

The orders of the General to direct their course as much as possible in the vicinity of the Italian frontier, though it lengthened their journey, somewhat mitigated its dreariness, and an hour after noon, after traversing some flinty fields, they observed in the distance an olive wood, beneath the pale shade of which, and among whose twisted branches and contorted roots, they had contemplated finding a halting-place. But here the advanced guard observed already an encampment, and one of them rode back to report the discovery.

A needless alarm; for after a due reconnaissance, they were ascertained to be friends, a band of patriots about to join the General in his encampment among the mountains. They reported that a division of the Italian army was assembled in force upon the frontier, but that several regiments had already signified to their commanders that they would not fight against Garibaldi or his friends. They confirmed also the news that the great leader himself was a prisoner at Caprera; that although his son Menotti by his command had withdrawn from Norola, his force was really increased by the junction of Ghirelli and the Roman legion, twelve hundred strong, and that five hundred riflemen would join the General in the course of the week.

A little before sunset they had completed the passage of the open country, and had entered the opposite branch of the Apennines, which they had long observed in the distance. After wandering among some rocky ground, they entered a defile amid hills covered with ilex, and thence emerging found themselves in a valley of some expanse and considerable cultivation; bright crops, vineyards in which the vine was married to the elm, orchards full of fruit, and groves of olive; in the distance blue hills that were becoming dark in the twilight, and in the centre of the plain, upon a gentle and wooded elevation, a vast pile of building, the exact character of which at this hour it was difficult to recognise, for even as Theodora mentioned to Lothair that they now beheld the object of their journey, the twilight seemed to vanish and the stars glistened in the dark heavens.

Though the building seemed so near, it was yet a considerable time before they reached the wooded hill, and though its ascent was easy, it was night before they halted in face of a huge gate flanked by high stone walls. A single light in one of the windows of the vast pile which it enclosed was the only evidence of human habitation.

The corporal sounded a bugle, and immediately the light moved and noises were heard; the opening of the hall doors, and then the sudden flame of torches, and the advent of many feet. The great gate slowly opened, and a steward and several serving men appeared. The steward addressed Theodora and Lothair, and invited them to dismount and enter what now appeared to be a garden with statues and terraces and fountains and rows of cypress, its infinite dilapidation not being recognisable in the deceptive hour; and he informed the escort that their quarters were prepared for them, to which they were at once attended. Guiding their Captain and his charge, they soon approached a double flight of steps, and ascending, reached the main terrace from which the building immediately rose. It was, in truth, a castle of the middle ages, on which a Roman prince, at the commencement of the last century, had engrafted the character of one of those vast and ornate villas then the mode, but its original character still asserted itself, and notwithstanding its Tuscan basement and its Ionic pilasters, its rich pediments and delicate volutes, in the distant landscape it still seemed a fortress in the commanding position which became the residence of a feudal chief.

They entered through a Palladian vestibule a hall which they felt must be of huge dimensions, though with the aid of a single torch it was impossible to trace its limits, either of extent or of elevation. Then bowing before them, and lighting as it were their immediate steps, the steward guided them down a long and lofty corridor, which led to

the entrance of several chambers, all vast, with little furniture, but their walls covered with pictures. At length he
opened a door and ushered them into a saloon, which was
in itself bright and glowing, but of which the lively air
was heightened by its contrast with the preceding scene.
It was lofty, and hung with faded satin in gilded panels
still bright. An ancient chandelier of Venetian crystal
hung illumined from the painted ceiling, and on the silver
dogs of the marble hearth a fresh block of cedar had just
been thrown and blazed with aromatic light.

A lady came forward and embraced Theodora, and then
greeted Lothair with cordiality. 'We must dine to-day
even later than you do in London,' said the Princess of
Tivoli, 'but we have been expecting you these two hours.'
Then she drew Theodora aside, and said, 'He is here; but
you must be tired, my best beloved. As some wise man
said: "Business to-morrow."'

'No, no,' said Theodora; 'now, now: I am never tired.
The only thing that exhausts me is suspense.'

'It shall be so. At present I will take you away to
shake the dust off your armour; and Serafino attend to
Captain Muriel.'

CHAPTER LVI.

WHEN they assembled again in the saloon there was an
addition to their party in the person of a gentleman of
distinguished appearance. His age could hardly have
much exceeded that of thirty, but time had agitated his
truly Roman countenance, one which we now find only in
consular and imperial busts, or in the chance visage of a
Roman shepherd or a Neapolitan bandit. He was a shade
above the middle height, with a frame of well-knit sym-

metry. His proud head was proudly placed on broad
shoulders, and neither time nor indulgence had marred his
slender waist. His dark brown hair was short and hya-
cinthine, close to his white forehead, and naturally showing
his small ears. He wore no whiskers, and his moustache
was limited to the centre of his upper lip.

When Theodora entered and offered him her hand he
pressed it to his lips with gravity and proud homage, and
then their hostess said, 'Captain Muriel, let me present you
to a Prince who will not bear his titles, and whom, therefore, I must call by his name—Romolo Colonna.'

The large folding doors, richly painted and gilt, though
dim from neglect and time, and sustained by columns of
precious marbles, were suddenly opened and revealed
another saloon, in which was a round table brightly lighted,
and to which the Princess invited her friends.

Their conversation at dinner was lively and sustained ;
the travels of the last two days formed a natural part, and
were apposite to commence with, but they were soon engrossed in the great subject of their lives; and Colonna,
who had left Rome only four-and-twenty hours, gave them
interesting details of the critical condition of that capital.
When the repast was concluded the Princess rose, and,
accompanied by Lothair, re-entered the saloon, but Theodora and Colonna lingered behind, and finally seating
themselves at the farthest end of the apartment in which
they had dined, became engaged in earnest conversation.

'You have seen a great deal since we first met at Belmont,' said the Princess to Lothair.

'It seems to me now,' said Lothair, 'that I know as much
of life then as I did of the stars above us, about whose
purposes and fortunes I used to puzzle myself.'

'And might have remained in that ignorance. The great
majority of men exist but do not live, like Italy in the last
century. The power of the passions, the force of the will,

the creative energy of the imagination, these make life, and
reveal to us a world of which the million are entirely
ignorant. You have been fortunate in your youth to have
become acquainted with a great woman. It developes all a
man's powers, and gives him a thousand talents.'

'I often think,' said Lothair, 'that I have neither powers
nor talents, but am drifting without an orbit.'

'Into infinite space,' said the Princess. 'Well, one might
do worse than that. But it is not so. In the long run
your nature will prevail, and you will fulfil your organic
purpose; but you will accomplish your ends with a completeness which can only be secured by the culture and
development you are now experiencing.'

'And what is my nature?' said Lothair. 'I wish you
would tell me.'

'Has not the divine Theodora told you?'

'She has told me many things, but not that.'

'How then could I know,' said the Princess, 'if she has
not discovered it?'

'But perhaps she has discovered it,' said Lothair.

'Oh! then she would tell you,' said the Princess, 'for she
is the soul of truth.'

'But she is also the soul of kindness, and she might wish
to spare my feelings.'

'Well, that is very modest, and I dare say not affected.
For there is no man, however gifted, even however con-
ceited, who has any real confidence in himself until he has
acted.'

'Well, we shall soon act,' said Lothair, 'and then I
suppose I shall know my nature.'

'In time,' said the Princess, 'and with the continued
inspiration of friendship.'

'But you too are a great friend of Theodora?'

'Although a woman. I see you are laughing at female
friendships, and, generally speaking, there is foundation

for the general sneer. I will own, for my part, I have
every female weakness, and in excess. I am vain, I am
curious, I am jealous, and I am envious; but I adore
Theodora. I reconcile my feelings towards her and my
disposition in this way. It is not friendship, it is worship.
And indeed there are moments when I sometimes think
she is one of those beautiful divinities that we once worshipped in this land, and who, when they listened to our
prayers, at least vouchsafed that our country should not be
the terrible wilderness that you crossed this day.'

In the meantime Colonna, with folded arms and eyes
fixed on the ground, was listening to Theodora.

'Thus you see,' she continued, 'it comes to this: Rome
can only be freed by the Romans. He looks upon the
secret societies of his own country as he does upon universal
suffrage: a wild beast, and dangerous, but which may be
watched and tamed and managed by the police. He listens,
but he plays with them. He temporises. At the bottom
of his heart, his Italian blood despises the Gauls. It must
be something deeper and more touching than this. Rome
must appeal to him, and in the ineffable name.'

'It has been uttered before,' said Colonna, looking up at
his companion, 'and ——'. And he hesitated.

'And in vain you would say,' said Theodora. 'Not so.
There was a martyrdom, but the blood of Felice baptised
the new birth of Italian life. But I am not thinking of
bloodshed. Had it not been for the double intrigues of
the Savoyards it need not then have been shed. We bear
him no ill will, at least not now, and we can make
great offers. Make them. The revolution in Gaul is ever
a mimicry of Italian thought and life. Their great affair of
the last century, which they have so marred and muddled,
would never have occurred had it not been for Tuscan
reform ; 1848 was the echo of our societies; and the Seine
will never be disturbed if the Tiber flows unruffled. Let

him consent to Roman freedom, and MADRE NATURA will
guarantee him against Lutetian barricades.'

'It is only the offer of Mary-Anne in another form,' said
Colonna.

'Guarantee the dynasty,' said Theodora. 'There is the
point. He can trust us. Emperors and kings break treaties
without remorse, but he knows that what is registered by
the most ancient power in the world is sacred.'

'Can republicans guarantee dynasties?' said Colonna,
shaking his head.

'Why what is a dynasty, when we are dealing with
eternal things? The casualties of life compared with infinite space. Rome is eternal. Centuries of the most degrading and foreign priestcraft, enervating rites brought
in by Heliogabalus and the Syrian emperors, have failed to
destroy her. Dynasties! Why, even in our dark servitude
we have seen Merovingian and Carlovingian kings, and
Capets and Valois and Bourbons and now Buonapartes.
They have disappeared, and will disappear like Orgetorix
and the dynasties of the time of Cæsar. What we want is
Rome free. Do not you see that everything has been preparing for that event? This monstrous masquerade of
United Italy, what is it but an initiatory ceremony to prove
that Italy without Rome is a series of provinces? Establish the Roman republic, and the Roman race will, as
before, conquer them in detail. And when the Italians
are thus really united, what will become of the Gauls?
Why, the first Buonaparte said that if Italy were really
united the Gauls would have no chance. And he was a
good judge of such things.'

'What would you have me do then?' said Colonna.

'See him, see him at once. Say everything that I have
said, and say it better. His disposition is with us. Convenience, all political propriety, counsel and would justify
his abstinence. A return to Rome would seem weak, fit-

ful, capricious, and would prove that his previous retirement was ill-considered and ill-informed. It would disturb
and alarm Europe. But you have, nevertheless, to fight
against great odds. It is MADRE NATURA against ST.
PETER's. Never was the abomination of the world so
active as at present. It is in the very throes of its fell
despair. To save itself, it would poison in the Eucharist.'

'And if I fail?' said Colonna.

'You will not fail. On the whole his interest lies on
our side.'

'The sacerdotal influences are very strong there. When
the calculation of interest is fine, a word, a glance, sometimes a sigh, a tear, may have a fatal effect.'

'All depends upon him,' said Theodora. 'If he were to
disappear from the stage, interference would be impossible.'

'But he is on the stage, and apparently will remain.'

'A single life should not stand between Rome and freedom.'

'What do you mean?'

'I mean that Romolo Colonna should go to Paris and
free his country.'

CHAPTER LVII.

WHEN Captain Muriel and his detachment returned to the
camp, they found that the force had been not inconsiderably
increased in their absence, while the tidings of the disposition of the Italian army, brought by the recruits and the
deserters from the royal standard, cherished the hopes of
the troops, and stimulated their desire for action. Theodora
had been far more communicative during their journey
back than in that of her departure. She was less absorbed,
and had resumed that serene yet over sympathising character which was one of her charms. Without going into

detail, she mentioned more than once to Lothair how relieved she felt by Colonna accepting the mission to Paris.
He was a person of so much influence, she said, and of such
great judgment and resource. She augured the most satisfactory results from his presence on the main scene of
action.

Time passed rapidly at the camp. When a life of constant activity is combined with routine, the hours fly.
Neither letter nor telegram arrived from Colonna, and
neither was expected; and yet Theodora heard from him,
and even favourably. One day, as she was going the rounds
with her husband, a young soldier, a new recruit, approached her, and pressing to his lips a branch of the olive
tree, presented it to her. On another occasion when she
returned to her tent, she found a bunch of fruit from the
same tree, though not quite ripe, which showed that the
cause of peace had not only progressed but had almost matured. All these communications sustained her sanguine
disposition, and full of happy confidence she laboured with
unceasing and inspiring energy, so that when the looked-
for signal came they might be prepared to obey it, and
rapidly gather the rich fruition of their glorious hopes.

While she was in this mood of mind a scout arrived from
Nerola, bringing news that a brigade of the French army
had positively embarked at Marseilles, and might be hourly
expected at Civita Vecchia. The news was absolute. The
Italian Consul at Marseilles had telegraphed to his government both when the first regiment was on board, and when
the last had embarked. Copies of these telegrams had been
forwarded instantly by a secret friend to the volunteers on
the southern frontier.

When Theodora heard this news she said nothing, but,
turning pale, she quitted the group round the General and
hastened to her own tent. She told her attendant, the
daughter of the custom-house officer at Narni, and a true

child of the mountains, that no one must approach her, not
even Colonel Campian, and the girl sate without the tent at
its entrance, dressed in her many-coloured garments, with
fiery eyes and square white teeth, and her dark hair braided
with gold coins and covered with a long white kerchief of
perfect cleanliness; and she had a poniard at her side and
a revolver in her hand, and she would have used both weapons sooner than that her mistress should be disobeyed.

Alone in her tent, Theodora fell upon her knees, and
lifting up her hands to heaven and bowing her head to the
earth, she said: ' O God! whom I have ever worshipped,
God of justice and of truth, receive the agony of my soul!'

And on the earth she remained for hours in despair.

Night came and it brought no solace, and the day returned, but to her it brought no light. Theodora was no
longer seen. The soul of the camp seemed extinct. The
mien of majesty that ennobled all; the winning smile that
rewarded the rifleman at his practice and the sapper at his
toil; the inciting word that reanimated the recruit and recalled to the veteran the glories of Sicilian struggles: all
vanished, all seemed spiritless and dull, and the armourer
clinked his forge as if he were the heartless hireling of a
king.

In this state of moral discomfiture there was one person
who did not lose his head, and this was the General. Calm,
collected, and critical, he surveyed the situation and indicated the possible contingencies. ' Our best, if not our
only, chance,' he said to Colonel Campian, ' is this: that
the Italian army now gathered in force upon the frontier
should march to Rome and arrive there before the French.
Whatever then happens, we shall at least get rid of the
great impostor, but in all probability the French and
Italians will fight. In that case I shall join the Savoyards,
and in the confusion we may do some business yet.'

' This embarkation,' said the Colonel, ' explains the ga-

x

thering of the Italians on the frontier. They must have
foreseen this event at Florence. They never can submit to
another French occupation. It would upset their throne.
The question is, who will be at Rome first.'

'Just so,' said the General; 'and as it is an affair upon
which all depends, and is entirely beyond my control, I
think I shall now take a nap.' So saying he turned into
his tent, and, in five minutes, this brave and exact man, but
in whom the muscular development far exceeded the nervous, was slumbering without a dream.

Civita Vecchia was so near at hand, and the scouts of the
General were so numerous and able, that he soon learnt
the French had not yet arrived, and another day elapsed
and still no news of the French. But, on the afternoon
of the following day, the startling but authentic information arrived, that, after the French army having embarked
and remained two days in port, the original orders had
been countermanded, and the troops had absolutely disembarked.

There was a cheer in the camp when the news was
known, and Theodora started from her desolation, surprised
that there could be in such a scene a sound of triumph.
Then there was another cheer, and though she did not
move, but remained listening and leaning on her arm, the
light returned to her eyes. The cheer was repeated, and
there were steps about her tent. She caught the voice of
Lothair speaking to her attendant, and adjuring her to tell
her mistress immediately that there was good news, and
that the French troops had disembarked. Then she heard
her husband calling Theodora.

The camp became a scene of excitement and festivity
which, in general, only succeeds some signal triumph.
The troops lived always in the air, except in the hours of
night, when the atmosphere of the mountains in the late
autumn is dangerous. At present they formed groups and

parties in the vicinity of the tents; there was their gay
canteen and there their humorous kitchen. The man of
the Gulf with his rich Venetian banter and the Sicilian
with his scaramouch tricks got on very well with the
gentle and polished Tuscan, and could amuse without
offending the high Roman soul; but there were some quips
and cranks and sometimes some antics which were not
always relished by the simpler men from the islands,
and the offended eye of a Corsican sometimes seemed to
threaten ' vendetta.'

About sunset, Colonel Campian led forth Theodora.
She was in female attire, and her long hair restrained
only by a fillet reached nearly to the ground. Her Olympian brow seemed distended; a phosphoric light glittered
in her Hellenic eyes; a deep pink spot burnt upon each of
those cheeks usually so immaculately fair.

The General and the chief officers gathered round her
with their congratulations, but she would visit all the
quarters. She spoke to the men in all the dialects of
that land of many languages. The men of the Gulf, in
general of gigantic stature, dropped their merry Venetian
stories and fell down on their knees and kissed the hem of
her garment; the Scaramouch forgot his tricks, and wept
as he would to the Madonna; Tuscany and Rome made
speeches worthy of the Arno and the Forum; and the
Corsicans and the islanders unsheathed their poniards and
brandished them in the air, which is their mode of de-
noting affectionate devotion. As the night advanced, the
crescent moon glittering above the Apennine, Theodora
attended by the whole staff, having visited all the troops,
stopped at the chief fire of the camp, and in a voice which
might have maddened nations sang the hymn of Roman
liberty, the whole army ranged in ranks along the valley
joining in the solemn and triumphant chorus.

CHAPTER LVIII.

This exaltation of feeling in the camp did not evaporate. All felt that they were on the eve of some great event, and that the hour was at hand. And it was in this state of enthusiasm, that couriers arrived with the intelligence that Garibaldi had escaped from Caprera, that he had reached Nerola in safety, and was in command of the assembled forces; and that the General was, without loss of time, to strike his camp, join the main body at a given place, and then march to Rome.

The breaking-up of the camp was as the breaking-up of a long frost and the first scent of spring. There was a brightness in every man's face and a gay elasticity in all their movements. But when the order of the day informed them that they must prepare for instant combat, and that in eight and forty hours they would probably be in face of the enemy, the hearts of the young recruits fluttered with strange excitement, and the veterans nodded to each other with grim delight.

It was nearly midnight when the troops quitted the valley through a defile in an opposite direction to the pass by which they had entered it. It was a bright night. Colonel Campian had the command of the division in advance, which was five hundred strong. After the defile, the country though hilly was comparatively open, and here the advanced guard was to halt until the artillery and cavalry had effected the passage, and this was the most laborious and difficult portion of the march; but all was well considered, and all went right. The artillery and cavalry by sunrise had joined the advanced guard who were bivouacking in the rocky plain, and about noon the

main columns of the infantry began to deploy from the
heights, and in a short time the whole force was in the
field. Soon after this some of the skirmishers who had
been sent forward returned, and reported the enemy in
force and in a strong position, commanding the intended
route of the invading force. On this the General resolved
to halt for a few hours, and rest and refresh the troops,
and to recommence their march after sunset, so that, without effort, they might be in the presence of the enemy by
dawn.

Lothair had been separated from Theodora during this
to him novel and exciting scene. She had accompanied
her husband, but when the whole force advanced in battle
array, the General had desired that she should accompany
the staff. They advanced through the night, and by dawn
they were fairly in the open country. In the distance, and
in the middle of the rough and undulating plain, was a
round hill with an ancient city, for it was a bishop's see,
built all about and over it. It would have looked like a
gigantic beehive, had it not been for a long convent on the
summit, flanked by some stone pines, as we see in the pictures of Gaspar and Claude.

Between this city and the invading force, though not
in a direct line, was posted the enemy in a strong position;
their right wing protected by one of the mounds common
in the plain, and their left backed by an olive wood of
considerable extent, and which grew on the last rocky
spur of the mountains. They were therefore, as regards
the plain, on commanding ground. The strength of the
two forces was not unequal, and the Papal troops were
not to be despised, consisting among others of a detachment of the legion of Antibes and the Zouaves. They had
artillery, which was well posted.

The General surveyed the scene, for which he was not
unprepared. Disposing his troops in positions in which

they were as much protected as possible from the enemy's
fire, he opened upon them a fierce and continuous cannon-
ade, while he ordered Colonel Campian and eight hundred
men to fall back among the hills, and following a circuitous
path, which had been revealed by a shepherd, gain the
spur of the mountains and attack the enemy in their rear
through the olive wood. It was calculated that this movement, if successful, would require about three hours, and
the General for that period of the time had to occupy the
enemy and his own troops with what were in reality feint
attacks.

When the calculated time had elapsed, the General became anxious, and his glass was never from his eye. He
was posted on a convenient ridge, and the wind, which
was high this day from the sea, frequently cleared the field
from the volumes of smoke; so his opportunities of observation were good. But the three hours passed, and there
was no sign of the approach of Campian, and he ordered
Sarano with his division to advance towards the mound
and occupy the attention of the right wing of the enemy;
but very shortly after Lothair had carried this order, and
four hours having elapsed, the General observed some confusion in the left wing of the enemy, and instantly counter-
manding the order, commanded a general attack in line.
The troops charged with enthusiasm, but they were encountered with a resolution as determined. At first they
carried the mound, broke the enemy's centre, and were
mixed up with their great guns; but the enemy fiercely
rallied, and the invaders were repulsed. The Papal troops
retained their position, and their opponents were in disorder
on the plain and a little dismayed. It was at this moment
that Theodora rushed forward, and waving a sword in one
hand, and in the other the standard of the Republic, exclaimed, 'Brothers, to Rome!'

This sight inflamed their faltering hearts, which after all

were rather confounded than dismayed. They formed and rallied round her, and charged with renewed energy at the very moment that Campian had brought the force of his division on the enemy's rear. A panic came over the Papal troops, thus doubly assailed, and their rout was complete. They retreated in the utmost disorder to Vitorbo, which they abandoned that night and hurried to Rome.

At the last moment, when the victory was no longer doubtful, and all were in full retreat or in full pursuit, a Zouave, in wantonness firing his weapon before he threw it away, sent a random shot which struck Theodora, and she fell. Lothair, who had never left her during the battle, was at her side in a moment, and a soldier, who had also marked the fatal shot; and, strange to say, so hot and keen was the pursuit, that though a moment before they seemed to be in the very thick of the strife, they almost instantaneously found themselves alone, or rather with no companions than the wounded near them. She looked at Lothair, but at first could not speak. She seemed stunned, but soon murmured, 'Go, go; you are wanted.'

At this moment the General rode up with some of his staff. His countenance was elate and his eye sparkled with fire. But catching the figure of Lothair kneeling on the field, he reined in his charger and said, 'What is this?' Then looking more closely, he instantly dismounted, and muttering to himself, 'This mars the victory,' he was at Theodora's side.

A slight smile came over her when she recognised the General, and she faintly pressed his hand, and then said again, 'Go, go; you are all wanted.'

'None of us are wanted. The day is won; we must think of you.'

'Is it won?' she murmured.

'Complete.'

'I die content.'

'Who talks of death?' said the General. 'This is a wound, but I have had some worse. What we must think of now are remedies. I passed an ambulance this moment. Run for it,' he said to his aide-de-camp. 'We must staunch the wound at once; but it is only a mile to the city, and then we shall find everything, for we were expected. I will ride on, and there shall be proper attendance ready before you arrive. You will conduct our friend to the city,' he said to Lothair, 'and be of good courage, as I am.'

CHAPTER LIX.

The troops were rushing through the gates of the city when the General rode up. There was a struggling and stifling crowd; cheers and shrieks. It was that moment of wild fruition, when the master is neither recognised nor obeyed. It is not easy to take a bone out of a dog's mouth; nevertheless the presence of the General in time prevailed, something like order was established, and before the ambulance could arrive, a guard had been appointed to receive it, and the ascent to the monastery, where a quarter was prepared, kept clear.

During the progress to the city Theodora never spoke, but she seemed stunned rather than suffering; and once, when Lothair, who was walking by her side, caught her glance with his sorrowful and anxious face, she put forth her hand and pressed his.

The ascent to the convent was easy, and the advantages of air and comparative tranquillity, which the place offered, counterbalanced the risk of postponing, for a very brief space, the examination of the wound.

They laid her on their arrival on a large bed, without poles or canopy, in a lofty white-washed room of considerable dimensions, clean and airy, with high open windows. There was no furniture in the room except a chair, a table, and a crucifix. Lothair took her in his arms and laid her on the bed; and the common soldier who had hitherto assisted him, a giant in stature with a beard a foot long, stood by the bedside crying like a child. The chief surgeon almost at the same moment arrived with an aide-de-camp of the General, and her faithful female attendant, and in a few minutes her husband, himself wounded and covered with dust.

The surgeon at once requested that all should withdraw except her devoted maid, and they waited his report without, in that deep sad silence which will not despair, and yet dares not hope.

When the wound had been examined and probed and dressed, Theodora in a faint voice said, 'Is it desperate?'

'Not desperate,' said the surgeon, 'but serious. All depends upon your perfect tranquillity, of mind as well as body.'

'Well I am here and cannot move; and as for my mind, I am not only serene but happy.'

'Then we shall get through this,' said the surgeon encouragingly.

'I do not like you to stay with me,' said Theodora. 'There are other sufferers besides myself.'

'My orders are not to quit you,' said the surgeon, 'but I can be of great use within these walls. I shall return when the restorative has had its effect. But remember, if I be wanted, I am always here.'

Soon after this Theodora fell into a gentle slumber, and after two hours woke refreshed. The countenance of the surgeon when he again visited her was less troubled; it was hopeful.

The day was now beginning to decline; notwithstanding the scenes of tumult and violence near at hand, all was here silent; and the breeze, which had been strong during the whole day, but which blew from the sea, and was very soft, played gratefully upon the pale countenance of the sufferer. Suddenly she said, 'What is that?'

And they answered and said, 'We heard nothing.'

'I hear the sound of great guns,' said Theodora.

And they listened, and in a moment both the surgeon and the maid heard the sound of distant ordnance.

'The Liberator is at hand,' said the maid.

'I dare say,' said the surgeon.

'No;' said Theodora looking distressed. 'The sounds do not come from his direction. Go and see, Dolores; ask and tell me what are those sounds.'

The surgeon was sitting by her side, and occasionally touching her pulse, or wiping the slight foam from her brow, when Dolores returned and said, 'Lady, the sounds are the great guns of Civita Vecchia.'

A deadly change came over the countenance of Theodora, and the surgeon looked alarmed. He would have given her some restorative, but she refused it. 'No, kind friend,' she said; 'it is finished. I have just received a wound more fatal than the shot in the field this morning. The French are at Rome. Tell me, kind friend, how long do you think I may live?'

The surgeon felt her pulse; his look was gloomy. 'In such a case as yours,' he said, 'the patient is the best judge.'

'I understand,' she said. 'Send then at once for my husband.'

He was at hand, for his wound had been dressed in the convent, and he came to Theodora with his arm in a sling, but with the attempt of a cheerful visage.

In the meantime, Lothair, after having heard the first, and by no means hopeless, bulletin of the surgeon, had been obliged to leave the convent to look after his men,

and having seen them in quarters and made his report to
the General, he obtained permission to return to the convent and ascertain the condition of Theodora. Arrived
there, he heard that she had had refreshing slumber, and
that her husband was now with her, and a ray of hope
lighted up the darkness of his soul. He was walking up
and down the refectory of the convent with that sickening
restlessness which attends impending and yet uncertain
sorrow, when Colonel Campian entered the apartment and
beckoned to him.

There was an expression in his face which appalled
Lothair, and he was about to enquire after Theodora, when
his tongue cleaved to the roof of his mouth and he could
not speak. The Colonel shook his head, and said in a
low, hollow voice, ' She wishes to see you, and alone.
Come.'

Theodora was sitting in the bed propped up by cushions
when Lothair entered, and as her wound was internal,
there was no evidence of her sufferings. The distressful
expression of her face when she heard the great guns of
Civita Vecchia had passed away. It was serious, but it
was serene. She bade her maid leave the chamber, and
then she said to Lothair, ' It is the last time I shall speak
to you, and I wish that we should be alone. There is
something much on my mind at this moment, and you can
relieve it.'

' Adored being,' murmured Lothair with streaming eyes,
' there is no wish of yours that I will not fulfil.'

' I know your life, for you have told it me, and you are
true. I know your nature; it is gentle and brave, but
perhaps too susceptible. I wished it to be susceptible only
of the great and good. Mark me: I have a vague but
strong conviction that there will be another, and a more
powerful, attempt to gain you to the Church of Rome. If
I have ever been to you, as you have sometimes said, an

object of kind thoughts, if not a fortunate, at least a faithful, friend ; promise me now, at this hour of trial, with all
the solemnity that becomes the moment, that you will never
enter that communion.'

Lothair would have spoken, but his voice was choked,
and he could only press her hand and bow his head.

'But promise me,' said Theodora.

'I promise,' said Lothair.

'And now,' she said, 'embrace me, for I wish that your
spirit should be upon me as mine departs.'

CHAPTER LX.

It was a November day in Rome, and the sky was as
gloomy as the heaven of London. The wind moaned
through the silent streets, deserted except by soldiers.
The shops were shut, not a civilian or a priest could be
seen. The Corso was occupied by the Swiss Guard and
Zouaves, with artillery ready to sweep it at a moment's
notice. Six of the city gates were shut and barricaded
with barrels full of earth. Troops and artillery were also
posted in several of the principal piazzas, and on some
commanding heights, and St. Peter's itself was garrisoned.

And yet these were the arrangements rather of panic than
precaution. The utmost dismay pervaded the council-
chamber of the Vatican. Since the news had arrived of
the disembarkation of the French troops at Marseilles, all
hope of interference had expired. It was clear that Berwick had been ultimately foiled, and his daring spirit and
teeming device were the last hope, as they were the ablest
representation, of Roman audacity and stratagem. The
Revolutionary Committee, whose abiding-place or agents
never could be traced or discovered, had posted every

part of the city during the night with their manifesto, announcing that the hour had arrived; an attempt, partially successful, had been made to blow up the barracks of the Zouaves; and the Cardinal Secretary was in possession of information that an insurrection was immediate, and that the city would be fired in four different quarters.

The Pope had escaped from the Vatican to the Castle of St. Angelo, where he was secure, and where his courage could be sustained by the presence of the Noble Guard with their swords always drawn. The six score of Monsignori, who in their different offices form, what is styled, the Court of Rome, had either accompanied his Holiness, or prudently secreted themselves in the strongest palaces and convents at their command. Later in the day, news arrived of the escape of Garibaldi from Caprera; he was said to be marching on the city, and only five and twenty miles distant. There appeared another proclamation from the Revolutionary Committee, mysteriously posted under the very noses of the guards and police, postponing the insurrection till the arrival of the Liberator.

The Papal cause seemed hopeless. There was a general feeling throughout the city and all classes, that this time it was to be an affair of Alaric or Genseric, or the Constable of Bourbon; no negotiations, no compromises, no conventions, but slaughter, havoc, a great judicial devastation, that was to extirpate all signs and memories of Mediæval and Semitic Rome, and restore and renovate the inheritance of the true offspring of the she-wolf. The very aspect of the place itself was sinister. Whether it were the dulness of the dark sky, or the frown of MADRE NATURA herself, but the old Seven Hills seemed to look askance. The haughty Capitol, impatient of its chapels, sighed once more for triumphs; and the proud Palatine, remembering the Cæsars, glanced with imperial contempt on the palaces of the Papal princelings that, in the course of ignominious ages, had been constructed out of the exhaustless womb of its still sovereign ruin. The Jews in their quarter spoke nothing, but exchanged a curious glance, as if to say, 'Has it come at last? And will they indeed serve her as she served Sion?'

This dreadful day at last passed, followed by as dreadful a night, and then another day equally gloomy, equally silent, equally panicstricken. Even insurrection would have been a relief amid the horrible and wearing suspense. On the third day the Government made some wild arrests of the wrong persons, and then came out a fresh proclamation from the Revolutionary Committee, directing the Romans to make no move until the advanced guard of Garibaldi had appeared upon Monte Mario. About this time the routed troops of the Pope arrived in confusion from Viterbo, and of course extenuated their discomfiture by exaggerating the strength of their opponents. According to them they had encountered not less than ten thousand men, who now having joined the still greater force of Garibaldi, were in full march on the city.

The members of the Papal party who showed the greatest spirit and the highest courage at this trying conjuncture, were the Roman ladies and their foreign friends. They scraped lint for the troops as incessantly as they offered prayers to the Virgin. Some of them were trained nurses, and they were training others to tend the sick and wounded. They organised a hospital service, and when the wounded arrived from Viterbo, notwithstanding the rumours of incendiarism and massacre, they came forth from their homes, and proceeded in companies, with no male attendants but armed men, to the discharge of their self-appointed public duties. There were many foreigners in the Papal ranks, and the sympathies and services of the female visitors to Rome were engaged for their countrymen. Princesses of France and Flanders might be seen by the tressel beds of many a suffering

soldier of Dauphiné and Brabant; but there were numerous
subjects of Queen Victoria in the Papal ranks: some
Englishmen, several Scotchmen, many Irish. For them
the English ladies had organised a special service. Lady
St. Jerome, with unflagging zeal, presided over this depart-
ment; and the superior of the sisterhood of mercy, that
shrank from no toil, and feared no danger in the fulfilment
of those sacred duties of pious patriots, was Miss Arundel.

She was leaning over the bed of one who had been cut
down in the olive wood by a sabre of Campian's force,
when a peal of artillery was heard. She thought that her
hour had arrived, and the assault had commenced.

'Most holy Mary!' she exclaimed, 'sustain me.'

There was another peal, and it was repeated, and again
and again at regular intervals.

'That is not a battle, it is a salute,' murmured the
wounded soldier.

And he was right; it was the voice of the great guns telling that the French had arrived.

The consternation of the Revolutionary Committee, no
longer sustained by Colonna, absent in France, was complete.
Had the advanced guard of Garibaldi been in sight, it
might still have been the wisest course to rise; but Monte
Mario was not yet peopled by them, and an insurrection
against the Papal troops, reanimated by the reported arrival
of the French, and increased in numbers by the fugitives
from Viterbo, would have been certainly a rash and probably a hopeless effort. And so, in the midst of confused
and hesitating councils, the first division of the French force
arrived at the gates of Rome, and marched into the gloomy
and silent city.

Since the interference of St. Peter and St. Paul against
Alaric, the Papacy had never experienced a more miraculous interposition in its favour. Shortly after this the wind
changed, and the sky became serene; a sunbeam played on

the flashing cross of St. Peter's; the Pope left the Castle of
Angelo, and returned to the Quirinal; the Noble Guard
sheathed their puissant blades; the six score of Monsignori
reappeared in all their busy haunts and stately offices; and
the Court of Rome, no longer despairing of the Republic,
and with a spirit worthy of the Senate after Cannæ, ordered
the whole of its forces into the field to combat its invaders,
with the prudent addition, in order to ensure a triumph, of
a brigade of French infantry armed with chassepots.

Garibaldi, who was really at hand, hearing of these events,
fell back on Monte Rotondo, about fifteen miles from the
city, and took up a strong position. He was soon attacked
by his opponents, and defeated with considerable slaughter,
and forced to fly. The Papal troops returned to Rome in
triumph, but with many wounded. The Roman ladies and
their friends resumed their noble duties with enthusiasm.
The ambulances were apportioned to the different hospitals,
and the services of all were required. Our own countrymen had suffered severely, but the skill and energy and
gentle care of Clare Arundel and her companions only increased with the greater calls upon their beautiful and
sublime virtues.

A woman came to Miss Arundel and told her that in
one of the ambulances was a young man whom they could
not make out. He was severely wounded, and had now
swooned; but they had reason to believe he was an Englishman. Would she see him and speak to him? And she
went.

The person who had summoned her was a woman of
much beauty, not an uncommon quality in Rome, and of
some majesty of mien, as little rare in that city. She was
said, at the time when some enquiry was made, to be Maria
Serafina de Angelis, the wife of a tailor in the Ripetta.

The ambulance was in the courtyard of the hospital of
the Santissima Trinita di Pellegrini. The woman pointed

to it, and then went away. There was only one person in the ambulance; the rest had been taken into the hospital, but he had been left because he was in a swoon, and they were trying to restore him. Those around the ambulance made room for Miss Arundel as she approached, and she beheld a young man, covered with the stains of battle, and severely wounded; but his countenance was uninjured though insensible. His eyes were closed, and his auburn hair fell in clusters on his white forehead. The sister of mercy touched the pulse to ascertain whether there yet was life, but, in the very act, her own frame became agitated, and the colour left her cheek, as she recognised—LOTHAIR.

CHAPTER LXI.

WHEN Lothair in some degree regained consciousness, he found himself in bed. The chamber was lofty and dim, and had once been splendid. Thoughtfulness had invested it with an air of comfort rare under Italian roofs. The fagots sparkled on the hearth, the light from the windows was veiled with hangings, and the draughts from the tall doors guarded against by screens. And by his bedside there were beautiful flowers, and a crucifix, and a silver bell.

Where was he? He looked up at the velvet canopy above, and then at the pictures that covered the walls, but there was no familiar aspect. He remembered nothing since he was shot down in the field of Mentana, and even that imperfectly.

And there had been another battle before that, followed by a catastrophe still more dreadful. When had all this happened, and where? He tried to move his bandaged form, but he had no strength, and his mind seemed weaker

Y

than his frame. But he was soon sensible that he was not
alone. A veiled figure gently lifted him, and another one
refreshed his pillows. He spoke, or tried to speak, but one
of them pressed her finger to her shrouded lips, and he
willingly relapsed into the silence which he had hardly
strength enough to break.

And sometimes these veiled and gliding ministers brought
him sustenance and sometimes remedies, and he complied
with all their suggestions, but with absolute listlessness ;
and sometimes a coarser hand interposed, and sometimes he
caught a countenance that was not concealed, but was ever
strange. He had a vague impression that they examined
and dressed his wounds, and arranged his bandages ; but
whether he really had wounds, and whether he were or
were not bandaged, he hardly knew, and did not care to
know. He was not capable of thought, and memory was
an effort under which he always broke down. Day after
day he remained silent and almost motionless alike in mind
and body. He had a vague feeling that, after some great
sorrows, and some great trials, he was in stillness and in
safety; and he had an indefinite mysterious sentiment of
gratitude to some unknown power, that had cherished him
in his dark calamities, and poured balm and oil into his
wounds.

It was in this mood of apathy that, one evening, there
broke upon his ear low but beautiful voices performing the
evening service of the Church. His eye glistened, his
heart was touched by the vesper spell. He listened with
rapt attention to the sweet and sacred strains, and when
they died away he felt depressed. Would they ever sound
again ?

Sooner than he could have hoped, for, when he woke in
the morning from his slumbers, which, strange to say, were
always disturbed, for the mind and the memory seemed to
work at night though in fearful and exhausting chaos, the

same divine melodies that had soothed him in the eve,
now sounded in the glad and grateful worship of matin
praise.

'I have heard the voice of angels,' he murmured to his
veiled attendant.

The vesper and the matin hours became at once the
epochs of his day. He was ever thinking of them, and
soon was thinking of the feelings which their beautiful
services celebrate and express. His mind seemed no
longer altogether a blank, and the religious sentiment was
the first that returned to his exhausted heart.

'There will be a requiem to-day,' whispered one of his
veiled attendants.

A requiem! a service for the dead; a prayer for their
peace and rest! And who was dead? The bright, the
matchless one, the spell and fascination of his life! Was it
possible? Could she be dead, who seemed vitality in its
consummate form? Was there ever such a being as Theodora? And if there were no Theodora on earth, why should
one think of anything but heaven?

The sounds came floating down the chamber till they
seemed to cluster round his brain; sometimes solemn,
sometimes thrilling, sometimes the divine pathos melting
the human heart with celestial sympathy and heavenly
solace. The tears fell fast from his agitated vision, and
he sank back exhausted, almost insensible, on his pillow.

'The Church has a heart for all our joys and all our
sorrows, and for all our hopes, and all our fears,' whispered
a veiled attendant, as she bathed his temples with fragrant
waters.

Though the condition of Lothair had at first seemed desperate, his youthful and vigorous frame had enabled him
to rally, and with time and the infinite solicitude which he
received, his case was not without hope. But though his
physical cure was somewhat advanced, the prostration of

his mind seemed susceptible of no relief. The services of
the Church accorded with his depressed condition; they
were the only events of his life, and he cherished them.
His attendants now permitted and even encouraged him to
speak, but he seemed entirely incurious and indifferent.
Sometimes they read to him, and he listened, but he never
made remarks. The works which they selected had a religious or ecclesiastical bias, even while they were imaginative; and it seemed difficult not to be interested
by the ingenious fancy by which it was worked out, that
everything that was true and sacred in heaven had its
symbol and significance in the qualities and accidents of
earth.

After a month passed in this manner, the surgeons having
announced that Lothair might now prepare to rise from
his bed, a veiled attendant said to him one day, ' There is a
gentleman here who is a friend of yours, and who would
like to see you. And perhaps you would like to see him
also for other reasons, for you must have much to say to
God after all that you have suffered. And he is a most
holy man.'

' I have no wish to see anyone. Are you sure he is not
a stranger ? ' asked Lothair.

' He is in the next room,' said the attendant.   ' He has
been here throughout your illness, conducting our services ;
often by your bedside when you were asleep, and always
praying for you.'

The veiled attendant drew back and waved her hand,
and some one glided forward and said in a low, soft voice,
' You have not forgotten me ? '

And Lothair beheld Monsignore Catesby.

' It is a long time since we met,' said Lothair, looking at
him with some scrutiny, and then all interest died away,
and he turned away his vague and wandering eyes.

' But you know me ? '

'I know not where I am, and I but faintly comprehend what has happened,' murmured Lothair.

'You are among friends,' said the Monsignore, in tones of sympathy.

'What has happened,' he added, with an air of mystery, not unmixed with a certain expression of ecstasy in his glance, 'must be reserved for other times, when you are stronger, and can grapple with such high themes.'

'How long have I been here?' enquired Lothair, dreamingly.

'It is a month since the Annunciation.'

'What Annunciation?'

'Hush!' said the Monsignore, and he raised his finger to his lip. 'We must not talk of these things, at least at present. No doubt the same blessed person that saved you from the jaws of death is at this moment guarding over your recovery and guiding it; but we do not deserve, nor does the Church expect, perpetual miracles. We must avail ourselves, under Divine sanction, of the beneficent tendencies of nature; and in your case her operations must not be disturbed at this moment by any excitement, except, indeed, the glow of gratitude for celestial aid, and the inward joy which must permeate the being of anyone who feels that he is among the most favoured of men.'

From this time Monsignore Catesby scarcely ever quitted Lothair. He hailed Lothair in the morn, and parted from him at night with a blessing; and in the interval Catesby devoted his whole life, and the inexhaustible resources of his fine and skilled intelligence to alleviate or amuse the existence of his companion. Sometimes he conversed with Lothair, adroitly taking the chief burthen of the talk; and yet, whether it were bright narrative or lively dissertation, never seeming to lecture or hold forth, but relieving the monologue when expedient by an interesting enquiry, which he was always ready in due time to answer himself, or softening the instruction by the playfulness of his mind and manner. Sometimes he read to Lothair, and attuned the mind of his charge to the true spiritual note by melting passages from À Kempis or Chrysostom. Then he would bring a portfolio of wondrous drawings by the mediæval masters, of saints and seraphs, and accustom the eye and thought of Lothair to the forms and fancies of the Court of Heaven.

One day Lothair, having risen from his bed for the first time, and lying on a sofa in an adjoining chamber to that in which he had been so long confined, the Monsignore seated himself by the side of Lothair, and, opening a portfolio, took out a drawing and held it before Lothair, observing his countenance with a glance of peculiar scrutiny.

'Well!' said Catesby after some little pause, as if awaiting a remark from his companion.

'Tis beautiful!' said Lothair. 'Is it by Raffaelle?'

'No; by Fra Bartolomeo. But the countenance, do you remember ever having met such an one?'

Lothair shook his head. Catesby took out another drawing, the same subject, the Blessed Virgin. 'By Giulio,' said the Monsignore, and he watched the face of Lothair, but it was listless.

Then he showed Lothair another and another and another. At last he held before him one which was really by Raffaelle, and by which Lothair was evidently much moved. His eye lit up, a blush suffused his pale cheek, he took the drawing himself and held it before his gaze with a trembling hand.

'Yes, I remember this,' he murmured, for it was one of those faces of Greek beauty which the great painter not infrequently caught up at Rome. The Monsignore looked gently round and waved his hand, and immediately there arose the hymn to the Virgin in subdued strains of exquisite melody.

On the next morning, when Lothair woke, he found on
the table by his side the drawing of the Virgin in a sliding
frame.

About this time the Monsignore began to accustom
Lothair to leave his apartment, and as he was not yet permitted to walk, Catesby introduced what he called an
English chair, in which Lothair was enabled to survey a
little the place which had been to him a refuge and a
home. It seemed a building of vast size, raised round an
inner court with arcades and windows, and, in the higher
story where he resided, an apparently endless number of
chambers and galleries. One morning, in their peram-
bulations, the Monsignore unlocked the door of a covered
way which had no light but from a lamp which guided
their passage. The opposite door at the end of this
covered way opened into a church, but one of a character
different from any which Lothair had yet entered.

It had been raised during the latter half of the sixteenth
century by Vignola, when, under the influence of the great
Pagan revival, the Christian Church began to assume the
character of an Olympian temple. A central painted
cupola of large but exquisite proportions, supported by
pilasters with gilded capitals, and angels of white marble
springing from golden brackets; walls encrusted with rare
materials of every tint, and altars supported by serpentine
columns of agate and alabaster; a blaze of pictures, and
statues, and precious stones, and precious metals, denoted
one of the chief temples of the sacred brotherhood of
Jesus, raised when the great order had recognised that the
views of primitive and medieval Christianity, founded on
the humility of man, were not in accordance with the age
of confidence in human energy, in which they were destined to rise, and which they were determined to direct.

Guided by Catesby, and leaning on a staff, Lothair
gained a gorgeous side chapel in which mass was cele-

brating; the air was rich with incense, and all heaven
seemed to open in the ministrations of a seraphic choir.
Crushed by his great calamities, both physical and moral,
Lothair sometimes felt that he could now be content if the
rest of his life could flow away amid this celestial fragrance and these gushing sounds of heavenly melody.
And absorbed in these feelings it was not immediately
observed by him that on the altar, behind the dazzling
blaze of tapers, was a picture of the Virgin, and identically
the same countenance as that he had recognised with emotion in the drawing of Raffaelle.

It revived perplexing memories which agitated him,
thoughts on which it seemed his brain had not now
strength enough to dwell, and yet with which it now
seemed inevitable for him to grapple. The congregation
was not very numerous, and when it broke up, several of
them lingered behind and whispered to the Monsignore,
and then, after a little time, Catesby approached Lothair
and said, ' There are some here who would wish to kiss
your hand, or even touch the hem of your garments. It
is troublesome, but natural, considering all that has
occurred and that this is the first time, perhaps, that they
may have met anyone who has been so favoured.'

' Favoured!' said Lothair; 'am I favoured? It seems
to me I am the most forlorn of men, if even I am that.'

' Hush!' said the Monsignore, 'we must not talk of
these things at present;' and he motioned to some who
approached and contemplated Lothair with blended curiosity and reverence.

These visits of Lothair to the beautiful church of the
Jesuits became of daily occurrence, and often happened
several times on the same day; indeed they formed the
only incident which seemed to break his listlessness. He
became interested in the change and variety of the services,
in the persons and characters of the officiating priests.

The soft manners of these fathers, their intelligence in the performance of their offices, their obliging carriage, and the unaffected concern with which all he said or did seemed to inspire them, won upon him unconsciously. The church had become his world; and his sympathies, if he still had sympathies, seemed confined to those within its walls.

In the meantime his physical advancement though slow was gradual, and had hitherto never been arrested. He could even walk a little alone, though artificially supported, and rambled about the halls and galleries full of a prodigious quantity of pictures, from the days of Raffael Sanzio to those of Raffael Mengs.

'The doctors think now we might try a little drive,' said the Monsignore one morning. 'The rains have ceased and refreshed everything. To-day is like the burst of spring.' And when Lothair seemed to shudder at the idea of facing anything like the external world, the Monsignore suggested immediately that they should go out in a close carriage, which they finally entered in the huge quadrangle of the building. Lothair was so nervous that he pulled down even the blind of his window; and the Monsignore, who always humoured him, half pulled down his own.

Their progress seemed through a silent land and they could hardly be traversing streets. Then the ascent became a little precipitous, and then the carriage stopped and the Monsignore said, 'Here is a solitary spot. We shall meet no one. The view is charming, and the air is soft.' And he placed his hand gently on the arm of Lothair, and, as it were, drew him out of the carriage.

The sun was bright, and the sky was bland. There was something in the breath of nature that was delightful. The scent of violets was worth all the incense in the world; all the splendid marbles and priestly vestments seemed hard and cold when compared with the glorious colours of the cactus and the wild forms of the golden and gigantic aloes.

The Favonian breeze played on the brow of this beautiful hill, and the exquisite palm trees, while they bowed their rustling heads, answered in responsive chorus to the antiphon of nature.

The dreary look that had been so long imprinted on the face of Lothair melted away.

''Tis well that we came, is it not?' said Catesby; 'and now we will seat ourselves.' Below and before them, on an undulating site, a city of palaces and churches spread out its august form, enclosing within its ample walls sometimes a wilderness of classic ruins, column and arch and theatre, sometimes the umbrageous spread of princely gardens. A winding and turbid river divided the city in unequal parts, in one of which there rose a vast and glorious temple, crowned with a dome of almost superhuman size and skill, on which the favourite sign of heaven flashed with triumphant truth.

The expression of relief which, for a moment, had reposed on the face of Lothair, left it when he said in an agitated voice, 'I at length behold ROME!'

CHAPTER LXII.

THE recognition of Rome by Lothair evinced not only a consciousness of locality, but an interest in it not before exhibited; and the Monsignore soon after seized the opportunity of drawing the mind of his companion to the past, and feeling how far he now realised the occurrences that immediately preceded his arrival in the city. But Lothair would not dwell on them. 'I wish to think of nothing,' he said, 'that happened before I entered this city: all I desire now is to know those to whom I am indebted for my preservation in a condition that seemed hopeless.'

'There is nothing hopeless with Divine aid,' said the Monsignore; 'but, humanly speaking, you are indebted for your preservation to English friends, long and intimately cherished. It is under their roof that you dwell, the Agostini palace, tenanted by Lord St. Jerome.'

'Lord St. Jerome!' murmured Lothair to himself.

'And the ladies of his house are those who, only with some slight assistance from my poor self, tended you throughout your most desperate state, and when we sometimes almost feared that mind and body were alike wrecked.'

'I have a dream of angels,' said Lothair; 'and sometimes I listened to heavenly voices that I seemed to have heard before.'

'I am sure you have not forgotten the ladies of that house?' said Catesby watching his countenance.

'No; one of them summoned me to meet her at Rome,' murmured Lothair, 'and I am here.'

'That summons was divine,' said Catesby, 'and only the herald of the great event that was ordained and has since occurred. In this holy city Miss Arundel must ever count as the most sanctified of her sex.'

Lothair relapsed into silence, which subsequently appeared to be meditation, for when the carriage stopped, and the Monsignore assisted him to alight, he said, 'I must see Lord St. Jerome.'

And in the afternoon, with due and preparatory announcement, Lord St. Jerome waited on Lothair. The Monsignore ushered him into the chamber, and, though he left them as it were alone, never quitted it. He watched them conversing, while he seemed to be arranging books and flowers; he hovered over the conference, dropping down on them at a critical moment, when the words became either languid or embarrassing. Lord St. Jerome was a hearty man, simple and high-bred. He addressed

Lothair with all his former kindness, but with some
degree of reserve, and even a dash of ceremony. Lothair
was not insensible to the alteration in his manner, but
could ascribe it to many causes. He was himself resolved
to make an effort, when Lord St. Jerome rose to depart,
and expressed the intention of Lady St. Jerome to wait on
him on the morrow. 'No, my dear Lord,' said Lothair;
'to-morrow I make my first visit, and it shall be to my
best friends. I would try to come this evening, but they
will not be alone; and I must see them alone, if it be only
once.'

This visit of the morrow rather pressed on the nervous
system of Lothair. It was no slight enterprise, and called
up many recollections. He brooded over his engagement
during the whole evening, and his night was disturbed.
His memory, long in a state of apathy, or curbed and
controlled into indifference, seemed endowed with unnatural
vitality, reproducing the history of his past life in rapid
and exhausting tumult. All its scenes rose before him,
Brentham, and Vauxe, and Muriel, and closing with one
absorbing spot, which, for a long time, it avoided, and in
which all merged and ended, Belmont. Then came that
anguish of the heart, which none can feel but those who in
the youth of life have lost some one infinitely fascinating
and dear, and the wild query why he too had not fallen on
the fatal plain which had entombed all the hope and
inspiration of his existence.

The interview was not so trying an incident as Lothair
anticipated, as often under such circumstances occurs.
Miss Arundel was not present; and in the second place,
although Lothair could not at first be insensible to a
change in the manner of Lady St. Jerome, as well as in
that of her lord, exhibiting as it did a degree of deference
and ceremony which with her towards him were quite
unusual, still the genial, gushing nature of this lively and

enthusiastic woman, full of sympathy, soon asserted itself, and her heart was overflowing with sorrow for all his sufferings, and gratitude for his escape.

'And after all,' she said, 'everything must have been ordained; and, without these trials and even calamities, that great event could not have been brought about which must make all hail you as the most favoured of men.'

Lothair stared with a look of perplexity, and then said, 'If I be the most favoured of men, it is only because two angelic beings have deigned to minister to me in my sorrow, with a sweet devotion I can never forget, and, alas! can never repay.'

CHAPTER LXIII.

Lothair was not destined to meet Clare Arundel alone or only in the presence of her family. He had acceded, after a short time, to the wish of Lady St. Jerome, and the advice of Monsignore Catesby, to wait on her in the evening, when Lady St. Jerome was always at home and never alone. Her rooms were the privileged resort of the very cream of Roman society and of those English who, like herself, had returned to the Roman Church. An Italian palace supplied an excellent occasion for the display of the peculiar genius of our countrywomen to make a place habitable. Beautiful carpets, baskets of flowers, and cases of ferns, and chairs which you could sit upon, tables covered with an infinity of toys, sparkling, useful, and fantastic, huge silken screens of rich colour, and a profusion of light, produced a scene of combined comfort and brilliancy which made everyone social who entered it, and seemed to give a bright and graceful turn even to the careless remarks of ordinary gossip.

Lady St. Jerome rose the moment her eye caught the

entry of Lothair, and, advancing, received him with an air of ceremony, mixed, however, with an expression of personal devotion which was distressing to him, and singularly contrasted with the easy and genial receptions that he remembered at Vauxe. Then Lady St. Jerome led Lothair to her companion whom she had just quitted, and presented him to the Princess Tarpeia-Cinque Cento, a dame in whose veins, it was said, flowed both consular and pontifical blood of the rarest tint.

The Princess Tarpeia-Cinque Cento was the greatest lady in Rome; had still vast possessions, palaces and villas and vineyards and broad farms. Notwithstanding all that had occurred, she still looked upon the kings and emperors of the world as the mere servants of the Pope, and on the old Roman nobility as still the Conscript Fathers of the world. Her other characteristic was superstition. So she was most distinguished by an irrepressible haughtiness and an illimitable credulity. The only softening circumstance was that, being in the hands of the Jesuits, her religion did not assume an ascetic or gloomy character. She was fond of society, and liked to show her wondrous jewels, which were still unrivalled, although she had presented His Holiness in his troubles with a tiara of diamonds.

There were rumours that the Princess Tarpeia-Cinque Cento had on occasions treated even the highest nobility of England with a certain indifference; and all agreed that to laymen, however distinguished, her Highness was not prone too easily to relax. But, in the present instance, it is difficult to convey a due conception of the graciousness of her demeanour when Lothair bent before her. She appeared even agitated, almost rose from her seat, and blushed through her rouge. Lady St. Jerome, guiding Lothair into her vacant seat, walked away.

'We shall never forget what you have done for us,' said the Princess to Lothair.

'I have done nothing,' said Lothair, with a surprised air.

'Ah, that is so like gifted beings like you,' said the Princess. 'They never will think they have done anything, even were they to save the world.'

'You are too gracious, Princess,' said Lothair; 'I have no claims to esteem which all must so value.'

'Who has, if you have not?' rejoined the Princess. 'Yes, it is to you and to you alone that we must look. I am very impartial in what I say, for, to be frank, I have not been of those who believed that the great champion would rise without the patrimony of St. Peter. I am ashamed to say that I have even looked with jealousy on the energy that has been shown by individuals in other countries; but I now confess that I was in error. I cannot resist this manifestation. It is a privilege to have lived when it happened. All that we can do now is to cherish your favoured life.'

'You are too kind, Madam,' murmured the perplexed Lothair.

'I have done nothing,' rejoined the Princess, 'and am ashamed that I have done nothing. But it is well for you, at this season, to be at Rome; and you cannot be better, I am sure, than under this roof. But when the spring breaks, I hope you will honour me, by accepting for your use a villa which I have at Albano, and which at that season has many charms.'

There were other Roman ladies in the room only inferior in rank and importance to the Princess Tarpeia-Cinque Cento; and in the course of the evening, at their earnest request, they were made acquainted with Lothair, for it cannot be said he was presented to them. These ladies, generally so calm, would not wait for the ordinary ceremony of life, but, as he approached to be introduced, sank to the ground with the obeisance offered only to royalty.

There were some cardinals in the apartment and several

monsignori. Catesby was there in close attendance on a
pretty English countess who had just 'gone over.' Her
husband had been at first very much distressed at the
event, and tore himself from the severe duties of the House
of Lords in the hope that he might yet arrive in time at
Rome to save her soul. But he was too late; and, strange
to say, being of a domestic turn, and disliking family dis-
sensions, he remained at Rome during the rest of the
session, and finally 'went over' himself.

Later in the evening arrived his Eminence Cardinal
Berwick, for our friend had gained and bravely gained the
great object of a churchman's ambition, and which even
our Laud was thinking at one time of accepting, although
he was to remain a firm Anglican. In the death-struggle
between the Church and the Secret Societies, Berwick had
been the victor, and no one in the Sacred College more
truly deserved the scarlet hat.

His Eminence had a reverence of radiant devotion for the
Princess Tarpeia-Cinque Cento, a glance of friendship for
Lady St. Jerome, for all a courtly and benignant smile;
but when he recognised Lothair, he started forward, seized
and retained his hand, and then seemed speechless with
emotion. 'Ah! my comrade in the great struggle,' he at
length exclaimed; 'this is indeed a pleasure, and to see
you here!'

Early in the evening, while Lothair was sitting by the
side of the Princess, his eye had wandered round the room,
not unsuccessfully, in search of Miss Arundel; and when
he was free he would immediately have approached her, but
she was in conversation with a Roman prince. Then when
she was for a moment free, he was himself engaged; and
at last he had to quit abruptly a cardinal of taste, who was
describing to him a statue just discovered in the baths of
Diocletian, in order to seize the occasion that again offered
itself.

Her manner was constrained when he addressed her, but she gave him her hand which he pressed to his lips. Looking deeply into her violet eyes he said, 'You summoned me to meet you at Rome; I am here.'

'And I summoned you to other things,' she answered, at first with hesitation and a blush; but then, as if rallying herself to the performance of a duty too high to allow of personal embarrassment, she added, 'all of which you will perform, as becomes one favoured by Heaven.'

'I have been favoured by you,' said Lothair, speaking low and hurriedly; 'to whom I owe my life and more than my life. Yes,' he continued, 'this is not the scene I would have chosen to express my gratitude to you for all that you have done for me, and my admiration of your sublime virtues; but I can no longer repress the feelings of my heart, though their utterance be as inadequate as your deeds have been transcendent.'

'I was but the instrument of a higher Power.'

'We are all instruments of a higher Power, but the instruments chosen are always choice.'

'Ay! there it is,' said Miss Arundel; 'and that is what I rejoice you feel. For it is impossible that such a selection could have been made, as in your case, without your being reserved for great results.'

'I am but a shattered actor for great results,' said Lothair, shaking his head.

'You have had trials,' said Miss Arundel; 'so had St. Ignatius, so had St. Francis, and great temptations; but these are the tests of character, of will, of spiritual power; the fine gold is searched. All things that have happened have tended and been ordained to one end, and that was to make you the champion of the Church of which you are now more than the child.'

'More than the child?'

'Indeed I think so. However, this is hardly the place

z

and occasion to dwell on such matters; and, indeed, I know
your friends, my friends equally, are desirous that your
convalescence should not be unnecessarily disturbed by
what must be, however delightful, still agitating thoughts;
but you touched yourself unexpectedly on the theme, and
at any rate you will pardon one who has the inconvenient
quality of having only one thought.'

'Whatever you say or think must always interest me.'

'You are kind to say so. I suppose you know that our
Cardinal, Cardinal Grandison, will be here in a few days?'

CHAPTER LXIV.

ALTHOUGH the reception of Lothair by his old friends and
by the leaders of the Roman world was in the highest
degree flattering, there was something in its tone which
was perplexing to him and ambiguous. Could they be
ignorant of his Italian antecedents? Impossible. Miss
Arundel had admitted, or rather declared, that he had experienced great trials, and even temptations. She could
only allude to what had occurred since their parting in
England. But all this was now looked upon as satisfactory, because it was ordained, and tended to one end;
and what was that end? His devotion to the Church of
Rome, of which they admitted he was not formally a child.

It was true that his chief companion was a priest, and
that he passed a great portion of his life within the walls
of a church. But the priest was his familiar friend in
England, who in a foreign land had nursed him with devotion in a desperate illness; and although in the great
calamities, physical and moral, that had overwhelmed him,
he had found solace in the beautiful services of a religion
which he respected, no one for a moment had taken ad-

vantage of this mood of his suffering and enfeebled mind
to entrap him into controversy, or to betray him into
admissions that he might afterwards consider precipitate
and immature. Indeed nothing could be more delicate
than the conduct of the Jesuit fathers throughout his communications with them. They seemed sincerely gratified
that a suffering fellow-creature should find even temporary
consolation within their fair and consecrated structure;
their voices modulated with sympathy; their glances
gushed with fraternal affection; their affectionate polite-
ness contrived, in a thousand slight instances, the selection
of a mass, the arrangement of a picture, the loan of a
book, to contribute to the interesting or elegant distraction
of his forlorn and brooding being.

And yet Lothair began to feel uneasy, and his uneasiness
increased proportionately as his health improved. He
sometimes thought that he should like to make an effort
and get about a little in the world; but he was very weak,
and without any of the resources to which he had been
accustomed throughout life. He had no servants of his
own, no carriages, no man of business, no banker; and
when at last he tried to bring himself to write to Mr.
Putney Giles, a painful task, Monsignore Catesby offered
to undertake his whole correspondence for him, and announced that his medical attendants had declared that he
must under no circumstances whatever attempt at present
to write a letter. Hitherto he had been without money,
which was lavishly supplied for his physicians and other
wants; and he would have been without clothes if the
most fashionable tailor in Rome, a German, had not been
in frequent attendance on him under the direction of
Monsignore Catesby, who in fact had organised his wardrobe as he did everything else.

Somehow or other Lothair never seemed alone. When
he woke in the morning the Monsignore was frequently

kneeling before an oratory in his room, and if by any
chance Lothair was wanting at Lady St. Jerome's reception, Father Coleman, who was now on a visit to the
family, would look in and pass the evening with him, as
men who keep a gaming table find it discreet occasionally
to change the dealer. It is a huge and even stupendous
pile, that Palazzo Agostini, and yet Lothair never tried to
thread his way through its vestibules and galleries, or
attempt a reconnaissance of its endless chambers without
some monsignore or other gliding up quite apropos, and
relieving him from the dulness of solitary existence during
the rest of his promenade.

Lothair was relieved by hearing that his former guardian,
Cardinal Grandison, was daily expected at Rome; and he
revolved in his mind whether he should not speak to his
Eminence generally on the system of his life, which he felt
now required some modification. In the interval, however,
no change did occur. Lothair attended every day the
services of the church, and every evening the receptions of
Lady St. Jerome; and between the discharge of these two
duties he took a drive with a priest, sometimes with more
than one, but always most agreeable men, generally in the
environs of the city, or visited a convent, or a villa, some
beautiful gardens, or a gallery of works of art.

It was at Lady St. Jerome's that Lothair met his former
guardian. The Cardinal had only arrived in the morning.
His manner to Lothair was affectionate. He retained
Lothair's hand and pressed it with his pale, thin fingers;
his attenuated countenance blazed for a moment with a
divine light.

'I have long wished to see you, sir,' said Lothair, 'and
much wish to talk with you.'

'I can hear nothing from you nor of you but what must
be most pleasing to me,' said the Cardinal.

'I wish I could believe that,' said Lothair.

The Cardinal caressed him ; put his arm round Lothair's neck and said, 'There is no time like the present. Let us walk together in this gallery,' and they withdrew naturally from the immediate scene.

'You know all that has happened, I daresay,' said Lothair with embarrassment and with a sigh, 'since we parted in England, sir.'

'All,' said the Cardinal. 'It has been a most striking and merciful dispensation.'

'Then I need not dwell upon it,' said Lothair, 'and naturally it would be most painful. What·I wish particularly to speak to you about is my position under this roof. What I owe to those who dwell under it no language can describe, and no efforts on my part, and they shall be unceasing, can repay. But I think the time has come when I ought no longer to trespass on their affectionate devotion, though, when I allude to the topic, they seem to misinterpret the motives which influence me, and to be pained rather than relieved by my suggestions. I cannot bear being looked upon as ungrateful, when in fact I am devoted to them. I think, sir, you might help me in putting all this right.'

'If it be necessary,' said the Cardinal; 'but I apprehend you misconceive them. When I last left Rome you were very ill, but Lady St. Jerome and others have written to me almost daily about you during my absence, so that I am familiar with all that has occurred, and quite cognisant of their feelings. Rest assured that, towards yourself, they are exactly what they ought to be and what you would desire.'

'Well I am glad,' said Lothair, 'that you are acquainted with everything that has happened, for you can put them right if it be necessary; but I sometimes cannot help fancying that they are under some false impression both as to my conduct and my convictions.'

'Not in the slightest,' said the Cardinal, 'trust me, my dear friend, for that. They know everything and appreciate everything; and great as, no doubt, have been your sufferings, feel that everything has been ordained for the best; that the hand of the Almighty has been visible throughout all these strange events; that His Church was never more clearly built upon a rock than at this moment; that this great manifestation will revive, and even restore, the faith of Christendom; and that you yourself must be looked upon as one of the most favoured of men.'

'Everybody says that,' said Lothair rather peevishly.

'And everybody feels it,' said the Cardinal.

'Well, to revert to lesser points,' said Lothair. 'I do not say I want to return to England, for I dread returning to England, and do not know whether I shall ever go back there; and at any rate I doubt not my health at present is unequal to the effort; but I should like some change in my mode of life. I will not say it is too much controlled, for nothing seems ever done without first consulting me; but, some how or other, we are always in the same groove. I wish to see more of the world; I wish to see Rome, and the people of Rome. I wish to see and do many things which, if I mention, it would seem to hurt the feelings of others, and my own are misconceived, but if mentioned by you all would probably be different.'

'I understand you, my dear young friend, my child, I will still say,' said the Cardinal. 'Nothing can be more reasonable than what you suggest. No doubt our friends may be a little too anxious about you, but they are the best people in the world. You appear to me to be quite well enough now to make more exertion than hitherto they have thought you capable of. They see you every day, and cannot judge so well of you as I who have been absent. I will charge myself to effect all your wishes. And we will begin by my taking you out to-morrow and your driving

with me about the city. I will show you Rome and the
Roman people.'

Accordingly, on the morrow, Cardinal Grandison and his
late pupil visited together Rome and the Romans. And first
of all Lothair was presented to the Cardinal Prefect of the
Propaganda, who presides over the ecclesiastical affairs of
every country in which the Roman Church has a mission,
and that includes every land between the Arctic and the
Southern Pole. This glimpse of the organised correspondence with both the Americas, all Asia, all Africa, all
Australia, and many European countries, carried on by a
countless staff of clerks in one of the most capacious buildings in the world, was calculated to impress the visitor
with a due idea of the extensive authority of the Roman
Pontiff. This institution, greater, according to the Cardinal, than any which existed in ancient Rome, was to
propagate the faith, the purity of which the next establishment they visited was to maintain. According to Cardinal
Grandison there never was a body the character of which
had been so wilfully and so malignantly misrepresented as
that of the Roman Inquisition. Its true object is reformation not punishment, and therefore pardon was sure to
follow the admission of error. True it was there were
revolting stories afloat, for which there was undoubtedly
some foundation, though their exaggeration and malice
were evident, of the ruthless conduct of the Inquisition;
but these details were entirely confined to Spain, and were
the consequences not of the principles of the Holy Office,
but of the Spanish race, poisoned by Moorish and Jewish
blood, or by long contact with those inhuman infidels.
Had it not been for the Inquisition organising and directing the mitigating influences of the Church, Spain would
have been a land of wild beasts; and even in quite modern
times it was the Holy Office at Rome which always stepped
forward to protect the persecuted, and, by the power of

appeal from Madrid to Rome, saved the lives of those who were unjustly or extravagantly accused.

'The real business however of the Holy Office now,' continued the Cardinal, 'is in reality only doctrinal ; and there is something truly sublime, essentially divine, I would say, in this idea of an old man, like the Holy Father, himself the object of ceaseless persecution by all the children of Satan, never for a moment relaxing his heaven-inspired efforts to maintain the purity of the faith once delivered to the Saints, and at the same time to propagate it throughout the whole world, so that there should be no land on which the sun shines that should not afford means of salvation to suffering man. Yes, the Propaganda and the Inquisition alone are sufficient to vindicate the sacred claims of Rome. Compared with them mere secular and human institutions, however exalted, sink into insignificance.'

These excursions with the Cardinal were not only repeated, but became almost of daily occurrence. The Cardinal took Lothair with him in his visits of business, and introduced him to the eminent characters of the city. Some of these priests were illustrious scholars, or votaries of science, whose names were quoted with respect and as authority in the circles of cosmopolitan philosophy. Then there were other institutions at Rome, which the Cardinal snatched occasions to visit, and which, if not so awfully venerable as the Propaganda and the Inquisition, nevertheless testified to the advanced civilisation of Rome and the Romans, and the enlightened administration of the Holy Father. According to Cardinal Grandison, all the great modern improvements in the administration of hospitals and prisons originated in the eternal city ; scientific ventilation, popular lavatories, the cellular or silent system, the reformatory. And yet these were nothing compared with the achievements of the Pontifical Government in education. In short, complete popular education only existed at Rome. Its schools were more numerous even than its fountains. Gratuitous instruction originated with the ecclesiastics; and from the night school to the university here might be found the perfect type.

'I really believe,' said the Cardinal, 'that a more virtuous, a more religious, a more happy and contented people than the Romans never existed. They could all be kept in order with the police of one of your counties. True it is the Holy Father is obliged to garrison the city with twelve thousand men of all arms, but not against the Romans, not against his own subjects. It is the Secret Societies of Atheism who have established their lodges in this city, entirely consisting of foreigners, that render these lamentable precautions necessary. They will not rest until they have extirpated the religious principle from the soul of man, and until they have reduced him to the condition of wild beasts. But they will fail, as they failed the other day, as Sennacherib failed. These men may conquer Zouaves and Cuirassiers, but they cannot fight against Saint Michael and all the Angels. They may do mischief, they may aggravate and prolong the misery of man, but they are doomed to entire and eternal failure.'

CHAPTER LXV.

Lady St. Jerome was much interested in the accounts which the Cardinal and Lothair gave her of their excursions in the city and their visits.

'It is very true,' she said, 'I ever knew such good people; and they ought to be; so favoured by Heaven, and leading a life which, if anything earthly can, must give them, however faint, some foretaste of our joys hereafter. Did your Eminence visit the Pellegrini?' This was the hospital where Miss Arundel had found Lothair.

The Cardinal looked grave. 'No,' he replied. 'My object was to secure for our young friend some interesting but not agitating distraction from certain ideas which, however admirable and transcendently important, are nevertheless too high and profound to permit their constant contemplation with impunity to our infirm natures. Besides,' he added, in a lower, but still distinct tone, 'I was myself unwilling to visit in a mere casual manner the scene of what I must consider the greatest event of this century.'

'But you have been there?' enquired Lady St. Jerome.

His Eminence crossed himself.

In the course of the evening Monsignore Catesby told Lothair that a grand service was about to be celebrated at the church of St. George: thanks were to be offered to the Blessed Virgin by Miss Arundel for the miraculous mercy vouchsafed to her in saving the life of a countryman, Lothair. 'All her friends will make a point of being there,' added the Monsignore, 'even the Protestants and some Russians. Miss Arundel was very unwilling at first to fulfil this office, but the Holy Father has commanded it. I know that nothing will induce her to ask you to attend; and yet, if I were you, I would turn it over in your mind. I know she said that she would sooner that you were present than all her English friends together. However, you can think about it. One likes to do what is proper.'

One does; and yet it is difficult. Sometimes in doing what we think proper, we get into irremediable scrapes; and often, what we hold to be proper, society in its caprice resolves to be highly improper.

Lady St. Jerome had wished Lothair to see Tivoli, and they were all consulting together when they might go there. Lord St. Jerome who, besides his hunters, had his drag at Rome, wanted to drive them to the place. Lothair sate opposite Miss Arundel, gazing on her beauty. It was like being at Vauxe again. And yet a great deal had happened since they were at Vauxe; and what? So far as they two were concerned, nothing but what should create or confirm relations of confidence and affection. Whatever may have been the influence of others on his existence, hers at least had been one of infinite benignity. She had saved his life, she had cherished it. She had raised him from the lowest depth of physical and moral prostration to health and comparative serenity. If at Vauxe he had beheld her with admiration, had listened with fascinated interest to the fervid expression of her saintly thoughts, and the large purposes of her heroic mind, all these feelings were naturally heightened now when he had witnessed her lofty and consecrated spirit in action, and when that action in his own case had only been exercised for his ineffable advantage.

'Your uncle cannot go to-morrow,' continued Lady St. Jerome, 'and on Thursday I am engaged.'

'And on Friday ——' said Miss Arundel, hesitating.

'We are all engaged,' said Lady St. Jerome.

'I should hardly wish to go out before Friday anywhere,' said Miss Arundel, speaking to her aunt, and in a lower tone.

Friday was the day on which the thanksgiving service was to be celebrated in the Jesuit church of St. George of Cappadocia. Lothair knew this well enough and was embarrassed: a thanksgiving for the mercy vouchsafed to Miss Arundel in saving the life of a fellow-countryman, and that fellow-countryman not present! All her Protestant friends would be there, and some Russians. And he not there! It seemed, on his part, the most ungracious and intolerable conduct. And he knew that she would prefer his presence to that of all her acquaintances together. It was more than ungracious on his part; it was ungrateful, almost inhuman.

Lothair sate silent, and stupid, and stiff, and dissatisfied with himself. Once or twice he tried to speak, but his tongue would not move, or his throat was not clear. And if he had spoken, he would only have made some trifling and awkward remark. In his mind's eye he saw, gliding about him, the veiled figure of his sick room, and he recalled with clearness the unceasing and angelic tenderness of which at the time he seemed hardly conscious.

Miss Arundel had risen and had proceeded some way down the room to a cabinet where she was accustomed to place her work. Suddenly Lothair rose and followed her. 'Miss Arundel!' he said, and she looked round, hardly stopping when he had reached her. 'Miss Arundel, I hope you will permit me to be present at the celebration on Friday?'

She turned round quickly, extending, even eagerly, her hand with mantling cheek. Her eyes glittered with celestial fire. The words hurried from her palpitating lips: 'And support me,' she said, 'for I need support.'

In the evening reception, Monsignore Catesby approached Father Coleman. 'It is done,' he said, with a look of saintly triumph. 'It is done at last. He will not only be present, but he will support her. There are yet eight and forty hours to elapse. Can anything happen to defeat us? It would seem not; yet when so much is at stake, one is fearful. He must never be out of our sight; not a human being must approach him.'

'I think we can manage that,' said Father Coleman.

CHAPTER LXVI.

The Jesuit church of St. George of Cappadocia was situate in one of the finest piazzas of Rome. It was surrounded with arcades, and in its centre the most beautiful fountain of the city spouted forth its streams to an amazing height, and in forms of graceful fancy. On Friday morning the arcades were festooned with tapestry and hangings of crimson velvet and gold. Every part was crowded, and all the rank and fashion and power of Rome seemed to be there assembling. There had been once some intention on the part of the Holy Father to be present, but a slight indisposition had rendered that not desirable. His Holiness, however, had ordered a company of his halberdiers to attend, and the ground was kept by those wonderful guards in the dress of the middle ages; halberds and ruffs, and white plumes, and party-coloured coats, a match for our beef-eaters. Carriages with scarlet umbrellas on the box, and each with three serving men behind, denoted the presence of the cardinals in force. They were usually brilliant equipages, being sufficiently new, or sufficiently now pur-chased, Garibaldi and the late commanding officer of Lothair having burnt most of the ancient coaches in the time of the Roman Republic twenty years before. From each carriage an eminence descended with his scarlet cap and his purple train borne by two attendants. The Princess Tarpeia-Cinque Cento was there, and most of the Roman princes and princesses and dukes and duchesses. It seemed that the whole court of Rome was there; monsignori and prelates without end. Some of their dresses, and those of the generals of the orders, appropriately varied the general effect, for the ladies were all in black, their heads covered only with black veils.

Monsignore Catesby had arranged with Lothair that
they should enter the church by their usual private way,
and Lothair therefore was not in any degree prepared for
the sight which awaited him on his entrance into it. The
church was crowded; not a chair nor a tribune vacant.
There was a suppressed gossip going on as in a public
place before a performance begins, much fluttering of fans,
some snuff taken, and many sugar plums.

'Where shall we find a place?' said Lothair.

'They expect us in the sacristy,' said the Monsignore.

The sacristy of the Jesuit church of St. George of
Cappadocia might have served for the ball-room of a palace.
It was lofty and proportionately spacious, with a grooved
ceiling painted with all the court of heaven. Above the
broad and richly gilt cornice floated a company of Seraphim
that might have figured as the Cupids of Albano. The
apartment was crowded, for there and in some adjoining
chambers were assembled the cardinals and prelates, and
all the distinguished or official characters, who, in a few
minutes, were about to form a procession of almost un-
equalled splendour and sanctity, and which was to parade
the whole body of the church.

Lothair felt nervous; an indefinable depression came over
him, as on the morning of a contest when a candidate enters
his crowded committee-room. Considerable personages
bowing, approached to address him : the Cardinal Prefect
of the Propaganda, the Cardinal Assessor of the Holy
Office, the Cardinal Pro-Datario, and the Cardinal Vicar of
Rome. Monsignori the Secretary of Briefs to Princes
and the Master of the Apostolic Palace were presented to
him. Had this been a conclave, and Lothair the future
Pope, it would have been impossible to have treated him
with more consideration than he experienced. They assured
him that they looked upon this day as one of the most interesting in their lives, and the importance of which to the

Church could not be overrated. All this somewhat encouraged him, and he was more himself when a certain
general stir, and the entrance of individuals from adjoining
apartments, intimated that the proceedings were about to
commence. It seemed difficult to marshal so considerable
and so stately an assemblage, but those who had the
management of affairs were experienced in such matters.
The acolytes and the thurifers fell into their places; there
seemed no end of banners and large golden crosses; great
was the company of the prelates, a long purple line, some
only in cassocks, some in robes, and mitred; then came a
new banner of the Blessed Virgin, which excited intense
interest, and every eye was strained to catch the pictured
scene. After this banner, amid frequent incense, walked
two of the most beautiful children in Rome, dressed as
angels with golden wings; the boy bearing a rose of
Jericho, the girl a lily. After these, as was understood,
dressed in black and veiled, walked six ladies, who were
said to be daughters of the noblest houses of England,
and then a single form with a veil touching the ground.

'Here we must go,' said Monsignore Catesby to Lothair,
and he gently but irresistibly guided him into his place.
'You know you promised to support her. You had better
take this,' he said, placing a lighted taper in his hand;
'it is usual, and one should never be singular.'

So they walked on, followed by the Roman princes,
bearing a splendid baldachin. And then came the pomp of
the cardinals, each with his train-bearers, exhibiting with
the skill of artists the splendour of their violet robes.

As the head of the procession emerged from the sacristy into the church, three organs and a choir, to which
all the Roman churches had lent their choicest voices,
burst into the Te Deum. Round the church and to all the
chapels, and then up the noble nave, the majestic procession moved, and then the gates of the holy place opening,

the cardinals entered and seated themselves, their train-bearers crouching at their knees, the prelates grouped themselves, and the banners and crosses were ranged in the distance, except the new banner of the Virgin, which seemed to hang over the altar. The Holy One seemed to be in what was recently a field of battle, and was addressing a beautiful maiden in the dress of a Sister of Mercy.

'This is your place,' said Monsignore Catesby, and he guided Lothair into a prominent position.

The service was long, but sustained by exquisite music, celestial perfumes, and the graceful movements of priests in resplendent dresses continually changing, it could not be said to be wearisome. When all was over, Monsignore Catesby said to Lothair, 'I think we had better return by the public way; it seems expected.'

It was not easy to leave the church. Lothair was detained, and received the congratulations of the Princess Tarpeia-Cinque Cento and many others. The crowd, much excited by the carriages of the cardinals, had not diminished when they came forth, and they were obliged to linger some little time upon the steps, the Monsignore making difficulties when Lothair more than once proposed to advance.

'I think we may go now,' said Catesby, and they descended into the piazza. Immediately many persons in their immediate neighbourhood fell upon their knees, many asked a blessing from Lothair, and some rushed forward to kiss the hem of his garment.

CHAPTER LXVII.

THE Princess Tarpeia-Cinque Cento gave an entertainment in the evening in honour of 'the great event.' Italian palaces are so vast, are so ill-adapted to the moderate establishments of modern times, that their grand style in general only impresses those who visit them with a feeling of disappointment and even mortification. The meagre retinue are almost invisible as they creep about the corridors and galleries, and linger in the sequence of lofty chambers. These should be filled with crowds of serving men and groups of splendid retainers. They were built for the days when a great man was obliged to have a great following; and when the safety of his person, as well as the success of his career, depended on the number and the lustre of his train.

The palace of the Princess Tarpeia was the most celebrated in Rome, one of the most ancient, and certainly the most beautiful. She dwelt in it in a manner not unworthy of her consular blood and her modern income. To-night her guests were received by a long line of foot servants in showy liveries, and bearing the badge of her house, while in every convenient spot pages and gentlemen ushers in courtly dress guided the guests to their place of destination. The palace blazed with light, and showed to advantage the thousand pictures which, it is said, were there enshrined, and the long galleries full of the pale statues of Grecian gods and goddesses and the busts of the former rulers of Rome and the Romans. The atmosphere was fragrant with rare odours, and music was heard amid the fall of fountains in the dim but fancifully illumined gardens.

The Princess herself wore all those famous jewels which

A A

had been spared by all the Goths from the days of Brennus
to those of Garibaldi, and on her bosom reposed the celebrated transparent cameo of Augustus, which Cæsar himself is said to have presented to Livia, and which Benvenuto Cellini had set in a framework of Cupids and rubies.
If the weight of her magnificence were sometimes distressing, she had the consolation of being supported by the arm
of Lothair.

Two young Roman princes, members of the Guardia
Nobile, discussed the situation.

'The English here say,' said one, 'that he is their richest
man.'

'And very noble, too,' said the other.

'Certainly, truly noble; a kind of cousin of the Queen.'

'This great event must have an effect upon all their
nobility. I cannot doubt they will all return to the Holy
Father.'

'They would if they were not afraid of having to restore
their church lands. But they would be much more happy
if Rome were again the capital of the world.'

'No shadow of doubt. I wonder if this young prince
will hunt in the Campagna?'

'All Englishmen hunt.'

'I make no doubt he rides well, and has famous horses,
and will sometimes lend us one. I am glad his soul is
saved.'

'Yes; it is well, when the Blessed Virgin interferes, it
should be in favour of princes. When princes become
good Christians it is an example. It does good. And this
man will give an impulse to our opera, which wants it,
and, as you say, he will have many horses.'

In the course of the evening Miss Arundel, with a beaming face but of deep expression, said to Lothair, 'I could
tell you some good news had I not promised the Cardinal
that he should communicate it to you himself. He will see

you to-morrow. Although it does not affect me personally, it will be to me the happiest event that ever occurred, except, of course, one.'

'What can she mean?' thought Lothair. But at that moment Cardinal Berwick approached him, and Miss Arundel glided away.

Father Coleman attended Lothair home to the Agostini Palace, and when they parted said with much emphasis, 'I must congratulate you once more on the great event.'

On the following morning, Lothair found on his table a number of the Roman journal published that day. It was customary to place it there, but in general he only glanced at it, and scarcely that. On the present occasion his own name caught immediately his eye. It figured in a long account of the celebration of the preceding day. It was with a continually changing countenance, now scarlet, now pallid as death; with a palpitating heart, a trembling hand, a cold perspiration, and at length a disordered vision, that Lothair read the whole of an article, of which we now give a summary:

'Rome was congratulated on the service of yesterday, which celebrated the greatest event of this century. And it came to pass in this wise. It seems that a young English noble, of the highest rank, family, and fortune (and here the name and titles of Lothair were accurately given), like many of the scions of the illustrious and influential families of Britain, was impelled by an irresistible motive to enlist as a volunteer in the service of the Pope, when the Holy Father was recently attacked by the Secret Societies of Atheism. This gallant and gifted youth, after prodigies of valour and devotion, had fallen at Mentana in the sacred cause, and was given up for lost. The day after the battle, when the ambulances laden with the wounded were hourly arriving at Rome from the field, an English lady, daughter of an illustrious house, celebrated

throughout centuries for its devotion to the Holy See, and
who during the present awful trial had never ceased in
her efforts to support the cause of Christianity, was employed, as was her wont, in offices of charity, and was
tending with her companion sisters her wounded countrymen at the hospital La Consolazione, in the new ward
which has been recently added to that establishment by
the Holy Father.

  ‘ While she was leaning over one of the beds, she felt a
gentle and peculiar pressure on her shoulder, and, looking
round, beheld a most beautiful woman, with a countenance
of singular sweetness and yet majesty. And the visitor
said, “ You are attending to those English who believe in
the Virgin Mary. Now at the Hospital Santissima Trinitá
di Pellegrini there is in an ambulance a young Englishman
apparently dead, but who will not die if you go to him
immediately and say you came in the name of the Virgin.”

  ‘ The influence of the stranger was so irresistible that
the young English lady, attended by a nurse and one of
the porters of La Consolazione, repaired instantly to the
Di Pellegrini, and there they found in the courtyard, as
they had been told, an ambulance, in form and colour and
equipment unlike any ambulance used by the papal troops,
and in the ambulance the senseless body of a youth, who
was recognised by the English lady as her young and
gallant countryman. She claimed him in the name of
the Blessed Virgin, and, after due remedies, was permitted
to take him at once to his noble relatives, who lived in the
Palazzo Agostini.

  ‘ After a short time much conversation began to circulate
about this incident. The family wished to testify their
gratitude to the individual whose information had led to
the recovery of the body, and subsequently of the life of
their relation ; but all that they could at first learn at La Consolazione was, that the porter believed the woman was Maria

Serafina di Angelis, the handsome wife of a tailor in the
Strada di Ripetta. But it was soon shown that this could
not be true, for it was proved that, on the day in question,
Maria Serafina di Angelis was on a visit to a friend at La
Riccia; and, in the second place, that she did not bear the
slightest resemblance to the stranger who had given the
news. Moreover, the porter of the gate being required to
state why he had admitted any stranger without the accustomed order, denied that he had so done; that he was in
his lodge and the gates were locked, and the stranger had
passed through without his knowledge.

'Two priests were descending the stairs when the stranger came upon them, and they were so struck by the peculiarity of her carriage, that they turned round and looked
at her, and clearly observed at the back of her head a sort
of halo. She was out of their sight while they were making
this observation, but in consequence of it they made enquiries of the porter of the gate, and remained in the courtyard till she returned.

'This she did a few minutes before the English lady and
her attendants came down, as they had been detained by
the preparation of some bandages and other remedies,
without which they never moved. The porter of the gate
having his attention called to the circumstance by the
priests, was most careful in his observations as to the halo,
and described it as distinct. The priests then followed the
stranger, who proceeded down a long and solitary street,
made up in a great degree of garden and convent walls,
and without a turning. They observed her stop and speak
to two children, and then, though there was no house to
enter and no street to turn into, she vanished.

'When they had reached the children they found each of
them holding in its hand a beautiful flower. It seems the
lady had given the boy a rose of Jericho, and to his sister
a white and golden lily. Enquiring whether she had

spoken to them, they answered that she had said, "Let
these flowers be kept in remembrance of me; they will
never fade." And truly, though months had elapsed, these
flowers had never faded, and, after the procession of yesterday, they were placed under crystal in the chapel of the
Blessed Virgin in the Jesuit church of St. George of
Cappadocia, and may be seen every day, and will be seen
for ever in primeval freshness.

'This is the truthful account of what really occurred
with respect to this memorable event, and as it was ascertained by a Consulta of the Holy Office, presided over by
the Cardinal Prefect himself. The Holy Office is most
severe in its inquisition of the truth, and though it well
knows that the Divine presence never leaves His Church,
it is most scrupulous in its investigations whenever any
miraculous interposition is alleged. It was entirely by its
exertions that the somewhat inconsistent and unsatisfactory
evidence of the porter of the gate, in the first instance, was
explained, cleared, and established; the whole chain of
evidence worked out; all idle gossip and mere rumours
rejected; and the evidence obtained of above twenty witnesses of all ranks of life, some of them members of the
learned profession, and others military officers of undoubted
honour and veracity, who witnessed the first appearance of
the stranger at the Pellegrini, and the undoubted fact of
the halo playing round her temples.

'The Consulta of the Holy Office could only draw one
inference, sanctioned by the Holy Father himself, as to the
character of the personage who thus deigned to appear
and interpose; and no wonder that in the great function
of yesterday, the eyes of all Rome were fixed upon Lothair
as the most favoured of living men.'

He himself now felt as one sinking into an unfathomable
abyss. The despair came over him that involves a man
engaged in a hopeless contest with a remorseless power.

All his life during the last year passed rushingly across his mind. He recalled the wiles that had been employed to induce him to attend a function in a Jesuits' chapel in an obscure nook of London; the same agencies had been employed there; then, as now, the influence of Clare Arundel had been introduced to sway him when all others had failed. Belmont had saved him then. There was no Belmont now. The last words of Theodora murmured in his ear like the awful voice of a distant sea. They were the diapason of all the thought and feeling of that profound and passionate spirit.

That seemed only a petty plot in London, and he had since sometimes smiled when he remembered how it had been baffled. Shallow apprehension! The petty plot was only part of a great and unceasing and triumphant conspiracy, and the obscure and inferior agencies which he had been rash enough to deride had consummated their commanded purpose in the eyes of all Europe, and with the aid of the great powers of the world.

He felt all the indignation natural to a sincere and high-spirited man, who finds that he has been befooled by those whom he has trusted; but summoning all his powers to extricate himself from his desolate dilemma, he found himself without resource. What public declaration on his part could alter the undeniable fact, now circulating throughout the world, that in the supernatural scene of yesterday he was the willing and the principal actor? Unquestionably he had been very imprudent, not only in that instance but in his habitual visits to the church; he felt all that now. But he was lorn and shattered, infinitely distressed both in body and in mind; weak and miserable; and he thought he was leaning on angelic hearts, when he found himself in the embrace of spirits of another sphere.

In what a position of unexampled pain did he not now find himself! To feel it your duty to quit the faith in which you have been bred must involve an awful pang; but to be a renegade without the consolation of conscience, against your sense, against your will, alike for no celestial hope and no earthly object, this was agony mixed with self-contempt.

He remembered what Lady Corisande had once said to him about those who quitted their native church for the Roman communion. What would she say now? He marked in imagination the cloud of sorrow on her imperial brow and the scorn of her curled lip.

Whatever happened he could never return to England, at least for many years, when all the things and persons he cared for would have disappeared, or changed, which is worse; and then what would be the use of returning? He would go to America, or Australia, or the Indian Ocean, or the interior of Africa; but even in all these places, according to the correspondence of the Propaganda, he would find Roman priests and active priests. He felt himself a lost man; not free from faults in this matter, but punished beyond his errors. But this is the fate of men who think they can struggle successfully with a supernatural power.

A servant opened a door and said in a loud voice, that, with his permission, his Eminence, the English Cardinal, would wait on him.

CHAPTER LXVIII.

IT is proverbial to what drowning men will cling. Lothair, in his utter hopelessness, made a distinction between the Cardinal and the conspirators. The Cardinal had been absent from Rome during the greater portion of the residence of Lothair in that city. The Cardinal was his father's friend, an English gentleman, with an English education, once an Anglican, a man of the world, a man of honour, a good, kind-hearted man. Lothair explained the apparent and occasional co-operation of his Eminence with the others, by their making use of him without a due consciousness of their purpose on his part. Lothair remembered how delicately his former guardian had always treated the subject of religion in their conversations. The announcement of his visit instead of aggravating the distresses of Lothair, seemed, as all these considerations rapidly occurred to him, almost to impart a ray of hope.

'I see,' said the Cardinal, as he entered serene and graceful as usual, and glancing at the table, 'that you have been reading the account of our great act of yesterday.'

'Yes; and I have been reading it,' said Lothair reddening, 'with indignation; with alarm; I should add, with disgust.'

'How is this?' said the Cardinal, feeling or affecting surprise.

'It is a tissue of falsehood and imposture,' continued Lothair; 'and I will take care that my opinion is known of it.'

'Do nothing rashly,' said the Cardinal. 'This is an official journal, and I have reason to believe that nothing appears in it which is not drawn up, or well considered, by truly pious men.'

'You yourself, sir, must know,' continued Lothair, 'that the whole of this statement is founded on falsehood'

'Indeed I should be sorry to believe,' said the Cardinal, 'that there was a particle of misstatement, or even exaggeration, either in the base or the superstructure of the narrative.'

'Good God!' exclaimed Lothair. 'Why! take the very first allegation, that I fell at Mentana fighting in the ranks of the Holy Father. Every one knows that I fell

fighting against him, and that I was almost slain by one of
his chassepots. It is notorious; and though, as a matter
of taste, I have not obtruded the fact in the society in
which I have been recently living, I have never attempted
to conceal it, and have not the slightest doubt that it must
be as familiar to every member of that society as to your
Eminence.'

'I know there are two narratives of your relations with
the battle of Mentana,' observed the Cardinal quietly.
'The one accepted as authentic is that which appears in
this journal; the other account, which can only be traced
to yourself, bears no doubt a somewhat different character;
but considering that it is in the highest degree improbable,
and that there is not a tittle of confirmatory or collateral
evidence to extenuate its absolute unlikelihood, I hardly
think you are justified in using, with reference to the
statement in this article, the harsh expression which I am
persuaded, on reflection, you will feel you have hastily
used.'

'I think,' said Lothair with a kindling eye and a burning
cheek, 'that I am the best judge of what I did at Mentana.'

'Well, well,' said the Cardinal with dulcet calmness,
'you naturally think so; but you must remember you
have been very ill, my dear young friend, and labouring
under much excitement. If I were you, and I speak as
your friend, I hope your best one, I would not dwell too
much on this fancy of yours about the battle of Mentana.
I would myself always deal tenderly with a fixed idea:
harsh attempts to terminate hallucination are seldom successful. Nevertheless, in the case of a public event, a
matter of fact, if a man finds that he is of one opinion and
all orders of society of another, he should not be encouraged
to dwell on a perverted view; he should be gradually
weaned from it.'

'You amaze me!' said Lothair.

'Not at all,' said the Cardinal. 'I am sure you will benefit by my advice. And you must already perceive that, assuming the interpretation which the world without exception places on your conduct in the field to be the just one, there really is not a single circumstance in the whole of this interesting and important statement, the accuracy of which you yourself would for a moment dispute.'

'What is there said about me at Mentana makes me doubt of all the rest,' said Lothair.

'Well, we will not dwell on Mentana,' said the Cardinal with a sweet smile; 'I have treated of that point. Your case is by no means an uncommon one. It will wear off with returning health. King George IV. believed that he was at the battle of Waterloo, and indeed commanded there; and his friends were at one time a little alarmed; but Knighton, who was a sensible man, said, " His Majesty has only to leave off Curaçoa, and rest assured he will gain no more victories." The rest of this statement, which is to-day officially communicated to the whole world, and which in its results will probably be not less important even than the celebration of the Centenary of St. Peter, is established by evidence so incontestable, by witnesses so numerous, so various, in all the circumstances and accidents of testimony so satisfactory, I may say so irresistible, that controversy on this head would be a mere impertinence and waste of time.'

'I am not convinced,' said Lothair.

'Hush!' said the Cardinal, 'the freaks of your own mind about personal incidents, however lamentable, may be viewed with indulgence, at least for a time. But you cannot be permitted to doubt of the rest. You must be convinced, and on reflection you will be convinced. Remember, sir, where you are. You are in the centre of Christendom, where truth, and where alone truth resides.

Divine authority has perused this paper and approved it.
It is published for the joy and satisfaction of two hundred
millions of Christians, and for the salvation of all those
who unhappily for themselves are not yet converted to the
faith. It records the most memorable event of this century. Our Blessed Lady has personally appeared to her
votaries before during that period, but never at Rome.
Wisely and well she has worked in villages and among the
illiterate as at the beginning did her Divine Son. But
the time is now ripe for terminating the infidelity of the
world. In the eternal city, amid all its matchless learning
and profound theology, in the sight of thousands, this
great act has been accomplished, in a manner which can
admit of no doubt, and which can lead to no controversy.
Some of the most notorious atheists of Rome have already
solicited to be admitted to the offices of the Church; the
Secret Societies have received their death-blow; I look to
the alienation of England as virtually over. I am panting
to see you return to the home of your fathers and recon-
quer it for the Church in the name of the Lord God of
Sabaoth. Never was a man in a greater position since
Godfrey or Ignatius. The eyes of all Christendom are
upon you as the most favoured of men, and you stand
there like Saint Thomas.'

'Perhaps he was as bewildered as I am,' said Lothair.

'Well, his bewilderment ended in his becoming an
apostle, as yours will. I am glad we have had this conversation, and that we agree; I knew we should. But
now I wish to speak to you on business, and very grave.
The world assumes that being the favoured of Heaven you
are naturally and necessarily a member of the Church.
I, your late guardian, know that is not the case, and
sometimes I blame myself that it is not so. But I have
ever scrupulously refrained from attempting to control
your convictions; and the result has justified me. Heaven

has directed your life, and I have now to impart to you
the most gratifying intelligence that can be communicated
by man, and that the Holy Father will to-morrow himself
receive you into the bosom of that Church of which he
is the divine head. Christendom will then hail you as its
champion and regenerator, and thus will be realised the
divine dream with which you were inspired in our morning
walk in the park at Vauxe.'

CHAPTER LXIX.

It was the darkest hour in Lothair's life. He had become
acquainted with sorrow; he had experienced calamities
physical and moral. The death of Theodora had shaken
him to the centre. It was that first great grief which
makes a man acquainted with his deepest feelings, which
detracts something from the buoyancy of the youngest
life, and dims, to a certain degree, the lustre of existence.
But even that bereavement was mitigated by distractions
alike inevitable and ennobling. The sternest and highest
of all obligations, military duty, claimed him with an un-
faltering grasp, and the clarion sounded almost as he
closed her eyes. Then he went forth to struggle for a
cause which at least she believed to be just and sublime;
and if his own convictions on that head might be less assured
or precise, still there was doubtless much that was inspiring
in the contest, and much dependent on the success of himself
and his comrades that tended to the elevation of man.

But, now, there was not a single circumstance to sustain
his involved and sinking life. A renegade, a renegade
without conviction, without necessity, in absolute violation
of the pledge he had given to the person he most honoured
and most loved, as he received her parting spirit! And

why was all this? and how was all this? What system
of sorcery had encompassed his existence? For he was
spell-bound, as much as any knight in fairy tale whom
malignant influences had robbed of his valour and will and
virtue. No sane person could credit, even comprehend,
his position. Had he the opportunity of stating it in a
court of justice to-morrow, he could only enter into a
narrative which would decide his lot as an insane being.
The magical rites had been so gradual, so subtle, so multifarious, all in appearance independent of each other, though
in reality scientifically combined, that while the conspirators had probably effected his ruin both in body and in
soul, the only charges he could make against them would
be acts of exquisite charity, tenderness, self-sacrifice, personal devotion, refined piety, and religious sentiment of
the most exalted character.

What was to be done? And could anything be done?
Could he escape? Where from and where to? He was
certain, and had been for some time, from many circumstances, that he was watched. Could he hope that the
vigilance which observed all his movements would scruple
to prevent any which might be inconvenient? He felt
assured that, to quit that palace alone, was not in his
power. And were it, whither could he go? To whom
was he to appeal? And about what was he to appeal? Should he appeal to the Holy Father? There
would be an opportunity for that to-morrow. To the
College of Cardinals, who had solemnised yesterday with
gracious unction his spiritual triumph? To those congenial spirits, the mild Assessor of the Inquisition, or
the President of the Propaganda, who was busied at that
moment in circulating throughout both the Americas, all
Asia, all Africa, all Australia, and parts of Europe, for the
edification of distant millions, the particulars of the miraculous scene in which he was the principal actor? Should

be throw himself on the protection of the ambiguous minister of the British Crown, and invoke his aid against a conspiracy touching the rights, reason, and freedom of one of Her Majesty's subjects? He would probably find that functionary inditing a private letter to the English Secretary of State, giving the minister a graphic account of the rare doings of yesterday, and assuring the minister, from his own personal and ocular experience, that a member of one of the highest orders of the British peerage carried in the procession a lighted taper after two angels with amaranthine flowers and golden wings.

Lothair remained in his apartments; no one approached him. It was the only day that the Monsignore had not waited on him. Father Coleman was equally reserved. Strange to say, not one of those agreeable and polite gentlomen, fathers of the oratory, who talked about gems, torsos, and excavations, and who always more or less attended his levée, troubled him this morning. With that exquisite tact which pervades the hierarchical circles of Rome, everyone felt that Lothair, on the eve of that event of his life which Providence had so long and so mysteriously prepared, would wish to be undisturbed.

Restless, disquieted, revolving all the incidents of his last year, trying, by terrible analysis, to ascertain how he ever could have got into such a false position, and how he could yet possibly extricate himself from it, not shrinking in many things from self-blame, and yet not recognising on his part such a degree of deviation from the standard of right feeling, or even of common sense, as would authorise such an overthrow as that awaiting him, high rank and boundless wealth, a station of duty and of honour, some gifts of nature, and golden youth, and a disposition that at least aspired, in the employment of these accidents of life and fortune, at something better than selfish gratification, all smashed, the day drew on.

Drew on the day, and every hour it seemed his spirit was more lone and dark. For the first time the thought of death occurred to him as a relief from the perplexities of existence. How much better had he died at Mentana! To this pass had arrived the cordial and brilliant Lord of Muriel, who enjoyed and adorned life, and wished others to adorn and to enjoy it; the individual whom, probably, were the majority of the English people polled, they would have fixed upon as filling the most enviable of all positions, and holding out a hope that he was not unworthy of it. Born with every advantage that could command the sympathies of his fellow-men, with a quick intelligence and a noble disposition, here he was at one-and-twenty ready to welcome death, perhaps even to devise it, as the only rescue from a doom of confusion, degradation, and remorse.

He had thrown himself on a sofa, and had buried his face in his hands to assist the abstraction which he demanded. There was not an incident of his life that escaped the painful inquisition of his memory. He passed his childhood once more in that stern Scotch home, that, after all, had been so kind, and, as it would seem, so wise. The last words of counsel and of warning from his uncle, expressed at Muriel, came back to him. And yet there seemed a destiny throughout these transactions which was irresistible! The last words of Theodora, her look, even more solemn than her tone, might have been breathed over a tripod, for they were a prophecy, not a warning.

How long he had been absorbed in this passionate reverie he knew not, but when he looked up again it was night, and the moon had touched his window. He rose and walked up and down the room, and then went into the corridor. All was silent; not an attendant was visible; the sky was clear and starry, and the moonlight fell on the tall, still cypresses in the vast quadrangle.

Lothair leant over the balustrade and gazed upon the

moonlit fountains. The change of scene, silent and yet
not voiceless, and the softening spell of the tranquillising
hour were a relief to him. And after a time he wandered
about the corridors, and after a time he descended into the
court. The tall Swiss, in his grand uniform, was closing
the gates which had just released a visitor. Lothair motioned that he too wished to go forth, and the Swiss obeyed
him. The threshold was passed, and Lothair found himself for the first time alone in Rome.

Utterly reckless he cared not where he went or what
might happen. The streets were quite deserted, and he
wandered about with a strange curiosity, gratified as he
sometimes encountered famous objects he had read of, and
yet the true character of which no reading ever realises.

The moonlight becomes the proud palaces of Rome,
their corniced and balconied fronts rich with deep shadows
in the blaze. Sometimes he encountered an imperial
column; sometimes he came to an arcadian square flooded
with light and resonant with the fall of statued fountains.
Emerging from a long straggling street of convents and
gardens, he found himself in an open space full of antique
ruins, and among them the form of a colossal amphitheatre that he at once recognised.

It rose with its three tiers of arches and the huge wall that
crowns them, black and complete in the air; and not until
Lothair had entered it could he perceive the portion of the
outer wall that was in ruins, and now bathed with the
silver light. Lothair was alone. In that huge creation;
once echoing with the shouts, and even the agonies, of
thousands, Lothair was alone.

He sate him down on a block of stone in that sublime
and desolate arena, and asked himself the secret spell of
this Rome that had already so agitated his young life, and
probably was about critically to affect it. Theodora lived
for Rome and died for Rome. And the Cardinal, born and

bred an English gentleman, with many hopes and honours,
had renounced his religion, and, it might be said, his
country, for Rome. And for Rome, to-morrow, Catesby
would die without a pang, and sacrifice himself for Rome,
as his race for three hundred years had given, for the same
cause, honour and broad estates and unhesitating lives.
And these very people were influenced by different motives, and thought they were devoting themselves to opposite ends. But still it was Rome: Republican or Cæsarian,
papal or pagan, it still was Rome.

Was it a breeze in a breezeless night that was sighing
amid these ruins? A pine tree moved its head on a
broken arch, and there was a stir among the plants that
hung on the ancient walls. It was a breeze in a breezeless
night that was sighing amid the ruins.

There was a tall crag of ancient building contiguous to
the block on which Lothair was seated, and which on his
arrival he had noted, although, long lost in reverie, he had
not recently turned his glance in that direction. He was
roused from that reverie by the indefinite sense of some
change having occurred which often disturbs and termi-
nates one's brooding thoughts. And looking round, he
felt, he saw, he was no longer alone. The moonbeams fell
upon a figure that was observing him from the crag of ruin
that was near, and as the light clustered and gathered round
the form, it became every moment more definite and distinct.

Lothair would have sprung forward, but he could only
extend his arms: he would have spoken, but his tongue
was paralysed.

'Lothair,' said a deep, sweet voice that never could be
forgotten.

'I am here,' he at last replied.

'Remember!' and she threw upon him that glance, at
once serene and solemn, that had been her last, and was
impressed indelibly upon his heart of hearts.

Now, he could spring forward and throw himself at her feet; but alas! as he reached her, the figure melted into the moonlight, and she was gone: that divine Theodora, who, let us hope, returned at least to those Elysian fields she so well deserved.

CHAPTER LXX.

'THEY have overdone it, Gertrude, with Lothair,' said Lord St. Jerome to his wife. 'I spoke to Monsignore Catesby about it some time ago, but he would not listen to me; I had more confidence in the Cardinal and am disappointed; but a priest is ever too hot. His nervous system has been tried too much.'

Lady St. Jerome still hoped the best, and believed in it. She was prepared to accept the way Lothair was found senseless in the Coliseum as a continuance of miraculous interpositions. He might have remained there for a day or days and never have been recognised when discovered. How marvellously providential that Father Coleman should have been in the vicinity and tempted to visit the great ruin that very night!

Lord St. Jerome was devout, and easy in his temper. Priests and women seemed to have no difficulty in managing him. But he was an English gentleman, and there was at the bottom of his character a fund of courage, firmness, and common sense, that sometimes startled and sometimes perplexed those who assumed that he could be easily controlled. He was not satisfied with the condition of Lothair, 'a peer of England and my connection;' and he had not unlimited confidence in those who had been hitherto consulted as to his state. There was a celebrated English physician at that time visiting Rome, and Lord

St. Jerome, notwithstanding the multiform resistance of Monsignore Catesby, insisted he should be called in to Lothair.

The English physician was one of those men who abhor priests, and do not particularly admire ladies. The latter, in revenge, denounced his manners as brutal, though they always sent for him, and were always trying, though vainly, to pique him into sympathy. He rarely spoke, but he listened to everyone with entire patience. He sometimes asked a question, but he never made a remark.

Lord St. Jerome had seen the physician alone before he visited the Palazzo Agostini, and had talked to him freely about Lothair. The physician saw at once that Lord St. Jerome was truthful, and that though his intelligence might be limited, it was pure and direct. Appreciating Lord St. Jerome, that nobleman found the redoubtable doctor not ungenial, and assured his wife that she would meet on the morrow by no means so savage a being as she anticipated. She received him accordingly, and in the presence of Monsignore Catesby. Never had she exercised her distinguished powers of social rhetoric with more art and fervour, and never apparently had they proved less productive of the intended consequences. The physician said not a word, and merely bowed when exhausted nature consigned the luminous and impassioned Lady St. Jerome to inevitable silence. Monsignore Catesby felt he was bound in honour to make some diversion in her favour; repeat some of her unanswered inquiries, and reiterate some of her unnoticed views; but the only return he received was silence without a bow, and then the physician remarked, 'I presume I can now see the patient.'

The English physician was alone with Lothair for some time, and then he met in consultation the usual attendants. The result of all these proceedings was that he returned to the saloon, in which he found Lord and Lady St. Jerome,

Monsignore Catesby, and Father Coleman, and he then said, 'My opinion is that his Lordship should quit Rome immediately, and I think he had better return at once to his own country.'

All the efforts of the English Propaganda were now directed to prevent the return of Lothair to his own country. The Cardinal and Lady St. Jerome, and the Monsignore, and Father Coleman, all the beautiful young countesses who had 'gone over' to Rome, and all the spirited young earls who had come over to bring their wives back, but had unfortunately remained themselves, looked very serious, and spoke much in whispers. Lord St. Jerome was firm that Lothair should immediately leave the city, and find that change of scene and air which were declared by authority to be indispensable for his health, both of mind and body. But his return to England, at this moment, was an affair of serious difficulty. He could not return unattended, and attended too by some intimate and devoted friend. Besides it was very doubtful whether Lothair had strength remaining to bear so great an exertion, and at such a season of the year; and he seemed disinclined to it himself. He also wished to leave Rome, but he wished also in time to extend his travels. Amidst these difficulties a Neapolitan duke, a great friend of Monsignore Catesby, a gentleman who always had a friend in need, offered to the young English noble, the interesting young Englishman so favoured by heaven, the use of his villa on the coast of the remotest part of Sicily, near Syracuse. Here was a solution of many difficulties: departure from Rome, change of scene and air (sea air, too, particularly recommended), and almost the same as a return to England, without an effort; for was it not an island, only with a better climate, and a people with free institutions, or a taste for them, which is the same?

The mode in which Lady St. Jerome and Monsignore

Catesby consulted Lord St. Jerome on the subject, took the
adroit but insidious form of congratulating him on the
entire and unexpected fulfilment of his purpose. 'Are we
not fortunate?' exclaimed her Ladyship, looking up
brightly in his face, and gently pressing one of his arms.

'Exactly everything your Lordship required,' echoed
Monsignore Catesby, congratulating him by pressing the
other.

The Cardinal said to Lord St. Jerome in the course of
the morning, in an easy way, and as if he were not thinking too much of the matter, 'So you have got out of all
your difficulties.'

Lord St. Jerome was not entirely satisfied, but he thought
he had done a great deal, and, to say the truth, the effort
for him had not been inconsiderable; and so the result was
that Lothair, accompanied by Monsignore Catesby and
Father Coleman, travelled by easy stages, and chiefly on
horseback, through a delicious and romantic country, which
alone did Lothair a great deal of good, to the coast; crossed
the straits on a serene afternoon, visited Messina and
Palermo, and finally settled at their point of destination,
the Villa Catalano.

Nothing could be more satisfactory than the Monsignore's
bulletin, announcing to his friends at Rome their ultimate
arrangements. Three weeks' travel, air, horse exercise, the
inspiration of the landscape and the clime, had wonderfully
restored Lothair, and they might entirely count on his passing Holy Week at Rome, when all they had hoped and
prayed for would, by the blessing of the Holy Virgin, be
accomplished.

CHAPTER LXXI.

THE terrace of the Villa Catalano, with its orange and palm trees, looked upon a sea of lapis lazuli, and rose from a shelving shore of aloes and arbutus. The waters reflected the colour of the sky, and all the foliage was bedewed with the same violet light of morn which bathed the softness of the distant mountains, and the undulating beauty of the ever-varying coast.

Lothair was walking on the terrace, his favourite walk, for it was the only occasion on which he ever found himself alone. Not that he had any reason to complain of his companions. More complete ones could scarcely be selected. Travel, which they say tries all tempers, had only proved the engaging equanimity of Catesby, and had never disturbed the amiable repose of his brother priest: and then they were so entertaining and so instructive, as well as handy and experienced in all common things. The Monsignore had so much taste and feeling and various knowledge; and as for the reverend Father, all the antiquaries they daily encountered were mere children in his hands who, without effort, could explain and illustrate every scene and object, and spoke as if he had never given a thought to any other theme than Sicily and Syracuse, the expedition of Nicias and the adventures of Agathocles. And yet during all their travels Lothair felt that he never was alone. This was remarkable at the great cities such as Messina and Palermo, but it was a prevalent habit in less frequented places. There was a petty town near them, which he had never visited alone, although he had made more than one attempt with that view; and it was only on the terrace in the early morn, a spot whence he could be observed from the villa, and which did not easily communicate with the precipitous and surrounding scenery, that Lothair would indulge that habit of introspection which he had pursued through many a long ride, and which to him was a never-failing source of interest and even excitement.

He wanted to ascertain the causes of what he deemed the failure of his life, and of the dangers and discomfiture that were still impending over him. Were these causes to be found in any peculiarity of his disposition, or in the general inexperience and incompetence of youth ? The latter he was now quite willing to believe would lead their possessors into any amount of disaster, but his ingenuous nature hesitated before it accepted them as the self-complacent solution of his present deplorable position.

Of a nature profound and inquisitive, though with a great fund of reverence which had been developed by an ecclesiastical education, Lothair now felt that he had started in life with an extravagant appreciation of the influence of the religious principle on the conduct of human affairs. With him, when heaven was so nigh, earth could not be remembered ; and yet experience showed that, so long as one was on the earth, the incidents of this planet considerably controlled one's existence, both in behaviour and in thought. All the world could not retire to Mount Athos. It was clear, therefore, that there was a juster conception of the relations between religion and life than that which he had at first adopted.

Practically, Theodora had led or was leading him to this result ; but Theodora, though religious, did not bow before those altars to which he for a moment had never been faithless. Theodora believed in her immortality, and did not believe in death according to the ecclesiastical interpretation. But her departure from the scene, and the circumstances under which it had taken place, had unexpectedly and violently restored the course of his life to its old bent.

Shattered and shorn, he was willing to believe that he was again entering the kingdom of heaven, but found he was only under the gilded dome of a Jesuit's church, and woke to reality, from a scene of magical deceptions, with a sad conviction that even cardinals and fathers of the Church were inevitably influenced in this life by its interests and its passions.

But the incident of his life that most occupied, it might be said engrossed, his meditation was the midnight apparition in the Coliseum. Making every allowance that a candid nature and an ingenious mind could suggest for explicatory circumstances; the tension of his nervous system, which was then doubtless strained to its last point; the memory of her death-scene, which always harrowed and haunted him; and that dark collision between his promise and his life which then, after so many efforts, appeared by some supernatural ordination to be about inevitably to occur in that very Rome whose gigantic shades surrounded him; he still could not resist the conviction that he had seen the form of Theodora and had listened to her voice. Often the whole day when they were travelling, and his companions watched him on his saddle in silent thought, his mind in reality was fixed on this single incident, and he was cross-examining his memory as some adroit and ruthless advocate deals with the witness in the box, and tries to demonstrate his infidelity or his weakness.

But whether it were indeed the apparition of his adored friend or a distempered dream, Lothair not less recognised the warning as divine, and the only conviction he had arrived at throughout his Sicilian travels was a determination that, however tragical the cost, his promise to Theodora should never be broken.

The beautiful terrace of the Villa Catalano overlooked a small bay to which it descended by winding walks. The

water was deep, and in any other country the bay might
have been turned to good account, but bays abounded on
this coast, and the people, with many harbours, had no
freights to occupy them. This morn, this violet morn,
when the balm of the soft breeze refreshed Lothair, and the
splendour of the rising sun began to throw a flashing line
upon the azure waters, a few fishermen in one of the
country boats happened to come in, about to dry a net
upon a sunny bank. The boat was what is called a speronaro; an open boat worked with oars, but with a lateen
sail at the same time when the breeze served.

Lothair admired the trim of the vessel, and got talking
with the men as they eat their bread and olives, and a
small fish or two.

'And your lateen sail——?' continued Lothair.

'Is the best thing in the world, except in a white squall,'
replied the sailor, 'and then everything is queer in these
seas with an open boat, though I am not afraid of Santa
Agnese, and that is her name. But I took two English
officers who came over here for sport, and whose leave
of absence was out; I took them over in her to Malta,
and did it in ten hours. I believe it had never been done
in an open boat before, but it was neck or nothing with
them.'

'And you saved them?'

'With the lateen up the whole way.'

'They owed you much, and I hope they paid you well.'

'I asked them ten ducats,' said the man, 'and they paid
me ten ducats.'

Lothair had his hand in his pocket all this time, feeling,
but imperceptibly, for his purse, and when he had found it,
feeling how it was lined. He generally carried about him
as much as Fortunatus.

'What are you going to do with yourselves this morning?' said Lothair.

'Well, not much; we thought of throwing the net, but we have had one dip, and no great luck.'

'Are you inclined to give me a sail?'

'Certainly, signor.'

'Have you a mind to go to Malta?'

'That is business, signor.'

'Look here,' said Lothair, 'here are ten ducats in this purse, and a little more. I will give them to you if you will take me to Malta at once, but if you will start in a hundred seconds, before the sun touches that rock, and the waves just beyond it are already bright, you shall have ten more ducats when you reach the isle.'

'Step in, signor.'

From the nature of the course, which was not in the direction of the open sea, for they had to double Cape Passaro, the speronaro was out of sight of the villa in a few minutes. They rowed only till they had doubled the cape, and then set the lateen sail, the breeze being light but steady and favourable. They were soon in open sea, no land in sight. 'And if a white squall does rise,' thought Lothair, 'it will only settle many difficulties.'

But no white squall came; everything was favourable to their progress: the wind, the current, the courage and spirit of the men, who liked the adventure and liked Lothair. Night came on, but they were as tender to him as women, fed him with their least coarse food, and covered him with a cloak made of stuff spun by their mothers and their sisters.

Lothair was slumbering when the patron of the boat roused him, and he saw at hand many lights, and in a few minutes was in still water. They were in one of the harbours of Malta, but not permitted to land at midnight, and when the morn arrived, the obstacles to the release of Lothair were not easily removed. A speronaro, an open boat from Sicily, of course with no papers to prove their

point of departure: here were materials for doubt and
difficulty, of which the petty officers of the port know how
to avail themselves. They might come from Barbary, from
an infected port; plague might be aboard, a question of
quarantine. Lothair observed that they were nearly along-
side of a fine steam yacht, English, for it bore the cross of
St. George, and while on the quay, he and the patron of
the speronaro arguing with the officers of the port, a
gentleman from the yacht put ashore in a boat, of which
the bright equipment immediately attracted attention. The
gentleman landed almost close to the point where the
controversy was carrying on. The excited manner and
voice of the Sicilian mariner could not escape notice. The
gentleman stopped and looked at the group, and then suddenly exclaimed, 'Good heavens! my Lord, can it be you?'

'Ah! Mr. Phœbus, you will help me,' said Lothair, and
then he went up to him and told him everything. All
difficulties of course vanished before the presence of
Mr. Phœbus, whom the officers of the port evidently looked
upon as a being beyond criticism and control.

'And now,' said Mr. Phœbus, 'about your people and
your baggage.'

'I have neither servants nor clothes,' said Lothair, 'and
if it had not been for these good people, I should not have
had food.'

CHAPTER LXXII.

MR. PHŒBUS in his steam-yacht PAN, of considerable ad-
measurement and fitted up with every luxury and convenience that science and experience could suggest, was on
his way to an island which he occasionally inhabited, near
the Asian coast of the Ægean Sea, and which he rented
from the chief of his wife's house, the Prince of Samos.

Mr. Phœbus, by his genius and fame, commanded a large income, and he spent it freely and fully. There was nothing of which he more disapproved than accumulation. It was a practice which led to sordid habits and was fatal to the beautiful. On the whole, he thought it more odious even than debt, more permanently degrading. Mr. Phœbus liked pomp and graceful ceremony, and he was of opinion that great artists should lead a princely life, so that in their manners and method of existence they might furnish models to mankind in general, and elevate the tone and taste of nations.

Sometimes when he observed a friend noticing with admiration, perhaps with astonishment, the splendour or finish of his equipments, he would say, 'The world thinks I had a large fortune with Madame Phœbus. I had nothing. I understand that a fortune, and no inconsiderable one, would have been given, had I chosen to ask for it. But I did not choose to ask for it. I made Madame Phœbus my wife because she was the finest specimen of the Aryan race that I was acquainted with, and I would have no considerations mixed up with the high motive that influenced me. My father-in-law Cantacuzene, whether from a feeling of gratitude or remorse, is always making us magnificent presents. I like to receive magnificent presents, but also to make them; and I presented him with a picture which is the gem of his gallery, and which, if he ever part with it, will in another generation be contended for by kings and peoples.

'On her last birthday we breakfasted with my father-in-law Cantacuzene, and Madame Phœbus found in her napkin a cheque for five thousand pounds. I expended it immediately in jewels for her personal use; for I wished my father-in-law to understand that there are other princely families in the world besides the Cantacuzenes.'

A friend once ventured enquiringly to suggest whether

his way of life might not be conducive to envy and so disturb that serenity of sentiment necessary to the complete life of an artist. But Mr. Phœbus would not for a moment admit the soundness of the objection. 'No,' he said, 'envy is a purely intellectual process. Splendour never excites it: a man of splendour is looked upon always with favour; his appearance exhilarates the heart of man. He is always popular. People wish to dine with him, to borrow his money, but they do not envy him. If you want to know what envy is you should live among artists. You should hear me lecture at the Academy. I have sometimes suddenly turned round and caught countenances like that of the man who was waiting at the corner of the street for Benvenuto Cellini, in order to assassinate the great Florentine.'

It was impossible for Lothair in his present condition to have fallen upon a more suitable companion than Mr. Phœbus. It is not merely change of scene and air that we sometimes want, but a revolution in the atmosphere of thought and feeling in which we live and breathe. Besides his great intelligence and fancy, and his peculiar views on art and man and affairs in general, which always interested their hearer and sometimes convinced, there was a general vivacity in Mr. Phœbus and a vigorous sense of life which were inspiriting to his companions. When there was anything to be done, great or small, Mr. Phœbus liked to do it; and this, as he averred, from a sense of duty, since, if anything is to be done, it should be done in the best manner, and no one could do it so well as Mr. Phœbus. He always acted as if he had been created to be the oracle and model of the human race, but the oracle was never pompous or solemn, and the model was always beaming with good nature and high spirits.

Mr. Phœbus liked Lothair. He liked youth, and goodlooking youth; and youth that was intelligent and engaging and well-mannered. He also liked old men. But between fifty and seventy, he saw little to approve of in the dark sex. They had lost their good looks if they ever had any, their wits were on the wane, and they were invariably selfish. When they attained second childhood the charm often returned. Age was frequently beautiful, wisdom appeared like an aftermath, and the heart which seemed dry and deadened suddenly put forth shoots of sympathy.

Mr. Phœbus postponed his voyage in order that Lothair might make his preparations to become his guest in his island. 'I cannot take you to a banker,' said Mr. Phœbus, 'for I have none; but I wish you would share my purse. Nothing will ever induce me to use what they call paper money. It is the worst thing that what they call civilisation has produced; neither hue nor shape, and yet a substitute for the richest colour, and, where the arts flourish, the finest forms.'

The telegraph which brought an order to the bankers at Malta to give an unlimited credit to Lothair, rendered it unnecessary for our friend to share what Mr. Phœbus called his purse, and yet he was glad to have the opportunity of seeing it, as Mr. Phœbus one morning opened a chest in his cabin and produced several velvet bags, one full of pearls, another of rubies, others of Venetian sequins, Napoleons, and golden piastres. 'I like to look at them,' said Mr. Phœbus, 'and find life more intense when they are about my person. But bank notes, so cold and thin, they give me an ague.'

Madame Phœbus and her sister Euphrosyne welcomed Lothair in maritime costumes which were absolutely bewitching; wondrous jackets with loops of pearls, girdles defended by dirks with handles of turquoises, and tilted hats that, while they screened their long eyelashes from the sun, crowned the longer braids of their never-ending hair. Mr. Phœbus gave banquets every day on board his

yacht, attended by the chief personages of the island and
the most agreeable officers of the garrison. They dined
upon deck, and it delighted him, with a surface of sang-froid,
to produce a repast which both in its material and its
treatment was equal to the refined festivals of Paris. Sometimes they had a dance; sometimes in his barge, rowed by
a crew in Venetian dresses, his guests glided on the tranquil waters, under a starry sky, and listened to the exquisite melodies of their hostess and her sister.

At length the day of departure arrived. It was bright,
with a breeze favourable to the sail and opportune for the
occasion. For all the officers of the garrison and all
beautiful Valetta itself seemed present in their yachts and
barges to pay their last tribute of admiration to the enchanting sisters and the all-accomplished owner of the
'Pan.' Placed on the gallery of his yacht, Mr. Phœbus
surveyed the brilliant and animated scene with delight.
'This is the way to conduct life,' he said. 'If, fortunately
for them, I could have passed another month among these
people, I could have developed a feeling equal to the old
regattas of the Venetians.'

The Ægean isle occupied by Mr. Phœbus was of no inconsiderable dimensions. A chain of mountains of white
marble intersected it, covered with forests of oak, though
in parts precipitous and bare. The lowlands, while they
produced some good crops of grain, and even cotton and
silk, were chiefly clothed with fruit trees: orange and
lemon, and the fig, the olive, and the vine. Sometimes
the land was uncultivated, and was principally covered
with myrtles of large size and oleanders and arbutus and
thorny brooms. Here game abounded, while from the
mountain forests the wolf sometimes descended and spoiled
and scared the islanders.

On the seashore, yet not too near the wave, and on a
sylvan declivity, was a long pavilion-looking building,

painted in white and arabesque. It was backed by the
forest, which had a park-like character from its partial
clearance, and which, after a convenient slip of even land,
ascended the steeper country and took the form of wooded
hills, backed in due time by still sylvan yet loftier eleva-
tions, and sometimes a glittering peak.

'Welcome, my friend!' said Mr. Phœbus to Lothair.
'Welcome to an Aryan clime, an Aryan landscape, and an
Aryan race. It will do you good after your Semitic
hallucinations.'

CHAPTER LXXIII.

Mr. Phœbus pursued a life in his island partly feudal, partly
oriental, partly Venetian, and partly idiosyncratic. He
had a grand studio where he could always find interesting
occupation in drawing every fine face and form in his
dominions. Then he hunted, and that was a remarkable
scene. The ladies, looking like Diana or her nymphs, were
mounted on cream-coloured Anatolian chargers with golden
bells; while Mr. Phœbus himself, in green velvet and
seven-leagued boots, sounded a wondrous twisted horn rife
with all the inspiring or directing notes of musical and
learned venerie. His neighbours of condition came
mounted, but the field was by no means confined to cavaliers. A vast crowd of men in small caps and jackets and
huge white breeches, and armed with all the weapons of
Palikari, handjars and yataghans and silver sheathed mus-
kets of uncommon length and almost as old as the battle of
Lepanto, always rallied round his standard. The eques-
trians caracolled about the park, and the horns sounded
and the hounds bayed and the men shouted till the deer
had all scudded away. Then, by degrees, the hunters
entered the forest, and the notes of venerie became more

c c

faint and the shouts more distant. Then for two or three
hours all was silent, save the sound of an occasional shot
or the note of a stray hound, until the human stragglers
began to reappear emerging from the forest, and in due
time the great body of the hunt, and a gilded cart drawn
by mules and carrying the prostrate forms of fallow deer
and roebuck. None of the ceremonies of the chase were
omitted, and the crowd dispersed, refreshed by Samian
wine, which Mr. Phœbus was teaching them to make
without resin, and which they quaffed with shrugging
shoulders.

'We must have a wolf-hunt for you,' said Euphrosyne
to Lothair. 'You like excitement, I believe?'

'Well, I am rather inclined for repose at present, and I
came here with the hope of obtaining it.'

'We are never idle here; in fact that would be impossible with Gaston. He has established here an academy of
the fine arts and also revived the gymnasia; and my sister
and myself have schools, only music and dancing; Gaston
does not approve of letters. The poor people have of
course their primary schools with their priests, and Gaston
does not interfere with them, but he regrets their existence.
He looks upon reading and writing as very injurious to
education.'

Sometimes reposing on divans, the sisters received the
chief persons of the isle, and regaled them with fruits and
sweetmeats and coffee and sherbets, while Gaston's chi-
bouques and tobacco of Salonica were a proverb. These
meetings always ended with dance and song, replete,
according to Mr. Phœbus, with studies of Aryan life.

'I believe these islanders to be an unmixed race,' said
Mr. Phœbus. 'The same form and visage prevails
throughout; and very little changed in anything, even in
their religion.'

'Unchanged in their religion!' said Lothair with some
astonishment.

'Yes; you will find it so. Their existence is easy; their wants are not great, and their means of subsistence plentiful. They pass much of their life in what is called amusement: and what is it? They make parties of pleasure; they go in procession to a fountain or a grove. They dance and eat fruit, and they return home singing songs. They have, in fact, been performing unconsciously the religious ceremonies of their ancestors, and which they pursue, and will for ever, though they may have forgotten the name of the dryad or the nymph who presides over their waters.'

'I should think their priests would guard them from these errors,' said Lothair.

'The Greek priests, particularly in these Asian islands, are good sort of people,' said Mr. Phœbus. 'They marry and have generally large families, often very beautiful. They have no sacerdotal feelings, for they never can have any preferment; all the high posts in the Greek Church being reserved for the monks, who study what is called theology. The Greek parish priest is not at all Semitic; there is nothing to counteract his Aryan tendencies. I have already raised the statue of a nymph at one of their favourite springs and places of pleasant pilgrimage, and I have a statue now in the island, still in its case, which I contemplate installing in a famous grove of laurel not far off and very much resorted to.'

'And what then?' enquired Lothair.

'Well, I have a conviction that among the great races the old creeds will come back,' said Mr. Phœbus, 'and it will be acknowledged that true religion is the worship of the beautiful. For the beautiful cannot be attained without virtue, if virtue consists, as I believe, in the control of the passions, in the sentiment of repose, and the avoidance in all things of excess.'

One night Lothair was walking home with the sisters from a village festival, where they had been much amused.

c c 2

'You have had a great many adventures since we first met?' said Madame Phœbus.

'Which makes it seem longer ago than it really is,' said Lothair.

'You count time by emotion then?' said Euphrosyne.

'Well, it is a wonderful thing however it be computed,' said Lothair.

'For my part, I do not think that it ought to be counted at all,' said Madame Phœbus; 'and there is nothing to me so detestable in Europe as the quantity of clocks and watches.'

'Do you use a watch, my Lord?' asked Euphrosyne in a tone which always seemed to Lothair one of mocking artlessness.

'I believe I never wound it up when I had one,' said Lothair.

'But you make such good use of your time,' said Madame Phœbus, 'you do not require watches.'

'I am glad to hear I make good use of my time,' said Lothair, but a little surprised.

'But you are so good, so religious,' said Madame Phœbus. 'That is a great thing; especially for one so young.'

'Hem!' said Lothair.

'That must have been a beautiful procession at Rome,' said Euphrosyne.

'I was rather a spectator of it than an actor in it,' said Lothair with some seriousness. 'It is too long a tale to enter into, but my part in those proceedings was entirely misrepresented.'

'I believe that nothing in the newspapers is ever true,' said Madame Phœbus.

'And that is why they are so popular,' added Euphrosyne; 'the taste of the age being so decidedly for fiction.'

'Is it true that you escaped from a convent to Malta?' said Madame Phœbus.

'Not quite,' said Lothair, 'but true enough for conversation.'

'As confidential as the present, I suppose?' said Euphrosyne.

'Yes, when we are grave, as we are inclined to be now,' said Lothair.

'Then, you have been fighting a good deal,' said Madame Phœbus.

'You are putting me on a court martial, Madame Phœbus,' said Lothair.

'But we do not know on which side you were,' said Euphrosyne.

'That is matter of history,' said Lothair, 'and that, you know, is always doubtful.'

'Well, I do not like fighting,' said Madame Phœbus, 'and for my part I never could find out that it did any good.'

'And what do you like?' said Lothair. 'Tell me how would you pass your life?'

'Well, much as I do. I do not know that I want any change, except I think I should like it to be always summer.'

'And I would have perpetual spring,' said Euphrosyne.

'But, summer or spring, what would be your favourite pursuit?'

'Well, dancing is very nice,' said Madame Phœbus.

'But we cannot always be dancing,' said Lothair.

'Then we would sing,' said Euphrosyne.

'But the time comes when one can neither dance nor sing,' said Lothair.

'Oh! then we become part of the audience,' said Madame Phœbus, 'the people for whose amusement everybody labours.'

'And enjoy power without responsibility,' said Euphrosyne, 'detect false notes and mark awkward gestures.

How can anyone doubt of Providence with such a system of constant compensation!'

There was something in the society of these two sisters that Lothair began to find highly attractive. Their extraordinary beauty, their genuine and unflagging gaiety, their thorough enjoyment of existence, and the variety of resources with which they made life amusing and graceful, all contributed to captivate him. They had, too, a great love and knowledge both of art and nature, and insensibly they weaned Lothair from that habit of introspection which, though natural to him, he had too much indulged, and taught him to find sources of interest and delight in external objects. He was beginning to feel happy in this island, and wishing that his life might never change, when one day Mr. Phœbus informed them that the Prince Agathonides, the eldest son of the Prince of Samos, would arrive from Constantinople in a few days, and would pay them a visit. 'He will come with some retinue,' said Mr. Phœbus, 'but I trust we shall be able by our reception to show that the Cantacuzenes are not the only princely family in the world.'

Mr. Phœbus was confident in his resources in this respect, for his yacht's crew in their Venetian dresses could always furnish a guard of honour which no Grecian prince or Turkish pacha could easily rival. When the eventful day arrived he was quite equal to the occasion. The yacht was dressed in every part with the streaming colours of all nations, the banner of Gaston Phœbus waved from his pavilion, the guard of honour kept the ground, but the population of the isle were present in numbers and in their most showy costume, and a battery of ancient Turkish guns fired a salute without an accident.

The Prince Agathonides was a youth, good looking and dressed in a splendid Palikar costume, though his manners were quite European, being an attaché to the Turkish embassy at Vienna. He had with him a sort of governor, a secretary, servants in Mamlouk dresses, pipe-bearers, and grooms, there being some horses as presents from his father to Mr. Phœbus, and some rarely embroidered kerchiefs and choice perfumes and Persian greyhounds for the ladies.

The arrival of the young Prince was the signal for a series of entertainments in the island. First of all Mr. Phœbus resolved to give a dinner in the Frank style, to prove to Agathonides that there were other members of the Cantacuzene family besides himself who comprehended a firstrate Frank dinner. The chief people of the island were invited to this banquet. They drank the choicest grapes of France and Germany, were stuffed with truffles, and sate on little cane chairs. But one might detect in their countenances how they sighed for their easy divans, their simple dishes, and their resinous wine. Then there was a wolf-hunt, and other sport; a great day of gymnasia, many dances and much music; in fact, there were choruses all over the island, and every night was a serenade.

Why such general joy? Because it was understood that the heir apparent of the isle, their future sovereign, had in fact arrived to make his bow to the beautiful Euphrosyne, though he saw her for the first time.

CHAPTER LXXIV.

VERY shortly after his arrival at Malta, Mr. Phœbus had spoken to Lothair about Theodora. It appeared that Lucien Campian, though severely wounded, had escaped with Garibaldi after the battle of Mentana into the Italian territories. Here they were at once arrested, but not severely detained, and Colonel Campian took the first

opportunity of revisiting England, where, after settling his
affairs, he had returned to his native country, from which
he had been separated for many years. Mr. Phœbus
during the interval had seen a great deal of him, and the
Colonel departed for America under the impression that
Lothair had been among the slain at the final struggle.

'Campian is one of the best men I ever knew,' said
Phœbus. 'He was a remarkable instance of energy combined with softness of disposition. In my opinion, however, he ought never to have visited Europe: he was made
to clear the back woods, and govern man by the power of
his hatchet and the mildness of his words. He was fighting for freedom all his life, yet slavery made and slavery
destroyed him. Among all the freaks of fate nothing is
more surprising than that this Transatlantic planter should
have been ordained to be the husband of a divine being, a
true Hellenic goddess, who in the good days would have
been worshipped in this country and have inspired her
race to actions of grace, wisdom, and beauty.'

'I greatly esteem him,' said Lothair, 'and I shall write
to him directly.'

'Except by Campian, who spoke probably about you to
no one save myself,' continued Phœbus, 'your name has
never been mentioned with reference to those strange
transactions. Once there was a sort of rumour that you
had met with some mishap, but these things were contradicted and explained, and then forgotten: and people were
all out of town. I believe that Cardinal Grandison communicated with your man of business, and between them
everything was kept quiet, until this portentous account
of your doings at Rome, which transpired after we left
England and which met us at Malta.'

'I have written to my man of business about that,' said
Lothair, 'but I think it will tax all his ingenuity to explain, or to mystify it as successfully as he did the pre-

ceding adventures. At any rate, he will not have the
assistance of my Lord Cardinal.'

'Theodora was a remarkable woman on many accounts,'
said Mr. Phœbus, 'but particularly on this, that, although
one of the most beautiful women that ever existed, she was
adored by beautiful women. My wife adored her; Euphrosyne, who has no enthusiasm, adored her; the Princess of
Tivoli, the most capricious being probably that ever existed,
adored, and always adored, Theodora. I think it must
have been that there was on her part a total absence of
vanity, and this the more strange in one whose vocation in
her earlier life had been to attract and live on popular
applause; but I have seen her quit theatres ringing with
admiration and enter her carriage with the serenity of a
Phidian muse.'

'I adored her,' said Lothair, 'but I never could quite
solve her character. Perhaps it was too rich and deep for
rapid comprehension.'

'We shall never perhaps see her like again,' said Mr.
Phœbus. 'It was a rare combination, peculiar to the
Tyrrhenian sea. I am satisfied that we must go there to
find the pure Hellenic blood, and from thence it got to
Rome.'

'We may not see her like again, but we may see her
again,' said Lothair; 'and sometimes I think she is always
hovering over me.'

In this vein, when they were alone, they were frequently
speaking of the departed; and one day (it was before the
arrival of Prince Agathonides), Mr. Phœbus said to
Lothair, 'We will ride this morning to what we call the
grove of Daphne. It is a real laurel grove. Some of the
trees must be immemorial, and deserve to have been
sacred, if once they were not so. In their huge grotesque
forms you would not easily recognise your polished friends
of Europe, so trim and glossy and shrublike. The people

are very fond of this grove and make frequent processions
there. Once a year they must be headed by their priest.
No one knows why, nor has he the slightest idea of the
reason of the various ceremonies which he that day per-
forms. But we know, and some day he or his successors
will equally understand them. Yes, if I remain here long
enough, and I sometimes think I will never again quit the
isle, I shall expect some fine summer night, when there is
that rich stillness which the whispering waves only render
more intense, to hear a voice of music on the mountains
declaring that the god Pan has returned to earth.'

It was a picturesque ride, as every ride was on this
island, skirting the sylvan hills with the sea glimmering in
the distance. Lothair was pleased with the approaches to
the sacred grove: now and then a single tree with grey
branches and a green head, then a great spread of under-
wood, all laurel, and then spontaneous plantations of young
trees.

'There was always a vacant space in the centre of the
grove,' said Mr. Phœbus, 'once sadly overrun with wild
shrubs, but I have cleared it and restored the genius of the
spot. See!'

They entered the sacred circle and beheld a statue raised
on a porphyry pedestal. The light fell with magical effect
on the face of the statue. It was the statue of Theodora,
the placing of which in the pavilion of Belmont Mr.
Phœbus was superintending when Lothair first made his
acquaintance.

CHAPTER LXXV.

The Prince Agathonides seemed quite to monopolise the attention of Madame Phœbus and her sister. This was not very unreasonable, considering that he was their visitor, the future chief of their house, and had brought them so many embroidered pocket-handkerchiefs, choice scents and fancy dogs. But Lothair thought it quite disgusting, nor could he conceive what they saw in him, what they were talking about or laughing about, for, so far as he had been able to form any opinion on the subject, the Prince was a shallow-pated coxcomb without a single quality to charm any woman of sense and spirit. Lothair began to consider how he could pursue his travels, where he should go to, and when that was settled, how he should get there.

Just at this moment of perplexity, as is often the case, something occurred which no one could foresee, but which like every event removed some difficulties and introduced others.

There arrived at the island a despatch forwarded to Mr. Phœbus by the Russian Ambassador at Constantinople, who had received it from his colleague at London. This despatch contained a proposition to Mr. Phœbus to repair to the Court of St. Petersburgh, and accept appointments of high distinction and emolument. Without in any way restricting the independent pursuit of his profession, he was offered a large salary, the post of Court painter, and the Presidency of the Academy of Fine Arts. Of such moment did the Russian Government deem the official presence of this illustrious artist in their country, that it was intimated, if the arrangement could be effected, its conclusion might be celebrated by conferring on Mr.

Phœbus a patent of nobility and a decoration of a high class. The despatch contained a private letter from an exalted member of the Imperial family, who had had the high and gratifying distinction of making Mr. Phœbus's acquaintance in London, personally pressing the acceptance by him of the general proposition, assuring him of cordial welcome and support, and informing Mr. Phœbus that what was particularly desired at this moment was a series of paintings illustrative of some of the most memorable scenes in the Holy Land and especially the arrival of the pilgrims of the Greek rite at Jerusalem. As for this purpose he would probably like to visit Palestine, the whole of the autumn or even a longer period was placed at his disposal, so that, enriched with all necessary drawings and studies, he might achieve his more elaborate performances in Russia at his leisure and with every advantage.

Considering that the great objects in life with Mr. Phœbus were to live in an Aryan country, amid an Aryan race, and produce works which should revive for the benefit of human nature Aryan creeds, a proposition to pass some of the prime years of his life among the Mongolian race, and at the same time devote his pencil to the celebration of Semitic subjects, was startling.

'I shall say nothing to Madame Phœbus until the Prince has gone,' he remarked to Lothair: 'he will go the day after to-morrow. I do not know what they may offer to make me; probably only a Baron, perhaps a Count. But you know in Russia a man may become a Prince, and I certainly should like those Cantacuzenes to feel that after all their daughter is a Princess with no thanks to them. The climate is detestable, but one owes much to one's profession. Art would be honoured at a great, perhaps the greatest, Court. There would not be a fellow at his easel in the streets about Fitzroy Square who would not be

prouder. I wonder what the decoration will be. "Of a
high class;" vague. It might be Alexander Newsky.
You know you have a right, whatever your decoration, to
have it expressed, of course at your own expense, in brilliants. I confess I have my weakness. I should like to
get over to the Academy dinner (one can do anything in
these days of railroads) and dine with the R. A.s in my
ribbon and the star of the Alexander Newsky in brilliants.
I think every Academician would feel elevated. What I
detest are their Semitic subjects, nothing but drapery.
They cover even their heads in those scorching climes.
Can anyone make anything of a caravan of pilgrims? To
be sure, they say no one can draw a camel. If I went to
Jerusalem a camel would at last be drawn. There is
something in that. We must think over these things, and
when the Prince has gone talk it over with Madame Phœbus. I wish you all to come to a wise decision, without
the slightest reference to my individual tastes or, it may
be, prejudices.'

The result of all this was that Mr. Phœbus, without
absolutely committing himself, favourably entertained the
general proposition of the Russian Court; while, with
respect to their particular object in art, he agreed to visit
Palestine and execute at least one work for his Imperial
friend and patron. He counted on reaching Jerusalem
before the Easter pilgrims returned to their homes.

'If they would make me a Prince at once and give me
the Alexander Newsky in brilliants it might be worth
thinking of,' he said to Lothair.

The ladies, though they loved their isle, were quite
delighted with the thought of going to Jerusalem. Madame Phœbus knew a Russian Grand Duchess who had
boasted to her that she had been both to Jerusalem and
Torquay, and Madame Phœbus had felt quite ashamed
that she had been to neither.

'I suppose you will feel quite at home there,' said
Euphrosyne to Lothair.

'No; I never was there.'

'No; but you know all about those places and people,
holy places and holy persons. The Blessed Virgin did not,
I believe, appear to you. It was to a young lady, was it
not? We were asking each other last night who the
young lady could be.'

CHAPTER LXXVI.

TIME, which changes everything, is changing even the
traditionary appearance of forlorn Jerusalem. Not that
its mien, after all, was ever very sad. Its airy site, its
splendid mosque, its vast monasteries, the bright material
of which the whole city is built, its cupolaed houses of
freestone, and above all the towers and gates and battle-
ments of its lofty and complete walls, always rendered it a
handsome city. Jerusalem has not been sacked so often
or so recently as the other two great ancient cities, Rome
and Athens. Its vicinage was never more desolate than
the Campagna, or the state of Attica and the Morea in
1830.

The battlefield of western Asia from the days of the
Assyrian kings to those of Mehemet Ali, Palestine endured
the same devastation as in modern times has been the
doom of Flanders and the Milanese; but the years of
havoc in the Low Countries and Lombardy must be
counted in Palestine by centuries. Yet the wide plains of
the Holy Land, Sharon and Shechem and Esdraelon, have
recovered; they are as fertile and as fair as in old days; it
is the hill culture that has been destroyed, and that is the
culture on which Jerusalem mainly depended. Its hills

were terraced gardens, vineyards, and groves of olive trees. And here it is that we find renovation. The terraces are again ascending the stony heights, and the eye is frequently gladdened with young plantations. Fruit trees, the peach and the pomegranate, the almond and the fig, offer gracious groups; and the true children of the land, the vine and the olive, are again exulting in their native soil.

There is one spot, however, which has been neglected, and yet the one that should have been the first remembered, as it has been the most rudely wasted. Blessed be the hand which plants trees upon Olivet! Blessed be the hand that builds gardens about Sion!

The most remarkable creation, however, in modern Jerusalem is the Russian settlement which within a few years has risen on the elevated ground on the western side of the city. The Latin, the Greek, and the Armenian Churches had for centuries possessed enclosed establishments in the city, which, under the name of monasteries, provided shelter and protection for hundreds, it might be said even thousands, of pilgrims belonging to their respective rites. The great scale, therefore, on which Russia secured hospitality for her subjects was not in reality so remarkable as the fact that it seemed to indicate a settled determination to separate the Muscovite Church altogether from the Greek, and throw off what little dependence is still acknowledged on the Patriarchate of Constantinople. Whatever the motive, the design has been accomplished on a large scale. The Russian buildings, all well defended, are a caravanserai, a cathedral, a citadel. The consular flag crowns the height and indicates the office of administration; priests and monks are permanent inhabitants, and a whole caravan of Muscovite pilgrims and the trades on which they depend can be accommodated within the precinct.

Mr. Phœbus, his family and suite were to be the guests

of the Russian Consul, and every preparation was made to
insure the celebrated painter a becoming reception. Frequent telegrams had duly impressed the representative of
all the Russias in the Holy Land with the importance of
his impending visitor. Even the qualified and strictly
provisional acceptance of the Russian proposition by Mr.
Phœbus had agitated the wires of Europe scarcely less
than a suggested Conference.

'An artist should always remember what he owes to
posterity and his profession,' said Mr. Phœbus to Lothair, as they were walking the deck, 'even if you can
distinguish between them, which I doubt, for it is only by
a sense of the beautiful that the human family can be
sustained in its proper place in the scale of creation, and
the sense of the beautiful is a result of the study of the
fine arts. It would be something to sow the seeds of
organic change in the Mongolian type, but I am not
sanguine of success. There is no original fund of aptitude
to act upon. The most ancient of existing communities is
Turanian, and yet though they could invent gunpowder
and the mariner's compass, they never could understand
perspective. Man a-head there! tell Madame Phœbus to
come on deck for the first sight of Mount Lebanon.'

When the ' Pan ' entered the port of Joppa they observed
another English yacht in those waters; but before they
could speculate on its owner they were involved in all the
complications of landing. On the quay, the Russian Vice-
Consul was in attendance with horses and mules, and
donkeys handsomer than either. The ladies were delighted
with the vast orange gardens of Joppa, which Madame
Phœbus said realised quite her idea of the Holy Land.

'I was prepared for milk and honey,' said Euphrosyne,
'but this is too delightful,' as she travelled through lanes
of date-bearing palm-trees, and sniffed with her almond-
shaped nostrils the all-pervading fragrance.

They passed the night at Arimathea, a pretty village surrounded with gardens enclosed with hedges of prickly pear. Here they found hospitality in an old convent, but all the comforts of Europe and many of the refinements of Asia had been forwarded for their accommodation.

'It is a great homage to art,' said Mr. Phœbus, as he scattered his gold like a great seigneur of Gascony.

The next day, two miles from Jerusalem, the Consul met them with a cavalcade, and the ladies assured their host that they were not at all wearied with their journey, but were quite prepared, in due time, to join his dinner party, which he was most anxious they should attend, as he had 'two English lords' who had arrived, and whom he had invited to meet them. They were all curious to know their names, though that, unfortunately, the Consul could not tell them, but he had sent to the English Consulate to have them written down. All he could assure them was that they were real English lords, not travelling English lords, but in sober earnestness great personages.

Mr. Phœbus was highly gratified. He was pleased with his reception. There was nothing he liked much more than a procession. He was also a sincere admirer of the aristocracy of his country. 'On the whole,' he would say, 'they most resemble the old Hellenic race; excelling in athletic sports, speaking no other language than their own, and never reading.'

'Your fault,' he would sometimes say to Lothair, 'and the cause of many of your sorrows, is the habit of mental introspection. Man is born to observe, but if he falls into psychology he observes nothing, and then he is astonished that life has no charms for him, or that, never seizing the occasion, his career is a failure. No, sir, it is the eye that must be occupied and cultivated; no one knows the capacity of the eye who has not developed it, or the visions of beauty and delight and inexhaustible interest which it commands. To

a man who observes, life is as different as the existence of a
dreaming psychologist is to that of the animals of the field.'

'I fear,' said Lothair, 'that I have at length found out
the truth, and that I am a dreaming psychologist.'

'You are young and not irremediably lost,' said Mr.
Phœbus. 'Fortunately you have received the admirable
though partial education of your class. You are a good
shot, you can ride, you can row, you can swim. That imperfect secretion of the brain which is called thought has
not yet bowed your frame. You have not had time to read
much. Give it up altogether. The conversation of a
woman like Theodora is worth all the libraries in the
world. If it were only for her sake, I should wish to save
you, but I wish to do it for your own. Yes, profit by the
vast though calamitous experience which you have gained
in a short time. We may know a great deal about our
bodies, we can know very little about our minds.'

The 'real English lords' turned out to be Bertram and
St. Aldegonde returning from Nubia. They had left England about the same time as Lothair, and had paired together on the Irish Church till Easter, with a sort of secret
hope on the part of St. Aldegonde that they might neither
of them reappear in the House of Commons again until the
Irish Church were either saved or subverted. Holy week had
long passed, and they were at Jerusalem, not quite so near
the House of Commons as the Reform Club or the Carlton,
but still St. Aldegonde had mentioned that he was beginning to be bored with Jerusalem, and Bertram counted on
their immediate departure when they accepted the invitation to dine with the Russian Consul.

Lothair was unaffectedly delighted to meet Bertram and
glad to see St. Aldegonde, but he was a little nervous and
embarrassed as to the probable tone of his reception by
them. But their manner relieved him in an instant, for
he saw they knew nothing of his adventures.

'Well,' said St. Aldegonde, 'what have you been doing with yourself since we last met? I wish you had come with us and had a shot at a crocodile.'

Bertram told Lothair in the course of the evening that he found letters at Cairo from Corisande, on his return, in which there was a good deal about Lothair, and which had made him rather uneasy. 'That there was a rumour you had been badly wounded, and some other things,' and Bertram looked him full in the face; 'but I dare say not a word of truth.'

'I was never better in my life,' said Lothair, 'and I have been in Sicily and in Greece. However, we will talk over all this another time.'

The dinner at the Consulate was one of the most successful banquets that were ever given, if to please your guests be the test of good fortune in such enterprises. St. Aldegonde was perfectly charmed with the Phœbus family. He did not know which to admire most: the great artist, who was in remarkable spirits to-day, considering he was in a Semitic country, or his radiant wife, or his brilliant sister-in-law. St. Aldegonde took an early opportunity of informing Bertram that if he liked to go over and vote for the Irish Church he would release him from his pair with the greatest pleasure, but for his part he had not the slightest intention of leaving Jerusalem at present. Strange to say, Bertram received this intimation without a murmur. He was not so loud in his admiration of the Phœbus family as St. Aldegonde, but there is a silent sentiment sometimes more expressive than the noisiest applause, and more dangerous. Bertram had sat next to Euphrosyne and was entirely spell-bound.

The Consul's wife, a hostess not unworthy of such guests, had entertained her friends in the European style. The dinner-hour was not late, and the gentlemen who attended the ladies from the dinner-table were allowed to

remain some time in the saloon. Lothair talked much to
the Consul's wife, by whose side sat Madame Phœbus. St.
Aldegonde was always on his legs, distracted by the rival
attractions of that lady and her husband. More remote,
Bertram whispered to Euphrosyne, who answered him with
laughing eyes.

At a certain hour, the Consul, attended by his male
guests, crossing a court, proceeded to his divan, a lofty and
capacious chamber painted in fresco, and with no furniture
except the low but broad raised seat that surrounded the
room. Here, when they were seated, an equal number of
attendants (Arabs in Arab dress, blue gowns and red
slippers and red caps) entered, each proffering a long pipe
of cherry or jasmine wood. Then in a short time guests
dropped in, and pipes and coffee were immediately brought
to them. Any person who had been formally presented to
the Consul had this privilege, without any further invitation. The society often found in these consular divans in
the more remote places of the east, Cairo, Damascus, Jerusalem, is often extremely entertaining and instructive.
Celebrated travellers, distinguished men of science, artists,
adventurers who ultimately turn out to be heroes, eccentric characters of all kinds, are here encountered, and give
the fruits of their original or experienced observation without reserve.

'It is the smoking-room over again,' whispered St. Aldegonde to Lothair, 'only in England one is so glad to get
away from the women, but here, I must say, I should have
liked to remain behind.'

An individual in a Syrian dress, fawn-coloured robes
girdled with a rich shawl, and a white turban, entered.
He made his salute with grace and dignity to the Consul,
touching his forehead, his lip, and his heart, and took his
seat with the air of one not unaccustomed to be received, playing, until he received his chibouque, with a chaplet of beads.

'That is a good-looking fellow, Lothair,' said St. Aldegonde; 'or is it the dress that turns them out such swells? I feel quite a lout by some of these fellows.'

'I think he would be good-looking in any dress,' said Lothair. 'A remarkable countenance.'

It was an oval visage, with features in harmony with that form; large dark-brown eyes and lashes, and brows delicately but completely defined; no hair upon the face except a beard, full but not long. He seemed about the same age as Mr. Phœbus, and his complexion, though pale, was clear and fair.

The conversation, after some rambling, had got upon the Suez Canal. Mr. Phœbus did not care for the political or the commercial consequences of that great enterprise, but he was glad that a natural division should be established between the greater races and the Ethiopian. It might not lead to any considerable result, but it asserted a principle. He looked upon that trench as a protest.

'But would you place the Nilotic family in the Ethiopian race?' enquired the Syrian in a voice commanding from its deep sweetness.

'I would certainly. They were Cushim, and that means negroes.'

The Syrian did not agree with Mr. Phœbus; he stated his views firmly and clearly, but without urging them. He thought that we must look to the Pelasgi as the colonising race that had peopled and produced Egypt. The mention of the Pelasgi fired Mr. Phœbus to even unusual eloquence. He denounced the Pelasgi as a barbarous race: men of gloomy superstitions who, had it not been for the Hellenes, might have fatally arrested the human development. The triumph of the Hellenes was the triumph of the beautiful, and all that is great and good in life was owing to their victory.

'It is difficult to ascertain what is great in life,' said the

Syrian, 'because nations differ on the subject and ages.
Some, for example, consider war to be a great thing, others
condemn it. I remember also when patriotism was a
boast, and now it is a controversy. But it is not so difficult to ascertain what is good. For man has in his own
being some guide to such knowledge, and divine aid to
acquire it has not been wanting to him. For my part I
could not maintain that the Hellenic system led to virtue.'

The conversation was assuming an ardent character
when the Consul, as a diplomatist, turned the channel.
Mr. Phœbus had vindicated the Hellenic religion, the
Syrian, with a terse protest against the religion of nature,
however idealised, as tending to the corruption of man, had
let the question die away, and the Divan were discussing
dromedaries, and dancing girls, and sherbet made of pomegranate which the Consul recommended and ordered to be
produced. Some of the guests retired, and among them
the Syrian, with the same salute and the same graceful
dignity as had distinguished his entrance.

'Who is that man?' said Mr. Phœbus. 'I met him at
Rome ten years ago. Baron Mecklenburg brought him to
me to paint for my great picture of St. John, which is in
the gallery of Munich. He said in his way (you remember
his way) that he would bring me a face of Paradise.'

'I cannot exactly tell you his name,' said the Consul.
'Prince Galitzin brought him here and thought highly of
him. I believe he is one of the old Syrian families in the
mountain; but whether he be a Maronite, or a Druse, or
anything else, I really cannot say. Now try the sherbet.'

CHAPTER LXXVII.

THERE are few things finer than the morning view of
Jerusalem from the Mount of Olives. The fresh and
golden light falls on a walled city with turrets and towers
and frequent gates: the houses of freestone with terraced
or oval roofs sparkle in the sun, while the cupolaed pile of
the Church of the Holy Sepulchre, the vast monasteries,
and the broad steep of Sion crowned with the Tower of
David, vary the monotony of the general masses of building. But the glory of the scene is the Mosque of Omar as
it rises on its broad platform of marble from the deep
ravine of Kedron, with its magnificent dome high in the
air, its arches and gardened courts, and its crescents glittering amid the cedar, the cypress, and the palm.

Reclining on Olivet, Lothair, alone and in charmed
abstraction, gazed on the wondrous scene. Since his
arrival at Jerusalem he lived much apart, nor had he
found difficulty in effecting this isolation. Mr. Phœbus
had already established a studio on a considerable scale,
and was engaged in making sketches of pilgrims and
monks, tall donkeys of Bethlehem with starry fronts, in
which he much delighted, and grave Jellaheen sheiks who
were hanging about the convents in the hopes of obtaining
a convoy to the Dead Sea. As for St. Aldegonde and Bertram, they passed their lives at the Russian Consulate, or
with its most charming inhabitants. This morning, with
the Consul and his wife and the matchless sisters, as
St. Aldegonde always termed them, they had gone on an
excursion to the Convent of the Nativity. Dinner usually
reassembled all the party, and then the Divan followed.

'I say, Bertram,' said St. Aldegonde, 'what a lucky
thing we paired and went to Nubia! I rejoice in the

Divan, and yet somehow I cannot bear leaving these
women. If the matchless sisters would only smoke, by
Jove they would be perfect!'

'I should not like Euphrosyne to smoke,' said Bertram.

A person approached Lothair by the pathway from
Bethany. It was the Syrian gentleman whom he had met
at the Consulate. As he was passing Lothair, he saluted
him with the grace which had been before remarked, and
Lothair, who was by nature courteous, and even inclined a
little to ceremony in his manners, especially with those
with whom he was not intimate, immediately rose, as he
would not receive such a salutation in a reclining posture.

'Let me not disturb you,' said the stranger, 'or if we
must be on equal terms, let me also be seated, for this is a
view that never palls.'

'It is perhaps familiar to you,' said Lothair, 'but with
me, only a pilgrim, its effect is fascinating, almost overwhelming.'

'The view of Jerusalem never becomes familiar,' said
the Syrian, 'for its associations are so transcendent, so
various, so inexhaustible, that the mind can never anticipate its course of thought and feeling, when one sits, as
we do now, on this immortal mount.'

'I presume you live here?' said Lothair.

'Not exactly,' said his companion. 'I have recently
built a house without the walls, and I have planted my
hill with fruit-trees and made vineyards and olive-grounds;
but I have done this as much, perhaps more, to set an
example, which I am glad to say has been followed, as for
my own convenience or pleasure. My home is in the North
of Palestine on the other side of Jordan, beyond the Sea of
Galilee. My family has dwelt there from time immemorial;
but they always loved this city, and have a legend that
they dwelt occasionally within its walls, even in the days
when Titus from that hill looked down upon the temple.'

'I have often wished to visit the Sea of Galilee,' said Lothair.

'Well, you have now an opportunity,' said the Syrian; 'the North of Palestine, though it has no tropical splendour, has much variety and a peculiar natural charm. The burst and brightness of spring have not yet quite vanished: you would find our plains radiant with wild flowers, and our hills green with young crops; and though we cannot rival Lebanon, we have forest glades among our famous hills that when once seen are remembered.'

'But there is something to me more interesting than the splendour of tropical scenery,' said Lothair, 'even if Galilee could offer it. I wish to visit the cradle of my faith.'

'And you would do wisely,' said the Syrian, 'for there is no doubt the spiritual nature of man is developed in this land.'

'And yet there are persons at the present day who doubt, even deny, the spiritual nature of man,' said Lothair. 'I do not, I could not; there are reasons why I could not.'

'There are some things I know, and some things I believe,' said the Syrian. 'I know that I have a soul, and I believe that it is immortal.'

'It is science that by demonstrating the insignificance of this globe in the vast scale of creation has led to this infidelity,' said Lothair.

'Science may prove the insignificance of this globe in the scale of creation,' said the stranger, 'but it cannot prove the insignificance of man. What is the earth compared with the sun? a molehill by a mountain; yet the inhabitants of this earth can discover the elements of which the great orb consists, and will probably ere long ascertain all the conditions of its being. Nay, the human mind can penetrate far beyond the sun. There is no relation therefore between the faculties of man and the scale in creation of the planet which he inhabits.'

'I was glad to hear you assert the other night the spiritual nature of man in opposition to Mr. Phœbus.'

'Ah! Mr. Phœbus!' said the stranger with a smile. 'He is an old acquaintance of mine. And I must say he is very consistent, except in paying a visit to Jerusalem. That does surprise me. He said to me the other night the same things as he said to me at Rome many years ago. He would revive the worship of nature. The deities whom he so eloquently describes and so exquisitely delineates are the ideal personifications of the most eminent human qualities and chiefly the physical. Physical beauty is his standard of excellence, and he has a fanciful theory that moral order would be the consequence of the worship of physical beauty, for without moral order he holds physical beauty cannot be maintained. But the answer to Mr. Phœbus is, that his system has been tried and has failed, and under conditions more favourable than are likely to exist again; the worship of nature ended in the degradation of the human race.'

'But Mr. Phœbus cannot really believe in Apollo and Venus,' said Lothair. 'These are phrases. He is, I suppose, what is called a Pantheist.'

'No doubt the Olympus of Mr. Phœbus is the creation of his easel,' replied the Syrian. 'I should not, however, describe him as a Pantheist, whose creed requires more abstraction than Mr. Phœbus, the worshipper of nature, would tolerate. His school never care to pursue any investigation which cannot be followed by the eye, and the worship of the beautiful always ends in an orgy. As for Pantheism, it is Atheism in domino. The belief in a Creator who is unconscious of creating is more monstrous than any dogma of any of the Churches in this city, and we have them all here.'

'But there are people now who tell you that there never was any Creation, and therefore there never could have been a Creator,' said Lothair.

'And which is now advanced with the confidence of novelty,' said the Syrian, 'though all of it has been urged, and vainly urged, thousands of years ago. There must be design, or all we see would be without sense, and I do not believe in the unmeaning. As for the natural forces to which all creation is now attributed, we know they are unconscious, while consciousness is as inevitable a portion of our existence as the eye or the hand. The conscious cannot be derived from the unconscious. Man is divine.'

'I wish I could assure myself of the personality of the Creator,' said Lothair. 'I cling to that, but they say it is unphilosophical.'

'In what sense?' asked the Syrian. 'Is it more unphilosophical to believe in a personal God, omnipotent and omniscient, than in natural forces unconscious and irresistible? Is it unphilosophical to combine power with intelligence? Goethe, a Spinozist who did not believe in Spinoza, said that he could bring his mind to the conception that in the centre of space we might meet with a monad of pure intelligence. What may be the centre of space I leave to the dædal imagination of the author of "Faust;" but a monad of pure intelligence, is that more philosophical than the truth, first revealed to man amid these everlasting hills,' said the Syrian, 'that God made man in His own image?'

'I have often found in that assurance a source of sublime consolation,' said Lothair.

'It is the charter of the nobility of man,' said the Syrian, 'one of the divine dogmas revealed in this land; not the invention of Councils, not one of which was held on this sacred soil: confused assemblies first got together by the Greeks, and then by barbarous nations in barbarous times.'

'Yet the divine land no longer tells us divine things,' said Lothair.

'It may, or it may not, have fulfilled its destiny,' said
the Syrian. '"In My Father's house are many mansions,"
and by the various families of nations the designs of the
Creator are accomplished. God works by races, and one
was appointed in due season and after many developments
to reveal and expound in this land the spiritual nature of
man. The Aryan and the Semite are of the same blood
and origin, but when they quitted their central land they
were ordained to follow opposite courses. Each division of
the great race has developed one portion of the double
nature of humanity, till after all their wanderings they met
again, and, represented by their two choicest families, the
Hellenes and the Hebrews, brought together the treasures
of their accumulated wisdom and secured the civilisation of
man.'

'Those among whom I have lived of late,' said Lothair,
'have taught me to trust much in Councils, and to believe
that without them there could be no foundation for the
Church. I observe you do not speak in that vein, though
like myself you find solace in those dogmas which recognise
the relations between the created and the Creator.'

'There can be no religion without that recognition,' said
the Syrian, 'and no creed can possibly be devised without
such a recognition that would satisfy man. Why we are
here, whence we come, whither we go, these are questions
which man is organically framed and forced to ask himself,
and that would not be the case if they could not be
answered. As for Churches depending on Councils, the
first Council was held more than three centuries after the
Sermon on the Mount. We Syrians had churches in the
interval: no one can deny that. I bow before the Divine
decree that swept them away from Antioch to Jerusalem,
but I am not yet prepared to transfer my spiritual allegiance
to Italian Popes and Greek Patriarchs. We believe that
our family were among the first followers of Jesus, and

that we then held lands in Bashan which we hold now. We had a gospel once in our district where there was some allusion to this, and being written by neighbours, and probably at the time, I dare say it was accurate, but the Western Churches declared our gospel was not authentic, though why I cannot tell, and they succeeded in extirpating it. It was not an additional reason why we should enter into their fold. So I am content to dwell in Galilee and trace the footsteps of my divine Master; musing over His life and pregnant sayings amid the mounts He sanctified and the waters He loved so well.'

The sun was now rising in the heavens, and the hour had arrived when it became expedient to seek the shade. Lothair and the Syrian rose at the same time.

'I shall not easily forget our conversation on the Mount of Olives,' said Lothair, 'and I would ask you to add to this kindness by permitting me, before I leave Jerusalem, to pay my respects to you under your roof.'

'Peace be with you!' said the Syrian. 'I live without the gate of Damascus, on a hill which you will easily recognise, and my name is PARACLETE.'

CHAPTER LXXVIII.

TIME passed very agreeably to St. Aldegonde and Bertram at Jerusalem, for it was passed entirely at the Russian Consulate, or with its interesting and charming inmates, who were always making excursions, or, as they styled them, pilgrimages. They saw little of Lothair, who would willingly have conversed with his friend on many topics, but his friend was almost always engaged, and if by some chance they succeeded in finding themselves alone, Bertram appeared to be always preoccupied. One day he said to

Lothair, 'I tell you what, old fellow, if you want to know
all about what has happened at home, I will give you
Corisande's letters. They are a sort of journal which she
promised to keep for me, and they will tell you everything.
I found an immense packet of them on our return from
Cairo, and I meant to have read them here; but I do not
know how it is, I suppose there is so much to be seen here,
but I never seem to have a moment to myself. I have got
an engagement now to the Consulate. We are going to
Elisha's fountain to-day. Why do not you come?'

'Well, I am engaged too,' said Lothair. 'I have settled
to go to the Tombs of the Kings to-day, with Signor
Parmelete, and I cannot well get off; but remember the
letters.'

The box of letters arrived at Lothair's rooms in due
season, and their perusal deeply interested him. In their
pages, alike earnest and lively, and a picture of a mind of
high intelligence adorned with fancy and feeling, the name
of Lothair frequently appeared, and sometimes accompanied
with expressions that made his heart beat. All the rumours
of his adventures as they gradually arrived in England,
generally distorted, were duly chronicled, and sometimes
with comments, which intimated the interest they occasioned to the correspondent of Bertram. More than once
she could not refrain from reproaching her brother for
having left his friend so much to himself. 'Of all your
friends,' she said, 'the one who always most interested me,
and seemed most worthy of your affection.' And then she
deplored the absolute ruin of Lothair, for such she deemed
his entrance into the Roman Church.

'I was right in my appreciation of that woman, though
I was utterly inexperienced in life,' thought Lothair. 'If
her mother had only favoured my views two years ago,
affairs would have been different Would they have been
better? Can they be worse But I have gained expe-

rience. Certainly; and paid for it with my heart's blood.
And might I not have gained experience tranquilly, in the
discharge of the duties of my position at home, dear home?
Perhaps not. And suppose I never had gained experience,
I still might have been happy? And what am I now?
Most lone and sad. So lone and sad, that nothing but the
magical influence of the scene around me saves me from an
overwhelming despondency.'

Lothair passed his life chiefly with Paraclete, and a few
weeks after their first acquaintance, they left Jerusalem
together for Galilee.

The month of May had disappeared and June was advancing. Bertram and St. Aldegonde no longer talked
about their pair, and their engagements in the House of
Commons. There seemed a tacit understanding between
them to avoid the subject; remarkable on the part of
Bertram, for he had always been urgent on his brother-in-
law to fulfil their parliamentary obligation.

The party at the Russian Consulate had gone on a
grand expedition to the Dead Sea, and had been absent for
many days from Jerusalem. They were convoyed by one
of the sheiks of the Jordan valley. It was a most successful
expedition: constant adventure, novel objects and habits,
all the spell of a romantic life. The ladies were delighted
with the scenery of the Jordan valley, and the gentlemen
had good sport; St. Aldegonde had killed a wild boar, and
Bertram an ibex, whose horns were preserved for Brentham.
Mr. Phœbus intensely studied the camel and its habits.
He persuaded himself that the ship of the desert entirely
understood him. 'But it is always so,' he added. 'There
is no animal that in a week does not perfectly comprehend
me. Had I time and could give myself up to it, I have no
doubt I could make them speak. Nature has endowed me,
so far as dumb animals are concerned, with a peculiar
mesmeric power.'

At last this happy caravan was again within sight of the walls of Jerusalem.

'I should like to have remained in the valley of the Jordan for ever,' said St. Aldegonde.

'And so should I,' whispered Bertram to Euphrosyne, 'with the same companions.'

When they had returned to the Consulato, they found the post from England had arrived during their absence. There were despatches for all. It is an agitating moment, that arrival of letters in a distant land. Lord St. Aldegonde seemed much disturbed when he tore open and perused his. His countenance became clouded; he dashed his hand through his dishevelled locks; he pouted; and then he said to Bertram, 'Come to my room.'

'Anything wrong at home?'

'Not at home,' said St. Aldegonde. 'Bertha is all right. But a most infernal letter from Glyn, most insolent. If I do return I will vote against them. But I will not return. I have made up my mind to that. People are so selfish,' exclaimed St. Aldegonde with indignation. 'They never think of anything but themselves.'

'Show me his letter,' said Bertram. 'I have got a letter too; it is from the Duke.'

The letter of the Opposition whip did not deserve the epithets ascribed to it by St. Aldegonde. It was urgent and courteously peremptory; but, considering the circumstances of the case, by no means too absolute. Paired to Easter by great indulgence, St. Aldegonde was passing Whitsuntide at Jerusalem. The parliamentary position was critical, and the future of the Opposition seemed to depend on the majority by which their resolutions on the Irish Church were sent up to the House of Lords.

'Well,' said Bertram. 'I see nothing to complain of in that letter. Except a little more urgency, it is almost the same language as reached us at Cairo, and then you said Glyn was a capital fellow, and seemed quite pleased.'

'Yes, because I hated Egypt,' said St. Aldegonde. 'I hated the Pyramids, and I was disappointed with the dancing-girls; and it seemed to me that, if it had not been for the whip, we never should have been able to escape. But things are very different now.'

'Yes they are,' said Bertram in a melancholy tone.

'You do not think of returning?' said St. Aldegonde.

'Instantly,' replied Bertram. 'I have a letter from the Duke which is peremptory. The county is dissatisfied with my absence. And mine is a queer constituency; very numerous and several large towns; the popularity of my family gained me the seat, not their absolute influence.'

'My constituents never trouble me,' said St. Aldegonde.

'You have none,' said Bertram.

'Well, if I were member for a metropolitan district I would not budge. And I little thought you would have deserted me.'

'Ah!' sighed Bertram. 'You are discontented, because your amusements are interrupted. But think of my position, torn from a woman whom I adore.'

'Well, you know you must have left her sooner or later,' urged St. Aldegonde.

'Why?' asked Bertram.

'You know what Lothair told us. She is engaged to her cousin the Prince of Samos, and ——'

'If I had only the Prince of Samos to deal with I should care little,' said Bertram.

'Why, what do you mean?'

'That Euphrosyne is mine, if my family will sanction our union, but not otherwise.'

St. Aldegonde gave a long whistle, and he added, 'I wish Bertha were here. She is the only person I know who has a head.'

'You see, my dear Granville, while you are talking of your little disappointments, I am involved in awful difficulties.'

E E

'You are sure about the Prince of Samos?'

'Clear your head of that. There is no engagement of any kind between him and Euphrosyne. The visit to the island was only a preliminary ceremony, just to show himself. No doubt the father wishes the alliance; nor is there any reason to suppose that it would be disagreeable to the son; but, I repeat it, no engagement exists.'

'If I were not your brother-in-law, I should have been very glad to have married Euphrosyne myself,' said St. Aldegonde.

'Yes, but what am I to do?' asked Bertram rather impatiently.

'It will not do to write to Brentham,' said St. Aldegonde, gravely; 'that I see clearly.' Then, after musing a while, he added, 'I am vexed to leave our friends here and shall miss them sadly. They are the most agreeable people I ever knew. I never enjoyed myself so much. But we must think of nothing but your affairs. We must return instantly. The whip will be an excuse, but the real business will be Euphrosyne. I should delight in having her for a sister-in-law, but the affair will require management. We can make short work of getting home: steam to Marseilles, leave the yacht there, and take the railroad. I have half a mind to telegraph to Bertha to meet us there. She would be of great use.'

CHAPTER LXXIX.

LOTHAIR was delighted with Galileo, and particularly with the blue waters of its lake slumbering beneath the surrounding hills. Of all its once pleasant towns, Tiberias alone remains, and that in ruins from a recent earthquake. But where are Chorazin, and Bethsaida, and Capernaum? A group of hovels and an ancient tower still bear the magic

name of Magdala, and all around are green mounts and
gentle slopes, the scenes of miracles that softened the heart
of man, and of sermons that never tire his ear. Dreams
passed over Lothair of settling for ever on the shores of
these waters and of reproducing all their vanished happiness: rebuilding their memorable cities, reviving their
fisheries, cultivating the plain of Gennesaret and the country of the Gadarenes, and making researches in this cradle
of pure and primitive Christianity.

The heritage of Paraclete was among the oaks of Bashan,
a lofty land, rising suddenly from the Jordan valley, verdant
and well watered, and clothed in many parts with forest;
there the host of Lothair resided among his lands and people,
and himself dwelt in a stone and castellated building, a
portion of which was of immemorial antiquity, and where
he could rally his forces and defend himself in case of the
irruption and invasion of the desert tribes. And here one
morn arrived a messenger from Jerusalem summoning
Lothair back to that city, in consequence of the intended
departure of his friends.

The call was urgent and was obeyed immediately with
that promptitude which the manners of the East, requiring
no preparation, admit. Paraclete accompanied his guest.
They had to cross the Jordan, and then to trace their way
till they reached the southern limit of the plain of Esdraelon,
from whence they counted on the following day to reach
Jerusalem. While they were encamped on this spot, a
body of Turkish soldiery seized all their horses, which were
required, they said, by the Pacha of Damascus, who was
proceeding to Jerusalem attending a great Turkish general,
who was on a mission to examine the means of defence of
Palestine on the Egyptian side. This was very vexatious,
but one of those incidents of Eastern life against which it
is impossible to contend; so Lothair and Paraclete were
obliged to take refuge in their pipes beneath a huge and

solitary sycamore tree, awaiting the arrival of the Ottoman magnificoes.

They came at last, a considerable force of cavalry, then mules and barbarous carriages with the harem, all the riders and inmates enveloped in what appeared to be winding sheets, white and shapeless; about them eunuchs and servants. The staff of the Pachas followed, preceding the grandees who closed the march, mounted on Anatolian chargers.

Paraclete and Lothair had been obliged to leave the grateful shade of the sycamore tree, as the spot had been fixed on by the commander of the advanced guard for the resting-place of the Pachas. They were standing aside and watching the progress of the procession, and contemplating the earliest opportunity of representing their grievances to high authority, when the Turkish general, or the Seraskier, as the Syrians inaccurately styled him, suddenly reined in his steed, and said in a loud voice, 'Captain Muriel.'

Lothair recognised the well-known voice of his commanding officer in the Apennine, and advanced to him with a military salute. 'I must first congratulate you on being alive, which I hardly hoped,' said the General. 'Then let me know why you are here.'

And Lothair told him.

'Well, you shall have back your horses,' said the General; 'and I will escort you to El Khuds. In the meantime you must be our guest;' and he presented him to the Pacha of Damascus with some form. 'You and I have bivouacked in the open air before this, and not in so bland a clime.'

Beneath the shade of the patriarchal sycamore, the General narrated to Lothair his adventures since they were fellow-combatants on the fatal field of Mentana.

'When all was over,' continued the General, 'I fled with Garibaldi, and gained the Italian frontier at Terni. Here we were of course arrested by the authorities; but not very maliciously. I escaped one morning, and got among the mountains in the neighbourhood of our old camp. I had to wander about these parts for some time, for the Papalini were in the vicinity, and there was danger. It was a hard time; but I found a friend now and then among the country people, though they are dreadfully superstitious. At last I got to the shore, and induced an honest fellow to put to sea in an open boat on the chance of something turning up. It did in the shape of a brigantine from Elba bound for Corfu. Here I was sure to find friends, for the brotherhood are strong in the Ionian Isles. And I began to look about for business. The Greeks made me some offers, but their schemes were all vanity, worse than the Irish. You remember our Fenian squabble? From something that transpired, I had made up my mind, so soon as I was well equipped, to go to Turkey. I had had some transactions with the house of Cantacuzene, through the kindness of our dear friend whom we will never forget, but will never mention; and through them I became acquainted with the Prince of Samos, who is the chief of their house. He is in the entire confidence of Aali Pacha. I soon found out that there was real business on the carpet. The Ottoman army, after many trials and vicissitudes, is now in good case; and the Porte has resolved to stand no more nonsense either in this direction,' and the General gave a significant glance, ' or in any other. But they wanted a general; they wanted a man who knew his business. I am not a Garibaldi, you know, and never pretended to be. I have no genius, or volcanic fire, or that sort of thing; but I do presume to say, with fair troops, paid with tolerable regularity, a battery or two of rifled cannon, and a well-organised commissariat, I am not afraid of meeting any captain of my acquaintance, whatever his land or language. The Turks are a brave people, and there is nothing in their system, political or religious, which jars with my convictions. In the army,

which is all that I much care for, there is the career of
merit, and I can promote any able man that I recognise.
As for their religion, they are tolerant and exact nothing
from me; and if I had any religion except Madre Natura,
I am not sure I would not prefer Islamism; which is at
least simple, and as little sacerdotal as any organised creed
can be. The Porte made me a liberal offer and I accepted
it. It so happened that, the moment I entered their service,
I was wanted. They had a difficulty on their Dalmatian
frontier; I settled it in a way they liked. And now I am
sent here with full powers, and am a pacha of the highest
class, and with a prospect of some warm work. I do not
know what your views are, but, if you would like a little
more soldiering, I will put you on my staff; and, for aught
I know, we may find our winter-quarters at Grand Cairo,
they say a pleasant place for such a season.'

'My soldiering has not been very fortunate,' said
Lothair; 'and I am not quite as great an admirer of
the Turks as you are, General. My mind is rather on the
pursuits of peace, and twenty hours ago I had a dream of
settling on the shores of the Sea of Galilee.'

'Whatever you do,' said the General, 'give up dreams.'

'I think you may be right in that,' said Lothair, with
half a sigh.

'Action may not always be happiness,' said the General;
'but there is no happiness without action. If you will not
fight the Egyptians, were I you, I would return home and
plunge into affairs. That was a fine castle of yours I visited
one morning; a man who lives in such a place must be
able to find a great deal to do.'

'I almost wish I were there, with you for my companion,' said Lothair.

'The wheel may turn,' said the General; 'but I begin
to think I shall not see much of Europe again. I have
given it some of my best years and best blood; and if I

had assisted in establishing the Roman republic, I should not have lived in vain; but the old imposture seems to me stronger than ever. I have got ten good years in me yet; and, if I be well supported and in luck (for, after all, everything depends on fortune), and manage to put a couple of hundred thousand men in perfect discipline, I may find some consolation for not blowing up St. Peter's, and may do something for the freedom of mankind on the banks of the Danube.'

CHAPTER LXXX.

Mrs. Putney Giles in full toilette was standing before the mantelpiece of her drawing-room in Hyde Park Gardens, and watching with some anxiety the clock that rested on it. It was the dinner hour, and Mr. Putney Giles, particular in such matters, had not returned. No one looked forward to his dinner and a chat with his wife with greater zest than Mr. Putney Giles; and he deserved the gratification which both incidents afforded him, for he fairly earned it. Full of news and bustle, brimful of importance and prosperity, sunshiny and successful, his daily return home, which, with many, perhaps most, men is a process lugubriously monotonous, was in Hyde Park Gardens, even to Apollonia, who possessed many means of amusement and occupation, a source ever of interest and excitement.

To-day too, particularly, for their great client, friend, and patron, Lothair, had arrived last night from the Continent at Muriel House, and had directed Mr. Putney Giles to be in attendance on him on the afternoon of this day.

Muriel House was a family mansion in the Green Park. It was built of hewn stone during the last century; a Palladian edifice, for a time much neglected, but now restored and duly prepared for the reception of its lord

and master by the same combined energy and taste which
had proved so satisfactory and successful at Muriel Towers.

It was a long room, the front saloon at Hyde Park
Gardens, and the door was as remote as possible from the
mantelpiece. It opened suddenly, but only the panting
face of Mr. Putney Giles was seen, as he poured forth in
hurried words: 'My dear, dreadfully late, but I can dress
in five minutes. I only opened the door in passing, to tell
you that I have seen our great friend; wonderful man!
but I will tell you all at dinner, or after. It was not he
who kept me, but the Duke of Brecon. The Duke has been
with me two hours. I had a good mind to bring him home
to dinner, and give him a bottle of my '48. They like that
sort of thing; but it will keep,' and the head vanished.

The Duke of Brecon would not have dined ill had he
honoured this household. It is a pleasant thing to see an
opulent and prosperous man of business, sanguine and full
of health, and a little overworked, at that royal meal,
dinner. How he enjoys his soup! And how curious in his
fish! How critical in his entrée, and how nice in his
Welsh mutton! His exhausted brain rallies under the glass
of dry sherry, and he realises all his dreams with the aid
of claret that has the true flavour of the violet.

'And now, my dear Apollonia,' said Mr. Putney Giles,
when the servants had retired, and he turned his chair and
played with a new nut from the Brazils, 'about our great
friend. Well, I was there at two o'clock, and found him
at breakfast. Indeed, he said, that had he not given me an
appointment, he thought he should not have risen at all,
so delighted he was to find himself again in an English
bed. Well, he told me everything that had happened. I
never knew a man so unreserved, and so different from
what he was when I first knew him, for he never much
cared then to talk about himself. But no egotism, nothing
of that sort of thing: all his mistakes, all his blunders, as

he called them. He told me everything that I might
thoroughly understand his position, and that he might
judge whether the steps I had taken in reference to it were
adequate.'

'I suppose about his religion,' said Apollonia. 'What is
he, after all?'

'As sound as you are. But you are right; that was the
point on which he was most anxious. He wrote, you know,
to me from Malta, when the account of his conversion first
appeared, to take all necessary steps to contradict the
announcement, and counteract its consequences. He gave
me carte blanche, and was anxious to know precisely
what I had done. I told him that a mere contradiction,
anonymous or from a third person, however unqualified its
language, would have no effect in the face of a detailed
narrative, like that in all the papers, of his walking in procession and holding a lighted taper and all that sort of
thing. What I did was this. I commenced building, by
his direction, two new churches on his estate, and announced in the local journals, copied in London, that he
would be present at the consecration of both. I subscribed
in his name, and largely, to all the diocesan societies, gave
a thousand pounds to the Bishop of London's fund, and
accepted for him the office of steward for this year for the
Sons of the Clergy. Then, when the public feeling was
ripe, relieved from all its anxieties, and beginning to get
indignant at the calumnies that had been so freely circulated, the time for paragraphs had arrived, and one
appeared stating that a discovery had taken place of the
means by which an unfounded and preposterous account of
the conversion of a distinguished young English nobleman
at Rome had been invented and circulated, and would probably furnish the occasion for an action for libel. And now
his return and appearance at the Chapel Royal next
Sunday will clench the whole business.'

'And he was satisfied?'

'Most satisfied; a little anxious whether his personal friends, and particularly the Brentham family, were assured of the truth. He travelled home with the Duke's son and Lord St. Aldegonde; but they came from remote parts, and their news from home was not very recent.'

'And how does he look?'

'Very well; never saw him look better. He is handsomer than he was. But he is changed. I could not conceive in a year that anyone could be so changed. He was young for his years; he is now old for his years. He was, in fact, a boy; he is now a man; and yet it is only a year. He said it seemed to him ten.'

'He has been through a fiery furnace,' said Apollonia.

'Well, he has borne it well,' said Mr. Giles. 'It is worth while serving such a client, so cordial, so frank, and yet so full of thought. He says he does not in the least regret all the money he has wasted. Had he remained at home, it would have gone to building a cathedral.'

'And a Popish one!' said Apollonia. 'I cannot agree with him,' she continued, 'that his Italian campaign was a waste of money. It will bear fruit. We shall still see the end of the "abomination of desolation."'

'Very likely,' said Mr. Giles; 'but I trust my client will have no more to do with such questions either way.'

'And did he ask after his friends?' said Apollonia.

'Very much: he asked after you. I think he went through all the guests at Muriel Towers except the poor Campiana. He spoke to me about the Colonel, to whom it appears he has written; but Theodora he never mentioned, except by some periphrasis, some allusion to a great sorrow, or to some dear friend whom he had lost. He seems a little embarrassed about the St. Jeromes, and said more than once that he owed his life to Miss Arundel. He dwelt a good deal upon this. He asked also a great deal about the Brentham family. They seem the people whom he most affects. When I told him of Lady Corisande's approaching union with the Duke of Brecon, I did not think he half liked it.'

'But is it settled?'

'The same as. The Duke has been with me two hours to-day about his arrangements. He has proposed to the parents, who are delighted with the match, and has received every encouragement from the young lady. He looks upon it as certain.'

'I wish our kind friend had not gone abroad,' said Apollonia.

'Well, at any rate, he has come back,' said Mr. Giles; 'that is something. I am sure I more than once never expected to see him again.'

'He has every virtue and every charm,' said Apollonia, 'and principles that are now proved. I shall never forget his kindness at the Towers. I wish he were settled for life. But who is worthy of him? I hope he will not fall into the clutches of that Popish girl. I have sometimes, from what I observed at Muriel and other reasons, a dread misgiving.'

CHAPTER LXXXI.

IT was the first night that Lothair had slept in his own house, and, when he awoke in the morning, he was quite bewildered, and thought for a moment he was in the Palazzo Agostini. He had not reposed in so spacious and lofty a chamber since he was at Rome. And this brought all his recollection to his Roman life, and everything that had happened there. 'And yet, after all,' he said, 'had it not been for Clare Arundel, I should never have seen Muriel House. I owe to her my life.' His relations with the St. Jerome family were doubtless embarrassing, even painful; and yet his tender and susceptible nature could not for a moment tolerate that he should passively submit to an estrangement from those who had conferred on him so much kindness, and whose ill-considered and injurious courses, as he now esteemed them, were perhaps, and probably, influenced and inspired by exalted, even sacred motives.

He wondered whether they were in London; and if so, what should he do? Should he call, or should he write? He wished he could do something to show to Miss Arundel how much he appreciated her kindness, and how grateful he was. She was a fine creature, and all her errors were noble ones: enthusiasm, energy, devotion to a sublime cause. Errors, but are these errors? Are they not, on the contrary, qualities which should command admiration in anyone? and in a woman and a beautiful woman, more than admiration?

There is always something to worry you. It comes as regularly as sunrise. Here was Lothair under his own roof again, after strange and trying vicissitudes, with his health restored, his youth little diminished, with some strange memories and many sweet ones; on the whole, once more in great prosperity, and yet his mind harped only on one vexing thought, and that was his painful and perplexed relations with the St. Jerome family.

His thoughts were a little distracted from this harassing theme by the novelty of his house and the pleasure it gave him. He admired the double staircase and the somewhat heavy yet richly carved ceilings; and the look into the park, shadowy and green, with a rich summer sun and the palace in the distance. What an agreeable contrast to his hard noisy sojourn in a bran-new, brobdignagian hotel, as was his coarse fate when he was launched into London life. This made him think of many comforts for which he

ought to be grateful; and then he remembered Muriel
Towers, and how completely and capitally everything was
there prepared and appointed; and while he was thinking
over all this and kindly of the chief author of these satisfactory arrangements, and the instances in which that individual had shown, not merely professional dexterity and
devotion, but some of the higher qualities that make life
sweet and pleasant, Mr. Putney Giles was announced, and
Lothair sprung forward and gave him his hand with a
cordiality which repaid at once that perfect but large-
hearted lawyer for all his exertions, and some anxieties
that he had never expressed even to Apollonia.

Nothing in life is more remarkable than the unnecessary
anxiety which we endure, and generally occasion ourselves.
Between four and five o'clock, having concluded his long
conference with Mr. Putney Giles, Lothair, as if he were
traversing the principal street of a foreign town, or rather
treading on tip-toe like a prince in some enchanted castle,
ventured to walk down St. James's Street, and the very
first person he met was Lord St. Jerome!

Nothing could be more unaffectedly hearty than his
greeting by that good man and thorough gentleman. 'I
saw by the "Post" you had arrived,' said Lord St. Jerome,
' and we were all saying at breakfast how glad we should
be to see you again. And looking so well. Quite yourself! I never saw you looking better. You have been to
Egypt with Lord St. Aldegonde, I think? It was the
wisest thing you could do. I said to Gertrude when you
went to Sicily, "If I were Lothair, I would go a good deal
farther than Sicily.' You wanted change of scene and air,
more than any man I know.'

' And how are they all?' said Lothair; ' my first visit
will be to them.'

' And they will be delighted to see you. Lady St. Jerome
is a little indisposed; a cold caught at one of her bazaars.

She will hold them, and they say that no one ever sells so much. But still, as I often say, my dear Gertrude, would it not be better if I were to give you a cheque for the institution; it would be the same to them, and would save you a great deal of trouble. But she fancies her presence inspires others, and perhaps there is something in it.'

'I doubt not; and Miss Arundel?'

'Clare is quite well, and I am hurrying home now to ride with her. I shall tell her that you asked after her.'

'And offer her my kindest remembrances.'

'What a relief!' exclaimed Lothair when once more alone. 'I thought I should have sunk into the earth when he first addressed me, and now I would not have missed this meeting for any consideration.'

He had not the courage to go into White's. He was under a vague impression that the whole population of the metropolis, and especially those who reside in the sacred land bounded on the one side by Piccadilly and on the other by Pall Mall, were unceasingly talking of his scrapes and misadventures; but he met Lord Carisbrooke and Mr. Brancepeth.

'Ah! Lothair,' said Carisbrooke; 'I do not think we have seen you this season; certainly not since Easter. What have you been doing with yourself?'

'You have been in Egypt?' said Mr. Brancepeth. 'The Duke was mentioning at White's to-day that you had returned with his son and Lord St. Aldegonde.'

'And does it pay?' enquired Carisbrooke. 'Egypt? What I have found generally in this sort of thing is, that one hardly knows what to do with one's evenings.'

'There is something in that,' said Lothair, 'and perhaps it applies to other countries besides Egypt. However, though it is true I did return with St. Aldegonde and Bertram, I have myself not been to Egypt.'

'And where did you pick them up?'

'At Jerusalem.'

'Jerusalem! What on earth could they go to Jerusalem for?' said Lord Carisbrooke. 'I am told there is no sort of sport there. They say, in the Upper Nile, there is good shooting.'

'St. Aldegonde was disappointed. I suppose our countrymen have disturbed the crocodiles and frightened away the pelicans?'

'We were going to look in at White's; come with us.'

Lothair was greeted with general kindness; but nobody seemed aware that he had been long and unusually absent from them. Some had themselves not come up to town till after Easter, and had therefore less cause to miss him. The great majority, however, were so engrossed with themselves that they never missed anybody. The Duke of Brecon appealed to Lothair about something that had happened at the last Derby, and was under the impression, until better informed, that Lothair had been one of his party. There were some exceptions to this general unacquaintance with events which an hour before Lothair had feared fearfully engrossed society. Hugo Bohun was doubly charmed to see him, 'because we were all in a fright one day that they were going to make you a cardinal, and it turned out that, at the very time they said you were about to enter the conclave, you happened to be at the second cataract. What lies these newspapers do tell!'

But the climax of relief was reached when the noble and grey-headed patron of the arts in Great Britain approached him with polished benignity, and said, 'I can give you perhaps even later news than you can give me of our friends at Jerusalem. I had a letter from Madame Phœbus this morning, and she mentioned with great regret that you had just left them. Your first travels, I believe?'

'My first.'

'And wisely planned. You were right in starting out

and seeing the distant parts. One may not always have
the energy which such an expedition requires. You can
keep Italy for a later and calmer day.'

Thus, one by one, all the cerulean demons of the morn
had vanished, and Lothair had nothing to worry him. He
felt a little dull as the dinner hour approached. Bertram
was to dine at home, and then go to the House of Commons; St. Aldegonde concluding the day with the same
catastrophe, had in the most immoral manner, in the
interval, gone to the play to see 'School,' of which he had
read an account in 'Galignani' when he was in quarantine.
Lothair was so displeased with this unfeeling conduct on
his part that he declined to accompany him: but Lady
St. Aldegonde, who dined at Crecy House, defended her
husband, and thought it very right and reasonable that
one so fond of the drama as he, who had been so long
deprived of gratifying his taste in that respect, should
take the first opportunity of enjoying this innocent amusement. A solitary dinner at Muriel House, in one of those
spacious and lofty chambers, rather appalled Lothair, and
he was getting low again, remembering nothing but his
sorrows, when Mr. Pinto came up to him and said, 'The
impromptu is always successful in life; you cannot be
engaged to dinner, for everybody believes you are at
Jericho. What say you to dining with me? Less than
the Muses and more than the Graces, certainly, if you
come. Lady Beatrice has invited herself, and she is to
pick up a lady, and I was to look out for a couple of
agreeable men. Hugo is coming, and you will complete
the charm.'

'The spell then is complete,' said Lothair; 'I suppose a
late eight.'

CHAPTER LXXXII.

LOTHAIR was breakfasting alone on the morrow, when his servant announced the arrival of Mr. Ruby, who had been ordered to be in attendance.

'Show him up,' said Lothair, 'and bring me the despatch-box which is in my dressing-room.'

Mr. Ruby was deeply gratified to be again in the presence of a nobleman so eminently distinguished, both for his property and his taste, as Lothair. He was profuse in his congratulations to his Lordship on his return to his native land, while at the same time he was opening a bag, from which he extracted a variety of beautiful objects, none of them for sale, all executed commissions, which were destined to adorn the fortunate and the fair. 'This is lovely, my Lord, quite new, for the Queen of Madagascar; for the Empress this, Her Majesty's own design, at least almost. Lady Melton's bridal necklace, and my Lord's George, the last given by King James II.; broken up during the Revolution, but re-set by us from an old drawing with picked stones.'

'Very pretty,' said Lothair; 'but it is not exactly this sort of thing that I want. See,' and he opened the despatch-box, and took from out of it a crucifix. It was made of some Eastern wood, inlaid with mother-of-pearl; the figure carved in brass, though not without power, and at the end of each of the four terminations of the cross was a small cavity enclosing something, and covered with glass.

'See,' continued Lothair, 'this is the crucifix, given with a carved shell to each pilgrim who visits the Holy Sepulchre. Within these four cavities is earth from the

F F

four holy places: Calvary, Sion, Bethlehem, and Gethse-
mane. Now what I want is a crucifix, something of this
dimension, but made of the most costly materials; the
figure must be of pure gold; I should like the cross to be
of choice emeralds, which I am told are now more precious
even than brilliants, and I wish the earth of the sacred
places to be removed from this crucifix, and introduced in
a similar manner into the one which you are to make; and
each cavity must be covered with a slit diamond. Do you
understand?'

'I follow you, my Lord,' said Mr. Ruby, with glistening
eyes. 'It will be a rare jewel. Is there to be a limit as
to the cost?'

'None but such as taste and propriety suggest,' said
Lothair. 'You will of course make a drawing and an
estimate, and send them to me; but I desire despatch.'

When Mr. Ruby had retired, Lothair took from the
despatch-box a sealed packet, and looked at it for some
moments, and then pressed it to his lips.

In the afternoon, Lothair found himself again in the
saddle, and was riding about London, as if he had never
quitted it. He left his cards at Crecy House, and many
other houses, and he called at the St. Jeromes late, but
asked if they were at home. He had reckoned that they
would not be, and his reckoning was right. It was impossible to conceal from himself that it was a relief. Mr.
Putney Giles dined alone with Lothair this evening, and
they talked over many things; among others the approaching marriage of Lady Corisande with the Duke of Brecon.

'Everybody marries except myself,' said Lothair rather
peevishly.

'But your Lordship is too young to think of that yet,'
said Mr. Putney Giles.

'I feel very old,' said Lothair.

At this moment there arrived a note from Bertram,

saying his mother was quite surprised and disappointed
that Lothair had not asked to see her in the morning.
She had expected him as a matter of course at luncheon,
and begged that he would come on the morrow.

'I have had many pleasant luncheons in that house,'
said Lothair, 'but this will be the last. When all the
daughters are married nobody eats luncheon.'

'That would hardly apply to this family,' said Mr.
Putney Giles, who always affected to know everything, and
generally did. 'They are so united, that I fancy the
famous luncheons at Crecy House will always go on, and
be a popular mode of their all meeting.'

'I half agree with St. Aldegonde,' said Lothair grum-
bling to himself, 'that if one is to meet that Duke of
Brecon every day at luncheon, for my part I had rather
stay away.'

In the course of the evening there also arrived invitations to all the impending balls and assemblies for Lothair,
and there seemed little prospect of his again being forced
to dine with his faithful solicitor as a refuge from melancholy.

On the morrow he went in his brougham to Crecy
House, and he had such a palpitation of the heart when he
arrived, that for a moment he absolutely thought he must
retire. His mind was full of Jerusalem, the Mount of
Olives, and the Sea of Galilee. He was never nervous
there, never agitated, never harassed, no palpitations of the
heart, no dread suspense. There was repose alike of body
and soul. Why did he ever leave Palestine and Paraclete?
He should have remained in Syria for ever, cherishing in a
hallowed scene a hallowed sorrow, of which even the
bitterness was exalted and ennobling.

He stood for a moment in the great hall at Crecy House,
and the groom of the chambers in vain solicited his attention. It was astonishing how much passed through his

mind while the great clock hardly described sixty seconds.
But in that space he had reviewed his life, arrived at the
conclusion that all was vanity and bitterness, that he had
failed in everything, was misplaced, had no object and no
hope, and that a distant and unbroken solitude in some
scene where either the majesty of nature was overwhelming
or its moral associations were equally sublime, must be his
only refuge. In the meditation of the Cosmos, or in the
divine reverie of sacred lands, the burthen of existence
might be endured.

'Her Grace is at luncheon, my Lord,' at length said the
groom of the chambers, and Lothair was ushered into the
gay and festive and cordial scene. The number of the self-
invited guests alone saved him. His confusion was absolute, and the Duchess remarked afterwards that Lothair
seemed to have regained all his shyness.

When Lothair had rallied and could survey the scene, he
found he was sitting by his hostess; that the Duke, not a
luncheon man, was present, and, as it turned out afterwards,
for the pleasure of meeting Lothair. Bertram also was
present, and several married daughters, and Lord Montairy, and Captain Mildmay, and one or two others; and next
to Lady Corisande was the Duke of Brecon.

So far as Lothair was concerned, the luncheon was unsuccessful. His conversational powers deserted him. He answered in monosyllables, and never originated a remark.
He was greatly relieved when they rose and returned to the
gallery in which they seemed all disposed to linger. The
Duke approached him, and in his mood he found it easier to
talk to men than to women. Male conversation is of a
coarser grain, and does not require so much play of thought
and manner: discourse about Suez Canal, and Arab horses,
and pipes and pachas, can be carried on without any psycho-
logical effort, and by degrees banishes all sensibility. And
yet he was rather dreamy, talked better than he listened,

did not look his companion in the face as the Duke spoke,
which was his custom, and his eye was wandering.   Suddenly, Bertram having joined them and speaking to his
father, Lothair darted away and approached Lady Corisande,
whom Lady Montairy had just quitted.

'As I may never have the opportunity again,' said Lothair, 'let me thank you, Lady Corisande, for some kind
thoughts which you deigned to bestow on me in my absence.'

His look was serious ; his tone almost sad.   Neither was
in keeping with the scene and the apparent occasion ; and
Lady Corisande, not displeased, but troubled, murmured,
'Since I last met you, I heard you had seen much and suffered much.'

'And that makes the kind thoughts of friends more
precious,' said Lothair.   'I have few : your brother is the
chief, but even he never did me any kindness so great
as when he told me that you had spoken of me with
sympathy.'

'Bertram's friends are mine,' said Lady Corisande, 'but,
otherwise, it would be impossible for us all not to feel an
interest in ——, one of whom we had seen so much,' she
added with some hesitation.

'Ah ! Brentham !' said Lothair, 'dear Brentham !   Do
you remember once saying to me that you hoped you should
never leave Brentham ? '

'Did I say so ? ' said Lady Corisande.

'I wish I had never left Brentham,' said Lothair ; 'it
was the happiest time of my life.   I had not then a sorrow
or a care.'

'But everybody has sorrows and cares,' said Lady Corisande ; 'you have, however, a great many things which
ought to make you happy.'

'I do not deserve to be happy,' said Lothair, 'for I
have made so many mistakes.   My only consolation is

that one great error which you most deprecated I have escaped.'

'Take a brighter and a nobler view of your life,' said Lady Corisande; 'feel rather you have been tried and not found wanting.'

At this moment the Duchess approached them and interrupted their conversation; and soon after this Lothair left Crecy House, still moody but less despondent.

There was a ball at Lady Clanmorne's in the evening, and Lothair was present He was astonished at the number of new faces he saw, the new phrases he heard, the new fashions alike in dress and manner. He could not believe it was the same world that he had quitted only a year ago. He was glad to take refuge with Hugo Bohun as with an old friend, and could not refrain from expressing to that eminent person his surprise at the novelty of all around him.

'It is you, my dear Lothair,' replied Hugo, 'that is surprising, not the world; that has only developed in your absence. What could have induced a man like you to be away for a whole season from the scene! Our forefathers might afford to travel; the world was then stereotyped. It will not do to be out of sight now. It is very well for St. Aldegonde to do these things, for the great object of St. Aldegonde is not to be in society, and he has never succeeded in his object. But here is the new beauty.'

There was a stir and a sensation. Men made way and even women retreated; and, leaning on the arm of Lord Carisbrooke, in an exquisite costume that happily displayed her splendid figure, and radiant with many charms, swept by a lady of commanding mien and stature, self-possessed and even grave, when suddenly turning her head, her pretty face broke into enchanting dimples as she exclaimed, 'O! cousin Lothair!'

Yes, the beautiful giantesses of Muriel Towers had becomo the beauties of the season. Their success had been as sudden and immediate as it was complete and sustained.

'Well, this is stranger than all!' said Lothair to Hugo Bohun when Lady Flora had passed on.

'The only persons talked of,' said Hugo. 'I am proud of my previous acquaintance with them. I think Carisbrooke has serious thoughts; but there are some who prefer Lady Grizell.'

'Lady Corisande was your idol last season,' said Lothair.

'Oh! she is out of the running,' said Hugo; 'she is finished. But I have not heard yet of any day being fixed. I wonder when he marries whether Brecon will keep on his theatre.'

'His theatre!'

'Yes; the high mode now for a real swell is to have a theatre. Brecon has the Frolic; Kate Simmons is his manager, who calls herself Athalie du Montfort. You ought to have a theatre, Lothair; and if there is not one to hire, you should build one. It would show that you were alive again and had the spirit of an English noble, and atone for some of your eccentricities.'

'But I have no Kate Simmons who calls herself Athalie du Montfort,' said Lothair; 'I am not so favoured, Hugo. However, I might succeed Brecon, as I hardly suppose he will maintain such an establishment when he is married.'

'I beg your pardon,' rejoined Hugo. 'It is the thing. Several of our greatest swells have theatres and are married. In fact, a first-rate man should have everything, and therefore he ought to have both a theatre and a wife.'

'Well, I do not think your manners have improved since last year, or your morals,' said Lothair. 'I have half a mind to go down to Muriel, and shut myself up there.'

He walked away and sauntered into the ball-room. The

first forms he recognised were Lady Corisande waltzing
with the Duke of Brecon, who was renowned for this
accomplishment. The heart of Lothair felt bitter. He
remembered his stroll to the dairy with the Duchess at
Brentham, and their conversation. Had his views then
been acceded to how different would have been his lot!
And it was not his fault that they had been rejected. And
yet, had they been accomplished, would they have been
happy? The character of Corisande, according to her
mother, was not then formed, nor easily scrutable. Was it
formed now? and what were its bent and genius? And
his own character? It could not be denied that his mind
was somewhat crude then, and his general conclusions on
life and duty hardly sufficiently matured and developed to
offer a basis for domestic happiness on which one might
confidently depend.

And Theodora? Had he married then he should never
have known Theodora. In this bright saloon, amid the
gaiety of festive music, and surrounded by gliding forms
of elegance and brilliancy, his heart was full of anguish
when he thought of Theodora. To have known such
a woman and to have lost her! Why should a man
live after this? Yes; he would retire to Muriel, once
hallowed by her presence, and he would raise to her
memory some monumental fane, beyond the dreams even
of Artemisia, and which should commemorate alike her
wondrous life and wondrous mind.

A beautiful hand was extended to him, and a fair face,
animated with intelligence, welcomed him without a word.
It was Lady St. Jerome. Lothair bowed lowly and touched
her hand with his lip.

'I was sorry to have missed you yesterday. We had
gone down to Vauxe for the day, but I heard of you from
my Lord with great pleasure. We are all of us so happy
that you have entirely recovered your health.'

'I owe that to you, dearest lady,' said Lothair, 'and to those under your roof. I can never forget your goodness to me. Had it not been for you, I should not have been here or anywhere else.'

'No, no; we did our best for the moment. But I quite agree with my Lord, now, that you stayed too long at Rome under the circumstances. It was a good move, that going to Sicily, and so wise of you to travel in Egypt. Men should travel.'

'I have not been to Egypt,' said Lothair; 'I have been to the Holy Land, and am a pilgrim. I wish you would tell Miss Arundel that I shall ask her permission to present her with my crucifix, which contains the earth of the Holy Places. I should have told her this myself, if I had seen her yesterday. Is she here?'

'She is at Vauxe; she could not tear herself away from the roses.'

'But she might have brought them with her as companions,' said Lothair, 'as you have, I apprehend, yourself.'

'I will give you this in Clare's name,' said Lady St. Jerome, as she selected a beautiful flower and presented it to Lothair. 'It is in return for your crucifix, which I am sure she will highly esteem. I only wish it were a rose of Jericho.'

Lothair started. The name brought up strange and disturbing associations: the procession in the Jesuits' Church, the lighted tapers, the consecrated children, one of whom had been supernaturally presented with the flower in question. There was an awkward silence, until Lothair, almost without intending it, expressed a hope that the Cardinal was well.

'Immersed in affairs, but I hope well,' replied Lady St. Jerome. 'You know what has happened? But you will see him. He will speak to you of these matters himself.'

'But I should like also to hear from you.'

'Well, they are scarcely yet to be spoken of,' said Lady St. Jerome. 'I ought not perhaps even to have alluded to the subject; but I know how deeply devoted you are to religion. We are on the eve of the greatest event of this century. When I wake in the morning, I always fancy that I have heard of it only in dreams. And many, all this room, will not believe in the possibility of its happening. They smile when the contingency is alluded to, and if I were not present they would mock. But it will happen, I am assured it will happen,' exclaimed Lady St. Jerome, speaking with earnestness, though in a hushed voice. 'And no human imagination can calculate or conceive what may be its effect on the destiny of the human race.'

'You excite my utmost curiosity,' said Lothair.

'Hush! there are listeners. But we shall soon meet again. You will come and see us, and soon. Come down to Vauxe on Saturday; the Cardinal will be there. And the place is so lovely now. I always say Vauxe at Whitsuntide, or a little later, is a scene for Shakespeare. You know you always liked Vauxe.'

'More than liked it,' said Lothair; 'I have passed at Vauxe some of the happiest hours of my life.'

CHAPTER LXXXIII.

On the morning of the very Saturday on which Lothair was to pay his visit to Vauxe, riding in the park, he was joined by that polished and venerable nobleman who presides over the destinies of art in Great Britain. This distinguished person had taken rather a fancy to Lothair, and liked to talk to him about the Phœbus family; about the great artist himself, and all his theories and styles; but especially about the fascinating Madame Phœbus and the captivating Euphrosyne.

'You have not found time, I dare say,' said the nobleman, 'to visit the exhibition of the Royal Academy?'

'Well, I have only been here a week,' said Lothair, 'and have had so many things to think of, and so many persons to see.'

'Naturally,' said the nobleman; 'but I recommend you to go. I am now about to make my fifth visit there; but it is only to a single picture, and I envy its owner.'

'Indeed!' said Lothair. 'Pray tell me its subject, that I may not fail to see it.'

'It is a portrait,' said the nobleman; 'only a portrait, some would say, as if the finest pictures in the world were not only portraits. The masterpieces of the English school are portraits, and some day when you have leisure and inclination, and visit Italy, you will see portraits by Titian and Raffaelle and others, which are the masterpieces of art. Well, the picture in question is a portrait by a young English painter at Rome and of an English lady. I doubt not the subject was equal to the genius of the artist, but I do not think that the modern pencil has produced anything equal to it, both in design and colour and expression. You should see it by all means, and I have that opinion of your taste that I do not think you will be content by seeing it once. The real taste for fine art in this country is proved by the crowd that always surrounds that picture; and yet only a portrait of an English lady, a Miss Arundel.'

'A Miss Arundel?' said Lothair.

'Yes, of a Roman Catholic family; I believe a relative of the St. Jeromes. They were at Rome last year, when this portrait was executed.'

'If you will permit me,' said Lothair, 'I should like to accompany you to the Academy. I am going out of town this afternoon, but not far, and could manage it.'

So they went together. It was the last exhibition of the
Academy in Trafalgar Square. The portrait in question
was in the large room, and hung on the eye line; so, as the
throng about it was great, it was not easy immediately to
inspect it. But one or two R.A.s who were gliding about,
and who looked upon the noble patron of art as a sort of
divinity, insensibly controlled the crowd, and secured for
their friend and his companion the opportunity which they
desired.

'It is the finest thing since the portrait of the Cenci,'
said the noble patron.

The painter had represented Miss Arundel in her robe of
a sister of mercy, but with uncovered head. A wallet was
at her side, and she held a crucifix. Her beautiful eyes,
full of mystic devotion, met those of the spectator with a
fascinating power that kept many spell-bound. In the
background of the picture was a masterly glimpse of the
papal gardens and the wondrous dome.

'That must be a great woman,' said the noble patron
of art.

Lothair nodded assent in silence.

The crowd about the picture seemed breathless and awe-
struck. There were many women, and in some eyes there
were tears.

'I shall go home,' said one of the spectators; 'I do not
wish to see anything else.'

'That is religion,' murmured her companion. 'They may
say what they like, but it would be well for us if we were
all like her.'

It was a short half hour by the railroad to Vauxe, and
the station was close to the park gates. The sun was in its
last hour when Lothair arrived, but he was captivated by
the beauty of the scene, which he had never witnessed in
its summer splendour. The rich foliage of the great
avenues, the immense oaks that stood alone, the deer

glancing in the golden light, and the quaint and stately edifice itself, so finished and so fair, with its freestone pinnacles and its gilded vanes glistening and sparkling in the warm and lucid sky, contrasted with the chilly hours when the Cardinal and himself had first strolled together in that park, and when they tried to flatter themselves that the morning mist clinging to the skeleton trees was perhaps the burst of spring.

Lothair found himself again in his old rooms, and as his valet unpacked his toilette, he fell into one of his reveries.

'What,' he thought to himself, 'if life after all be only a dream. I can scarcely realise what is going on. It seems to me I have passed through a year of visions. That I should be at Vauxe again! A roof I once thought rife with my destiny. And perhaps it may prove so. And were it not for the memory of one event, I should be a ship without a rudder.'

There were several guests in the house, and when Lothair entered the drawing-room, he was glad to find that it was rather full. The Cardinal was by the side of Lady St. Jerome when Lothair entered, and immediately after saluting his hostess it was his duty to address his late guardian. Lothair had looked forward to this meeting with apprehension. It seemed impossible that it should not to a certain degree be annoying. Nothing of the kind. It was impossible to greet him more cordially, more affectionately than did Cardinal Grandison.

'You have seen a great deal since we parted,' said the Cardinal. 'Nothing could be wiser than your travelling. You remember that at Muriel I recommended you to go to Egypt, but I thought it better that you should see Rome first. And it answered: you made the acquaintance of its eminent men, men whose names will be soon in everybody's mouth, for before another year elapses Rome will be the cynosure of the world. Then, when the great questions

come on which will decide the fate of the human race for
centuries, you will feel the inestimable advantage of being
master of the situation, and that you are familiar with
every place and every individual. I think you were not very
well at Rome; but next time you must choose your season.
However, I may congratulate you on your present looks.
The air of the Levant seems to have agreed with you.'

Dinner was announced almost at this moment, and Lothair, who had to take out Lady Clanmorne, had no opportunity before dinner of addressing anyone else except his
hostess and the Cardinal. The dinner party was large, and
it took some time to reconnoitre all the guests. Lothair
observed Miss Arundel, who was distant from him and on
the same side of the table, but neither Monsignore Catesby
nor Father Coleman was present.

Lady Clanmorne chatted agreeably. She was content to
talk, and did not insist on conversational reciprocity. She
was a pure freetrader in gossip. This rather suited Lothair.
It pleased Lady Clanmorne to-day to dilate upon marriage
and the married state, but especially on all her acquaintances, male and female, who were meditating the surrender
of their liberty and about to secure the happiness of their
lives.

'I suppose the wedding of the season, the wedding of
weddings, will be the Duke of Brecon's,' she said. 'But
I do not hear of any day being fixed.'

'Ah!' said Lothair, 'I have been abroad and am very
deficient in these matters. But I was travelling with the
lady's brother, and he has never yet told me that his sister
was going to be married.'

'There is no doubt about that,' said Lady Clanmorne.
'The Duchess said to a friend of mine the other day, who
congratulated her, "that there was no person in whom she
should have more confidence as a son-in-law than the
Duke."'

'Most marriages turn out unhappy,' said Lothair, rather morosely.

'Oh! my dear Lord, what can you mean?'

'Well I think so,' he said doggedly. 'Among the lower orders, if we may judge from the newspapers, they are always killing their wives, and in our class we get rid of them in a more polished way, or they get rid of us.'

'You quite astonish me with such sentiments,' said Lady Clanmorne. 'What would Lady St. Jerome think if she heard you, who told me the other day that she believed you to be a faultless character? And the Duchess too, your friend's mamma, who thinks you so good, and that it is so fortunate for her son to have such a companion?'

'As for Lady St. Jerome, she believes in everything,' said Lothair; 'and it is no compliment that she believes in me. As for my friend's mamma, her ideal character, according to you, is the Duke of Brecon, and I cannot pretend to compete with him. He may please the Duchess, but I cannot say the Duke of Brecon is a sort of man I admire.'

'Well, he is no great favourite of mine,' said Lady Clanmorne; 'I think him overbearing and selfish, and I should not like at all to be his wife.'

'What do you think of Lady Corisande?' said Lothair.

'I admire her more than any girl in society, and I think she will be thrown away on the Duke of Brecon. She is clever and she has strong character, and, I am told, is capable of great affections. Her manners are good, finished and natural; and she is beloved by her young friends, which I always think a test.'

'Do you think her handsome?'

'There can be no question about that: she is beautiful, and her beauty is of a high class. I admire her much more than all her sisters. She has a grander mien.'

'Have you seen Miss Arundel's picture at the Academy?'

'Everybody has seen that: it has made a fury.'

'I heard an eminent judge say to-day, that it was the portrait of one who must be a great woman.'

'Well, Miss Arundel is a remarkable person.'

'Do you admire her?'

'I have heard first-rate critics say that there was no person to be compared to Miss Arundel. And unquestionably it is a most striking countenance: that profound brow and those large deep eyes; and then her figure is so fine. But, to tell you the truth, Miss Arundel is a person I never could make out.'

'I wonder she does not marry,' said Lothair.

'She is very difficult,' said Lady Clanmorne. 'Perhaps, too, she is of your opinion about marriage.'

'I have a good mind to ask her after dinner whether she is,' said Lothair. 'I fancy she would not marry a Protestant?'

'I am no judge of such matters,' said Lady Clanmorne; 'only I cannot help thinking that there would be more chance of a happy marriage when both were of the same religion.'

'I wish we were all of the same religion. Do not you?'

'Well, that depends a little on what the religion might be.'

'Ah!' sighed Lothair, 'what between religion and marriage and some other things, it appears to me one never has a tranquil moment. I wonder what religious school the Duke of Brecon belongs to? Very high and dry, I should think.'

The moment the gentlemen returned to the drawing-room Lothair singled out Miss Arundel, and attached himself to her.

'I have been to see your portrait to-day,' he said. She changed colour.

'I think it,' he continued, 'the triumph of modern art,

and I could not easily fix on any production of the old masters that excels it.'

'It was painted at Rome,' she said in a low voice.

'So I understood. I regret that when I was at Rome I saw so little of its art. But my health you know was wretched. Indeed, if it had not been for some friends, I might say for one friend, I should not have been here or in this world. I can never express to that person my gratitude, and it increases every day. All that I have dreamed of angels was then realised.'

'You think too kindly of us.'

'Did Lady St. Jerome give you my message about the earth from the holy places which I had placed in a crucifix, and which I hope you will accept from me, in remembrance of the past and your Christian kindness to me? I should have left it at St. James's Square before this, but it required some little arrangement after its travels.'

'I shall prize it most dearly, both on account of its consecrated character and for the donor's sake, whom I have ever wished to see the champion of our Master.'

'You never had a wish, I am sure,' said Lothair, 'that was not sublime and pure.'

CHAPTER LXXXIV.

They breakfasted at Vauxe, in the long gallery. It was always a merry meal, and it was the fashion of the house that all should be present. The Cardinal was seldom absent. He used to say, 'I feel more on equal terms with my friends at breakfast, and rather look forward to my banquet of dry toast.' Lord St. Jerome was quite proud of receiving his letters and newspapers at Vauxe earlier by far than he did at St. James's Square; and as all were supplied

with their letters and journals, there was a great demand
for news, and a proportional circulation of it. Lady Clanmorne indulged this passion for gossip amusingly one
morning, and read a letter from her correspondent, written
with the grace of a Sevigné, but which contained details of
marriages, elopements, and a murder among their intimate
acquaintance, which made all the real intelligence quite
insipid, and was credited for at least half an hour.

The gallery at Vauxe was of great length, and the break-
fast-table was laid at one end of it. The gallery was of
panelled oak, with windows of stained glass in the upper
panes, and the ceiling, richly and heavily carved, was entirely gilt, but with deadened gold. Though stately, the
general effect was not free from a certain character of
gloom. Lit, as it was, by sconces, this was at night much
softened; but on a rich summer morn, the gravity and repose of this noble chamber were grateful to the senses.

The breakfast was over; the ladies had retired, stealing
off with the 'Morning Post,' the gentlemen gradually dis-
appearing for the solace of their cigars. The Cardinal, who
was conversing with Lothair, continued their conversation
while walking up and down the gallery, far from the hearing of the servants, who were disembarrassing the break-
fast-table, and preparing it for luncheon. A visit to a
country house, as Pinto says, is a series of meals mitigated
by the new dresses of the ladies.

'The more I reflect on your travels,' said the Cardinal,
'the more I am satisfied with what has happened. I recognise the hand of Providence in your preliminary visit to
Rome and your subsequent one to Jerusalem. In the vast
events which are impending, that man is in a strong position who has made a pilgrimage to the Holy Sepulchre.
You remember our walk in the park here,' continued the
Cardinal; 'I felt then that we were on the eve of some
mighty change, but it was then indefinite, though to me

inevitable. You were destined, I was persuaded, to witness
it, even, as I hoped, to take no inconsiderable share in its
fulfilment. But I hardly believed that I should have been
spared for this transcendent day, and when it is consummated, I will gratefully exclaim, " Nunc me dimittis! " '

'You allude, sir, to some important matter which Lady
St. Jerome a few days ago intimated to me, but it was only
an intimation, and purposely very vague.'

'There is no doubt,' said the Cardinal, speaking with
solemnity, ' of what I now communicate to you. The Holy
Father, Pius IX., has resolved to summon an Œcumenical
Council.'

'An Œcumenical Council!' said Lothair.

'It is a weak phrase,' resumed the Cardinal, 'to say it
will be the greatest event of this century. I believe it will
be the greatest event since the Episcopate of St. Peter;
greater, in its consequences to the human race, than the
fall of the Roman Empire, the pseudo-Reformation, or the
Revolution of France. It is much more than three hundred years since the last Œcumenical Council, the Council
of Trent, and the world still vibrates with its decisions.
But the Council of Trent, compared with the impending
Council of the Vatican, will be as the mediæval world of
Europe compared with the vast and complete globe which
man has since discovered and mastered.'

'Indeed!' said Lothair.

'Why the very assembly of the Fathers of the Church
will astound the Freemasons, and the Secret Societies, and
the Atheists. That alone will be a demonstration of power
on the part of the Holy Father which no conqueror from
Sesostris to Napoleon has ever equalled. It was only the
bishops of Europe that assembled at Trent, and, inspired
by the Holy Spirit, their decisions have governed man for
more than three hundred years. But now the bishops of
the whole world will assemble round the chair of St. Peter,

and prove by their presence the catholic character of the Church. Asia will send its patriarchs and pontiffs, and America and Australia its prelates; and at home, my dear young friend, the Council of the Vatican will offer a striking contrast to the Council of Trent; Great Britain will be powerfully represented. The bishops of Ireland might have been counted on, but it is England also that will send her prelates now, and some of them will take no ordinary share in transactions that will give a new form and colour to human existence.'

'Is it true, sir, that the object of the Council is to declare the infallibility of the Pope?'

'In matters of faith and morals,' said the Cardinal quickly. 'There is no other infallibility. That is a secret with God. All that we can know of the decision of the Council on this awful head is that its decision, inspired by the Holy Spirit, must infallibly be right. We must await that decision, and, when made known, we must embrace it, not only with obedience, but with the interior assent of mind and will. But there are other results of the Council on which we may speculate; and which, I believe, it will certainly accomplish: first, it will show in a manner that cannot be mistaken that there is only one alternative for the human intellect: Rationalism or Faith; and, secondly, it will exhibit to the Christian powers the inevitable future they are now preparing for themselves.'

'I am among the faithful,' said Lothair.

'Then you must be a member of the Church Catholic,' said the Cardinal. 'The basis on which God has willed that His revelation should rest in the world is the testimony of the Catholic Church, which, if considered only as a human and historical witness, affords the highest and most certain evidence for the fact and the contents of the Christian religion. If this be denied, there is no such thing as history. But the Catholic Church is not only a human and historical witness of its own origin, constitution, and authority, it is also a supernatural and divine witness, which can neither fail nor err. When it œcumenically speaks, it is not merely the voice of the Fathers of the world; it declares what "it hath seemed good to the Holy Ghost and to us." '

There was a pause, and then Lothair remarked : 'You said, sir, that the Council would show to the civil powers of the Christian world the inevitable future they are preparing for themselves ? '

'Even so. Now mark this, my child. At the Council of Trent the Christian powers were represented, and properly so. Their seats will be empty at the Council of the Vatican. What does that mean ? The separation between Church and State, talked of for a long time, now demonstrated. And what does separation between Church and State mean ? That society is no longer consecrated. The civil governments of the world no longer profess to be Catholic. The faithful indeed among their subjects will be represented at the Council by their pastors, but the civil powers have separated themselves from the Church ; either by royal edict, or legislative enactment, or revolutionary changes, they have abolished the legal status of the Catholic Church within their territory. It is not their choice ; they are urged on by an invisible power that is anti-Christian, and which is the true, natural, and implacable enemy of the one visible and universal Church. The coming anarchy is called progress, because it advances along the line of departure from the old Christian order of the world. Christendom was the offspring of the Christian family, and the foundation of the Christian family is the sacrament of matrimony, the spring of all domestic and public morals. The anti-Christian societies are opposed to the principle of home. When they have destroyed the

hearth, the morality of society will perish. A settlement
in the foundations may be slow in sinking, but it brings all
down at last. The next step in de-Christianising the political life of nations is to establish national education without Christianity. This is systematically aimed at wherever
the revolution has its way. The period and policy of
Julian are returning. Some think this bodes ill for the
Church; no, it is the State that will suffer. The Secret
Societies are hurrying the civil governments of the world,
and mostly the governments who disbelieve in their
existence, to the brink of a precipice, over which monar-
chies and law and civil order will ultimately fall and perish
together.'

'Then all is hopeless,' said Lothair.

'To human speculation,' said the Cardinal; 'but none
can fathom the mysteries of Divine interposition. This
coming Council may save society, and on that I would
speak to you most earnestly. His Holiness has resolved
to invite the schismatic priesthoods to attend it and labour
to bring about the unity of Christendom. He will send an
ambassador to the Patriarch of the heresy of Photius, which
is called the Greek Church. He will approach Lambeth.
I have little hope of the latter, though there is more than
one of the Anglican bishops who revere the memory and
example of Laud. But I by no means despair of your
communion being present in some form at the Council.
There are true spirits at Oxford who sigh for unity. They
will form, I hope, a considerable deputation; but as, not
yet being prelates, they cannot take their seats formally in
the Council, I wish, in order to increase and assert their
influence, that they should be accompanied by a band of
powerful laymen, who shall represent the pious and pure
mind of England, the coming guardians of the land in the
dark hour that may be at hand. Considering your previous
knowledge of Rome, your acquaintance with its eminent

men and its language, and considering too, as I well know,
that the Holy Father looks to you as one marked out by
Providence to assert the truth, it would please me, and,
trust me, it would be wise in you, were you to visit Rome
on this sublime occasion, and perhaps put your mark on
the world's history.'

'It must yet be a long time before the Council meets,'
said Lothair, after a pause.

'Not too long for preparation,' replied the Cardinal.
'From this hour, until its assembling, the pulse of humanity
will throb. Even at this hour they are speaking of the
same matters as ourselves alike on the Euphrates and the
St. Lawrence. The good Catesby is in Ireland, conferring
with the bishops, and awakening them to the occasion.
There is a party among them narrow-minded and local,
the effects of their education. There ought not to be an
Irish priest who was not brought up at the Propaganda.
You know that admirable institution. We had some happy
hours at Rome together, may we soon repeat them! You
were very unwell there; next time you will judge of Rome
in health and vigour.'

CHAPTER LXXXV.

They say there is a skeleton in every house; it may be
doubted. What is more certain are the sorrow and perplexity which sometimes, without a warning and preparation, suddenly fall upon a family living in a world of
happiness and ease, and meriting their felicity by every
gift of fortune and disposition.

Perhaps there never was a circle that enjoyed life more,
and deserved to enjoy life more, than the Brentham family.
Never was a family more admired and less envied. Nobody

grudged them their happy gifts and accidents, for their demeanour was so winning, and their manners so cordial and sympathetic, that everyone felt as if he shared their amiable prosperity. And yet, at this moment, the Duchess, whose countenance was always as serene as her soul, was walking with disturbed visage and agitated step up and down the private room of the Duke; while his Grace, seated, his head upon his arm, and with his eyes on the ground, was apparently in anxious thought.

Now what had happened? It seems that these excellent parents had become acquainted, almost at the same moment, with two astounding and disturbing facts: their son wanted to marry Euphrosyne Cantacuzene, and their daughter would not marry the Duke of Brecon.

'I was so perfectly unprepared for the communication,' said the Duke, looking up, 'that I have no doubt I did not express myself as I ought to have done. But I do not think I said anything wrong. I showed surprise, sorrow; no anger. I was careful not to say anything to hurt his feelings; that is a great point in these matters: nothing disrespectful of the young lady. I invited him to speak to me again about it when I had a little got over my surprise.'

'It is really a catastrophe,' exclaimed the Duchess; 'and only think I came to you for sympathy in my sorrow, which, after all, though distressing, is only a mortification!'

'I am very sorry about Brecon,' said the Duke, 'who is a man of honour, and who would have suited us very well; but, my dear Augusta, I never took exactly the same view of this affair as you did: I was never satisfied that Corisande returned his evident, I might say avowed, admiration of her.'

'She spoke of him always with great respect,' said the Duchess, 'and that is much in a girl of Corisande's disposition. I never heard her speak of any of her admirers in the same tone; certainly not of Lord Carisbrooke; I was quite prepared for her rejection of him. She never encouraged him.'

'Well,' said the Duke, 'I grant you it is mortifying, infinitely distressing; and Brecon is the last man I could have wished that it should occur to; but, after all, our daughter must decide for herself in such affairs. She is the person most interested in the event. I never influenced her sisters in their choice, and she also must be free. The other subject is more grave.'

'If we could only ascertain who she really is,' said the Duchess.

'According to Bertram, fully our equal; but I confess I am no judge of Levantine nobility,' his Grace added, with a mingled expression of pride and despair.

'That dreadful travelling abroad!' exclaimed the Duchess. 'I always had a foreboding of something disastrous from it. Why should he have gone abroad, who has never been to Ireland, or seen half the counties of his own country?'

'They all will go,' said the Duke; 'and I thought, with St. Aldegonde, he was safe from getting into any scrape of this kind.'

'I should like to speak to Granville about it,' said the Duchess. 'When he is serious, his judgment is good.'

'I am to see St. Aldegonde before I speak to Bertram,' said the Duke. 'I should not be surprised if he were here immediately.'

One of the social mysteries is, 'how things get about!' It was not the interest of any of the persons immediately connected with the subject that society should be aware that the Lady Corisande had declined the proposal of the Duke of Brecon. Society had no right even to assume that such a proposal was either expected or contemplated. The Duke of Brecon admired Lady Corisande, so did many others; and many others were admired by the Duke of Brecon. The Duchess even hoped that, as the season was waning, it might break up, and people go into

the country or abroad, and nothing be observed. And
yet it 'got about.' The way things get about is through
the Hugo Bohuns. Nothing escapes their quick eyes and
slow hearts. Their mission is to peer into society, like
professional astronomers ever on the watch to detect the
slightest change in the phenomena. Never embarrassed
by any passion of their own, and their only social
scheming being to maintain their transcendent position,
all their life and energy are devoted to the discovery of
what is taking place around them; and experience, combined with natural tact, invests them with almost a supernatural skill in the detection of social secrets. And so it
happened that scarcely a week had passed before Hugo
began to sniff the air, and then to make fine observations
at balls, as to whom certain persons danced with, or did
not dance with; and then he began the curious process of
what he called putting two and two together, and putting
two and two together proved in about a fortnight that it
was all up between Lady Corisande and the Duke of Brecon.

Among others he imparted this information to Lothair,
and it set Lothair a-thinking; and he went to a ball that
evening solely with the purpose of making social observations like Hugo Bohun. But Lady Corisande was not
there, though the Duke of Brecon was, apparently in high
spirits, and waltzing more than once with Lady Grizell
Falkirk. Lothair was not very fortunate in his attempts
to see Bertram. He called more than once at Crecy
House too, but in vain. The fact is, Bertram was naturally entirely engrossed with his own difficulties, and the
Duchess, harassed and mortified, could no longer be at
home in the morning.

Her Grace, however, evinced the just appreciation of
character for which women are remarkable, in the confidence which she reposed in the good sense of Lord St.
Aldegonde at this crisis. St. Aldegonde was the only one

of his sons-in-law whom the Duke really considered and a
little feared. When St. Aldegonde was serious, his influ
ence over men was powerful. And he was serious now.
St. Aldegonde, who was not conventional, had made the
acquaintance of Mr. Cantacuzene immediately on his return
to England, and they had become friends. He had dined
in the Tyburnian palace of the descendant of the Greek
Emperors more than once, and had determined to make his
second son, who was only four years of age, a Greek merchant. When the Duke therefore consulted him on ' the
catastrophe,' St. Aldegonde took high ground, spoke of
Euphrosyne in the way she deserved, as one equal to an
elevated social position, and deserving it. ' But if you
ask me my opinion, sir,' he continued, ' I do not think,
except for Bertram's sake, that you have any cause to fret
yourself. The family wish her to marry her cousin, the
eldest son of the Prince of Samos. It is an alliance of the
highest, and suits them much better than any connection
with us. Besides, Cantacuzene will give his children large
fortunes, and they like the money to remain in the family.
A hundred or a hundred and fifty thousand pounds, perhaps more, goes a great way on the coasts of Asia Minor.
You might buy up half the Archipelago. The Cantacuzenes are coming to dine with us next week. Bertha is
delighted with them. Mr. Cantacuzene is so kind as to
say he will take Clovis into his counting-house. I wish I
could induce your Grace to come and meet him: then you
could judge for yourself. You would not be in the least
shocked were Bertram to marry the daughter of some of
our great merchants or bankers. This is a great merchant and banker, and the descendant of princes, and his
daughter one of the most beautiful and gifted of women,
and worthy to be a princess.'

' There is a good deal in what St. Aldegonde says,' said
the Duke afterwards to his wife. ' The affair takes rather

a different aspect. It appears they are really people of high consideration, and great wealth too. Nobody could describe them as adventurers.'

'We might gain a little time,' said the Duchess. 'I dislike peremptory decisions. It is a pity we have not an opportunity of seeing the young lady.'

'Granville says she is the most beautiful woman he ever met, except her sister.'

'That is the artist's wife?' said the Duchess.

'Yes,' said the Duke; 'I believe a most distinguished man, but it rather adds to the imbroglio. Perhaps things may turn out better than they first promised. The fact is, I am more amazed than annoyed. Granville knows the father, it seems, intimately. He knows so many odd people. He wants me to meet him at dinner. What do you think about it? It is a good thing sometimes to judge for oneself. They say this Prince of Samos she is half betrothed to is attaché to the Turkish Embassy at Vienna, and is to visit England.'

'My nervous system is quite shaken,' said the Duchess. 'I wish we could all go to Brentham. I mentioned it to Corisande this morning, and I was surprised to find that she wished to remain in town.'

'Well, we will decide nothing, my dear, in a hurry. St. Aldegonde says that, if we decide in that sense, he will undertake to break off the whole affair. We may rely on that. We need consider the business only with reference to Bertram's happiness and feelings. This is an important issue no doubt, but it is a limited one. The business is not of so disagreeable a nature as it seemed. It is not an affair of a rash engagement in a discreditable quarter from which he cannot extricate himself. There is no doubt they are thoroughly reputable people, and will sanction nothing which is not decorous and honourable. St. Aldegonde has been a comfort to me in this matter; and you will find out

a great deal when you speak to him about it. Things
might be worse. I wish I was as easy about the Duke
of Brecon. I met him this morning and rode with him, to
show there was no change in my feelings.'

CHAPTER LXXXVI.

The world goes on with its aching hearts and its smiling
faces, and very often, when a year has revolved, the world
finds out there was no sufficient cause for the sorrows or
the smiles. There is much unnecessary anxiety in the
world, which is apt too hastily to calculate the consequences of any unforeseen event, quite forgetting that, acute
as it is in observation, the world, where the future is concerned, is generally wrong. The Duchess would have liked
to bury herself in the shades of Brentham, but Lady Corisande, who deported herself as if there were no care at
Crecy House except that occasioned by her brother's rash
engagement, was of opinion that 'Mamma would only
brood over this vexation in the country,' and that it would
be much better not to anticipate the close of the waning
season. So the Duchess and her lovely daughter were seen
everywhere where they ought to be seen, and appeared the
pictures of serenity and satisfaction.

As for Bertram's affair itself, under the manipulation of
St. Aldegonde it began to assume a less anxious and more
practicable aspect. The Duke was desirous to secure his
son's happiness, but wished nothing to be done rashly. If,
for example, in a year's time or so, Bertram continued in
the same mind, his father would never be an obstacle to
his well-considered wishes. In the meantime an opportunity might offer of making the acquaintance of the young
lady and her friends.

And in the meantime the world went on, dancing and betting and banqueting, and making speeches, and breaking hearts and heads, till the time arrived when social stock is taken, the results of the campaign estimated and ascertained, and the dark question asked, 'Where do you think of going this year?'

'We shall certainly winter at Rome,' said Lady St. Jerome to Lady Clanmorne, who was paying a morning visit. 'I wish you could induce Lord Clanmorne to join us.'

'I wish so too,' said the lady, 'but that is impossible. He never will give up his hunting.'

'I am sure there are more foxes in the Campagna than at Vauxe,' said Lady St. Jerome.

'I suppose you have heard of what they call the double event?' said Lady Clanmorne.

'No.'

'Well, it is quite true; Mr. Bohun told me last night, and he always knows everything.'

'Everything!' said Lady St. Jerome; 'but what is it that he knows now?'

'Both the Ladies Falkirk are to be married, and on the same day.'

'But to whom?'

'Whom should you think?'

'I will not even guess,' said Lady St. Jerome.

'Clare,' she said to Miss Arundel, who was engaged apart, 'you always find out conundrums. Lady Clanmorne has got some news for us. Lady Flora Falkirk and her sister are going to be married, and on the same day. And to whom, think you?'

'Well, I should think that somebody has made Lord Carisbrooke a happy man,' said Miss Arundel.

'Very good,' said Lady Clanmorne. 'I think Lady Flora will make an excellent Lady Carisbrooke. He is not quite as tall as she is, but he is a man of inches. And now for Lady Grizell.'

'My powers of divination are quite exhausted,' said Miss Arundel.

'Well, I will not keep you in suspense,' said Lady Clanmorne. 'Lady Grizell is to be Duchess of Brecon.'

'Duchess of Brecon!' exclaimed both Miss Arundel and Lady St. Jerome.

'I always admired the ladies,' said Miss Arundel. 'We met them at a country house last year, and I thought them pleasing in every way, artless and yet piquant; but I did not anticipate their fate being so soon sealed.'

'And so brilliantly,' added Lady St. Jerome.

'You met them at Muriel Towers,' said Lady Clanmorne. 'I heard of you there: a most distinguished party. There was an American lady there, was there not? a charming person, who sang and acted, and did all sorts of things.'

'Yes; there was. I believe, however, she was an Italian, married to an American.'

'Have you seen much of your host at Muriel Towers?' said Lady Clanmorne.

'We see him frequently,' said Lady St. Jerome.

'Ah! yes, I remember; I met him at Vauxe the other day. He is a great admirer of yours,' Lady Clanmorne added, addressing Miss Arundel.

'Oh! we are friends, and have long been so,' said Miss Arundel, and she left the room.

'Clare does not recognise admirers,' said Lady St. Jerome gravely.

'I hope the ecclesiastical fancy is not reviving,' said Lady Clanmorne. 'I was half in hopes that the lord of Muriel Towers might have deprived the Church of its bride.'

'That could never be,' said Lady St. Jerome; 'though, if it could have been, a source of happiness to Lord St.

Jerome and myself would not have been wanting. We greatly regard our kinsman, but between ourselves,' added Lady St. Jerome in a low voice, ' it was supposed that he was attached to the American lady of whom you were speaking.'

' And where is she now ? '

' I have heard nothing of late. Lothair was in Italy at the same time as ourselves, and was ill there, under our roof; so we saw a great deal of him. Afterwards he travelled for his health, and has now just returned from the East.'

A visitor was announced, and Lady Clanmorne retired.

Nothing happens as you expect. On his voyage home Lothair had indulged in dreams of renewing his intimacy at Crecy House, around whose hearth all his sympathies were prepared to cluster. The first shock to this romance was the news he received of the impending union of Lady Corisande with the Duke of Brecon. And what with this unexpected obstacle to intimacy, and the domestic embarrassments occasioned by Bertram's declaration, he had become a stranger to a roof which had so filled his thoughts. It seemed to him that he could not enter the house either as the admirer of the daughter or as the friend of her brother. She was probably engaged to another, and as Bertram's friend and fellow-traveller, he fancied he was looked upon by the family as one who had in some degree contributed to their mortification. Much of this was imaginary, but Lothair was very sensitive, and the result was that he ceased to call at Crecy House, and for some time kept aloof from the Duchess and her daughter, when he met them in general society. He was glad to hear from Bertram and St. Aldegonde that the position of the former was beginning to soften at home, and that the sharpness of his announcement was passing away. And when he had clearly ascertained that the contemplated union of Lady

Corisande with the Duke was certainly not to take place, Lothair began to reconnoitre, and try to resume his original position. But his reception was not encouraging, at least not sufficiently cordial for one who by nature was retiring and reserved. Lady Corisande was always kind, and after some time he danced with her again. But there were no invitations to luncheon from the Duchess; they never asked him to dinner. His approaches were received with courtesy, but he was not courted.

The announcement of the marriage of the Duke of Brecon did not, apparently, in any degree distress Lady Corisande. On the contrary, she expressed much satisfaction at her two young friends settling in life with such success and splendour. The ambition both of Lady Flora and Lady Grizell was that Corisande should be a bridesmaid. This would be a rather awkward post to occupy under the circumstances, so she embraced both, and said that she loved them both so equally, that she would not give a preference to either, and therefore, though she certainly would attend their weddings, she would refrain from taking part in the ceremony.

The Duchess went with Lady Corisande one morning to Mr. Ruby's to choose a present from her daughter to each of the young ladies. Mr. Ruby in a back shop poured forth his treasures of bracelets, and rings, and lockets. The presents must be similar in value and in beauty, and yet there must be some difference between them; so it was a rather long and troublesome investigation, Mr. Ruby as usual varying its monotony, or mitigating its wearisomeness, by occasionally, or suddenly, exhibiting some splendid or startling production of his art. The parure of an Empress, the bracelets of Grand-Duchesses, a wonderful fan that was to flutter in the hands of Majesty, had all in due course appeared, as well as the black pearls and yellow diamonds that figure and flash on such occasions, before eyes so favoured and so fair.

At last (for, like a prudent general, Mr. Ruby had always a great reserve), opening a case, he said, 'There!' and displayed a crucifix of the most exquisite workmanship and the most precious materials.

'I have no hesitation in saying the rarest jewel which this century has produced. See! the figure by Monti; a masterpiece. Every emerald in the cross a picked stone. These corners, your Grace is aware,' said Mr. Ruby condescendingly, 'contain the earth of the holy places at Jerusalem. It has been shown to no one but your Grace.'

'It is indeed most rare and beautiful,' said the Duchess, 'and most interesting too, from containing the earth of the holy places. A commission, of course?'

'From one of our most eminent patrons,' and then he mentioned Lothair's name.

Lady Corisande looked agitated.

'Not for himself,' said Mr. Ruby.

Lady Corisande seemed relieved.

'It is a present to a young lady, Miss Arundel.'

Lady Corisande changed colour, and turning away, walked towards a case of works of art, which was in the centre of the shop, and appeared to be engrossed in their examination.

CHAPTER LXXXVII.

A DAY or two after this adventure of the crucifix, Lothair met Bertram, who said to him, 'By the bye, if you want to see my people before they leave town, you must call at once.'

'You do not mean that,' replied Lothair, much surprised. 'Why, the Duchess told me, only three or four days ago,

that they should not leave town until the end of the first
week of August. They are going to the weddings.'

'I do not know what my mother said to you, my dear
fellow, but they go to Brentham the day after to-morrow,
and will not return. The Duchess has been for a long
time wishing this, but Corisande would stay. She thought
they would only bother themselves about my affairs, and
there was more distraction for them in town. But now
they are going, and it is for Corisande they go. She is not
well, and they have suddenly resolved to depart.'

'Well, I am very sorry to hear it,' said Lothair; 'I shall
call at Crecy House. Do you think they will see me?'

'Certain.'

'And what are your plans?'

'I have none,' said Bertram. 'I suppose I must not
leave my father alone at this moment. He has behaved
well; very kindly, indeed. I have nothing to complain of.
But still all is vague, and I feel somehow or other I ought
to be about him.'

'Have you heard from our dear friends abroad?'

'Yes,' said Bertram, with a sigh, 'Euphrosyne writes to
me; but I believe St. Aldegonde knows more about their
views and plans than I do. He and Mr. Phœbus correspond
much. I wish to heaven they were here, or rather that we
were with them,' he added, with another sigh. 'How
happy we all were at Jerusalem! How I hate London!
And Brentham worse. I shall have to go to a lot of agri-
cultural dinners and all sorts of things. The Duke expects
it, and I am bound now to do everything to please him.
What do you think of doing?'

'I neither know nor care,' said Lothair, in a tone of
great despondency.

'You are a little hipped.'

'Not a little. I suppose it is the excitement of the last
two years that has spoiled me for ordinary life. But I

find the whole thing utterly intolerable, and regret now
that I did not rejoin the staff of the General. I shall never
have such a chance again. It was a mistake; but one is
born to blunder.'

Lothair called at Crecy House. The hall-porter was not
sure whether the Duchess was at home, and the groom of
the chambers went to see. Lothair had never experienced
this form. When the groom of the chambers came down
again, he gave her Grace's compliments, but she had a
headache, and was obliged to lie down, and was sorry she
could not see Lothair, who went away livid.

Crecy House was only a few hundred yards from St.
James's Square, and Lothair repaired to an accustomed
haunt. He was not in a humour for society, and yet he
required sympathy. There were some painful associations
with the St. Jerome family, and yet they had many
charms. And the painful associations had been greatly
removed by their easy and cordial reception of him, and
the charms had been renewed and increased by subsequent
intercourse. After all, they were the only people who had
always been kind to him. And if they had erred in a
great particular, they had been animated by pure, and even
sacred, motives. And had they erred? Were not his
present feelings of something approaching to desolation a
fresh proof that the spirit of man can alone be sustained
by higher relations than merely human ones? So he
knocked at the door, and Lady St. Jerome was at home.
She had not a headache; there were no mysterious whisper-
ings between hall-porters and grooms of the chamber, to
ascertain whether he was one of the initiated. Whether it
were London or Vaux, the eyes of the household proved
that he was ever a welcome and cherished guest.

Lady St. Jerome was alone, and rose from her writing-
table to receive him. And then, for she was a lady who
never lost a moment, she resumed some work, which did

not interfere with their conversation. Her talking resources were so happy and inexhaustible, that it signified little that her visitor, who was bound in that character to have something to say, was silent and moody.

'My Lord,' she continued, 'has taken the Palazzo Agostini for a term. I think we should always pass our winters at Rome under any circumstances; but (the Cardinal has spoken to you about the great event) if that comes off, of which, between ourselves, whatever the world may say, I believe there is no sort of doubt, we should not think of being absent from Rome for a day during the Council.'

'Why! it may last years,' said Lothair. 'There is no reason why it should not last as long as the Council of Trent. It has in reality much more to do.'

'We do things quicker now,' said Lady St. Jerome.

'That depends on what there is to do. To revive faith is more difficult than to create it.'

'There will be no difficulty when the Church has assembled,' said Lady St. Jerome. 'This sight of the universal Fathers coming from the uttermost ends of the earth to bear witness to the truth will at once sweep away all the vain words and vainer thoughts of this unhappy century. It will be what they call a great fact, dear Lothair; and when the Holy Spirit descends upon their decrees, my firm belief is the whole world will rise as it were from a trance, and kneel before the divine tomb of St. Peter.'

'Well, we shall see,' said Lothair.

'The Cardinal wishes you very much to attend the Council. He wishes you to attend it as an Anglican, representing with a few others our laity. He says it would have the very best effect for religion.'

'He spoke to me.'

'And you agreed to go?'

'I have not refused him. If I thought I could do any good, I am not sure I would not go,' said Lothair; 'but from what I have seen of the Roman Court, there is little hope of reconciling our differences. Rome is stubborn. Now, look at the difficulties they make about the marriage of a Protestant and one of their own communion. It is cruel, and I think on their part unwise.'

'The sacrament of marriage is of ineffable holiness,' said Lady St. Jerome.

'I do not wish to deny that,' said Lothair, 'but I see no reason why I should not marry a Roman Catholic if I liked, without the Roman Church interfering and entirely regulating my house and home.'

'I wish you would speak to Father Coleman about this,' said Lady St. Jerome.

'I have had much talk with Father Coleman about many things in my time,' said Lothair, 'but not about this. By the bye, have you any news of the Monsignore?'

'He is in Ireland, arranging about the Œcumenical Council. They do not understand these matters there as well as we do in England, and his Holiness, by the Cardinal's advice, has sent the Monsignore to put things right.'

'All the Father Colemans in the world cannot alter the state of affairs about mixed marriages,' said Lothair; 'they can explain, but they cannot alter. I want change in this matter, and Rome never changes.'

'It is impossible for the Church to change,' said Lady St. Jerome, 'because it is Truth.'

'Is Miss Arundel at home?' said Lothair.

'I believe so,' said Lady St. Jerome.

'I never see her now,' he said discontentedly. 'She never goes to balls, and she never rides. Except occasionally under this roof, she is invisible.'

'Clare does not go any longer into society,' said Lady St. Jerome.

'Why?'

'Well, it is a secret,' said Lady St. Jerome, with some disturbance of countenance, and speaking in a lower tone; 'at least, at present; and yet I can hardly on such a subject wish that there should be a secret from you: Clare is about to take the veil.'

'Then I have not a friend left in the world,' said Lothair, in a despairing tone.

Lady St. Jerome looked at him with an anxious glance. 'Yes,' she continued, 'I do not wish to conceal it from you, that for a time we could have wished it otherwise; it has been, it is a trying event for my Lord and myself: but the predisposition, which was always strong, has ended in a determination so absolute, that we recognise the Divine purpose in her decision, and we bow to it.'

'I do not bow to it,' said Lothair; 'I think it barbarous and unwise.'

'Hush! hush! dear friend.'

'And does the Cardinal approve of this step?'

'Entirely.'

'Then my confidence in him is entirely destroyed,' said Lothair.

CHAPTER LXXXVIII.

It was August, and town was thinning fast. Parliament still lingered, but only for technical purposes; the political struggle of the session having terminated at the end of July. One social event was yet to be consummated: the marriages of Lothair's cousins. They were to be married on the same day, at the same time, and in the same place. Westminster Abbey was to be the scene, and as it was understood that the service was to be choral, great expectations of ecclesiastical splendour and effect were much anticipated by the fair sex. They were however doomed to disappointment, for although the day was fine, the attendance numerous and brilliant beyond precedent, Lord Culloden would have 'no popery.' Lord Carisbrooke, who was a ritualist, murmured, and was encouraged in his resistance by Lady Clanmorne and a party, but as the Duke of Brecon was high and dry, there was a want of united action, and Lord Culloden had his way.

After the ceremony, the world repaired to the mansion of Lord Culloden in Belgrave Square, to inspect the presents, and to partake of a dinner called a breakfast. Cousin Lothair wandered about the rooms, and had the satisfaction of seeing a bracelet with a rare and splendid sapphire which he had given to Lady Flora, and a circlet of diamond stars which he had placed on the brow of the Duchess of Brecon. The St. Aldegondes were the only members of the Brentham family who were present. St. Aldegonde had a taste for marriages and public executions, and Lady St. Aldegonde wandered about with Lothair, and pointed out to him Corisande's present to his cousins.

'I never was more disappointed than by your family leaving town so early this year,' he said.

'We were quite surprised.'

'I am sorry to hear your sister is indisposed.'

'Corisande! she is perfectly well.'

'I hope the Duchess's headache is better,' said Lothair. 'She could not receive me when I called to say farewell, because she had a headache.'

'I never knew Mamma have a headache,' said Lady St. Aldegonde.

'I suppose you will be going to Brentham?'

'Next week.'

'And Bertram too?'

'I fancy that we shall be all there.'

'I suppose we may consider now that the season is really over?'

'Yes; they stayed for this. I should not be surprised if everyone in these rooms had disappeared by to-morrow.'

'Except myself,' said Lothair.

'Do you think of going abroad again?'

'One might as well go,' said Lothair, 'as remain.'

'I wish Granville would take me to Paris. It seems so odd not to have seen Paris. All I want is to see the new streets and dine at a café.'

'Well, you have an object; that is something,' said Lothair. 'I have none.'

'Men have always objects,' said Lady St. Aldegonde. 'They make business when they have none, or it makes itself. They move about, and it comes.'

'I have moved about a great deal,' said Lothair, 'and nothing has come to me but disappointment. I think I shall take to croquet, like that curious gentleman I remember at Brentham.'

'Ah! you remember everything.'

'It is not easy to forget anything at Brentham,' said Lothair. 'It is just two years ago. That was a happy time.'

'I doubt whether our re-assembling will be quite as happy this year,' said Lady St. Aldegonde, in a serious tone. 'This engagement of Bertram is an anxious business; I never saw Papa before really fret. And there are other things which are not without vexation; at least to Mamma.'

'I do not think I am a great favourite of your Mamma,' said Lothair. 'She once used to be very kind to me, but she is so no longer.'

'I am sure you mistake her,' said Lady St. Aldegonde, but not in a tone which indicated any confidence in her remark. 'Mamma is anxious about my brother, and all that.'

' I believe the Duchess thinks that I am in some way or
other connected with this embarrassment; but I really had
nothing to do with it, though I could not refuse my testimony to the charms of the young lady, and my belief she
would make Bertram a happy man.'

' As for that, you know, Granville saw a great deal more
of her, at least at Jerusalem, than you did, and he has said
to Mamma a great deal more than you have done.'

' Yes; but she thinks that had it not been for me, Bertram would never have known the Phœbus family. She
could not conceal that from me, and it has poisoned her
mind.'

' Oh ! do not use such words.'

' Yes; but they are true. And your sister is prejudiced
against me also.'

' That I am sure she is not,' said Lady St. Aldegonde
quickly. ' Corisande was always your friend.'

' Well, they refused to see me, when we may never meet
again for months, perhaps for years,' said Lothair, ' perhaps
never.'

' What shocking things you are saying, my dear Lord,
to-day ! Here, Lord Culloden wants you to return thanks
for the bridesmaids. You must put on a merry face.'

The dreary day at last arrived, and very quickly, when
Lothair was the only person left in town. When there is
nobody you know in London, the million that go about are
only voiceless phantoms. Solitude in a city is a trance.
The motion of the silent beings with whom you have no
speech or sympathy only makes the dreamlike existence
more intense. It is not so in the country: the voices of
nature are abundant, and from the hum of insects to the
fall of the avalanche, something is always talking to you.

Lothair shrank from the streets. He could not endure
the dreary glare of St. James's and the desert sheen of
Pall Mall. He could mount his horse in the Park, and soon

lose himself in suburban roads that he once loved. Yes! it
was irresistible; and he made a visit to Belmont. The house
was dismantled, and the gardens shorn of their lustre; but
still it was there, very fair in the sunshine, and sanctified
in his heart. He visited every room that he had frequented,
and lingered in her boudoir. He did not forget the now
empty pavilion, and he plucked some flowers that she once
loved, and pressed them to his lips, and placed them near
his heart. He felt now what it was that made him unhappy: it was the want of sympathy.

He walked through the Park to the residence of Mr.
Phœbus, where he had directed his groom to meet him. His
heart beat as he wandered along, and his eye was dim with
tears. What characters and what scenes had he not become
acquainted with since his first visit to Belmont! And even
now, when they had departed, or were absent, what influence were they not exercising over his life, and the life of
those most intimate with him! Had it not been for his
pledge to Theodora, it was far from improbable that he
would now have been a member of the Roman Catholic
Church, and all his hopes at Brentham, and his intimacy
with the family on which he had most reckoned in life for
permanent friendship and support, seemed to be marred
and blighted by the witching eyes of that mirthful Euphrosyne, whose mocking words on the moonlit terrace at Belmont first attracted his notice to her. And then, by association of ideas, he thought of the General, and what his
old commander had said at their last interview, reminding
him of his fine castle, and expressing his conviction that
the lord of such a domain must have much to do.

'I will try to do it,' said Lothair, 'and I will go down to
Muriel to-morrow.'

CHAPTER LXXXIX.

LOTHAIR, who was very sensible to the charms of nature, found at first relief in the beauties of Muriel. The season was propitious to the scene. August is a rich and leafy month, and the glades and avenues and stately trees of his parks and pleasaunces seemed at the same time to soothe and gladden his perturbed spirit. Muriel was still new to him, and there was much to examine and explore for the first time. He found a consolation also in the frequent remembrance that these scenes had been known to those whom he loved. Often in the chamber, and often in the bower, their forms arose; sometimes their voices lingered in his ear; a frolic laugh, or whispered words of kindness and enjoyment. Such a place as Muriel should always be so peopled. But that is impossible. One cannot always have the most agreeable people in the world assembled under one's roof. And yet the alternative should not be the loneliness he now experienced. The analytical Lothair resolved that there was no happiness without sympathy.

The most trying time were the evenings. A man likes to be alone in the morning. He writes his letters and reads the newspapers, attempts to examine his steward's accounts, and if he wants society can gossip with his studgroom. But a solitary evening in the country is gloomy, however brilliant the accessories. As Mr. Phœbus was not present, Lothair violated the prime principles of a first-class Aryan education, and ventured to read a little. It is difficult to decide which is the most valuable companion to a country eremite at his nightly studies, the volume that keeps him awake or the one that sets him a-slumbering.

At the end of a week Lothair had some good sport on

his moors, and this reminded him of the excellent Campian, who had received and answered his letter. The Colonel, however, held out but a faint prospect of returning at present to Europe, though, whenever he did, he promised to be the guest of Lothair. Lothair asked some of his neighbours to dinner, and he made two large parties to slaughter his grouse. They were grateful and he was popular, but 'we have not an idea in common,' thought Lothair, as wearied and uninterested he bade his last guest his last good-night. Then Lothair paid a visit to the Lord Lieutenant, and stayed two nights at Agramont Castle. Here he met many county notables, and 'great was the company of the preachers ;' but the talk was local or ecclesiastical, and after the high-spiced condiments of the conversation to which he was accustomed, the present discourse was insipid even to nausea. He sought some relief in the society of Lady Ida Alice, but she blushed when she spoke to him, and tittered when he replied to her; and at last he found refuge in pretty Mrs. Ardenne, who concluded by asking him for his photograph.

On the morrow of his return to Muriel, the servant bringing in his letters, he seized one in the handwriting of Bertram, and discarding the rest, devoured the communication of his friend, which was eventful.

It seems that the Phœbus family had returned to England, and were at Brentham, and had been there a week. The family were delighted with them, and Euphrosyne was an especial favourite. But this was not all. It seems that Mr. Cantacuzene had been down to Brentham, and stayed, which he never did anywhere, a couple of days. And the Duke was particularly charmed with Mr. Cantacuzene. This gentleman, who was only in the earlier term of middle age, and looked younger than his age, was distinguished in appearance, highly polished, and singularly acute. He appeared to be the master of great wealth, for he offered to

make upon Euphrosyne any settlement which the Duke
desired. He had no son, and did not wish his sons-in-law
to be sighing for his death. He wished his daughters,
therefore, to enjoy the bulk of their inheritance in his lifetime. He told the Duke that he had placed one hundred
thousand pounds in the names of trustees on the marriage
of Madame Phœbus, to accumulate, 'and when the genius
and vanity of her husband are both exhausted, though I
believe they are inexhaustible,' remarked Mr. Cantacuzene,
'it will be a nest's egg for them to fall back upon, and at
least save them from penury.' The Duke had no doubt
that Mr. Cantacuzene was of imperial lineage. But the
latter portion of the letter was the most deeply interesting
to Lothair. Bertram wrote that his mother had just observed that she thought the Phœbus family would like to
meet Lothair, and begged Bertram to invite him to Brentham. The letter ended by an urgent request that, if disengaged, he should arrive immediately.

Mr. Phœbus highly approved of Brentham. All was art,
and art of a high character. He knew no residence with
an aspect so thoroughly Aryan. Though it was really a
family party, the house was quite full; at least, as Bertram
said to Lothair on his arrival, 'there is only room for you,
and you are in your old quarters.'

'That is exactly what I wished,' said Lothair.

He had to escort the Duchess to dinner. Her manner
was of old days. 'I thought you would like to meet your
friends,' she said.

'It gives me much pleasure, but much more to find myself again at Brentham.'

'There seems every prospect of Bertram being happy.
We are enchanted with the young lady. You know her, I
believe, well? The Duke is highly pleased with her father,
Mr. Cantacuzene; he says one of the most sensible men he
ever met, and a thorough gentleman, which he may well

be, for I believe there is no doubt he is of the highest descent: emperors they say, princes even now. I wish you could have met him, but he would only stay eight-and-forty hours. I understand his affairs are vast.'

'I have always heard a considerable person; quite the head of the Greek community in this country; indeed, in Europe generally.'

'I see by the morning papers that Miss Arundel has taken the veil.'

'I missed my papers to-day,' said Lothair, a little agitated, 'but I have long been aware of her intention of doing so.'

'Lady St. Jerome will miss her very much. She was quite the soul of the house.'

'It must be a great and painful sacrifice,' said Lothair; 'but, I believe, long meditated. I remember when I was at Vauxe, nearly two years ago, that I was told this was to be her fate. She was quite determined on it.'

'I saw the beautiful crucifix you gave her at Mr. Ruby's.'

'It was a homage to her for her great goodness to me when I was ill at Rome: and it was difficult to find anything that would please or suit her. I fixed on the crucifix, because it permitted me to transfer to it the earth of the holy places, which were included in the crucifix, that was given to me by the monks of the Holy Sepulchre when I made my pilgrimage to Jerusalem.'

In the evening St. Aldegonde insisted on their dancing, and he engaged himself to Madame Phœbus. Bertram and Euphrosyne seemed never separated; Lothair was successful in inducing Lady Corisande to be his partner.

'Do you remember your first ball at Crecy House?' asked Lothair. 'You are not nervous now?'

'I would hardly say that,' said Lady Corisande, 'though I try not to show it.'

'It was the first ball for both of us,' said Lothair. 'I

have not danced so much in the interval as you have. Do
you know, I was thinking just now, I have danced oftener
with you than with anyone else?'

'Are not you glad about Bertram's affair ending so well?'

'Very; he will be a happy man. Everybody is happy, I
think, except myself.'

In the course of the evening, Lady St. Aldegonde, on the
arm of Lord Montairy, stopped for a moment as she passed
Lothair, and said: 'Do you remember our conversation
at Lord Culloden's breakfast? Who was right about
mamma?'

They passed their long summer days in rambling and
riding, and in wondrous new games which they played in the
hall. The striking feature, however, were the matches at
battledore and shuttlecock between Madame Phœbus and
Lord St. Aldegonde, in which the skill and energy displayed
were supernatural, and led to betting. The evenings were
always gay; sometimes they danced; more or less they
always had some delicious singing. And Mr. Phœbus arranged some tableaux most successfully.

All this time Lothair hung much about Lady Corisande;
he was by her side in the riding parties, always very near
her when they walked, and sometimes he managed unconsciously to detach her from the main party, and they almost
walked alone. If he could not sit by her at dinner, he
joined her immediately afterwards, and whether it were a
dance, a tableau, or a new game, somehow or other he
seemed always to be her companion.

It was about a week after the arrival of Lothair, and
they were at breakfast at Brentham, in that bright room
full of little round tables which Lothair always admired,
looking, as it did, upon a garden of many colours.

'How I hate modern gardens,' said St. Aldegonde.
'What a horrid thing this is! One might as well have a
mosaic movement there. Give me ....

peas, and wallflowers. That is my idea of a garden. Corisande's garden is the only sensible thing of the sort.'

'One likes a mosaic pavement to look like a garden,' said Euphrosyne, 'but not a garden like a mosaic pavement.'

'The worst of these mosaic beds,' said Madame Phœbus, 'is, you can never get a nosegay, and if it were not for the kitchen-garden, we should be destitute of that gayest and sweetest of creations.'

'Corisande's garden is, since your first visit to Brentham,' said the Duchess to Lothair. 'No flowers are admitted that have not perfume. It is very old-fashioned. You must get her to show it you.'

It was agreed that after breakfast they should go and see Corisande's garden. And a party did go: all the Phœbus family, and Lord and Lady St. Aldegonde, and Lady Corisande, and Bertram and Lothair.

In the pleasure-grounds of Brentham were the remains of an ancient garden of the ancient house that had long ago been pulled down. When the modern pleasure-grounds were planned and created, notwithstanding the protests of the artists in landscape, the father of the present Duke would not allow this ancient garden to be entirely destroyed, and you came upon its quaint appearance in the dissimilar world in which it was placed, as you might in some festival of romantic costume upon a person habited in the courtly dress of the last century. It was formed upon a gentle southern slope, with turfen terraces walled in on three sides, the fourth consisting of arches of golden yew. The Duke had given this garden to Lady Corisande, in order that she might practise her theory, that flower-gardens should be sweet and luxuriant, and not hard and scentless imitations of works of art. Here, in their season, flourished abundantly all those productions of nature which are now banished from our once delighted senses: huge bushes of honeysuckle, and bowers of sweet-pea and sweetbriar, and

jessamine clustering over the walls, and gillyflowers
scenting with their sweet breath the ancient bricks from
which they seemed to spring. There were banks of violets
which the southern breeze always stirred, and mignonette
filled every vacant nook. As they entered now, it seemed
a blaze of roses and carnations, though one recognised in a
moment the presence of the lily, the heliotrope, and the
stock. Some white peacocks were basking on the southern
wall, and one of them, as their visitors entered, moved and
displayed its plumage with scornful pride. The bees were
busy in the air, but their homes were near, and you might
watch them labouring in their glassy hives.

'Now, is not Corisande quite right?' said Lord St. Aldegonde, as he presented Madame Phœbus with a garland of
woodbine, with which she said she would dress her head at
dinner. All agreed with him, and Bertram and Euphrosyne
adorned each other with carnations, and Mr. Phœbus
placed a flower on the uncovered head of Lady St. Aldegonde, according to the principles of high art, and they
sauntered and rambled in the sweet and sunny air amid a
blaze of butterflies and the ceaseless hum of bees.

Bertram and Euphrosyne had disappeared, and the rest
were lingering about the hives while Mr. Phœbus gave
them a lecture on the apiary and its marvellous life. The
bees understood Mr. Phœbus, at least he said so, and thus
his friends had considerable advantage in this lesson in
entomology. Lady Corisande and Lothair were in a distant corner of the garden, and she was explaining to him
her plans ; what she had done and what she meant to do.

'I wish I had a garden like this at Muriel,' said Lothair.

'You could easily make one.'

'If you helped me.'

'I have told you all my plans,' said Lady Corisande.

'Yes; but I was thinking of something else when you
spoke,' said Lothair.

'That is not very complimentary.'

'I do not wish to be complimentary,' said Lothair, 'if compliments mean less than they declare. I was not thinking of your garden, but of you.'

'Where can they have all gone?' said Lady Corisande, looking round. 'We must find them.'

'And leave this garden?' said Lothair. 'And I without a flower, the only one without a flower? I am afraid that is significant of my lot.'

'You shall choose a rose,' said Lady Corisande.

'Nay; the charm is that it should be your choice.'

But choosing the rose lost more time, and when Corisande and Lothair reached the arches of golden yew, there were no friends in sight.

'I think I hear sounds this way,' said Lothair, and he led his companion farther from home.

'I see no one,' said Lady Corisande, distressed, and when they had advanced a little way.

'We are sure to find them in good time,' said Lothair. 'Besides, I wanted to speak to you about the garden at Muriel. I wanted to induce you to go there and help me to make it. Yes,' he added, after some hesitation, 'on this spot, I believe on this very spot, I asked the permission of your mother two years ago to express to you my love. She thought me a boy, and she treated me as a boy. She said I knew nothing of the world, and both our characters were unformed. I know the world now. I have committed many mistakes, doubtless many follies, have formed many opinions, and have changed many opinions; but to one I have been constant, in one I am unchanged, and that is my adoring love for you.'

She turned pale, she stopped, then gently taking his arm, she hid her face in his breast.

He soothed and sustained her agitated frame, and sealed with an embrace her speechless form. Then, with soft

I I 2

thoughts and softer words, clinging to him he induced her
to resume their stroll, which both of them now wished
might assuredly be undisturbed. They had arrived at the
limit of the pleasure-grounds, and they wandered into the
park and into its most sequestered parts. All this time
Lothair spoke much, and gave her the history of his life
since he first visited her home. Lady Corisande said little,
but when she was more composed, she told him that from
the first her heart had been his, but everything seemed
to go against her hopes. Perhaps at last, to please her
parents, she would have married the Duke of Brecon, had
not Lothair returned; and what he had said to her that
morning at Crecy House had decided her resolution, whatever might be her lot, to unite it to no one else but him.
But then came the adventure of the crucifix, and she
thought all was over for her, and she quitted town in
despair.

'Let us rest here for a while,' said Lothair, 'under the
shade of this oak;' and Lady Corisande reclined against its
mighty trunk, and Lothair threw himself at her feet. He
had a great deal still to tell her, and among other things,
the story of the pearls, which he had wished to give to
Theodora.

'She was, after all, your good genius,' said Lady
Corisande. 'I always liked her.'

'Well now,' said Lothair, 'that case has never been
opened. The year has elapsed, but I would not open it,
for I had always a wild wish that the person who opened
it should be yourself. See, here it is.' And he gave her
the case.

'We will not break the seal,' said Lady Corisande.
'Let us respect it for her sake: ROMA!' she said, examining it; and then they opened the case. There was
the slip of paper which Theodora at the time had placed

upon the pearls, and on which she had written some unseen words. They were read now, and run thus:

'THE OFFERING OF THEODORA TO LOTHAIR'S BRIDE.'

'Let me place them on you now,' said Lothair.

'I will wear them as your chains,' said Corisande.

The sun began to tell them that some hours had elapsed since they quitted Brentham House. At last a soft hand which Lothair retained, gave him a slight pressure, and a sweet voice whispered, 'Dearest, I think we ought to return.'

And they returned almost in silence. They rather calculated that, taking advantage of the luncheon-hour, Corisande might escape to her room; but they were a little too late. Luncheon was over, and they met the Duchess and a large party on the terrace.

'What has become of you, my good people?' said her Grace; 'bells have been ringing for you in every direction. Where can you have been!'

'I have been in Corisande's garden,' said Lothair, 'and she has given me a rose.'

LONDON: PRINTED BY
SPOTTISWOODE AND CO., NEW-STREET SQUARE
AND PARLIAMENT STREET